DEATH WAS NEVER THE END...

Death's true face, that awful blinding darkness and midnight sunrise spilling from behind the remnants of his human masks, swallowing up the moon and sun and all parts of the sky—I mourned the sight of it, the feel of his presence, that all-encompassing everything and suffocating womb. I mourned it like a lost lover. I wanted him back. I wanted it all back.

PRAISE FOR THE RESURGAM TRILOGY:

DUST

"A massively entertaining and seriously revisionist zombie novel... smart, scary and viscerally real."

–*Booklist (starred review)*

FRAIL

"A great, unsettling portrait of raw hunger and hope."

– *Jeff Long, author of* Deeper *and* The Descent

"A gritty and personal post-zombie novel with a clear-voiced, strong female narrator and a fresh new perspective on a saturated genre."

–*Shelf Awareness*

ALSO IN THE RESURGAM TRILOGY:

DUST
FRAIL

Joan Frances Turner

First edition published 2014.

For information, address
Candlemark & Gleam LLC,
102 Morgan Street, Bennington, VT 05201
info@candlemarkandgleam.com

ISBN: 978-1-936460-55-7
eBook ISBN: 978-1-936460-56-4

Library of Congress Cataloging-in-Publication Data
In Progress

Cover art by RB Griffiths

Map by Alan Caum

Composition by Kate Sullivan
Typeface: ElectraLH

Editor: Kate Sullivan

Proofreader: Aliza Becker

www.candlemarkandgleam.com

In loving memory of **C.**,
who lives on, somewhere else.

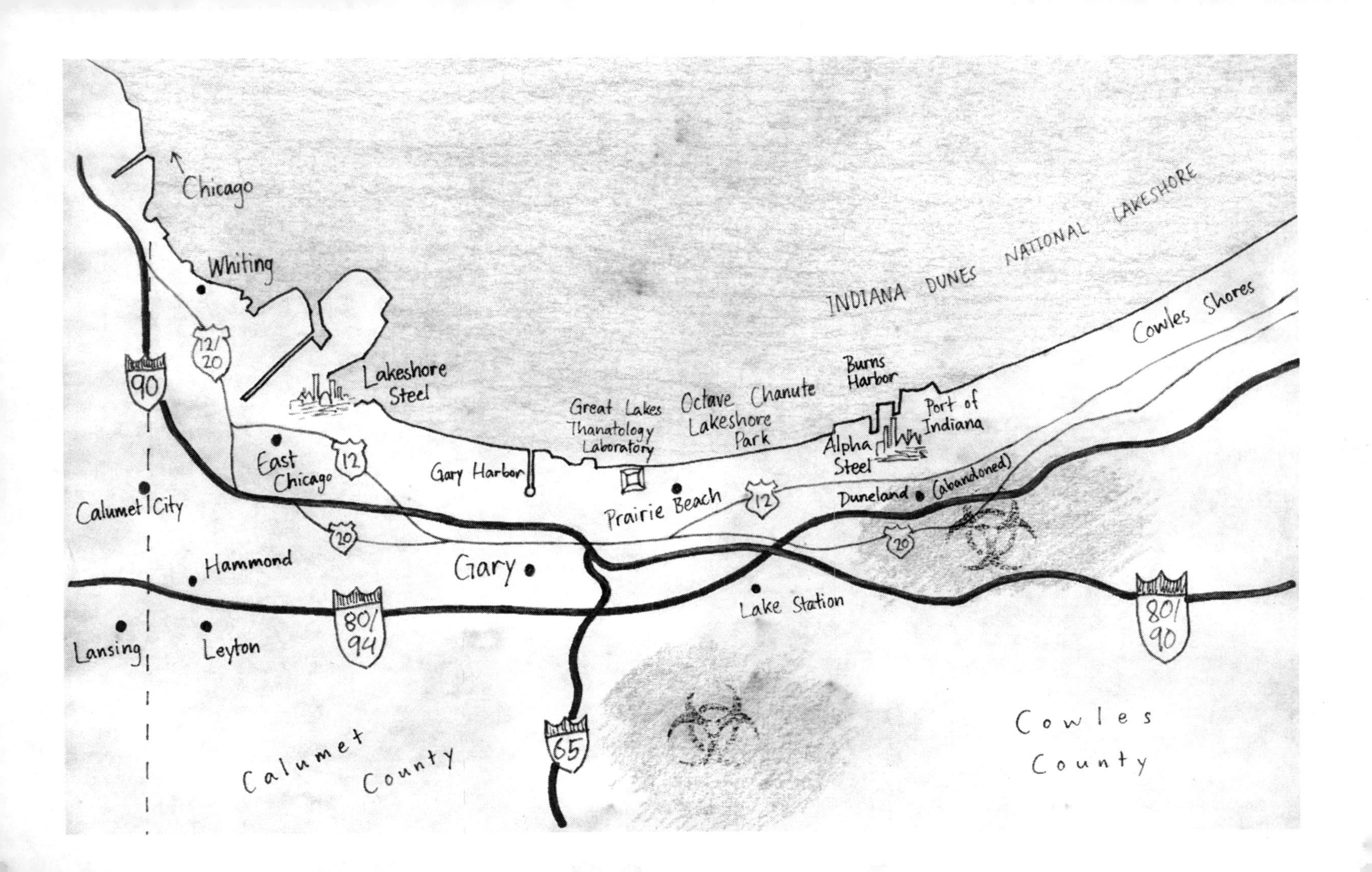
Chicago
Whiting
INDIANA DUNES NATIONAL LAKESHORE
Cowles Shores
12/20
90
Lakeshore Steel
Burns Harbor
Great Lakes Thanatology Laboratory
Octave Chanute Lakeshore Park
Port of Indiana
Alpha Steel
East Chicago
12
Gary Harbor
Calumet City
Prairie Beach
Duneland
(abandoned)
20
Hammond
Gary
Lake Station
80/94
80/90
Lansing
Leyton
65
Calumet County
Cowles County

DOUBT

ONE
AMY

The world may be good as ended, but there's still a Shop-Wel pharmacy every fifty yards. That's a beautiful thing, really, to know that even after we're all dead, after we're all walking around dead, the potato chips and rubbing alcohol and tweezers and condoms and snack-pack ravioli will all live to see another—

I think I'm getting ahead of myself. It's hard not to, so much has happened in just a few months. Zombies, proper zombies—they already feel like the vaguest of memories. The world we thought we knew—is it already just any old story, a random folktale? Once upon a time, children, just a few short months ago, most people stayed dead when they died, but some just didn't. They rose up, tunneled out, wandered the earth like vagrants, killing and eating whatever got in their way: wild animals, pets, people. It'd been that way for hundreds of years, thousands. Their numbers grew, slowly, and living humans built fences, sounded alarms, hired security teams with flamethrowers to hold them all back. Everyone knows that much, but nobody ever figured out *why* they were coming back, or what to do about it. There were laboratories, secret ones, or supposed to be secret, built to study the problem. A big one in Gary, Indiana, on the Prairie Beach side along the lake. You didn't ask what they did. Someone should have. We all should have.

But it's a little late for that now, and there's a deserted Shop-Wel sitting there right for the foraging and I was hungry. Starving, in fact, my stomach a sour shriveled pumpkin-seed in that way I'd never grown used to, even last winter after the plague, so when we stumbled into what remained of Sandy Shores and I saw the big red-mortar-blue-pestle sign, I turned straight off the road. My mother marched right behind me, skirting the door's shattered glass, and my dog, my ghost dog, Old Nick Drake, sniffed and picked his way inside. Stephen, Lisa, Naomi clinging to Lisa's hand—they peered frowning into the broad, intact side windows, looking for squatters and interlopers who'd got here before us, but the whole place, the whole town, was empty. You get a feeling after a while for when a place is truly deserted, for when that heavy-hanging sense of an aborted, interrupted *presence* around you, like rain thick in the air, has passed: not a sound turned echo, like just after a death, but an echo dispersed to failing memory, indistinguishable shadow.

Some store shelves were overturned, a few cans of something bean-thick yet runny exploded all over the floor, but it was half-hearted looting at best and we all fanned out, grabbing bagged boxed pull-top snacks, warm sodas still in the chill case (we left the milk strictly alone), bottles of antacids, arthritis tablets, aspirin. My ravioli was right there waiting on a collapsed metal shelf, a good dozen little containers or more; I sat down in the aisle, wrenched the plastic top off one and finger-spooned it in, licking the side of my hand clean of gummy sugared tomato. Cheese-filled, this kind, coating my tongue in a thick salty paste.

Once upon a time, not long ago, there *were* zombies; this was their time, the sunset, this was when they all came out to play—I'd be looking over my shoulder with every bite. But not anymore. The labs sprayed something, like a pesticide, that was supposed to kill zombies dead for good. It killed them, all right. And most of humankind, too. A man-made plague. The only survivors were the few immune, like me, Naomi, Stephen, my mother, and the few others like my friend Lisa who got sick unto death, passed through the other side of illness, became something inhuman and impervious to disease, injury, mortality. Exes, I called them: ex-humans, ex-zombies. They were supposed to be untouchable, something that could never die, but we'd killed them, me and my mother and Stephen, they were coming for us and somehow we tore up their untouchable flesh and—

"Nick?" I said, and held out the little plastic tub for him to lick the sauce. "Don't you want any?"

Nick sniffed and declined it when I opened another one just for him, keeping his eyes on my fast-moving fingers—not like begging but like my hand was strange, dangerous, a thing needing vigilant inspection. That thick fur too deep black to carry a sheen, those watery sulphur-pisshole eyes taking every bit of me in... surely even ghost dogs needed to eat, but he hadn't since he first started following me, all those weeks ago. Not one bite, not that I'd ever seen. I picked up his can and started in, soft wet pasta like waterlogged paper, stringy bits of beef drowned in sweet tomato.

Once upon a time, there was a dog who'd been a spirit, a chimera, a ghost sent by Death itself to track a murderer. Casper the Unfriendly Bloodhound. Then, sometime between Ms. Acosta's death and my own, he became true, living flesh. I didn't know how, wouldn't ask why, because he'd defended us, gotten us out of Prairie Beach alive; whether he meant to be or not, he was maybe the truest friend I'd ever had. The others didn't want to hear that, not for a second. The others had no idea just what they defied, when they tried to pretend Nick wasn't there.

"Anti-inflammatory," Stephen read from the side of a bottle, standing at the end of the aisle while the others hit the dry goods. "Might help your eye—"

"Nothing's gonna help this eye," I said, but I stretched out my sauce-smeared hand anyway for two pills, swallowed them barely checking what they were. Stephen didn't look any great shakes himself, face bruised, cut throat scabbing over just like mine, blood not all his own dried stiff on his clothes and mouth, the fingers clutching a half-drunk Coke trembling with fatigue. I reached for a third ravioli and Stephen handed me a pull-top can of peaches and the rest of his bag of Hott Stix, as good a lunch as any I'd got in a long time; in Paradise City, the human settlement where he and I had met, where we both sang, tap-danced, and rolled over playing dead for our supper, they didn't bother with midday meals at all. The exes who ran the place, they only fed us human serfs just enough to keep us going, keep us distracted. The other humans, the frails, they rioted and set the place on fire after we left, that's what Lisa said and she had the singed smell all in her hair and clothes to prove it. I wanted to ask her about that, just what she saw and did before it all went up, but I knew she'd never give me a straight answer.

"Is there a pet aisle here?" I asked. I hadn't looked. "Dog food or kibble or something? Nick—"

"Can fend for himself just fine," Stephen said, gulping down more Coke and clutching the bottle like it might grow legs and run away. He and Nick—they'd met only hours ago, but already Stephen's unease, his strange faltering hesitance in Nick's presence, snaked up between the two of them like a smell. "We don't need him getting used to one kind of food we might never find again. Dogs can eat anything."

"This dog *won't* eat anything," I retorted, and Nick just stared impassive at us both as I licked Hott Stix traces from my fingers, deep radioactive red against the orangey traces of tomato. I stuck powdery fingertips in the ravioli and stirred, a little cayenne for the sauce. "He's never eaten anything, even those squirrels he chased in the woods he just let go—"

"Then we hardly need to start worrying about him now, do we?"

The little edge to Stephen's voice was something I was growing used to, the prick and jab of a rusty safety pin that slipped loose whenever he was nervous, tired, felt the absence of memory inside him acute as the emptiness of a room: the diffuse, bleak emptiness of a room where someone died. We'd both died that day, he and I, but it'd happened to him, to my mother, again and again, the very act of it an acid eating through their memories, their selves—dead today. Because the lab didn't just study zombies, back before the plague. They also lured in or kidnapped human beings: addicts, prostitutes, homeless people, prisoners, anyone and everyone filed under Riddance, Good. Like my mother. Like Stephen. They experimented on them, killing them over and over, bringing them back to life again and again. It destroyed their memories, their sense of who they once were, their minds' avenues stretching back only to the lab's own sandy-shore backyard. Most test subjects just plain died.

And now, even though there were meant to be no more labs, they'd done it to him again. And to me. We'd died, this very day, and come back again this very day, and real human beings, like I'd thought I was for so long, they couldn't do that. I thought that over like I'd been trying not to and then grabbed another can of fruit, even though I had the distended, slightly ill feeling I'd already eaten too much.

"Nick got me this far," I said, and left it there because I didn't want a fight. "But I guess he's not sick. He doesn't look sick, anyway. Take some of those things for your own face, your jaw looks awful."

"You look worse," he replied. Rancor faded, easily as it flared, his fingers so light at my temple pulling strands of hair away from my swollen eye. "Billy packs a nasty punch, I should know."

"I don't want to talk about Billy," I said, and flexed my sore stained fingers that Billy and Mags, the king and queen of Paradise City, tried to break, to bite right off like the zombies they still were inside. Mags that I'd killed, when her kind—those who got the plague, survived it, and came out transformed—were meant to be impervious, immortal, when their flesh knitted together in seconds right before your eyes and nothing in this life could kill them. But I'd killed her. And killed something inside Billy, who loved her and only her, when I did it. Ms. Acosta, back in Lepingville, she and I were the town's only human survivors and she'd had no family, but maybe there was someone else, a Billy to her Mags. Maybe now that spring had come, a friend, a long-lost someone, would go looking for her and find her body how I'd left it and—

I don't want to talk about Billy. Ever.

Stephen sat in the aisle next to me, gulping the rest of his Coke with his back half-turned on Nick. Lisa came over, sway-footed with the faint bruising of exhaustion beneath her eyes, stepping gingerly over a splat puddle of exploded chili cans.

"I propose we stop here, for the evening," she announced, spitting out the words harsh and hard like her plague-twisted tongue couldn't help doing. "Maybe the night. Naomi's worn out—"

"No, I'm not," Naomi said, from the other end of the aisle. Kids her age—I'm only seventeen and the energy shooting from their ears still makes me feel old. She was cradling a flimsy coloring book, a little box of crayons, a bag of potato chips half her height. "Can I color while you sleep?"

Lisa actually glared at her, the unique feverish hostility of love all in her eyes. Just like she'd looked at me, back in the woods this morning when she came for me. Rescued me. Naomi was another of her rescues, motherless and fatherless and thrown on Paradise's awful mercies before Lisa stepped in; she'd lost a daughter of her own, Lisa had, long before all of this started. Leukemia. Only three, four years old. Sometimes I thought Lisa tried, a lot harder than she should, to forget Naomi wasn't really Karen, her dead little girl. Just like she tried so hard to forget I wasn't really Judy, Jenny, whatshername, her little sister.

"If you even think of wandering off by yourself," Lisa told Naomi, "while we're sleeping? If you even vaguely contemplate considering it? I will kill you. I'm not kidding, I will take both my hands and wring your little scrawny neck—"

It shouldn't have been funny to hear her talking like that, an ex-human with all her strength to an actual little girl, but Stephen laughed and I laughed and Naomi, unafraid, just swelled with indignation. "I'm not wandering anywhere!" she declared, swiftly setting down her chips and toys like we were about to accuse her of shoplifting. "I want to stay with the doggy."

The doggy, quite politely, wanted nothing to do with her, but she was a stubborn kid and Nick was patient enough that she kept trying. He looked up from where he sat with paws pressing at my thigh and gave her a searching stare that lit her up with false hope, made her run over to clutch him round the neck and bury her face in its furry crook. He suffered it in silence, like he always did. Stephen, a little flicker of disquiet crossing his face at the sight, bent his head and finished off my ravioli.

Soft rustlings, a shuffling sound, as my mother came dragging down the aisle; she had backpacks slung over her arm, plain utilitarian red and blue, plus sparkle-flowered pink nylon stuffed with cans, pills, boxes, bottles tenting and spiking the thin porous cloth. An armful of those cheap six-a-pack white cotton socks, fleece blankets, jars of vitamins. I remembered the safehouse back in Leyton, the kit bags of ready supplies I'd had to toss aside when I thought something was after me (and it was), and regretted all over again the tornado Lisa and I got caught in leaving town, everything we took as our own flung into the trees and smashed beyond repair. Nick, though, Nick had been there all along, whether I saw him or not; following us, following me, making sure we got where we were going. Following me like he had since I'd killed Ms. Acosta. Leading me toward my own, briefest of deaths.

The thing that had followed me here, flushing me out and chasing me miles across the county until I ended up in Prairie Beach, the lab's backyard—my birthplace, my new birthplace—maybe it had planned the tornado, another obstacle to push me closer into its path. You should've warned me, Nick, I know you *verr only follow-ink orrd-uhs* but your master... you should've warned me how vicious he can get. Your master. My master. I reached an arm up silently to my mother and she sank down cross-legged beside us, deflated and fading fast.

"Bedding," she said, nodding toward the blankets as she set them down. "There's travel pillows too. I can't go any farther than this. Just now." She glanced toward Lisa. "Sorry."

"Why apologize?" Lisa asked, in the same careful, measured tone, the formality of two friends mending fences after a horrible, friendship-ending fight. Only hours they'd known each other, and already this guarded intimacy that could shatter at the slightest push. "I need to sleep, too. Whatever they say, nobody here's superhuman."

Her eyes flitted to Nick, still suffering Naomi's petting with a dignified indifference, then she looked away. I pretended I didn't see it, getting up to help lay out our makeshift bedding. I brushed my mother's shoulder reaching over her and she raised her hand like I had, stroking idly at my arm; I combed fingers through her hair, tugging out tangles as though she were my little girl instead. Checking, constantly, like we had been since the lab, to make sure we really were both still there.

Before the plague, before I found out why she didn't have and never talked about family, my mother was a security worker, an anti-zombie patroller. A good job, important, great pay for a single mom. That's when she killed my own father, even though he was already dead. Undead. Stretching his hand out to her, trying to say her name. She killed him not because he was something different, outside us all, but because on the inside, where it counted, he was exactly like her. She like him. And all of us, together, only human-shaped shells around a—

We kept finding excuses to touch each other but it was like we were doing it from across a chasm, the barest, split-second brushes of fingertips like gathering sustenance for more months, years, of being entirely alone. It was her choice to leave me, to walk out when I was fifteen, after she killed him, because she thought she was too dead a thing to raise a living child, half-crazy from obliterating something too much like herself; I understood that now, a little, understood the killing part of it all too well, but still, she left. Left me to the elements—and the elementals, while she was at it. If she hadn't—

If she hadn't. If I hadn't. If the whole world were bunnies and rainbows and disease hadn't scorched it down to dirt and salt. I folded a blanket, made a smaller thicker square of one for Naomi, just to have something to do with my hands. Stephen had already taken several and wrapped them around his shoulders, indifferent to this effort to make the linoleum beneath us soft.

"So what exactly is this sister of yours going to do?" my mother asked, handing out pillows. "I mean, when we show up."

Lisa's sister, the ex-zombie. The one that we'd all fled the remnants of Gary to try and find. Because Lisa claimed she knew something about everything that'd happened to us all, that might still keep happening. Lisa shrugged, her arms jerking in a little whip-snap as she tried airing out her fleece. No point in that, it all smelled of dust and mold and stale corn chips. "Nobody's in any danger of getting roasted over a spit, if that's what you—"

"I never said that." My mother's voice was sharp, impatient with tiredness. Full of rusty pins and needles of its own. "I've seen as much as anyone during all this, I'm not—"

"Kidding. I was kidding. I swear." Lisa pulled at a lank handful of hair, ragged and uneven from past tuggings, still acrid with the lingering smell of ash. "She'll rant about how I'm dragging the whole world in like a lot of stray cats, do I think she's running a fucking foster home, then she'll pipe down to a dull grumble and maybe actually listen when I talk." She gave me and Stephen a wary look. "Let me do the talking. She doesn't like people—even when she was human, she always liked animals more. And she was never diplomatic. It's nothing personal."

"She'd better not be looking for a body servant," Stephen muttered, punching a pillow trying to get it to soften up. "Or a cook. I've had a bellyful of that."

"She'll be looking to be let be," Lisa said, adding another blanket to Naomi's pile. "Don't even try talking to Linc, her friend Linc. He's a quiet fellow anyway, Silent Cal, but he's a stubborn son of a bitch who just won't see reason, Renee's at least a little more—"

"She wants peace and quiet, but here we are to tell her the world's turned upside down, and we need her to do Christ knows what to help fix it, and if she doesn't, then something or other might happen, we don't know what, or then again it might not." Stephen considered this scenario, giving me a look close to amusement. "And she won't have certain *issues* with— "

"I thought we agreed on where we were going." My mother looked not just wary but stricken, like someone standing under a crumbling ceiling watching another of its struts weaken, collapse. "For God's sake, hours of walking just to— "

"I didn't say to turn back." Stephen turned on his side toward the shelves, his back to us all, clutching the pillow with tense fingertips. "I just said, I'm not expecting anything when we get there but more shit. You go on and handle it, Lisa. Just like you said you would."

Silence, for a moment, as Stephen made a great show of settling in for siesta. Then Naomi crawled onto her blankets, murmuring futile endearments in Nick's ear and crunching handfuls of potato chips. I lay next to my mother, Nick a warm bit of pillow at the tops of our heads, and dutifully closed my eyes because there was nothing left to say to each other. I was vibrating with nerves and no way I'd ever sleep but it was less awkward this way, I'd just let my thoughts go adrift and—

When I opened my eyes again, my shoulders were aching, the thin fleece rucked up uncomfortably at my back, and the store windows looked out on darkness. I rose slowly to my feet, snaking with great care from our pile of limbs so I didn't wake anyone, and discovered too late how pleasantly warm that little nest had been. Crayons forgotten, Naomi lay with her chip-stuffed mouth half-open and arms not quite circling Nick's neck; he surprised me with his closed eyes and the gentle rise and fall of his chest—wouldn't eat but he was happy to sleep. Of course, there was nothing *but* sleep, where he came from.

Lisa and my mother were stretched out rigid, like thin wooden planks side by side in a buckling old floor; Stephen was his own nest of fleece, a tuft of dark hair sticking out of the top. I smoothed the tuft down and went down the aisle, still wrapped in my own blanket, slowly approaching the door. Foolish to consider waking Nick for protection, foolish to think what was outside might've tired of us when I knew—we know firsthand, don't we, Nick—that such things never tire, but maybe he changed his mind and wandered off to bother other Paradise City refugees, wretched crazy Natalie we'd left behind at the lab—

The lab wanted to unlock control of life and death, let folks choose how long they lived and when they'd die with no rot, no decay, no sickness or age. My mother the lab rat got away; she escaped. She had me. And then my father died. And then years later, after she killed what was left of him, she lost her head, ran away without me, and they found her. And kept her. Their property. Their rules.

And now, it'd started again. Natalie, another of the lab rats—the last surviving rat—still just a kid, but she learned as they worked on her, she remembered what she'd been taught. She lured us in, Stephen and me, killed us and brought us both back, held my mother half-hostage so she could hold some perverted family reunion: I owed her that much, really, she gave me my mother back. And we got away. And here we were, all the family I had left, off to find Lisa's family; there were answers there, Lisa said, supposed, hoped. Me, I couldn't imagine what anyone, anywhere could tell us. If I'd learned just one useful thing, this past autumn, winter, spring, it was that nobody ever *tells* you what you need to know. You have to work it out yourself, without words. You have to acknowledge you always knew it, all along, and just couldn't stand to admit it.

The sky outside the pharmacy was a deep, chalky ashen-black, the half moon and dottings of stars sparks of hot white flame in smoldering charcoal. The man stood there in the middle of the empty street, bare silvery head and bare pale toes pointed toward our makeshift lodgings, waxen hands folded against his expanse of long black coat. And his face... he had no face; every time I tried concentrating long enough to discern mouth, eyes, the shape of chin or forehead, it was like my own eyes couldn't help sliding away, seeing only a half-scribbled pencil sketch crumpled in the trash.

One of Natalie's sketches, he looked like, the ones pinned all over the walls of her laboratory prison room (my mother's cell, Stephen's, what had they looked like, had they even had windows like hers?). He'd been following us since we left the lab and Prairie Beach, so quiet and just far enough behind us we could almost forget—but turn around, let your sights drift to the side, and there he was. Never came an inch closer. Never retreated one step. He was all loyalty and all constancy, and what he wanted from us, where he needed us to go, we wouldn't find that out until it was right upon us, just like how Nick led me lamb-stupid toward my own death but I still never suspected it'd be from Natalie's knife—

He shifted from foot to foot, whitish feet narrow and bony with one of the big toes bulging a bit, crooked upward; human feet with all their asymmetries and imperfections, their color not artifice but anemia. It wasn't Death. I'd seen Death, the thing, the entity, taking the forms of so many different dead people, but this wasn't Death and I'd known that in my bones before Death ever told me so. It wasn't what Stephen thought either, a Scissor Man, one of those damaged lab experiments recycled for guard duty, cleanup crew, goon squad. This was something waiting for us to forget ourselves, turn our heads, realize only too late the cold hardness we lay upon wasn't the lino floor of an abandoned pharmacy, but the stone of a sacrificial altar.

Soft rustlings behind me, rodent or canine or human; I didn't turn around, I was too busy trying to fix in my mind some shape, any shape, for the features of that candle-wax face. Stephen came quietly up beside me, hair still standing on end, gazing at the man in black with an equanimity he could never manage with Nick.

"We should have slept in shifts," he said, his shoulder pressing against mine in a faint bony tap through layers of matted fleece. "He's bound to try and come inside."

"He won't," I said. I was very sure of that. "He's had the perfect chance already, but there he is."

"I wish he *had* come in," Stephen said, and in the compressed tightness of his voice I sensed the yearning for more fights, more fists and feet, release from the clenched-up, tooth-aching tension of not knowing where we were going or what we'd find or what our uninvited guest might do when we got there. "He wants something from us? Let him try and grab it, I mean, we're all right where he wants us, right now—"

"We've got no clue what he wants," I pointed out. "Maybe it's not even us. It's got to be something where we're going."

I pressed a palm to my bad eye, wincing at the tenderness like a burn, the vague nausea that came both from pain and the nasty spongy sensation of swollen flesh. Hands hurt. Eye hurt. Arms, throat, back, madly itching feet, skin still winter-cracked after dozens of lotion-slicks and weeks of spring—I'd given up on all that, on the soft constant throb behind one temple ever going away. Stephen pressed his own palm over mine.

"He must know me," he said, and as he gently pulled my fingers away, his own jumped, twitching with tension. "It must be someone I knew from before, at the lab, wanting to grab all the lab rats before that Natalie gets us back. There must be different factions, fighting, even now—I know there were. Before." A derisive little sound, aimed at himself. "Even if I've got no names. Or faces."

Stephen's ruined memory was the wound he kept worrying at because it never healed, the blistering stone stuck in his shoe. Every time they experimented on you, you lost more of yourself, lowered inch by inch into Lethe until your head went under, until what little was left of you drowned. "It isn't," I said, again, for the fourth or seventh or sixty-third time. "It's nobody you knew. It's nothing like what you think. He just appeared, like he's always been there, like he can't help but—you have to trust me about this, Stephen. This is exactly what happened with Nick."

From the corner of my eye I saw Stephen crane his neck,

looking behind us where Nick still lay, then swivel back to gaze at me.

"Nick's a real dog," he said, and the "real" was like a politeness, something we'd all merely agreed to say was true. "You keep saying that, even though he appeared out of nowhere and he never eats anything and he stares right through you and me and everyone like some kind of four-legged laser beam— "

"We wouldn't be here if it weren't for him." I was muttering under my breath, so nobody else would wake up, and the words came out almost in a hiss. "I know you haven't *forgotten* he got us away from Natalie, back in the lab, he— "

"Your mother got us out. Not him." His brows had knitted up tight, the old thundercloud lowering over his face like another fresh bruise. "Lucy got us out of the lab. Without her, we'd still be wandering in circles."

"I'd never have *found* the lab without Nick." Frustration drew my temples, my aching forehead, even tighter. "I've never have found you, my mother... it's just, he knows things, okay? He's keyed into something we aren't, at least not like we should be, and he can sense what might happen next, like a smell, and lead me to— "

"So which is it?" Stephen's eyes were hard with a sudden, untoward triumph, a cop who didn't care his confession was coming by the business end of a baton. "Which is it? A real dog? Or some sort of— " He flung a hand at the air. " —ghost? Like that, that phantom, that Angel of Death you said you saw— "

"*Said* I saw—I saw it, Stephen, I saw *him*." All those weeks I thought I was crazy, that I'd snapped inside from the blood on my hands and in my mind and that it was all a hallucination— I'd seen it all turn real, delusion made flesh, and now Stephen wanted to take that away from me. It wasn't fair, it wasn't *fair*. "I saw him and I keep seeing him because he's here, everywhere around us, Natalie might be fucked in the head but she was totally right about— "

"Is Nick real, or isn't he?" More baton, every word a hard, stinging tap. "Which is it? You can't have it both ways, Amy— "

"I can't?" I bit back a shout. "Everything that's happened, I can't? Since when? Where the hell have you even been during all this, for Christ's sake?"

I glared at him, waiting for him to lose his temper in earnest and give that baton a real swing. Just try it. Why was he acting like this, why now? He'd believed me since before the lab, all the way back in Paradise; we'd known each other and believed each other on sight and now he was backtracking like all the others had been right, everyone who'd dismissed us both as tainted, stone crazy. It couldn't be he'd forgotten, forgotten so soon everything we'd seen, could it? Maybe he really had, maybe it was all his memory. But Lisa, and my mother, I could tell they didn't really believe me either. (Naomi, she didn't count; six-year-olds would believe anything.) Everything that happened, everything we'd seen just hours ago—why didn't any of them want to believe me?

Stephen reached out a hand again, touched my hair with slow caution like he was certain I'd jerk away. I stood still, just watching, and he stroked it, rested fingers on my shoulder, let his arm drop back down to his side.

"Scissors," he said. "Your mother found some." He jabbed an absent, almost brutal finger at his own throat. "And one of those little sewing hooks, that pulls out stitched threads. We can get rid of these, they itch like crazy when—"

"Tell me about it." All the way here over miles of road, congealing into one big expanse of potholes always circling the same dead steel mill, coke plant, used car lot—all that way, the soft ceaseless itch was like a tiny nest of millipedes, scuttling endlessly back and forth across my windpipe; my fingers kept twitching to crush all their dry dead filament-legs into powder, tear them from the burrows they'd scored in my skin. I pictured something laying eggs there, like a zombie hatching beetles and flies, and shuddered. "Tomorrow, before we leave."

"Tomorrow," he repeated.

He stood there for a moment, awkward, all the anger drained away. Then he leaned forward, gave my mouth a fleeting kiss, and walked back to the tangle of limbs, warm blankets, low steady sleepers' breath. I didn't turn around. We both needed to be alone, just now.

Tomorrow. If we kept our pace, we might cross the county line tomorrow, find the beach farther east at Cowles Shores, meet Lisa's sister and those friends of hers and it'd all be a big old party—ex-humans, ex-zombies, real live people all sharing and caring and merry like Christmas. Just like Paradise City, one big happy family of gimcrack lords and shellshocked serfs and how had I ever managed to kill Mags, to do that to poor murderous Billy whom she'd left behind in her impossible dying, *how*? Lisa's sister sees things we don't, knows things we don't, that's Lisa's story and so we'll find out everything, somehow, if we just keep walking and walking toward her for the rest of our lives, then all of this will be explained. Tomorrow, and tomorrow, and tomorrow.

Toenails, clicking softly behind me, and then something leaning against my shin: Nick, waiting discreetly until Stephen was settled in and sleeping before fleeing his presence for mine. Rough, shaggy, unkempt fur, the bones beneath it hard smooth planes and the flesh warm and solid and alive: a real dog. Every bit as real even when he was still something that melted into air, just like Death appearing and disappearing before my eyes, just like that man outside I couldn't see and couldn't stop seeing was nothing corporeal, but he was still real as real.

Flesh isn't reality; I'd figured that out with startling speed once I realized I wasn't crazy after all—it's just a testimony to reality, something you can touch and feed and love and hurt as a stand-in, a symbol, for the thing that's really there. Like Lisa's statues, inside the ruined church where she'd insisted on stopping on the way here. I'd craned my head inside, as we all stood there awkwardly waiting for her to finish, and saw her crouched silently before an impassive ash-gray Virgin Mary, thin slender fingers on one of its outstretched hands all broken off (someone surely tried to eat them, at the worst of the plague). It wasn't the statue getting the love, of course—that was just the stand-in. We're all just statues of ourselves; all our bodies, souls solidified. The sculpting clay rots away, all that was there before it still stands. Before he was there, Nick was there. Both at once.

Souls. I hadn't been raised that way, to think about souls. We were agnostics. I'd thought I was, anyway.

They weren't getting rid of Nick. They all wanted to, I knew that, all but Naomi (and I'd appeal to her if I had to, if they all told me Nick had to go, I'm not proud). He helped save us, back in the lab, gave us our avenue of escape, and this is the thanks he gets. Even if the only reason he saved us, just like last time, was to deliver us to something else, to what's waiting outside. To that statue of a man, all livid wax and impassive stone... but those knobbly feet aren't any artwork, stop just fucking standing there and move, for Christ's sake, twitch a finger, sneeze cough fart do *something* halfway human before I—

Nothing. And nothing.

Lisa's sister knows things we don't. *Lisa* says. I wonder if she knows, if the man outside knows I've killed three people, all in a row, in just under a year: one for autumn, two for spring. That's serial killer numbers. Who'd ever believe how it happened? You'd have to be crazy, snapped, to think any of it was true. And it's *all* true.

"Three," I told Nick, a soft murmur though this was a confession he'd already heard over and over again, before ever I spoke it aloud. "An ex and two humans makes three."

He stretched his head up toward my palm and I stroked his fur, ran a hand up and down his snout.

People aren't very imaginative, really; they like stories best when they know they're true. And what I know to be true, is this: like everyone else's, my own flesh and blood is just a statue, a stand-in for what I really am, but I don't know what that real thing *is*. I never have. I confessed it to Stephen, that feeling of unoccupied housing and hollow plaster-space all inside me—inside him too, just like me, such an overpowering rush of love and relief when he said *Then it's not just me*—but the spaces don't magically fill up just because a mother, a lover, a sort-of older sister come to help you, listen to you, try and save you. There's something inside me that was never human, never right, long before any of this happened, and I could blame it for making me a killer, but I chose that fate. A choice made from rage or fear or a warped notion of justice is still choosing. The hollowness inside me didn't make me evil. I did that. I chose.

No matter where I am, whatever I do or think or feel, it's always like I'm somewhere else at the same time, the way Nick is flesh but still a ghost, the way the man outside is following our path but on his own road entirely. Life hits me in the face, overpowers me physically or psychically like it hasn't stopped doing since I thought my mother died, but even as every part of me feels it, even as it thuds through me like my one truest heartbeat and I choke on it all, drown in my own blood, somehow I'm always somewhere else, standing aside, forever watching the watcher inside me. Depressed, I bet someone would say (had said and said and said, after my mother disappeared, tone-deaf broken records all). No. That's such a useful word, *depression*, a damp musty flattened-fleece blanket to throw over anything someone else doesn't want to think is real. I might very well be *depressed* but I'm much more than that: I'm absent. Absentminded, but also absent-bodied; here, and not. Living in the moment, as everyone does because they have to—and yet, I've never been here. I never have, all my life, been entirely here.

Is that why it seems like I can see things, sometimes, before anyone else can? Jenny-Jessie-Ginny-Lisa's sister, whatever her name is, does that happen to her too? Nick, Death himself, they weren't even the half of it. Though I knew now it had really happened, that I hadn't imagined it, what it *meant* I didn't know at all. You, outside, you faceless thin-fingered slab-footed thing only yards away, but still somewhere I can't follow—do you know? You must. I've died once already, walked unknowing straight to my own execution. Is it happening again, are you taking me there again? Taking all of us? Stephen's right: if you are, then just walk right in and do it now.

Come on. Do it. You can hear me. I know I don't have to say a word for you to hear what I'm thinking.

The spring that had started off so hot, dry and hot, was rolling over itself and going cold; the wind outside picked up, rattling the shattered door's metal frame, rushing up the legs of my jeans, whipping the blanket-edges hard around my ears. The man outside was still. Even as the tree branches bent and twisted under the assault, his sickly-pale moonlight hair, the hem of his long black coat, they merely stirred, ruffled faintly, and then subsided.

What are you?

He uncurled his fingers. Stretched them out, long and straight. Then folded them again, resting so decorous against his coatfront.

What am I?

Still and decorous, like prayer. I don't pray. Not like Lisa. There's nothing out there that wants to hear it.

Where are you taking us? And wherever it is, will I end up back where I was, all alone?

The moonlight dimmed and faded as the wind increased, the clouds growing thicker in preparation for rain. Whatever fell from the sky, however furious the rush of water, he'd never soak to the skin, it'd never touch him. As the first large, fat drops came down, I went as close to the doorway as I dared, stretching a hand outside just to watch the water roll down my palm, my sleeve go damp and then dark, clinging to me saturated and wet; not like him, never like him. No matter what I was, not him.

I wrung the cloth out as best I could and retreated inside, to try and sleep.

TWO

NATALIE

They were gone.

Everyone was gone!

It wasn't fair, I didn't plan it this way—I was going to stay at Paradise City long enough I'd get to be Amy's friend, I'd explain things to her. Where she really came from. Where her mother really came from (I couldn't believe it, how much they both looked alike, I'd searched months and months for anyone else from my real family, my lab family, and here they just fell right into my lap). We were going to be friends. She'd bring Stephen along, of course. I was so happy when they fell in love but of course they would, they're the same type, same blood, how would they not fall in love forever? How could she not see right away we were supposed to be friends?

But I couldn't stand how they treated me in Paradise. I couldn't take it anymore, humans treating me like dirt when it's folks like *me* who should be telling *them* what to do, so I left early and then Phoebe, that rotten crazy bitch Phoebe, *she* jumped the gun and told the lab workers, my workers, about who Amy really was. She guessed it, she turned them in.

If I ever found Phoebe, I'd kill her. I sat there rocking back and forth, under the big pine tree in the woods behind the lab where I'd gone to cry, and I prayed and hoped that she'd died in that fire. I kept hearing that the humans set Paradise City on fire—they couldn't stand things there anymore either. I hoped they all died in it.

It wasn't my fault things turned out this way!

I was going to show Amy everything, the laboratory space, the dissection rooms, the rooms where I grew up. Where her mother stayed, all that time, when they were experimenting on her. I saw Amy sneaking around looking, the nosy bitch who thought her shit doesn't stink—except *he* wouldn't want her if she were that kind of virgin, the kind who never did anything wrong and never had any dirt on her. Smile and smile and pretend that blood on your teeth is just a little old lipstick smear. *I* made her just like Stephen, like her mother, like me. *I* did!

I did it, and why wasn't she happy? How could she not be happy! I killed her, dropped her like a stone sinking-drowning in a sea no one but us can cross, and then I dove right in and retrieved her from the full-fathom-five bottom where no one but us can dive. I brought her back from all that brand new and one of us. I made her *what she was always supposed to be* and gave her a mother, a boyfriend, a best friend just like her. We could've been best friends, if she'd just let me explain! She was always inside out all her life, without ever knowing it, and I turned her true face out to the world and if I could've just explained that, if she'd just *shut up and let me talk*, she'd have understood and been happy about it. She'd be my best friend.

And she would have talked to *him* about me. Death, the Friendly Man, who came and went and was there for me and loved me all the time I was growing up and then he was gone, he just vanished—I was always so good, but he left me. I loved him and it turned out he was nothing. It was like thinking you had a pet bird, a big beautiful black bird strutting along on a pure-white parapet right outside your window, back and forth, any time day or night you cared to look, and then he collapses into a heap of black feathers and falls like a stone and when you rush to catch him you realize, he never was: it was always a heap of rotten feathers, a dirty discarded rag, an old leather boot squashed and huddled up on itself like something nesting. What a joke. What a nasty trick—

I had to stop crying so hard, I felt sick. Choking on snot like some nasty lab bitty-baby. It was usually so pretty up here on the ridge, the white gravel road winding outside the lab and the whole sweep of dunes and water right in front of you, the woods and the lab yard dark green shadows behind. It was like having your own country estate and I would've shown Amy the Aquatorium, its columns concrete gray instead of marble white but still like a pretty little Greek temple cake-crumbling into the sands. Up on the second floor where it's all open space you can see the whole horizon, all the way out across the lake to Chicago. Chicago's gone now, I suppose. I never even got to see it.

It was nice here, though. Didn't need Chicago. The lab would have beach parties here and I got to go too, for summer solstice and the Fourth of July and Labor Day and Birth-Day, the day they found out one of their experiments could bear a living child—did you know that, Amy? Did you know dozens, hundreds of people you never even knew gathered here for *your birthday* with barbecue and sparklers and cake and you got everything, you always got everything. Your mom might've run away but she was still contributing, they were still researching her in the wild. You too. I could've showed them to you, all the files and field notes they kept on you and your mother. I even saved some of them after the plague hit and the sick people were looting the lab, so hungry they were eating paper. I was saving them for you, Amy! All of it!

I decided to burn them. Never mind Birth-Day, you all could go ahead and die out there without my secret of what could bring you back, and I'd have a Death-Day, I'd take everything about you and burn it all up. Right away. I crawled out from under the pine tree, trudged over the weed-gone lawn and through the back door, and I was home. My home.

There were rusty red streaks still smearing the floor, my floor, where I'd fought with that filthy thing Amy called a pet dog, but here were all my drawings, my desk with the special locked drawer she didn't open, my little filing cabinet. My doll. There'd been boxes of files about Amy and her mother but what I'd salvaged just filled up that one little desk drawer. The thought of how she hadn't even thought to look in there, passed right over *herself* by spying on me, it made me feel even better as I jabbed the drawer-key into the lock.

Bent warped key, soft cheap metal, the lock rattling loose in its base—it was all so cheap, all the used-up banged-up things they gave me, not like precious Amy's barbeque-sparklers-layer cake Birth-Day with no expense spared. Didn't matter, not anymore, what I had here was worth ten thousand parties. I had everything that was left: her mother's real name, experiment logs, some of those reports Amy's pediatrician and her dad's sister and a couple of neighbors sent in because humans really are tattling scum who'll do anything for a little money, hospital records—the damn drawer stuck halfway open; I'd stuffed too many papers inside. I snaked fingers in to try and edge the papers away from the drawer seams, ease them out—

Cold in here, like those high-up windows I could never force open had suddenly broken, given way in a storm, letting early March air rush in. But it was almost May. I'd been sweating trying to break open my own stupid lock but my arms and back went tense with the chill, a fresh strong punishing breeze with a damp green smell of springtime, and then I started to shiver. So cold, even in dead January this room never got so cold. The drawer wouldn't move, I couldn't get my fingers far enough in to grab. I hated this desk, I hated this room, I was such a special-special experiment but not like that bitch Amy, who got her own white desk with flowers on it and a chair to match when she was twelve (her aunt tattled about the birthday, her aunt tattled about everything), all I ever got was this gray metal ugliness with a shortened leg they were going to throw away—

"Turn around," he said, behind me.

His voice was soft, quiet, velvety-damp just like the air: sharp and freezing as all of January, rich and scent-filled like the middle of May. It made my head spin. You, again. After all this time. Go away, it was Amy you really loved. All the work we did here, the work I was still doing, was so I never had to love you again.

"Turn around, Miss Beach," he said. Even quieter.

Natalie Beach. That was how we got written up in the files, us lab rats, like medieval people whose last names were all Of-The-Nearest-Village. I never found out what my parents were really called, or what happened to them. I yanked two-handed at the drawer, felt its frame buckle and warp.

"You can leave now," I said. Cool as March, keeping all my love to myself. My fear. "I don't need you anymore." Let the drawer snap loose from the frame, go flying from the desk like a tooth pulled from a mouth with twine and a slamming door. "You only ever pretended to be my friend, go talk to precious Amy if that's who you—"

"Amy will die soon." Soft as soft now, a sneering croon, like a lullaby for a baby its mother hates from birth. "That much, at least, will make you happy. Be a polite little freak of nature and turn around."

My teeth banged together with the cold, clicking sharp and hard like the teeth of the zombie I'd seen die out in the woods when I was six or seven: it succumbed to old age, rotted and crumbled down to a walking skeleton, shaking itself to powder there in the April violets and needle-stick beach grass. I'd never be warm again, I'd never—I threaded my hands into my sleeves, sweatshirt fleece spotted and ruined with dog's blood and mine, and cringing and shivering in all my love and fear, I turned around.

Death can take on any face he wants, when he calls on you, the face of any dead person he's already claimed as his. Gray hair, this time. Little wire-rimmed glasses. Khakis and neatly tucked-in flannel shirt, the clothes of a lab man heading out for field work. A nasty, torn-up nylon backpack, bulging and stained dark brown with something's old blood, slung easy over one shoulder. He smiled at me and my skin went numb with the encroaching ice.

"Hey, kiddo," he said.

Feeling your heart leap up and dance for someone you'd sworn to hate is like hurting so much you pass out, your own insides tormenting you into oblivion, and then getting hauled upright and forced awake so the torture can start all over again. His colorless eyes saw straight through me and into my jumped-up heart and my fingers were tinged blue; it wasn't him doing that, this part of the world was well used to frost in May. I shoved my hands in my pockets and clenched my fingers, rubbing against the cloth to try and coax them back to life.

"Hell of a greeting," he said, "after so long away."

His voice had a weight that stretched out its softness, distorted it, like fistfuls of coins in a sock. "I called and called for you and you never came," I said, backed against the warped desk drawer like he'd come for my papers, Amy's papers. Like he gave a damn about things like that. "When I was younger, and they were still experimenting on me. After the plague, when I was the only one left here. After I started our experiments again. All that time." I laughed. "We're getting rid of you, that's the whole point. We're figuring out how to control when life ends, how to keep folks from dying at all. And I, me, I've found out how to make it happen, what the real secret is to cheat death—and it's right here, on this beach. It's right here. So I don't need you anymore."

He was standing across the room and then suddenly he was right next to me, inches away, and I never saw him move. Nose to nose, no human breath from him to warm my freezing face, and his raised-up hands didn't touch me but somehow I still went stumbling backwards grabbing at the air, clutching the desk for balance as he pulled the broken drawer out so smooth and light. He didn't touch my papers but they spilled out anyway, of their own accord, fluttering all over the floor in a dry drifting snow.

"Well?" he said, and slammed the drawer shut so hard the whole desk, my arms gripping it, shuddered. "Aren't you happy you've got your Friendly Man back? Here-boy good-boy coming running whenever you want him?" Smiling, smiling wider, his words a throaty hiss. "Baby cried and cried for papa, now baby's got him back."

This wasn't his house, he couldn't talk to me like this. This was *my* house, all my laboratory now. He'd always been so nice to me before. "I told you, I know what you're about." Stronger, louder than that, dammit, Grandma who ran all the scientific testing on me always said to straighten up and look people in the eye. I'm using my loudest straighten-up voice right now and I still sound like a weak little girl. "I know what your secret is, I know why this beach is so important to you. We found it, all of us here, the lab found out how to control life and death. It's right here in the sands. I've killed two people, with my own hands, and brought them back alive. I don't need you anymore—"

"Baby's got papa back and if she's very, very good, he'll swear never, ever to leave her again, no matter what she does. Isn't that just what you always wanted, deep down in your rotten dragged-back stinking dead insides? Or maybe there's some second thoughts now, rattling around that tiny little mind?" Slam, went the drawer, slam again, his stretched-out arm shoving and banging it shut. Again. Again. "Aren't you glad you've got me?" Again. "How d'you like me?" Again. "D'you like your blue-eyed boy?"

That slamming drawer vibrated all through me like a blow, a hard bruising fist, but I couldn't let go of the desk. No matter where I turned my head, we were face to face and his light clear eyes, stolen human-mask eyes, they tugged at something in me like I really was rotten inside, rotten as the dead things that survived the autumn sickness, and that was the part of me that yearned to have him back. "I think you have to go away now," I said, and something dragged the words out of me, in a whisper, like they were all flattened and scraped against a cold concrete floor. "This isn't your house anymore. We dug up your secret. We know how to make dead people live again—not as zombies. As *people*. You can't stop it. And you have to leave."

He tilted his head, his eyes soft with amusement. "Go away now," he repeated. Slam. "Is that begging, perhaps? Is that how you tell me you're scared, under all that idiot talk about my *secrets*?" Slam. Slam. "Don't just spit out nonsense you've heard the grownups say. You're far too old for that." Slam. "Old enough to talk." Slam. "Reason." Slam. "Argue. Old enough to die. But then, nothing on earth's ever too young to die."

Slam, thud, slam, reverberating through my arms and shoulders and back and jaw, wrenching me between his hands like I was a dry half-broken branch. The drawer banged home and pulled back faster and faster and then it was a volley, a frenzy of clanging steel and jolting blows shredding me into splinters and I screamed, my fingers flying away from the desktop frantic to save me. I stumbled backwards, didn't fall, wrapped my arms around myself but they couldn't keep me still; I shook and trembled with the rattling echoes inside me, the screech of tortured metal ringing in my ears.

He reached an arm toward me, to jolt and break me just like he had that desk, and I cringed and squeezed my eyes shut. When I opened them again, he was holding something out—my papers, the whole lot of them from all over the floor, gathered up tight and crumpling in his fist. He couldn't have picked them all up so fast. Bits of them fell to the floor again, like torn-off corners, and then, there in his hand, they all crumbled so softly into pulp, into dust.

"You won't need these anymore," he told me, watching them disintegrate. "Amy won't need them either. Not where she's going. There's nothing your researchers"—that word, in his quiet mouth, was a snake poised to strike—"can tell anyone anymore, to do them any good."

My desk was ruined now, the frame buckled and bent and the lock-up drawer twisted nearly in half, hanging forlorn from the edge of its runners like it'd melted. The vibrations of it were still banging all through me, my whole skin prickling and painful as the warmth, spring warmth, slowly flowed back. I wasn't going to let him think he'd really scared me.

"We can do lots of things now," I said. "We can bring dead people back. I can. Us lab rats, we're new, a new kind of human. When we die, we can bring each other back. This isn't your house anymore. We've kicked Death out."

"You think you have me figured out," he said, and he was cheerful again, quietly genial, his face thoughtful as he surveyed the tiny anthills of dust littering my floor. "Because you know. You're in possession of all the facts."

He smiled, a real smile, open and sweet like the old days. "You know all the facts. Well, know this, when the time comes: you had a chance to stop me. All you had to do was leave this place—let it sit, find another roof, tell each other all sorts of ghost stories about the God-knows-what-went-on-here as it rots in the sand. You did, for a bit, last fall—remember, when the folks trying to shelter here gave up, headed east? But then you came back." He didn't move a step but he was still inches from me again, eye to eye. "*You* came back. My little prodigal daughter, crying for her fatted calf. Telling old father he's not welcome in his own home anymore, he has to clear out."

Something stirred in the dust piles, the little paper trails, shifting, settling, crawling out of the center. Ants. They were actual anthills now, all around us, with tiny black dots busily heading in and darting out as they set up housekeeping at our feet.

"You threw me out," he said, and watched impassively as a line of ants reached the summit of his shoe. "Can't even set a foot out of doors without getting kicked out of my own home—you can't even imagine how long it took me to get used to it all, to make what's mine really *mine*, but you don't care. Don't give a damn. So I'm out." His voice was so soft, so suffocatingly soft. "All your experiments, setting up to take the Grim Reaper's scythe away, so I can't claim a single solitary soul until they decide when to die, how to die, all on their own. And *then* you have the gall to turn around and beg, sob, cry for me to come back, daddy, come baaaack—and I do, I do just that, and after all that fuss you throw me out. You want me gone that badly? Maybe I'll just go. Forever. Not *one single part of me* ever to return."

The ants struggled over the scuffed toe of his shoe, its dirt-caked sides, in a futile search for food. His other foot reached out and nudged; a cluster of ants scattered, running frantically back and forth, their sandhill a flattened heap and the rice-grains of their eggs crushed to glassine specks of powder. He laughed.

"Don't," I said. A weak little whisper. I hadn't meant to say it.

"My first mistake," he said, smiling too hard and too wide, "was thinking all this was over and done. All that nasty upstart lab-ratting of years and years, grabbing at my scythe and spitting in my face, the plague took good care of all of that and all of you—" He chuckled, a smothered explosion. "And the best part is that it wasn't my doing, it was all of yours. I just admired from a distance, laughed my head off, reaped one truly stunning man-made whirlwind. Because I was foolish enough to think that *finished* it, that nobody left standing would ever again defy me like that, face to face. You, though—you're dragging all your kind right back into it, a little palace coup, dangling it in front of them knowing they can't refuse—so!" He shrugged, let his painfully stretched-out mouth relax. "You'll all have to suffer. Every one of you, everywhere. You could have left, you could have stopped this. You had the chance. You, Natalie. And you threw it away."

"I don't believe you," I said. Ants trekked around my toes, seeking the hiding places they'd lost. "I don't."

"Of course you don't. But that's all right. That's half the fun."

He was too far away for his arm to reach but still right there in my face, a dizzying mirror-refraction turned solid, patting my shoulder all good-kiddo with happiness dancing in his eyes. "And when you realize just how wrong you were—sorry, you just blew your last chance! You, my sweet Amy, all her funny little friends—"

"Amy," I said, and I was supposed to be cool and nonchalant

and make him understand just how unwelcome he was but that name made tears threaten to spill all over again, ignited an angry little coal in my chest. "It's always Amy, Amy gets presents and friends and *you* and why do you like her better? You help her, you rescue her, I know it's you who sent that horrible ghost dog to guide her here and get her out of—why? Why is it never *me*?"

His hand on my shoulder tightened and from each pressing fingertip a plume of crawling unpleasantness, the sickly heat of nausea, went traveling down and through me like a little nest of snakes.

"Because," he whispered, "she might've turned her back on me, but she never spit in my *face*."

He was back where he was supposed to be now, on the other side of the room, self-contained as a bird strutting over the soft loose ridges of sand above the lake. Right there in front of me and completely unreachable, like the thick, dark borderline where lake met sky.

"I wouldn't waste time envying Amy, if I were you," he said. Squatting down, laying an opened palm against the infested blood-spattered floor. He hadn't even asked whose blood it was. "She's going to die too. That should make you happy. They'll all die, everywhere, thanks to you—no matter what happens, you can rest assured it's all you—but I admit it, some deaths you regret a lot more than others. Some of those others? You just don't give a damn at all."

He looked up at me. "I love a killer. But what I hate, more than anything else alive, is a thief. Like you."

The thick ribbon-clusters of ants crawled in a steady, obedient line up his fingers, into his waiting palm, no panic or retreating when he closed his fingers around them and kept opening them up empty. All of them, so dutiful and happy, diving into the abyss. Then he took up his rucksack and was back on his feet.

"I've got things to do," he said. "I've got to leave, I'm a busy man. Thanks to you." His eyes flashed with a dark hollow sheen, then softened. Warm and kind as the old days. "But don't you get lonely, now. I'll be seeing you again. Very soon. Before we all part ways forever."

He turned on his heel and vanished, leaving me there in the cold and the dust.

THREE
LUCY

"I told you he was nothing but a Scissor Man." Stephen reached over to Amy, pulled the plastic travel slicker's hood up from its slide down her neck. Thank God I'd thought to grab some rain gear, cheap and flimsy as it was—we woke up to puddles in the store aisle and it hadn't stopped spitting, pouring, spitting since we started walking. "He finally got sick of us, or didn't like his odds, and left."

Amy kept her head down, not looking at him, me, anyone. The wind had made short work of her hood even when it stayed put, blowing in volleys of droplets so her hair was plastered to her cheeks, to that swollen-shut eye that made me wince inside whenever I saw it. My handiwork, that eye, even though I'd rather have died than hit my own child (I got more than enough of that, growing up, that's one of the few memories no lab-table time could erase). That and her fight-swollen fingers and torn-up throat and her expression permanently hardened, setting in its own rough sharp stone, even when she smiled or laughed or cried—that's what I've made of my own child, by leaving her behind. The flash-fire craziness of thinking, at the time, that I was doing right by her wasn't half enough excuse.

"It wasn't a Scissor Man," she finally said. Her voice was short and terse, little clipped-off syllables like her father's when he was impatient. Her "real" father, not my Mike. "I keep telling you that and telling you that, I know what sort of thing he is and if we can't see him just now, it doesn't mean jack. He's still there. So don't get too excited."

Her voice, his face, like they'd been arguing about this all night. Maybe they had been, for all I knew; I fell over drained dry on a heap of fleece and all of a sudden it was morning and we were shivering with the chill and rain, the strange man-shaped apparition who'd been trailing us all yesterday up and vanished. Not a trace left. "Either way," I said, "at least we don't have to see him following us—"

"So what?" Amy shook her head, exasperated at him, me, all of us. "Nobody wants to get it, do they? He's *still there*, whatever we do, and God only knows where he's taking us."

"There's nothing—" Stephen shook his head as he pushed aside another tree branch, inky-slender like a living brushwork line; a shower of tender green buds, small and fine as paper-punch holes, shook free and stuck to our damp plastic slickers and the skin of our hands. Sandy Shores had given way to open woods, former subdivisions gone to prairie. "Okay. Fine then, Amy, we're dancing to his tune, right now. He's here pulling all the strings and we only think we're walking, so why the hell are we even bothering at all?"

"So what, you want to go back to Prairie Beach?" Amy's voice was sharp and angry but her face was wary, almost fearful, like we might all just run off and leave her alone in the woods with a man who wasn't there. I couldn't much blame her for thinking that. "I can't stop you, I guess. No strings on you, you can do whatever you want."

"Do you think I'm crazy? I never *said* that, I just—"

"Dear God," Lisa muttered, from up ahead. "Will everybody

just stop bickering—"

"No," Amy said flatly, shoving her fists in her pockets. "Not over something this important."

Lisa kept on trudging forward, skinny shoulders hunched and those big broad paddle-feet splashing though the thin watery mud. I didn't like her, didn't like her narrow suspicious face and soaked rattails of dishwater hair and that plague-dog's voice whose every syllable barked and growled and snapped—she'd been good to me, better than good to my daughter, she'd never leave her own child standing in the dust like I had, but I just did not *like* her. Her little girl, Naomi, clutched her hand and had eyes only for her, just like it should be. Amy lingered behind them with me and Stephen, reaching out stroking fingers at soothing intervals like she had to keep checking we were there, but it was when Lisa spoke that she really listened. Her eyes would grow alert and her head tilt to attention, like that stray dog we all wished she'd just left behind at Prairie Beach, and when Lisa said not to bicker, defiance gave way to silence. Me, though, I still didn't know what to say to anyone. Quiet as that dog, that Nick, that we all wished she'd left behind.

What was I expecting? I was lucky she hadn't spat in my face. Three years of letting her think I was dead. Because I'd thought it was better that way. I was the only one to blame that someone else was her... her big sister, now. Well, she'd always wanted a sister. At least when she was little. And without Lisa I didn't know the way to Cowles Shores, much less what we'd actually do when we got there.

I kept turning my head to see if the man had come again, the man who wasn't there. There was nobody behind us but I still felt like he was there, staring at me, waiting his moment to show himself in the flesh and ambush and pounce. Lab-rat jitters, only natural after spending your whole life tracked and followed everywhere whether you knew it or not. Even when she was small, Amy just took it as normal that windows always had curtains closed, that I could never sit with my back to a door; when Mike's sister put me there, one Thanksgiving, Amy switched all the place settings around while us grownups were in the kitchen. Nobody ever really understood our little ways but us.

Naomi yanked hard at Lisa's hand, then harder, like she was trying to pull it out and keep it in her pocket. "Can we stop soon?" she pleaded, in that little seesaw whine every child's got patented. "I'm tired."

"We just got started," Stephen muttered. Nick, padding along in the mud, brushed against Stephen's shin and I saw Stephen stiffen at the touch, then migrate pointedly to Amy's other side. "If you're tired, ask Lisa to pick you up."

"What am I already carrying?" Lisa said, sharp and brusque, brandishing the supply-stuffed backpacks weighing down her arms, piled on her shoulders. She'd insisted on shouldering our latter-day luggage herself, reminding us how strong that plague-body was compared with us who'd never been ill, and Amy and Stephen ignored my protests, obligingly loading her down. "You'll have to walk, Naomi, you're a big girl—"

"I never asked to be picked up." Naomi craned her head around, glaring at Stephen. "I just want to stop, just for a minute. He's not the boss of me."

"Thank God." Stephen glared right back. "I want this, I want that, when are we gonna stoooooop—"

"You're the one whining, not her." Lisa stomped one foot into a mud-puddle, then paused to stare with grim satisfaction at her saturated boot. "Knock it off."

Stephen mouthed something that made Amy shove an elbow hard into his side, but she was almost laughing. So Lisa wasn't the revered general of this army after all? That shouldn't have made me feel better. Naomi marched along in silence for another mile, then tugged at Lisa's hand again. "I think Nick needs to stop too," she said.

Nick. His inky-brushstroke ears twitched at hearing himself mentioned, but he didn't look up, just kept plodding along tireless and steady because it wasn't Amy who'd said his name. Amy's boy he was, Amy's—something inside me twitched like Nick's ears, thinking of that archaic, superstitious, perfectly suited word: *familiar.* Except familiars do the witch's bidding and if anyone were the witch here it was Nick, Nick who Amy credited with leading her away from home and bringing her to me. She'd heard him, his tireless scratching and barking, while the rest of us had only silence. And she'd killed someone. She'd killed someone, my little girl—maybe to defend herself, maybe something else, and whatever had happened, it was me who'd left her to that, to the elements. The beasts. To the protection of something that hadn't been real until she called it up and made it real. Or maybe it called itself up. Nick might've been some kind of flesh and blood—technically speaking—but whenever I looked at him, I saw nothing but a dark moving splotch, a blight. Like the hole a flame burns in a photograph, taking bigger and stronger shape as everything around it melts.

Stephen was right, however gracelessly he said it. I did not like that dog.

Naomi pivoted on her heel, walking backwards now with arms out at her sides to keep from hitting the trees; bored with walking, bored with us, bored with everything but the black dog-shaped blight that barely noticed her. "Miss Lucy," she ventured, her respectful little-girl's name for me, "I really think he needs to rest—"

"That dog, or whatever the hell he is, is just fine." Stephen gazed back at her, and there was a hardness in his eyes that would've made Naomi quiet down fast if she hadn't already seen so much—too much for someone five times her age. "You can pet him and play up to him until you drive the rest of us crazy, but he doesn't like you, d'you get it? He doesn't *care.* Stop wasting your time. If you're not her"—he jerked his chin toward Amy, her hand cradling Nick's huge, indifferent head-"then he doesn't wanna know."

I saw Lisa's shoulders twitch, somewhere under their lumpy load of nylon, but she didn't say anything. Naomi marched on in silence, neat little steps still tramping in reverse, frowning crestfallen down at her shoes. Not looking at Nick anymore.

"He does like me," she insisted at last, small and timid. "He— "

"I've had it." Stephen snapped a bending branch straight off a tree, barely missing a step as he reached up and wrenched it away. Gray and dead, that branch, the whole tree looking like it had sickened and withered months back. "I've seriously had it."

"You are not her father." The mud beneath Lisa's shoes was firmer now, cake-packed deep, but her toes plowed through it like boat prows slicing the surface of a lake. Her voice was stone scraping at metal. "Understand me? All the shit Billy and them put her through, everything that happened, you even *think* now you're gonna turn around and— "

"I'm not putting anyone through anything," Stephen hissed back. "I'm trying to talk some sense into her head."

"Calm down," I said, as if anyone would listen. "Everyone just calm down."

"You're not my father," Naomi reminded Stephen, almost shouting. "You're never my father."

"You're right about that," Stephen said, a false brightness in his voice that presaged trouble. "Because maybe if I were, you'd actually listen when I say that so-called dog is nothing you should be within a hundred feet of, much less trying to make some sort of *pet*, and if Lisa actually had half the sense Amy keeps telling me she does, then she'd— "

"Okay," said Amy, stepping between him and Naomi. "We're stopping." She slid her arms from the limp, waterlogged rain slicker and threw it at Stephen like she was aiming for his face. "Right here. We can all dry off, and— "

"We have to keep moving," said Lisa, swaying with her parcels, stubborn and angry. I'd step between her and Amy, if I had to. We'd have words. "I want to get to Cowles tonight."

"Or what? Or your sister gets mad 'cause her dinner got cold waiting, and kicks us all out?" Amy stroked Nick's head with agitated vigor, almost scrubbing it, her fingers tight and tense. "She doesn't even know we're coming. She could kick us all out anyway. And some of us, you know, we can't walk forever, we're still just barely human enough that we need to—"

"Let's just go." Stephen had the rain slicker crumpled in a big deflated ball, fingers tugging its rubbery edges like a dog's teeth gnawing a chew toy. "All right? Just forget I said a damned thing, and—"

"We're stopping because I said we're stopping, all right? God! You and Naomi and all of it, you're driving me up a fucking wall, okay? Naomi can rest and try to play with Nick and Lisa can take a load off and everybody can just calm the hell down! Ten minutes, fifteen! Believe it or not, fifteen minutes off shift, we can still somehow get to the damned beach before tomorrow!"

Silence. As I reached up and pulled strands of hair away from her bad eye, Amy brushed a hand against her throat, her sliced, stitched-up throat that made me want to cry every time I looked at it. More of my own handiwork, in leaving her. And with every passing hour, she seemed closer and closer to forgetting it was even there.

"Also," she muttered, "I really, really have to pee."

The rain was dying down. We raised our arms to cool the sweat from those plastic slickers, scraped mud off our shoes, laid the slickers down as tarps over a wet tree trunk toppled on its side in a clearing of cottonwoods. Amy, Lisa, and Naomi all went off to pee. Stephen and I sat there on our log, knee to knee, in silence.

Remnants of houses fringed our patch of forest all around, standing like great grayish ruffles of fungi ringing an invisible oak. Every man-made surface had WARNING: CONDEMNED stamped over it in regulation waterproof red, the color still fresh and bright even after months, maybe years of hard sunlight, snow, rain. Nick sniffed all around our log and all around the dirt, and when he got to Stephen's feet, Stephen drew back, rising abruptly from our perch.

"I'm gonna walk around a little," he said, throwing a vague arm toward the waist-high backyard grasses. "Clear my head."

He walked off without waiting for an answer. The rancor of just moments before had vanished, abruptly as a swift-moving storm passing over a prairie; he looked almost confused now, as if something outside him had been driving his temper and tongue. Maybe sharing close quarters with three women and a little girl he barely knew was a lot to ask of him, of any boy that age. Maybe getting killed and brought back as much as he had, every last cell grist for someone else's mill, maybe it just screwed you up for good. It'd explain a lot about my own life, right after Amy was born, when I was trying so hard for her sake to be an ordinary average human. So much for that.

It was weirdly quiet here; no birdsong, no branches snapping in the wind, no soft scuttling sounds of animals in the underbrush. Everything was muted, silenced, as if the rain had been a heavy smothering blanket muffling the sky and ground. Nick ignored me and sniffed round and round one particular tree, probably chasing some elusive squirrel. Lisa had piled the backpacks at the end of the log, garish and bumpy like painted rocks, and I rummaged inside one for lunch: a bar of Honey-Kissed Bunches Of... some silage or other, best not to ask. The chocolate chips were like little bits of something charred, and the crispy rice had gone soft. Naomi came back, alone, and I handed her a bar of her own.

"Where's Lisa?" I asked.

"Over there," she said, angling her head toward the backyards as she sat back beside me and unwrapped her granola bar. Her face scrunched up suddenly in conspiratorial child-mirth. "She has to poop," she confided, giggling a little as she tore clumsily at the paper. "I didn't want to look."

"I don't blame you," I said, shoving her shredded granola wrapper in my pocket. Something about the way she drummed her heels against the log, a slow steady left-right-left of pink and silver sneakers gone gray with mud, it reminded me of Amy at that same age: even her restlessness was thoughtful, methodical.

As she made short work of the bar, Nick suddenly abandoned his tree and, as if he wanted to prove he wasn't just angling for food (though really, I'd never seen him eat anything at all), sat himself beside Naomi and put his nose to her empty palm. Her whole face lit up with joy and she wrapped arms around his neck, hugged him hard, and was rewarded with a considered, careful thump of the tail. Whap against the ground, pause, whap again. Then stop.

"See?" she said, reproving and triumphant like I'd tried to come between them. "Nick likes me just fine. I know he does."

Nick snuffled and scratched hard at an ear and let her hug him until she was satisfied. Those watery eyes of his, red-rimmed, always looking like they're about to stream over with tears... I didn't like him, I didn't like Naomi touching him, but there was no reason at all she shouldn't pet him if she wanted. Stick her finger right through that burnt melted hole in the photograph. "Nick's a stray," I said, not using the word I was really thinking. "We don't know what he's like with people, or if he's used to them. Stephen was just afraid you might get bitten."

The look of scorn Naomi threw me might've made me laugh, if things were different. "He's jealous of Nick," she said, scratching the dog behind the ears; whether or not Nick was used to humans, she was definitely accustomed to dogs. "He thinks Amy loves Nick better than him. And he's scared of Nick. He's scared of everything, but he thinks nobody can tell." Her face fell, as her fingernails patiently worked Nick's fur. "I don't know why he's so scared. Stephen was nice to me, before. He brought me extra food, and helped me hide when Papa Billy was angry at me. Now all of a sudden, he's mad at me all the time."

Papa Billy. Amy had told me about Mags and Billy, about how Lisa had claimed Naomi as her own. She seemed to make a habit of that, this Lisa, with other people's daughters. Mama Mags, who my Amy killed in the Prairie Beach woods, and Papa Billy, her furious, grieving, monstrous widower—had they been little Naomi's real parents? Alive and human, once, then turned by the plague? I couldn't ask, didn't want to know. She saw it all happen yesterday, little Naomi, and there was nothing we could do about that. She saw me like that, too, just yesterday, with the blood of supposed fellow humans all over and in my mouth. Feverish with biting and tearing flesh, flushed with a glorious liberation from scruples and care and letting bygones be. It had been there inside me all along, that need, that instinct, even as I tried so hard to appear normal, human, to be patient, methodical—

"Sometimes," I said, "people get angry when they're afraid. They say things they wouldn't if they were thinking straight. Stephen's been very afraid. Like we all have. It'll all be better once we get to Cowles." I didn't believe that, not really, but I had to. "Everyone will calm down again."

Naomi wriggled on her plastic cushion, hopped off the log, and dragged away the draped slicker to settle herself on the wet, rough bark. The damp of the tree trunk seeped right through her pink corduroy pants; Lisa wouldn't be at all happy when she saw it, but we didn't have any changes of clothes. "I had a bad dream last night," Naomi said. "It felt like I couldn't breathe."

I put a hand to her forehead: only as warm as it should be and the damp was from rain, not fever-sweat. "Are you getting a cold?" Just our luck if that happened, but then, it was something of a miracle none of us had gotten sick yet.

"I mean in the dream. Not for real." She was drumming her heels again, slow, steady, right and left. Nick sat at her side, watery eyes trained on her face. "We were walking to the beach, like we are now. Then this giant dark thing, like a shadow, or a big hand smushing an anthill, it came down on top of everything and it was like we were the anthill, and I couldn't see or think or breathe at all. In the dream. Then I woke up." Her feet pedaled faster. "I think Amy is right—that man who was following us is a monster. Even though you can't see him, he's still there. But Nick saved us."

Her eyes studied the muddy ground, a thick dead dirt-caked stick arching up like a tiny dinosaur struggling in its tarpit. "Stephen, in the dream, he was fighting with someone I couldn't see, and he fell over covered in blood. But Nick saved him. Nick can fight better than he can, maybe that's why he's scared of him."

She opened her fingers, exposing a sticky last remnant of granola, and held it out to Nick. He didn't even sniff it, and finally she gave up and shoved it in her own mouth. I craned my neck toward the backyards, but nobody was in sight. Where was Lisa anyway, gastric call of the wild or not? And Amy? Billy had already attacked her once; there was more than one monstrous thing that might be following us.

"I'll be right back," I said. Nick wouldn't leave without Amy, that much at least I could say of him. "Stay here with Nick—"

"You should pee now, if you have to," Naomi advised me. "Lisa said we're not stopping again until we get to Cowles."

Lisa can quit thinking she's in charge of this expedition, sister or no sister. Even if she stepped up for Amy when I wasn't there.

The thickets of trees diminished to a thin scrim as I walked toward the lost backyards; Stephen was right there, walking back and forth in the grasses a few yards away, lost in thought. He wouldn't leave here without Amy either. Despite the rain, there were tiny patches of dead grass everywhere I looked, poking up in the midst of deep green like wheat stalks, like the islands of sharp-edged beach grasses that broke up the Lake Michigan sands. The thought of Prairie Beach—not the lab, but the land around it—gave me a pang and I shoved it aside, concentrating on the thought of Cowles Shores. I hadn't visited there since my first civic security training exercises, when Amy was barely a year old. At the farthest edge of the trees was a little spot of light brown, another of strawberry red: Lisa and Amy, sitting shoulder to shoulder with their backs to me down in the long grass. I walked closer.

"...like even when I'm right here, sitting and talking, I'm always somewhere else." Amy's voice was low, clear, carrying back to me where I stood still in the trees. "I mean, not even like I'm standing aside watching myself, even though it can feel like that, it's more that I'm always two places at once." Her hand snaked up, tugged at the grass stems. "And I don't know where the other place even is."

"Nobody's thinking right anymore," Lisa said. Her consonants snapped and her vowels scratched glass even when she tried to keep it low; even Naomi sometimes winced at the sound of her voice. A strange plague-remnant. "The entire world's just been upended, everything's changed-everything you've seen—that wasn't even a year ago, Amy. Not even one year." Silence. "And barely weeks since..."

"Since I killed Ms. Acosta."

Those words sent a hot unpleasant thrill through me, listening: not horror or agony at the confession, but a ferocious desire to stand between her and any accusers, snarl them into silence. Don't you say a word against her, Lisa, not one word.

"Since you killed Ms. Acosta," Lisa repeated. Her hesitation hung in the air like rain. "Amy, when people are pushed to their absolute limits, beyond their limits, sometimes everything just— "

"Have you ever just wanted to die?"

The heat inside me pooled, liquefied: a sickening sensation like my insides were a wax candle, bits melting in drips and streaming away.

"If you keep talking like that," Lisa said, and for once the nail-pounding harshness of her words was a relief, "or thinking like it, I'm going straight to your mother and— "

"For God's sake," Amy said, almost wearily scornful, "I'm not going to kill myself. I swear. On your stupid rosary beads, I swear it." Her hands reached back, tugging at handfuls of ponytail until a slipping elastic inched back in place. "After everything that's happened, it'd be pretty stupid to do that—there's no point. Besides, I don't want to be—have *you* ever wanted to die?"

I waited.

"Many times," Lisa said. "Even if you don't count right after Karen died—a lot of times."

"So before the plague, too?"

"Before the plague, too." Her laugh was a convulsive bark that made my whole skin prickle. "Especially before the plague."

A bird called from up overhead, the trees just behind me:

something whose crooning chirp started out low and rose high and then swiftly muted itself again. I didn't know what it was. Then I heard the croaky braying of a crow, a few yards away. The first bird's voice spiraled higher and higher once more but then, before that second low note, it abruptly stopped singing. No crow sounds, either. Just silence.

"I don't want to die," Amy was saying, calm and unhurried like she was working it all out for herself, out loud, for the first time. "I never wanted to die, I mean, I wasn't afraid of dying, exactly, but I never—when I look at other people and how they live, how they're alive, it's like they're doing it in a totally different way and I'm just standing there, watching them, imitating." Her arms stretched over her head, each hand grasping the opposing elbow. "And it's got nothing to do with the plague, or everyone dying, or what Natalie did—or even what I did. That's the thing. Like, ever since I was born, I've been... traveling. Somewhere else."

The sadness unspooling between them both was like a thread, a spun ribbon, knotting them together in a great capacious net while the rest of us swam free outside. Except I knew the feel of that net too, the texture of that rough rope cutting into my hands; I'd almost swear I'd known it in the ghost times, the most-forgotten times, before the laboratory became my whole life. But what could I have ever said to her, my own daughter, if she'd confided all this in me? No words in any language are as cloying, self-serving, as selfishly solicitous as *I know just what you mean*.

Lisa shifted where she sat, tugging on another strand of hair. It was a miracle she hadn't pulled herself bald. "Look, Amy, everything that's happened since—"

"It's got nothing to do with that." She didn't sound angry, or frustrated that Lisa didn't *know just what she meant*; in fact, there was almost a buoyancy to her words now, the ballast of confession tossed overboard. "It's from a long time before—you can't tell my mom. Okay? She'd just start in again about how it's all her fault and if she'd just stayed—well, it was okay before, you know, I mean years ago, because it really was only her and me and we almost never talked to anyone else. I didn't even really know enough other people to feel different. I didn't have any friends. I didn't know how you talk to people, how to get friends. Then I learned how to pretend at it, use their language, but—"

"Lots of people have trouble making friends," Lisa said. "It doesn't make them freaks."

Silence again, like Amy was thinking that one over. Or just being polite. "But it does make them friendless," she said. "Okay, see, I can see how all of you look at Nick, I'm not blind, but I spent all that time running away from him and now it's like he's the only real friend I ever—"

I'd taken a step closer, then closer again to hear them better and I startled some large possum-like thing that went scuttling off in a crackling volley of dry twigs. And there I was, nothing between them and me but a half-dead lilac bush. They both turned swiftly and Amy's face shut up fast and tight with suspicion, like in the old days whenever Mike's sister tried kissing her hello; it shoved me farther away than the strongest set of hands. Lisa looked from Amy to me, then back again, waiting virtuously for her cue.

"I got worried about you," I said, my voice hardening as I turned to Lisa. "When Naomi came back all by herself."

Lisa gave me this tight little nod, her eyes searing me with a clean defiant heat of *don't even ask*, and suddenly all I could think about was what Naomi said, about how Lisa'd had to shit. Had she dug a hole and buried it, like you were supposed to do camping, or was it lying somewhere away from here for the flies to find, or had this whole privileged conversation happened right in the same spot, Lisa's shit sitting right at their feet? I couldn't smell anything, but then Lisa's shit didn't stink anyway, now did it. My skin prickled harder and my heart was beating in a bad way, sharp and drum-tight, and as Amy got to her feet, I pivoted and turned away—

A possum. The thing that gave me away was a possum, I'd guessed right. Now it lay curled up not five feet away from me, dead. Playing possum. It had to be from how I'd startled it. But I'd seen so many dead things back at the lab and I just knew, I knew looking at it; it'd died quietly right beside me, and I hadn't sensed a thing. It lay cradled in the mud and leaves and a damp gray netting of dead branches—so many, like someone had been gathering tinder and then dropped armfuls without ever building the fire. Something touched my arm as I stared at it and I jumped, then saw Amy standing beside me, her apprehension turning to fear.

"Mom," she said, "look." She pointed back into the trees, the path we'd all followed. Lisa was coming up too, gazing where Amy's arm led. "Before, when we came down here, it was..."

Green. It had been all sorts of colors not half an hour before, green with spring and brown with mud and purple-pink-white with blossoms, with only a few dead branches here and there—and now the soil was covered in them. The whole ground was a nest of gray twigs, dropping steadily from overhead, and the new, soft spring leaves had turned colorless and withered. The forsythia bush just ahead of us, that yellow everyone calls "butter" even though it's so much thicker and brighter a color, all its flowers were decayed and dropped to the ground.

The bird I'd heard singing, something brown-speckled but yellow as the petals had been—I knew it was the same one, I just *knew*—lay there in the twigs not just dead but swollen with decay, industrious carpets of tiny dark insects already working at feathers and flesh. Close by lay the crow, its wizened feet pointed suddenly and forever at the sky. All where we'd walked were huge, new bald patches of gray, brown, black; it was all falling to pieces like that poor little bird, like a great ripe fruit spotted with a sudden, deep rot.

Lisa just stared, at the bushes, the birds, and then wild-eyed and already breathless she was running through the trees, back to the clearing. Amy and I stood gripping each other's hands, too scared to move, too scared to speak aloud. We held our breaths, held them like it might trick whatever was out there into leaving us be, and then I heard Lisa's voice, a rising-falling chorus of feverish relief, and the higher-pitched sound of a protesting child.

Amy shuddered. I squeezed her hands harder and there was

Lisa, still half-running as she headed toward us, Naomi in her arms and Nick trotting close at her feet.

"I don't need to be carried!" Naomi kept saying, trying and failing to squirm out of Lisa's iron plague-dog grasp. "I'm not a baby, I don't need to—Lisa, look, the birds." Her head twisted around and she stared, stricken. "Poor little birds."

Her face convulsed as she tried not to cry; then she snuffled and mopped her eyes and turned back to Lisa with an air of reproof. "We need our bags," she said. "You left them."

"I'll go get them," Lisa said, her grinding voice coming from somewhere far away; she didn't move, didn't set Naomi down. Her arms were trembling. Nick kept making a circuit around the clearing, sniffing not just at the birds but at the dead bushes and branches, at the poor possum. Dogs loved dead things and loved rolling in them and I was bracing myself for that, but all he did was sniff and pace, round and around, over and over. Amy watched him in silence, and we all watched her, and finally she stepped back and out of my grasp.

"Here, boy," she said, a quaver in her voice. "Come on."

Nick abandoned his rootings-around and trotted obediently toward her without a moment's hesitation. They both headed back toward the long grass where she and Lisa had sat, and we all followed her, as if surely she knew the path like we didn't, as if she'd been leading the way all along. The sun had finally come out in earnest, weak and clouded over but still steady against our backs. Amy headed slowly around the uneven perimeter of the woods, the thick tangle of former backyards still alive and green and flowering with weeds. Still untouched. She came to an abrupt stop and we all looked warily around us, waiting for the man, with his long black coat and pale cropped hair. Waiting for him to appear before us, his face that none of us had ever quite seen lit up with triumph: *How'd you like all that back there, huh? How'd you like that? What makes you think I won't do it to you?*

But he wasn't there, not anymore, at least not where we could see him. Only Stephen, still walking up and down alone in the long grass not fifteen yards away, hands thrust deep into his pockets and dark head bent under the weight of his own thoughts. Amy turned to me and I could feel her pent-up urgency to speak, to speak now and say something I needed to hear, something even Lisa and that boy had never...

Quick as I observed it, the moment passed, and she turned away.

"Stephen?" she called, startlingly loud in the too quiet, rotten woods. "You ready? We're gonna head out."

FOUR

NATALIE

"You gotta come see this," he kept saying. Over and over. You gotta, you gotta—I didn't have to do anything. This is my house now, it's always been *my* house, I'm in charge here and if I want to walk up and down the hallway the whole day, then I will. If I want to not talk to anyone, then I won't. Amy and all my other real family hate me, my Friendly Man just shows up to be horrible and say things that don't make any sense. I might as well just walk up and down. The man, his dirty blond hair clipped short, his voice almost southern-sounding like you hear sometimes even this far north, I knew he'd worked here for years but I couldn't remember his name. Like it mattered. He grabbed at my arm and I yanked it away, almost hissing.

"Leave me alone," I said. "Just leave me alone."

"Kid—"

"Don't *call* me *kid*." Hissing for real, from behind my teeth, trying to make my face a slitty little Halloween mask like an actual cat. If I'd had fur to make stand on end, make me look and feel like a big deal you didn't mess with, my man would've treated me better. "Don't you ever call me that, I—"

"*Miss Beach*." He looked past patience and I didn't care. His skin, the patina of worked-in grime all over his clothes... he looked as close and musty as the hallway smelled and his big thick-necked body seemed somehow to blend into the floor and walls, dissolve into it, one great aura of unclean. "Ms. Beach, whatever the hell you want, I must *humbly request* you come with me and see what's going on outside. I don't know if I'm seeing things, or—"

"So ask one of the others." I shook his hand free and rubbed a finger against the wall, the protective glass covering a huge photograph of the lab staff circa... 1925, the writing said, even though their clothes looked awfully modern for that. Long rows of men in suits where only the collars looked really old-fashioned, one or two women in straight up-and-down dresses and short fussy hair. "I know they're still wandering around here even though I told everyone to leave, I'd be paying your salary but nobody listens. Go ask them."

His thick curve of a mouth, pink lips rubbery and flabby all at once, he twisted it up like I'd just shoved something sour into his cheek. "I can't," he said, and something flitted fish-like across his face and swam away again, that look when you can't decide whether to run from something or hit it in the face. "I can't. You'll see why. For fuck's sake, you wanna be in charge here so bad, this is something you gotta see."

The layers of dust over the photograph glass left all the faces in shadow, dust so thick you couldn't even make a proper clean line with your fingertip. If Amy thinks she's too good for a little dirt she can just shut the hell up and grab a mop. I don't have time for that, I've got serious work.

I don't have time for this either. "So what is it, anyway?"

Because nobody around here listens to me, he just turned around and headed out the hall, like he was just so sure I'd drop everything and run after him, and since nobody tells me anything unless I go looking for it, I followed him out, through the A-Wing and across Residency and out the old double back doors. The beach was just a rumor back here, a quiet prickling sensation that traveled through the air so everything felt lighter, cleaner, and at the same time ponderous with the sheer weight of water. The grass was up around my shins, the woods bordering the lab grounds on three sides thick with leaves and blooms; at the far edge of the trees, a deer nibbled away, too used to humans to do more than stop and look up when it heard us. I was about to ask where the hell he was taking me anyway, I wasn't getting lured into the woods on some pretense so he could kill me and take over, when he stopped in his tracks and pointed a few feet in front of us, down in the dandelions.

"Okay," I said. "So what?"

The bodies weren't torn or bitten up like what Stephen and Amy's mother had done, when they fought everybody off. These just lay there staring sightless at the sky, intact, dead. I squatted down to touch one and she was cold and stiff, clothes soaked through from the saturated grass and last night's rain. "So what am I supposed to do with this?" I asked him, as he paced back and forth with fingers curled tight over his gun holster. "So you guys were stupid enough to get into another fight yesterday, before they left, you should've just let them go—"

"This is nothing to do with those frea—with yesterday, okay, you get it? Do I have to spell it out?" He halted in his tracks and stood there big and bristling angry, but with hunched-up shoulders like he was cringing away from some invisible hand about to slap him sideways. "This just happened now. It just happened, what, half an hour ago. We were out here, talking shit over, and I turn around—I mean, literally, I turn around 'cause I think I hear someone coming out the back—and when I turn my head again, boom. Gone." He waved a hand at the bodies. "All dead. Right in front of me. Or, in back of me."

Why are the people who work for me so stupid? "They're stiff," I said. "Full-blown rigor, they've been dead for—"

"I know they're stiff. I know they're cold. I know what it looks like—and whatever it looks like, it was just a half hour ago."

He was pacing around again, walking a perimeter of the bodies like a dog sniffing tracks, that filthy dog of Amy's who hated me most of all. "You gotta do something," he said. "You think you're in charge of this shithole now, they're supposed to have taught you all kinds of medical shit, you've gotta do something. You've gotta bring them back."

Like it was that easy, you just snap your fingers and whoever you decide to bring back—even under the very best conditions, the best test subjects, it didn't work anything like that. Like I'd even waste my time bringing one of his stupid friends back, if it did. "I can't do that," I said. "How long did you work here, anyway? You know it's not that simple, a lot of times you do everything right and dead people just stay— "

"You have to do something!" He had my arms now, digging in the fingertips hard and abrading like how it'd felt when that drawer kept slamming, all inside my bones. "They were right here, we were all right there, then I turn my head and they all just fucking drop like something flipped a switch—you think you're in charge around here, you gotta get your ass in there and figure out what happened, how to— "

"Let go of me."

"This is just like before." Still had his hands on me, the grinding pressure of his fingers boring straight through to my bones, stuck drawer slam-slam-slam. His eyes were big and luminous with panic. "Just like before, when everyone here started getting sick and then everyone else, everywhere. You fuckers went and did it again."

"You let go of me," I said, quiet, calm as you please, "or I won't 'figure out' a damn thing."

He let go. The hatred smoking and heating him up all inside like a brazier felt good to see—it didn't bother me at all when weak little humans or plague-dogs hated me because they were so jealous. Because the world was mine now, not theirs—and not my man's either, I didn't care how much he tried to scare me. He was a liar. "I don't have time for this," I said, and turned right around to go back inside. "You bring them inside if you want, I can't stop you, and I'll look at them *if* I get a chance, but I'm not promising—"

"Oh, shit."

His voice sounded torn in two, pain and shock and fear all twisted up and made into sound, and that's what made me turn around again.

It had stormed during the night and my first thought was that somehow lightning hit the trees while I was sleeping and I didn't hear it, hit them so hard it fried them from the inside and then all the land around them too. Except lightning didn't work like that and the trees didn't look scorched or heat-blackened, they were just gray and bare and dead. And those trees had been living just seconds before, living and covered in tiny pretty green leaves like those salads they used to serve in the lab refectory, bushes exuberant with tiny pink and white bits of lace, branching sprays of deep red berries, maples letting off winged seedlings like candy thrown from a parade float. Gone. The grass, the unmown weedy grass almost up to my knees, that was still living, but the deer who'd gone right back to its lunch after it saw us was lying there in the clover and dandelions. Lying still.

The lab man whose name I couldn't remember, his arm was reaching in vain up to the trees, the wall of sticks that'd been trees, like he could entreat them not to do what they'd gone and done. His face was drawn and white. "What'd y'all go and do?" he asked softly. The southern in him was coming out stronger now he was really frightened, hillbilly drawl, those families that came up here a hundred years ago or more to work the steel mills and still sounded like they'd barely left Alabama. "The hell did you—now everything's getting sick." He started to laugh and the laughter was a scary sound, scarier than the wall of sticks. "Wasn't enough just to kill *people*, now everything everywhere's getting sick, I can't believe you went and did it again—"

"You shut up," I whispered, Halloween-mask hissing, and then I was running toward the deer, the green grass it should've been bending down to eat. It just lay there on its side, big pretty liquid stupid deer-eyes wide open and a mouthful of clover, torn-off bits of creeping Charlie, still wedged in its teeth. I pushed at it with my fingertips, ready to jump back, in case this was some sort of prey-animal trick and it might any moment spring back to its feet. Playing possum.

It just lay there.

Those things my man said to me, back in my room, they were lies. The thing about everyone suffering because of me, because I had his secret and I wouldn't leave. I knew lies when I heard them, nobody ever said anything to me but lies. Except him, a long time ago. He was lying, and even if he weren't he couldn't have meant things like flowers and deer. They never did anything to him. Trees. He couldn't stop me, couldn't stop our work, trying to scare me with a few dead trees.

He was lying! It was all a trick!

The deer felt cold and stiff when I touched it, like it'd been lying there for hours. I got up, my bent leg already cramped beneath me, and brushed the dirt off my shins. "Hey," I shouted to Lab Man, Hillbilly Scaredy-Boy. Jerkface pronouncing *Miss Beach* so precise and proper, over-enunciated, trying to make it sound like another word. "Come help me carry this back in. You wanted me to look at your stupid friends, okay, fine. But this first. Come and help me!"

No answer. Because nobody was standing there anymore.

I walked back to where we'd both been, slow as you please, because all that happened was he got disgusted standing there waiting for me, went off down the hillside, still whining and crying about how I cared more about some dumb animal than his buddies. That's all. Because I know lies when I hear them. I'm no fool.

The other bodies were still there and he was next to them, curled up on his side just like the deer, one hand on his holster though his gun wasn't drawn and the other arm still stretched out, full length, like he was grabbing for a dandelion from where he lay. Eyes wide open, liquid-clear with fright. Cold and stiff. Like he'd been there for hours.

No more dandelions. In the time it took me to walk from the deer back to him, all those bursts of yellow suddenly went damp rotten brown, right there in the grass, and died.

FIVE
JESSIE

"Well?" I asked. "What d'you think?"

Renee frowned, squinted. "Do you want an honest answer?"

Why the hell do people always say that? If I didn't give a shit what they actually thought about something, I wouldn't waste my time asking. "Spit it out," I said.

"Well—" She squinted harder, looking her own face up and down as it stared back at her from the paper, then she broke into a grin. "You ain't no Picasso. But we already knew that, right?" She ran her hand along a cheekbone, like she was checking its measurements against the drawing. "And you didn't put my nose totally out of joint, so I like it. It's good."

Renee broke her nose last autumn—shattered it, actually—fighting over food with the other Prairie Beach refugees, and even though it healed right off like these new bodies do, it never looked quite the same as it did before: it skewed to the side in a way Linc and I barely noticed and Renee couldn't stop thinking about. Her fingers reached up constantly and unconsciously, stroking and tracing the bridge-slope like she could coax it back where it'd been. I'd offered to re-break it for her, see if a strategic blow from the right might push it over left, but she always said no. She'd had her last fight, she kept saying, even though I wasn't angling to fight her at all. Those last buried bits of hoocow in her kept showing up, like some burrowing thing inside her had turned over all her earth; it made Linc impatient, those sudden outbursts of delicacy, but I kept telling him, she was barely out of the ground a month before everything started changing for good. Barely that. You had to make allowances, like it or not.

"I really do like it," she insisted. Teresa's rings clinked and rattled on her thin fingers, the faintest little wind-chime sound, as they traveled from cheek to nose and back again. "I'm not just saying that—"

"Okay already, I asked you once. I ain't no Picasso. And you ain't no Botticelli." She laughed and I laid the drawing out next to the others on the old short-legged table I'd stuck in my cabin for a desk, reaching for a pencil. "What month is it?"

"May. I think." She frowned. "You better ask Linc, but I'm pretty sure it's May."

I wrote that down at the bottom left corner, then leafed through all the others; May's nose was less flattering but more accurate than April's, hair texture was a lot truer to life than December's, still couldn't draw hands for shit but I gave up on those back in January. In November, Linc had brought back some art pencils and a tattered yellowed book called *The Mind of the Artist Within*—he said it'd been a big thing for a while, back when he was still alive; a lot of hoo-babble inside about Jung and Myers-Briggs types and accessing the right side of the brain, but in between the bullshit was line and perspective and other actual useful stuff, full of drawings for examples, and the babble plus Renee's face to practice on helped pass the time.

Passing the time, all the time, that was our job now, just like it'd been before. When we weren't hunting, Linc had his books and the garden. I had the notebook and a half, page after scribbled page, where I'd tried writing down everything that happened to me, to us, then gave up because I can't write for shit and tore out the rest of the pages for pictures. Renee did most of our foraging now and was constantly trying to work out how to make a solar oven, weatherize the cabins, build a chicken coop, and a thousand other things every bit as useless as my sitting around trying to pencil her hair just right.

I blamed Lisa for all that, Lisa who kept reminding and reminding Renee of her long-lost hoodom for no good reason whatsoever and then just took off, with barely any warning, mumbling something about how she wasn't doing anyone any good staying here and wanting to find out what actually became of things while she was sick and blah blah fucking blah just say you can't stand the sight of us anymore, why don't you? She never forgave me for saving her, I knew she hadn't; never forgave me for pulling her out of the sands as something more than human, not quite human, why the hell was everything for her still and always about the fucking humans? They had their world, whatever was left of it, and I didn't care what. I had mine. Frankly, I liked my company a hell of a lot more.

I hoped Linc was telling the truth when he said he foraged all my art stuff from an elementary school, that he didn't get it from our new neighbors down the road. Always showing up here, that bunch, no warning, acting all please-pretty and howdy-neighbor-God-bless-you and you *couldn't scare them away* for love or blood, they drove me insane. Linc hated humans as much as I did, maybe even more, but I still caught him talking to them in the woods and he just shrugged, said *They might be useful idiots, sometime.* Half of that was right, anyway.

Once, I asked them to keep an eye out for Lisa, but they said nobody new or old had come their way all winter. All spring.

Useful chattering jabbering idiots, for when we needed some kind of noise, any noise, in the empty space where our music once was. The unheard music, secret harmonies, that we had when we were properly undead, humming and pulsing through our flesh like blood through a living heart. I could *almost* remember what it sounded like, that music that would burst forth like spring thunderstorms with no pattern, no warning, into unfathomably sad arpeggios and unbearably exuberant waltzes that all of us heard, all together. Listening and rising and dancing, our rotten shambling mismatched limbs seized and transformed into one great, graceful, glorious body—

But we weren't dead anymore, and if you asked those hoos down the road, we weren't properly alive either, not how they judged it. We weren't *anything* anymore. We were just here.

Renee kept watching me as I stacked up my pencil drawings and put them back under the lake-stone paperweight in proper May to November order. Watching my hand as it jerked instinctively away from the paperweight's searing, unnatural heat and I pretended that nothing had happened, as I so casually picked it up once again.

"You're sure you're okay," she said.

Here we go. Goddammit, I did not want to talk about this right now. "I said I'm fine. Can you take my damn word for anything, or—"

"About this? Not really, no." She glared at me, hard and suspicious, then sighed and tapped her ring-rattling fingers on the tabletop. "Another funny dream, last night. The sky went dark but there was still light underneath it, somehow—like it wasn't really getting dark at all, but a layer of asphalt or black wax or—something—was pressing down, squashing out all the light. And then all the air." She shuddered a little, a delicate shoulder-shiver as her fingers, covered in corpse-trophy rings, rubbed nervously back and forth. "I woke up feeling like I was gasping for air—I hate that feeling, don't you hate that feeling?"

I hate having to breathe at all, is what I hate. Those hoos down the road might not think we're alive like them, like that'd be some kind of precious prize, but just like them, I'm now a prisoner of the *air*. Constant, ceaseless, relentless dependency, no more tunneling back safe underground, not with these sorry lungs, and because Renee's right back to what she was used to and Lisa didn't want to hear it, I never said anything about how breath was an awful weight, a burden. Linc had the same dream as Renee, just a few nights back, of something dark like a hand or a big box-lid stamping everything down. The exact same dream. He woke up choking, and even though all the beach-cabin doors and windows were wide open, I had to take him outside, walk with him along the shoreline for a good half-hour before he felt like he was breathing again.

"You're just feeling the weather change," I said. "Remember those tornadoes a few weeks back?" They never got close enough to do damage but I could still see them out in the distance, dark columnar clouds on the far end of the sickly green sky, the heavy-weighted air pressing down so we all got terrible headaches. "Fucks with your head, all that."

Renee thought that one over. "Weather change," she said. "Fucks with your head. That must be it." She glanced at me. "It couldn't be anything else out there, fucking with us. Right?"

I stared out of the cabin's wide-open window, at Linc's vegetable garden up the ridge; it'd been a warm rainy winter and a cool rainy spring but the dirt still looked drought-dry, nothing but gray chalky crumbly powder thick with the ruins of roots. "Weather," I repeated, sharp and impatient. "Air pressure, all of that, it fucks with your head like crazy, makes you moody as—"

"Jessie."

Her eyes bored so hard into me it made me miss the old days, the days when she was so new from the ground and so shit-scared of everything that I only had to bare my teeth and she'd burst into tears. Her dream, Linc's dream, the exact same dream I'd had last night, the night before, the night before that and that and that. Each time I woke up choking, weighted down with a genuine suffocating fear that wrang my lungs to limp rags, sent me staggering to the window for what was never enough air; when I tried to piece the dream together, all I could remember was a great, vague chasm, opening wider and wider to swallow the light, the air, the darkness of the night. A great nothingness. I wasn't lying, when Renee kept asking me if I'd dreamed about anything and I kept telling her, nothing.

"I don't know what the hell you want from me, Renee." I turned back to my drawings, shuffling and straightening them to show I was busy, very busy, that this conversation was long since over. "Because I mean, I'm fucking done playing detective, especially about some stupid dream, after what happened the last—"

"I know you and Linc have had the same dream. The same time I started having it—a week ago, ten days. I know you've both seen... something. Before. I mean, months before this. Walking around the woods. Keeping tabs on us."

She glared at me, her shoulders curling automatically into the old aggressive stance—not a fighting posture, all the real fight'd gone out of us three, but a hunched-up, tensed-up *I see you, I know you, whatever meat you're trying to steal you can drop it in the dirt right now.* Not as hopelessly hoocow as all that, after all, if she still knew how to talk properly. "You know what I mean, Jessie. It's like Lisa said once, you've seen a lot of stuff, all along the way, that you haven't talked about ever, and I never liked to push it because of... Joe, and everything, but..." Her shoulders sagged and for a split second she looked like her old, clueless 'maldie self, the embalmed-up thing that used to follow me around like a lost cat mewing for a cuddle. "Is *something else* involved in this?"

The last time I saw Joe, I don't talk about. That's what made the notebook project stop. The last time I saw Death, he was walking around our woods enjoying a refreshing stroll, nothing to do and nothing more to say to me, and he vanished so quick he barely even arrived. Linc saw him too. We didn't discuss it. I never told Lisa because I didn't want to scare her, and I never told Renee because he came and he left and that was that, and—and the truth was that I'd gone soft lately, soft and aimless like something big and strong and I-see-what-you-got-there inside me had collapsed and rotted away for good, all my strings cut so nothing inside me could get up and dance. Maybe this is what it felt like back in the old days, being a dusty, when your last remaining flesh went to dry powder as all the insects left you and the need to feed, to fight slowly trickled away for good. Like how serene Florian was, that quiet resignation shorn of any fear or anger flowing through him, right before he went to dust. I lost my own chance to find out what that was like.

"I don't know what you want from me, Renee," I said. That's my story and I'm sticking to it. "I really don't. I haven't seen anything. Anyone."

Renee considered this. Then she reached into her jacket pocket and held out the contents cupped like a Communion wafer in her palm. "I picked this up last night on the shore," she said. "Just like the paperweight. Go on. Just touch it."

Our lone souvenir from the old days, since I refused to draw Sam or Joe or Annie or anyone else who'd died: Lake Michigan beach stones, the kind we could find right outside our door any time we wanted. The paperweight, though, that was one of Florian's, that he'd carried with him for decades or centuries, that got us all out of Prairie Beach. Linc and Renee were weirdly superstitious, avoided the tokens he'd carried—the things that had saved them, and me—like they were radioactive, but I carried a few everywhere I went because I felt strange and bereft without them, because in ways I couldn't understand, they were just like me. Dead, inert, yet somehow still alive.

I touched it. Uncomfortably hot—hot enough to burn skin if we'd all still had human fingers, not these hands we could shove straight into live flames and pull back barely touched—just like my paperweight, and a faint vibration coming from inside it, against my skin, as though the stone were a planet whose tiny earthquakes threatened to split it open at the seams. Just like my paperweight.

"Warm from your pocket," I said.

"Jessie? You know it means something." She pulled more from her pocket and laid them out on the table, pink and black and striated green all in a neat little line. "I don't know what it means, but—"

"But we know it's something." Linc was standing there in the doorway, the afternoon sun turning him to a skinny ungainly shadow. He'd changed the least of any of us, the same old scarecrow dead or alive. "And that you'd be able to guess better than us. New drawing?"

"The old one," I said, as he came in and slid an arm around my shoulders, examining what he could see of May-Renee around the paperweight. "Better than you? Why could I guess any better than you? You saw... something strange too, in the woods, last fall. Just like me. So why would I know any better than you? Those new little friends of yours, the hoos down in Hootown, they have anything to say about any of this?"

"My friends," Linc repeated, his mouth twitching in a swift, mirthless little smile. He curled his fingers around the paperweight, weighed it thoughtfully in his palm. "Nothing, not a damned thing. Why would they? Why are you dragging the *children* into this, anyway?"

Linc's dislike of humanity was quieter than mine, more polite, but it was a steady, vibrant flicker inside him that never wavered or went out. He'd been a card-carrying misanthrope even before he died, with good reason for it, and was more than happy to prove he'd jumped the hoo fence with his first proper hunt; he wouldn't tell me who he killed, though I was sure it was no stranger, but every now and then he liked to remind me how much I'd missed out, not tasting their flesh back when that didn't feel like a cousin to cannibalism. Our new neighbors—I wondered if they realized yet that his calm measured ways, his please-God-don't-hit-me-again face he'd inherited from his awful first life, they meant absolutely nothing when you got him angry. They'd learn. I'd laugh.

Renee had her arms folded now, staring at me like I was her little kid who just got into the cookies. Like I'd been holding out on—all right, I had been, but so had Linc, who hadn't believed there was anything beyond these lives until he got sick. Linc saw him—it—too, walking around among the elms and the lilacs. Gazing down at our vegetable garden like it was the most interesting thing in the world. But that was all last year, before the winter.

"I haven't seen it here," I said, hard and brusque because it was nothing but the truth and she'd still never believe it. "I haven't seen it here all winter, all spring— "

"It's not like we need to see it, though," Linc said, slowly, that fucking irritating habit he had of weighing every side of an argument to see which one fit best inside his head. "It's not like it has to announce itself. I mean, it didn't bother before."

I picked up my paperweight again, feeling the heat. The insistent little vibrato emanating from inside, like the time I'd had one split itself open right there in my palm. Eternity, that's what I'd thought it sounded like when I held a shaking stone to my ear like a shell; not just some dry airy semblance of the sea, reverberating through thin little tunnels pink-veined like a cat's ear, but the actual, barely contained noise of something huge and mighty and constrained in a tiny carrying box. I put this one up to my ear in turn, hearing that familiar low, insistent hum.

"I don't know what it means," I said, feeling drained and deflated, like we'd been fighting in earnest and I'd had all the fight beaten out of me. "I mean, if he's here—here we are."

I fought him off, the last time, but I wasn't sure I'd do it again. I didn't want to say that out loud, though: it always got Renee upset. I stared up at another of my drawings, October, a clumsy sketch of our cabins up here on the ridge that Linc had insisted on pinning to the wall. From the corner of my eye, I saw Linc exchange a wary look with Renee; here it comes, I thought. Here it comes.

"Don't," Linc said to her. Weary with the knowledge she'd do it anyway, as if they'd argued about it over and over again out of my presence. "Renee, for the eightieth damned time, just let it go."

"Jessie." Renee's teeth settled on her bottom lip, gnawing, like that little bit of pain lent courage. "If you could somehow talk to him again, maybe— "

"No."

"If we could just find out why he's doing this. If he's doing this— "

"Doing *what*? You're both losing your minds over some half-assed nightmare and what the fuck do you think anyway, this is some kind of shaman thing? I channel it or summon it or some mystic bullshit like that?" I shoved the paperweight into my pocket. "He doesn't talk *to* me, he talks *at* me, and he hasn't done that since we were all so sick and as far as I'm concerned, it all means less than nothing—"

"It has to be something!" Renee shouted. "Or are you just keeping it to yourself again? Like you think I'm still too stupid to handle it?"

"I'm not listening to this," I said. "I'm not listening to any more—"

"Jessie." Linc was holding up his hands, a peace-plea he knew was doomed.

"D'you even know what you're asking me?" The gnawing, sickly little spark that had flickered to life inside me when we all started to wake up suffocating, when I went just yesterday into the trees and found kitty-Mags, kitty-Joe, the whole colony of feral cats who shared our woods lying dead in the underbrush, it flared up now like a burst of fountain water. I was hot and hollow as the inside of those lake stones, like something was trying to melt me down, but I'm not anything's fucking candle-wax, I've never let fear turn me runny soft. "You've got no idea what it's like actually *seeing* him, face to face. None. You think there's any talking to it, that it knows us? Needs to know anything but itself?" I was laughing now. I couldn't help it. "This was all your idea, right, Renee? Jesus Christ, everything that's happened and you're still just a fucking 'maldie. I thought you were smarter than that. But that thing, it's like looking at the whole universe at once except that part of it can talk, and you think it gives a damn whether we live or die!"

"I told you," Linc said to Renee as I pushed through the doorway, stumbling when I shoved past him. He was almost laughing, too. "I told you, and told—"

"Jessie!" Renee yelled, as my feet hit the sands, as I started marching down the ridge to get away. "If he wants us for real this time—I never said to try and talk him out of it!"

The beach grasses, dry and sharp and crusted with sand, bent and bowed into the wind; the sky was clouding over again, turning an ashy pearl as the sunset crept up, afternoon starting to diminish into night. I kept going.

I heard footsteps behind me and then Linc's sharp, reproving voice. Renee still had just enough hoocow in her to think earnest hand-holding talk could solve anything; thank God Linc had some damned sense. Some. The sands spread out ahead of me, a big curving sweep of beige raked into fabric-folds by the winds; nobody's footsteps marked it but our own, nobody's tracks and traces but the gulls. When I stood right on top of the ridge, bare toes pressed hard against the shifting ground and all that clean open space below, I could pretend it'd only ever been the gulls and grasses, that I just dreamed it all up myself from nothing. My own private landscape, sketched freehand.

A good drawing pencil makes a muted, crinkly scratch against crisp new paper. I hated the sound of it. I hated the way the tin foil rustled, when Renee tried wrapping another bent, sagging cardboard box into a useless solar oven. (Cake, Lisa said that once, if we had an oven we could bake a cake. What the hell would I do with a damned cake? Did she ever understand that meat was all that tasted like anything to the rest of us, anymore?) I hated Linc's tuneless, sing-song muttering as he dug sandy-soil seedbeds, snapped a thrashing rabbit's neck, leafed through our salvage piles from the Cowles County Library for the eighty-eighth time. All of it was nothing but goddamned useless noise, just like the rush of the lake waters, the winter wind, the spring thunder—none of it, magnified eighty-eight times over, could never do a thing to shatter the quiet inside us all. I was nothing *but* music, once;

its electricity sang night and day all through my supposedly dead flesh, whenever I slept, whenever I woke, but now all that was gone. All I had left, all any of us had left, was the deadbeat pulse of a pumping heart, the nasty little sucking sound of our own hoo breath. Worthless. It was worthless. We'd all gone stone deaf.

The beach, looking at it, walking on it, it felt like the only thing we had or did that made any true sense, that wasn't just distraction or marking time. Like our only happy thing. Even hunting—hunting!—didn't feel like that anymore. It was just another endless, never-finished chore in the long line of perpetual chores that made up living again. Our new neighbors, down the road, how the hell did they put up with having to cook and serve their food all hoo-proper on top of it all? I'd go crazy. Crazier.

Maybe this is how Teresa felt, back in the first-born days of the sickness, when she stopped hunting altogether, started demanding all the rest of us in the gang fetch her food. Maybe we're all getting sick again, like before. But it's not that I can't eat, that I'm not hungry. It's that even as I need to do it, as I can't stop feeling it, satiation's gone from bliss to fleeting pleasure to work and I just don't see the point of it at all anymore.

Neither does Linc, but then, he never did. The discussions we've had, late at night, when we were sure Renee and especially Lisa were both asleep: *I've tried it,* Linc said, *I've tried all this, living and dead, and I'm like Sam was: I just don't like it. Jessie, if we ever get the choice back and can decide for ourselves, again—*

I didn't know what to say, back then, lying with foreheads touching and fingers twined together, hearing the rustles and calls and cries of nighttime through the newfound barriers of walls and window. We'd fought for this life-afterlife-after-death, all of us had; we'd wrenched it back and dropped it into our own waiting laps and how am I supposed to promise to give it up again, say a fuck-you that big and then agree to just get fucked in turn? So I didn't promise to give up on life, not then, because I couldn't decide and because even if I said yes, even if I wanted to right then and there, we'd been left no choice. Just like poor Sam, who tried so hard to get out of his human life and then just woke up again, right where he was, as one of us. At least now Sam, my old Sam, he had what he'd always wanted. He was gone.

Enough! Annie, back in the old days, she'd look at me right now and go, *Girl, you're turning soft, what you need is a good goddamned fight.* Her, Joe, always right there to give me one. I missed that, the constant mad twitching urge to kick, punch, bite, wrench necks and break bones, do *something* with all the energy pulsing inside me. Did I miss that? Would fists and feet be anything now but another dutiful task? I didn't even know that feeling now anyway. It all drained straight out of me when I became a new sort of human. Inhuman. I'd had no choice.

And if Renee wanted her Big Answers so bad, she could fucking well find them herself. Whatever this was—if it was anything at all—we'd just get through it, like we had the sickness, and not waste time asking any damned questions.

Because when we weren't looking and we still thought we owned ourselves, that life and death might actually be in our own hands, *getting through it* had become our one duty, our sole and endless chore. Because one way or another, we just didn't have any choice.

Sitting on the last bit of powdery piled-up sand before it all went damp and smooth from the tides, it felt like being on a little island unto itself divorced from the rest of the beach. I perched at the edge of the dry with my heels dug into the wet, the lake rolling inward in a heavy, easy wave that never quite reached my toes, and when I looked up again I saw a vast, dark figure silhouetted against the horizon, walking slow and easy toward me over the surface of the waters.

A muscle in my leg wrenched and twisted as I struggled to my feet. The ashen pearl sky, the sun swelling up flame-colored and full as sunset crept closer, they made a pale illuminated border all around him, a corona, his darkness like the burnt-out hole in a photograph someone set on fire. The great shadow of him took shape as he came closer and it was Jim, my brother, it was my father, it was poor blinded Lillian from the undead days and it was Ben who'd died alongside Sam and it was me, it was my own self and my dead departed face coming toward me faster and faster, walking so easy on the Lake Michigan waters. I was smiling at myself standing so small and astonished here on the beach, pleased to meet me. Every step I took from horizon to shore covered miles in a single moment. I was inches away from myself now, smiling and holding my arms out in greeting and all around me was that same border of pearly light, fiery rays of sun, blinding suffocating light all outside and inside me, inside the arms I'd wrap around me in ceaseless, perpetual embrace, nothing but night—

I was lying on my side half-coated in wet sand, no memory of stumbling or falling. I took in shallow gulps of air, like a beached fish, and my whole chest was one hollow constricted ache; something had passed straight through it, seizing my breath as it went, then tossed it back to me as an afterthought. I pulled myself upright, whipping my head around to take in the woods to my left, bluish silhouette of dead steel mills on the horizon to my right, the sands themselves and the now-empty dune ridges above and the dark undisturbed tidal sweep of lake waters. I squinted and then stared into the swelling blood-orange sun, in search of his lingering, thieving shadow—and there was nothing. He—it—had passed straight through me, and was gone.

God damn you, Renee. God *damn* you for being right.

With gleaming spots still dancing before my eyes, I rushed back up the ridge, urgent strides kicking up cascades and miniature sandstorms with every step, and back on level ground I ran past the thickening clumps of dune grass, down the dirty sand that became sandy dirt with each new step, along the trodden-down path our feet had made before Lisa's empty beach house, Renee's, the one Linc and I shared. I nearly thudded straight into Linc as I rounded the corner of our house, the one farthest in the woods and nearest the outside road. When he instinctively threw his hands out in self-defense, I grabbed his forearms, let my fingertips sink in to assure myself he really was flesh, that he wasn't that sunset specter that could take the form of anything that'd died.

"Down on the beach," I managed, out of breath, cursing the fucking air for crippling me once again. "I saw—"

"Tell me later," Linc said, glancing over his shoulder. "I was just about to find you."

"What d'you mean, 'tell me later'? Linc, down on the beach, what Renee said, I saw—"

"Jessie?" He jerked his chin toward the trees. "It's just right now we've got company. Hoo company."

"Oh, fuck." I started laughing again because this was too much, too goddamned much in one day. "For the love of God, tell them to fuck off back to their little Garden of Eden, right now I can't take any of their—"

"It's not them," Linc said, his face closing up like it always did when something beyond him had him angry. "Just... come with me."

He turned for the woods. I followed, puzzled, brushing off drying sand as we passed the cottonwoods and oak that grew thickly in this part of the forest, the little cluster of pine trees that signaled the approach of the white gravel roadside and the faded, weatherbeaten sign marking the beach. The trees were still shedding pale new spring leaves for the fuller deeper growth of approaching summer, growing so close together they made a natural green-tinged tunnel of the road. As we emerged, Renee was standing there, looking tense and lost for words, and as the last sunspot streaks faded from my vision, I could see why.

Weighted down by a half-dozen backpacks bursting at the seams, her eyes ringed bruise-blue from fatigue, Lisa swayed from foot to foot on the gravel like she was poised for flight, like the backpacks were folded-up wings that would unfurl and carry her up toward the dying sun. Standing next to her was a little knot of strangers, humans I hadn't seen in the settlement down the road: a red-haired girl maybe the age I was when I died; older skewbald-redhead, obviously a sister or mother; tall skinny boy with dark hair and a tense, wary face; a kiddie not more than seven clutching hard at Lisa's hand. A great black dog, shaggy-furred and with watery, red-rimmed, strangely beatific eyes, sitting obediently by the red-haired girl's side, watching the hoos do their hoodom thing with an expression of elevated patience.

All of them, except the dog, looked like they might drop where they stood; all of them, except the dog, kept glancing from Lisa to me and back like they were expecting bad trouble, like they'd been told to anticipate a fight. Because fucking with humans is still one of the few pleasures we've all got left, I gave them a deliberate, calculated smile, a sarcastic little bow of the head. Lisa didn't smile back.

"Long time," she said, calm and measured, like all the others weren't even there. "Good to see you again, Jessie."

"Is it?" I asked. Linc and Renee, the hoo strangers, they didn't say anything. They just watched.

"Yes," she said quietly. Blinking hard, all of a sudden, a convulsive little muscle-twitch subsiding soon as it arrived. "It is."

I thought that one over. Long enough for the mother-red to start looking truly nervous, the kiddie to frown and give an anxious, instinctive tug on Lisa's sleeve.

"So put your goddamned *luggage* down, already," I replied. "How the hell many miles did you walk around like that, anyway? You look like the hunchback of Notre Dame's daughter."

SIX
NATALIE

All my drawings. My desk with the special locked drawer, broken now, that Amy couldn't open. My filing cabinet. My doll. I huddled in the far corner of my room, holding Sukie my doll I named after my favorite of the old lab staff clutched close to my chest, waiting. The residential doors only lock from the outside and the desk was too heavy for me to move by myself, nobody left to help me block the door, when he came to kill me that wouldn't stop him anyway. When my man returned to kill me, like he was destroying everything else that was mine: the oak trees, the lilacs, the deer, anyone who could help me out. Before he comes back for me.

Unless he was going to kill everything else and leave me here, all by myself, the only thing still alive. Temporarily.

The windows here were too far up to look or climb through, so I didn't have to see what was happening outside. Was it everywhere now, all the dying, all the—I couldn't be this afraid, it was ridiculous to be afraid when *I had his secret*. I knew exactly what brought dead things back to life, I'd *brought* them back, if I could do it with people there was no way I couldn't figure out how with cottonwoods and anthills and rabbits. I had his secret right here, where nobody would think to look for it and even if they did, they couldn't use it like I could. That's why I was so important to Grandma, when she ran this whole lab; even among all the *Homo novus*, us new people their experiments created, I was special. He couldn't do a thing to me. He had to know he couldn't—

There was a sound, beyond my closed door, faint but unmistakable, close down the hallway. A sort of moaning sound, laughing and moaning all at once.

I missed Grandma. People laughed at me here, when I called her that, but she never did. She had this way of looking at someone, all level and unyielding just the same way she always carried her back, her long swoop of a neck perfectly straight and dignified, and when she gave them that stare—bright blue eyes that sparked and smoldered, when she was angry, like coals feeding a peculiar flame—people shut their mouths quick and scuttled to do what she'd told them. And she was always right, what she told them, if she hadn't gotten sick and then vanished during those horrible few first weeks of the plague things around here would've been different, I wouldn't have had to rebuild everything myself from the ground up. If she were here, right now, she'd stare Death himself straight in the face, just like she'd been doing through the experiments all along. She'd spark right back at him not the least afraid and he'd snivel and cringe for favor, oh did you think I *wasn't* a Friendly Man anymore, how could you think that of me, or even better he'd just turn tail and run away—

That sound was growing louder. Like a man singing, horrible slurred off-key singing like someone drunk, except without a single recognizable word. It was words to whoever was singing, though, it was words to him in some secret language or other long since dead. Somehow I knew that. Somehow I knew that without ever having seen him.

If it were Death coming for me he'd have long since come in by now. He didn't wait around for introductions, he never had.

I felt for my knife, my little surgical scalpel I'd salvaged for safekeeping, almost lost for good when I dropped it fighting Amy's filthy dog. The singing was getting louder, I felt like I knew that voice—

"Open the fuckin' door!"

The doors only lock from the outside so nothing could keep him from coming in, but he kept shaking the handle so it shook and shuddered in its metal frame until I thought of Death and the desk drawer and almost lost my nerve all over again. I wasn't answering it, though, I didn't have to do anything *he* said, not anymore. The rattling got louder and my teeth clicked and ground in turn.

"Stop that!" I shouted. I held tighter onto Sukie, clutched the scalpel until my fingers hurt. "This isn't your house, get out!"

Drunken-sounding laughter, loud and phlegmy like a cold-cough caught in someone's throat. "I'll get out when I'm good and ready to get out, there ain't anyone left here but us two chickenshits so just *open the goddamned door*!"

I didn't budge. The door was slowly going rusted and warped, a loosening tooth in the lab's great spacious mouth; it creaked and shook as it opened, the outside deadbolt rattling and ready to fall out in one piece. He stood there swaying in the doorway, clutching the frame two-handed like he might fall over, his pale bare toes flexed and poised against the floor as if the doorway were a barre and he were about to go up en pointe.

"You look like shit," Billy said. Looking me up and down, staring at the dried blood streaks like it was all something brand new. Like he didn't even know what blood looked like anymore.

"You look worse," I said. I was on my feet now, my little knife extended. "Stay away from me."

Billy'd always been a big pale fattened-up thing, a walking waxen puffball ever ready to burst his poison straight in your face, but now he looked shrunken and diminished, like something inside him really had blown up. His suit jacket hung in loose folds around his torso, his shoulders hunched forward like he might pitch to the floor at any second, his face was drawn and tired and flushed like he'd just wept himself sick and was quietly gathering breath to do it again—all for that Mags? That nasty bellowing bitch who led him everywhere by the nose, thought we were all her little barnyard pigs? I laughed when she died, when Amy killed her without even meaning to. Still wish I'd done it. The look she'd have had on her face, seeing me do it...

"What do you want," I said. Flat and terse, no fear, like someone from a movie.

He didn't budge from the doorway, just grinned hollow and sad from beneath those hollow sad eyes and swayed back and forth, forth and back. "So they left you behind, too, huh. Figures."

"This is where I *live*," I told him. Teeth gritted. "This is where I live, I told them to get the hell out of—what do you want, anyway? More human slaves? Well, I'm not human, I never have been. So you can just get the hell out."

Not one word got through, I could tell just by his eyes. He shuffled his feet, bleary and confused, his head hanging down.

"I saw somethin' out there," he said. Arms still raised, fat waxen fingers curled over the doorframe. "Out in the woods. I saw something... out in the woods. Walking around. Spreading place to place like another fucking disease, doing its thing." Falling forward the short, stubby length of his own arms, pitching back where he stood. Over and over. "Doing its thing. And you don't wanna know what it is."

"I already know about it." I lowered my knife. He wasn't even seeing me, never mind wanting to hurt me. "So it's spread even further? Is it everywhere?"

"I ran to it." He laughed and shook his head, ran a hand over the darker blond stubble at his jaw. "I ran to it, see, 'cause I can run now like I couldn't ever run before, I never get over how fast I can move. Didn't you always say that, Mags? They might *think* old Billy's a fat slow swelled-up slug, but he sure can stir his rotten stumps when he wants to, he'll have you down in the mud neck-snapped and open-faced like a sandwich before you can scream help or goddamn you—she always said that." Tears streaked down his pale dirty face, making clean damp tracks in the dried mud, then subsided again. "You always said that. And now, you're—just lying there in the leaves. For the animals to eat. Like something true dead."

He looked up at me again, and smiled. "Except, no more animals. Looks like. Everywhere I go. That thing, out there, it's taking 'em."

Something deep in my stomach stirred and coiled around itself, tight and hurtful. That deer. Animals never did anything bad to me, the couple I'd killed to test I knew what I was doing I'd felt really sorry about afterward. Everywhere he goes.

"I ran toward it," Billy kept saying, again and again. Like a chant. "I ran toward it, but I couldn't reach—it was like, not a mirage, I knew it was really there, but like it was hidden behind some door or wall that I couldn't see and so every time I almost got to it, it threw me back." Shaking his head ruefully. "Threw me back like a fucking fish off the line. And then it just, went away."

"He does that," I said quietly. "All the time."

He didn't look half sad enough about it. Nobody really understands, even when they see it for themselves. "Hey! Doesn't matter, though, you know why, kid?" He was leaning forward again, all huddled-up shoulders and a face full of happy conspiracy. "Know why? 'Cause I'm getting there. I know I'm getting there. Not now, though, it's not time yet—but later. Later on. After I take care of business. And then I'm gonna run. I'm gonna run like I can run now, like I never could before, I'm gonna crash right through that big old invisible wall and just keep on going and going."

He smiled at me again, at me this time and not the open air. I felt good as certain now he wouldn't hurt me but something about the sharp, tight curve of his mouth made the coiled thing inside me knot itself up harder, tug and twist. "So why the hell tell it to me?" I said.

Billy thought that one over. Nodding his head at someone

I couldn't see. "You can't stay here, you know. You think you're safe, he told me you'd think you were tucked up all tight in this little stinking shithole but your Friendly Man? He knows where you are."

His smile was wider, harder, those long sharp-edged inhuman teeth a flash of incongruous good health, predatory eagerness in a face made gaunt and withered by grief. A death's-head grin. "He knows where you are. And wherever you go? Whatever you do? He'll find you."

I never told anyone I called Death the Friendly Man. Nobody except Amy and her horrible friends, and they wouldn't have said it to Billy. "Who told you that?" I demanded. "Who told you I used to call him—"

"We've gotta go," he said. His smile didn't waver. "You and I. We've gotta go, we've gotta get to what's waiting for us. I'll never get through the wall otherwise." He leaned forward, half-bowed, defeated red-rimmed eyes alight with the pleasure of telling me something I didn't want to hear. "It's waiting for both of us. You, and me. You can stay here and let it find ya"—a single thick, damp potato-wedge of a finger traced a line across his throat, ear to ear—"or you can meet it out in the open. Your choice. Either way, once I find it again? I know what I'm gonna do."

His voice was thick with satisfaction, the pride of a well thought-out plan, but the tears had started again. Stay here, and die. Because *he* knew just where I was, and he wasn't happy. Or meet him out in the open, in the arena of ground and sky, and—

He thought he could kill me. He really thought that, that he could send Billy—Billy!—to finish me off, that he could threaten me and trick me into—I put my knife away, thrust hands in my pockets glaring at Billy. "Who told you I was in here?"

The corners of Billy's mouth curled up again, subsided before a real smile broke out. "A man you can't see."

"Did he tell you to try and kill me?"

"A man you can't see, behind a wall I can't bust through."

"Because you can't kill me. You can't. And he can't either." I cradled Sukie tighter in the crook of one arm, for strength. "He can't kill anybody anymore, not without them deciding it's time to die. That's why he's so angry. That's why he's trying to scare—"

"You can stay here, and rot," Billy said. Jacket flapping around his diminished chest, pants loose and sliding on his hips, another full-flowering, poisonous tree dropping its fruit and withering before my eyes. "Or you can meet it out in the open."

He couldn't kill me. He couldn't send Billy to kill me. He knew that now, knew our science was that far beyond him, that was why he was so angry. He couldn't threaten me, not with Billy or dead-tinder trees or any other show-trick. He wanted to meet me out in the open, with *respect*, like the hero of some old movie meets the mortal enemy he can't help but admire. And Billy was just the collateral damage, Billy even knew he was but with Mags gone, he didn't care. Okay. Stop hiding away like some sad little human coward. Meet the Friendly Enemy-Man out in the open, fight him with everything I've got, show him all his old tricks meant crap. Obsolete. Less than nothing.

And then, everything that was his, all the power, would be mine.

Sukie was small and pliable enough I could bend her double, her bare dirty cloth feet touching the top of her yarn hair, and stuff her into my jacket pocket. I reached over to the dented gray metal desktop, grabbed for a couple of lake stones I'd used as paperweights—brick red, a mucky grayish-green threaded in pink—and when I felt the heat radiating from their surface I wrapped my hand in an old T-shirt for protection, gritted my teeth against the pain as I shoved them in my other pocket. The awful heat gnawed straight through the jacket cloth into my side and hip and leg, but they'd acted funny like this before and they couldn't actually burn anything and I wasn't leaving them behind just because of a little pain. I was tougher than anyone thought, than they ever wanted to think. I'd put up with a lot worse.

I took a deep breath and crossed the room, stood there until Billy retreated almost meekly from the threshold. He fell in beside me, shoulder to shoulder, stinking of muck and sweat, and we went down the hallway to the lab's front entrance.

"Where are we going?" I asked, as we crossed the tall half-dead yard grass for the white gravel road, the noise of our feet on the stone-powder like someone softly, tentatively chewing something crunchy. "Where are we supposed to go, to meet him?"

"Leave that up to me," said Billy. One of his puffy pale doll-feet caught a sharp fragmented edge, bled in spots against the white, healed over again in moments. "He told me to fetch you, tells me everything I need to know—so you just leave that well up to me."

Meet him out in the open, the Friendly Man, in an arena of his choosing. Fight to the death, or rather, to the eternity. Okay. You asked for it. You'll find out just what Grandma taught me, just what we learned about how to beat you back forever.

Billy, as we walked, started singing under his breath, some old song Mags used to like about a girl named Dinah in Carolina and as he warbled off key the waterworks opened up in earnest; he wept and sang and sang and wept while the road narrowed until it was barely wide enough for a single small car, wound right back into the depths of the woods. I ignored him. Let it all just blend into the background, like the sounds of birds and wind-rustled leaves and small scuttling animals that should've been there, but weren't. Don't worry, I was on my way to get it back. I'd get it all back.

SEVEN
LISA

Jessie just stood there, glaring at us, not giving an inch. Jessie never gave an inch, not when she was alive, not after she died, so one thing at least was still reassuringly familiar. She rocked back on her heels, skinny arms folded, her face twisted up like she'd realized she was about to smile and had to stomp on the urge in its cradle. That was familiar, too. Linc hovered close to the trees, poised to flee, like the wild animal he still was; Renee, beside him, smiled an actual smile, but didn't step between us. She, at least, could still remember her own humanity, a few niceties of behavior here and there, like me—but Linc, Jessie, they'd shaken off the last traces of domestication so far back they'd never retrieve it for trying. Unfair of me to keep hoping, I knew that, but I was exhausted far past the point of sympathy. The three of them didn't look much better.

"So you're back," Jessie said. She kept her eyes strictly on me, like it was only us two standing here on the beach, watching as I slid our luggage off my arms and let it thud softly against the sand. I didn't mind playing pack mule—it gave me something to do, besides pretending not to see Amy's mother shooting daggers at me every time she thought my head was turned—but I didn't want Jessie getting the idea I'd just been expected, ordered, to do it and meekly obeyed because I was just that soft-hearted, soft-headed. She assumed the worst of everything on two legs often enough as it was.

"I'm back," I said.

"Your cabin's still empty. Other than the mice."

From Jessie, that was practically a ticker-tape parade. Naomi was clutching at my leg, nervous and wanting to be picked up, and I patted her head and flung my free arm out for introductions. "This is Amy. And Lucy, her mother, and this is Amy's friend Stephen—"

But she'd walked right past everything on two legs, kneeling next to Nick and almost crooning in his ear. "What's *your* name? Hmm?" She stroked his head with an easy, calm hand. "Can you tell me?"

Nick's tail thumped against the gravel, with more eagerness than I'd ever seen him show anyone who wasn't Amy. "You a good boy? Hmm? What's your name?"

"That's Nick," Naomi volunteered, almost beaming that he'd made friends so quickly. "Like Old Nick, which is what you call the devil, but he's nice—"

"And who the hell are you?"

Naomi flinched and shut her mouth tight, hands curling even tighter around my shin. Right out of the box. Goddammit, Jessie, couldn't you just try for even five minutes? Couldn't I quit expecting miracles for even two minutes? I decided not to take notice. "And this is Naomi."

Jessie glanced at her, uninterested, then with obvious reluctance pulled herself away from Nick and back to her feet. "They can't stay here."

Right out of the box. "Amy, Stephen, Lucy, Naomi, this is Linc—like Lincoln—and Renee, and Jessie." I'm not taking notice, Jessie. I'm too tired for that. "And this is typical."

"And this is *sensible*." Jessie brushed away bits of gravel stuck to her knees, her palms hard and sweeping like she was trying to rub right through to the skin. "There's a human settlement right down the road, about a mile. They started moving in just after you left. I guess the kiddie can stay here with you, if you're gonna whine and cry about it otherwise, but—"

"It's not like we're crowded here," Linc interrupted, like a casual afterthought. His usual method of getting his way with Jessie, by pretending it was all the same to him one way or another. From the corner of my eye, I saw Amy start at the sound of his voice, rumbling and deep in a way she probably never expected from that sallow scarecrow body. "Lisa and the kiddie can double up with Renee—all right, Renee?" Renee just shrugged. "And the rest of them can have the empty cabin."

He turned to me. "There's a couple more cabins, but they've mostly fallen apart. Never thought we'd have to get around to fixing them, there's so little company—looks like you've had yourself a hell of a winter, Lisa."

"You don't know the half of it," Stephen said, before I could answer. His voice was hard and flat, but not hostile: trying to sound as casual and assured as Linc, coming so close to pulling it off. Amy and Lucy just stared at the ground, waiting.

Jessie ran fingers through her hair, the same old scraggly auburn snarls and knots; I suspected she kept forgetting she even had to comb it at all. That was never a crowning Porter family glory anyway, our hair. The look in her eyes, it wasn't all the old hostility, the kneejerk misanthropy I'd never been able to stop taking to heart—she looked spooked, plain and simple, and a little disoriented. Like we'd just shaken her out of some horribly vivid nightmare and she was still in that in-between state, those first few startled seconds of consciousness, before the rush of relief from realizing that none of it had happened. Or the terrible reverse, a dream where everything was put quietly right, everything was back as she'd expected—we'd expected—it would always be, and then, she'd woken up. She reached down again, scratching Nick between the ears.

"Double up, for now," she said. "Like Linc said. For *now*. And clean up after yourselves. I don't want any fucking dogshit all over Florian's beach."

"... and so we left Natalie behind, at the lab." I blinked into the encroaching sunset, watching the sky turn swollen orange and tender pink. I'd never stopped missing the sunsets at the lake. "What was left of the lab, that is. And we've been walking ever since, to get here. We didn't start seeing anything really strange, though, until this afternoon—"

"And now I keep seeing it everywhere," Stephen said, stretching his legs out on the sand. We'd all been telling our story in bits and pieces, interrupting each other to fill in what we'd forgotten or never saw. "No rhyme or reason. Some places, big ones, they're completely untouched. Like here." He ran a hand through his hair, sighing, and gave Lucy a glance like she'd understand better than any of us. Lab rat solidarity. "It's just, I keep thinking—"

"Tell her about the man," Amy broke in, around a bite of beef jerky. We still had enough Shop-Wel snacks to last for days, a mercy since I was too tired to hunt and almost laughed at myself for hoping Jessie might offer food. "The one following us."

"It was a Scissor Man," Stephen said, a thread of impatience in his voice. "He followed us for a while, he realized there wasn't any point, he left. There's no more to it than that."

"And I keep telling you there's a lot more to it than that. You just won't listen to me, because—"

"Because *you're wrong*."

Even in the draining, fading light, I could see the tension making his every muscle clench up tight, how badly he needed to fall over and sleep. Maybe because she was as bad off or worse,

Amy decided to ignore it. "Just like I was wrong, thinking I saw a black dog following me. All the way from Lepingville. Just like that, Stephen?"

All the time we'd been talking, Jessie just sat there cross-legged with her elbows on her knees, face unreadable, she and Linc and Renee silent as church. Now, seeing this, she sat up straighter, her narrow angular face lighting up from the inside; I could feel her sudden eagerness for an argument, an outright fight, anything at all *different* from the long months before. Amy saw it too, her back stiffening and eyes narrowing. Even in the failing light I could read the dislike plain on her face, dislike and what almost looked like embarrassment: she'd almost done for another ex what Billy always loved to see, the apple cart overturned and humans fighting it out for his entertainment. It wasn't like that with Jessie—she'd have been just as glad to see me and Linc go at it—but Amy would never believe that. Stephen must've been on Amy's wavelength, too, because he shrugged, letting the whole discussion lie where they'd dropped it, and swiveled his head around to stare at the water. Then he sat up straighter and frowned.

"What's he doing?" Stephen demanded, a furrow cutting into his forehead as he stared at Nick.

Nick was a dark streak below us on the ridge, hurtling himself down to the waterline, back up, then down again, running and panting and barking. Once out of Jessie's direct line of fire, Naomi had reverted to an overtired strung-out little bat out of hell, gone hooting and hollering after Nick as he took off on a tear for the shore; as she hurtled by, I just pressed a package of cheese crackers into her hand and decided to let her run it off, keeping an eye trained on them both from where I sat. The lake was as calm as I'd ever seen it, the water almost ice-still—no danger of a rip current pulling either of them in—but as they both veered into the wetter sand and the lake splashed at their ankles, Stephen jumped to his feet, running headlong toward the shore with me in close pursuit.

"What's the matter?" I shouted at his back. "Stephen, they're fine, they're just—"

But Stephen was sliding at double speed down the sand ridge, waving his arms furiously at them both; before I could catch up, he'd waded shoe-deep into the water and had Naomi tight by the arm, hauling her away from Nick and the shoreline as she let out squalls of angry protest. Nick ran ceaseless rings around them both, barking in agitation as Naomi tried and failed to pull free, and when I barreled past him, he just kept on looping around us like we were a pole stuck in the sand, with him leashed to us and only free to turn in circles. Stephen was unyielding, Naomi almost purple with indignation.

"Let me go!" she shouted as I took her by the shoulders, trying to tug her away from Stephen. "We were playing, I wanna go play with him!"

"Did you see him?" Stephen's grip slackened, but he still wouldn't let her go; the cords in his torn-up neck bulged out, the scars criss-crossing his skin swollen and as livid as Naomi's own face. "Did you see it? He wasn't just playing! He was leading her straight into the water, he—"

"He wasn't doing anything! We were playing, let me go!"

Stephen finally let go and Naomi sat down hard in the sand as Amy, Renee, and the others came running up to us. "Nick wasn't doing anything!" she entreated me, almost drowned out by the barking that only kept getting louder. "I wasn't going in the water, it's too cold and I wouldn't go swimming all by myself anyway, not without a grownup, I'm not stupid like Stephen thinks I am—"

"Is she okay?" Renee asked. "Is everything all right?"

"Hoo melodramatics," Jessie said, in a disdainful drawl I knew far too well. "That's all."

"With a heaping spoonful of kiddie hysterics thrown in," added Linc. They both stayed put, though, didn't turn their backs on us and walk off to the cabins, and I knew that meant they were just as disconcerted as everyone else.

"I'm telling you, he was leading her *into* the water!" Stephen's arms dangled by his sides, as if without Naomi to animate them they were limp, purposeless puppet hands, but his eyes, his voice—they were tense with conviction. "I saw it, I'm not just imagining—she was too excited to know what he was doing, he was leading her in, little by little—"

"*He was not*!" Naomi was kneeling against the sand now, her fists hitting it in fury. "We were just playing, we stayed right on the shore! He wouldn't hurt anyone! You hate him so much you'd say anything to make everyone mad at him, and look how upset he is now and it's your fault!"

Nick whipped past us in his dozenth-some circuit, barely noticing Stephen or Naomi in his cloud of noise and dust. Amy squatted down with her hands on her thighs, whistling calm and soft, and he scrambled to a stop at her feet with his sides heaving, his jaundiced eyes luminous and frenetic.

"You have to calm down, boy," she murmured, stroking his coarse, inky fur. Her eyes flickered toward Stephen. "I saw them too, Stephen—they were just playing on the shore. They just got their feet wet. Paws wet. Whatever. He wasn't doing anything to her."

Stephen seemed to think that over for a moment, then his eyes sought out mine, Lucy's, all the rest of us who didn't know what to make of Nick and weren't sure we wanted to. He wanted us to back him up, that much was clear, agree that whatever Nick was playing at, it was nothing good, but I'd seen only what Amy had and if I'd thought Nick had anything actually malevolent about him, the slightest hint of it, I wouldn't have let him within a mile of Naomi in the first place. Lucy shook her head. I did too. Stephen turned back to Amy.

"Tell them," he said, his puppet hands gaining life again, balling into slow fists just like Naomi's. "Nick likes to *lead* people into a lot of dangerous places, doesn't he?" Amy was silent. "Doesn't he? Isn't that what he does? Amy, you know what I'm talking about. You know exactly what I mean. *Tell* them."

Amy was still squatting at Nick's side, chin down and all her concentration focused on stroking the back of his neck. Her nails dug in, giving him a good scratch, and as Lucy watched her, an echo of Stephen's frown appeared on her own face.

"Not unless," Amy said softly, "that's where they already wanted to go."

Stephen opened his mouth, then closed it again; we wouldn't agree with him, wouldn't second his lying eyes, and almost imperceptibly, his shoulders started to sag with confusion, with doubt. I wanted to say something, assure him that I'd seen plenty of things in my time that I'd sworn were real and true only to turn out to be empty echoes from my own brain, but that would've only made it worse. Naomi snuffled and grabbed at my hand, the empty cheese-cracker wrapper balled up in our mutual grasp. Her fingers were oily from her snack, and thinly coated in sand. She was gritting her teeth.

"I don't like you anymore," she hissed at Stephen.

Nick nuzzled at Amy's hand, then headed off in a lively trot that took him in a parabolic loop up the ridge, then back down where the light rucked-up sands became dark and smooth; over and over, he approached the shoreline and then veered away, kicking up tiny arcs of spray in each paw's wake, gazing fixedly at some undefined spot far out in the water. We stood there, watching him, as the night approached. Stephen picked absently, roughly, at the sutures in his throat, stopping only when Amy lifted his hand away and took it in her own; the look in his eyes, as he watched Nick watching the water, wasn't anger or dislike or frustration. It was fear.

I could have discounted that, could have chalked it up to the pure exhaustion from our ordeal in the lab, in the woods, on the road, making him see what had never been there at all; I could have, except that Jessie, hanging back in the shadows, and Amy, clasping his hand in both her own, looked just as frightened as he did. Just as frightened as I felt. All the more because I—because we—had no idea why.

EIGHT

AMY

When I woke up the next morning, I saw thin gray light streaming through my cabin's grimy, half-broken window and Nick curled up right beside me, still wide awake, mercifully quiet but every muscle in him on tensed-up high alert. I rubbed his nose and he made a little whining sound, like I was affronting his dignity by doing something so playful at a time like this; I rubbed it more vigorously and he wagged his tail. Stephen and my mother, pressed close on either side of me, stirred but didn't wake up.

"You have to give me better hints than last night," I whispered to Nick. "I know you can. Is this about the dead trees? The birds?"

He just gazed up at me, full of silent reproach. Lassie he wasn't. He wasn't even Taffy, our neighbor's old golden retriever who'd hobble up stiff-legged with arthritis and bark at you all genial wanting to tell you about her amazing day; I was glad she'd got cancer and been put to sleep before any of this started, before the plague.

What had Nick seen, out there on the horizon, and how was

I supposed to get that Jessie to say what it was? Was this what Lisa meant, when she said Jessie saw things she, Lisa, couldn't?

Dead birds falling from nests built in dead trees, small curled-up corpses landing on dead bushes and springing off the tight whorls of dead twig-branches to fall dead to the ground. Everything here, though, it all looked so green and new and fine, just like it was supposed to. Death itself, was it—he—trying to scare us? But he'd sent Nick to look after me, Nick who saved us and helped get us out of the lab. Stephen didn't understand that, that Nick led me into the place where I was meant to die but then got us all back out again, that he never took me anywhere I didn't want, didn't desperately *need* to go. He didn't kill me. He just didn't *save* me, not until he was supposed to.

What happened last night, to make Stephen start seeing things? I knew he didn't want Nick there, nobody else but Naomi did, but he wouldn't make up stories to turn me against Nick; he really thought Nick was trying to pull Naomi into the water. I could tell. Was he just nerved up, or was he *seeing* things? Like how for the longest time, nobody except me could see Nick... but that never meant that Nick wasn't always there?

This all didn't start happening until the creature following us, the man in black I knew wasn't Death, had disappeared. Not Death, and not any damned Scissor Man. This was fact. Even if everything else was guesswork.

"Show yourself," I said, very softly, to the air. As if I could summon him back, make some sort of incantation to whatever wanted to play with us anew. "Come back, and show yourself."

I waited. I really did wait, I really did hope for a few seconds, because being scared makes magic, that stupid arbitrary trivial magic you just made up in your head and whose kindergarten ritual only you can master, start to seem not only possible but likely. Come on, now. Come back.

Nick was waiting with me. I could feel it, I could see it in his eyes. He didn't know just what this was either, I was suddenly certain; he just knew it was wrong, he just knew it shouldn't be there and by God he was *going* to scare it away. Good dog. Don't listen to Stephen, don't you listen to anyone. Stephen, don't you even fucking think about trying to make me choose.

"We'll figure it out," I told Nick, soft into his big dark ear. "We have to."

The sunlight looked strangely muted and heavy in here and it smelled, a musty airless smell like an old memory of milk gone sour. It was probably all of us more than the cabin. Shifting carefully so I didn't wake anyone, I got up and headed out.

The backs of the cabins faced the woods. There was an old fire pit outside one of the other cabins, a square brick-bordered dirt ditch with a healthy orange flame already crackling in the middle. Jessie, Linc, and Renee were squatting in front of it, their hands all right in the fire, roasting bits of meat that dripped spattering fat on the dirt and the brick border and then shoving them in their mouths, tearing at the stuff hard and eager, barely even looking at what they ate. Their fingers, their skin—the fire didn't touch them, it did nothing to them at all. What they ate was hanging from a tree a few yards away, field-dressed, its antlers dangling useless inches above the ground; they must've been up already for hours.

It was each other they kept staring at as they ate, intent and heated and shutting the whole world out; like a ritual, like this was a closeness speech or sex or mother-love could never hope to match. I stepped back; I'd interrupted an intimacy I'd never wanted to see, but just then Jessie crammed the last hunk of deer meat in her mouth, licked fat from her unscorched fingers, looked up at me with a baleful stare that made me want to go running for Lisa. I made myself glare back. I'd killed one of her own kind—though just how, I still didn't know—and she knew it.

"Well," Jessie said. She got up from where she sat, mud

clinging to her jeans. "That's one chore done."

Right off, when we met, I saw her family resemblance to Lisa: same thin angular features, same sharp clear eyes always darting back and forth like they just knew someone was up to something right behind them, same tense posture like runners about to spring from the blocks. Linc and Renee gazed up at her, looking like they wanted to protest, but then they lowered their heads and finished their meat.

Jessie marched back to the dangling stag, reached in and casually, efficiently tore long strips of flesh from its carcass in a way that made me feel a little sick—a stupid feeling, I'd always eaten meat, I'd snared and dressed rabbits, squirrels, even possum plenty of times since last autumn. But it was something about the way she didn't bother with a knife, just dug in her fingers so thick with dried blood that the nails looked like one continuous scab. She tossed the meat to Renee, who obligingly held it to the flame. Renee, who was tall and blonde and even with her hair chopped too short, was like something from a magazine or an old art movie from the Sixties, the ones with beautiful European girls robbing banks and then sitting in cafés explaining it was all because of existentialism. You couldn't help but keep looking at Renee. Linc, with his long gaunt body folding up at the elbows and knees like a camping knife, sallow pitted skin and big mop of dark chaotic springy hair falling into his eyes, looked so comically ugly that in a way, a weird oppositional way, he and Renee almost matched. He was all Jessie's, though, that much I had figured out.

"Where's Lisa?" Jessie asked me. "She never could manage to get up before noon."

I shrugged. Lisa'd been up at dawn plenty of times when we were traveling from Leyton to Gary. It wasn't my place to get involved, Lisa had made that much clear, but Jessie seemed to expect more of an answer. I didn't have one, and the rich smell of roasting meat filled my nostrils and my mouth was watering so much I'd forgotten about feeling sick, when two people I'd never seen before emerged from the trees: a short, round woman with black hair shorn close like Renee's and a calm cheerful face; a man tall and thin, gingery reddish hair with thick streaks of gray, pale blue eyes sunk into a face webbed with lines you could tell were premature, from bad living and hard treatment instead of encroaching age. He smiled at me, uneven teeth leaping from the thatch of a half-grown beard. I tried smiling back, but the effort faltered and I wondered where Lisa was, or my mother.

"No berries yet," said the woman—fully human, from her voice—setting down a battered wicker picnic basket whose withes were starting to split open; she pulled out plates, some paper, some china, all mismatched. "I was hoping at least for an early strawberry or two, but I always was a dreamer—here you go." She handed me a plate, thin stiff orange plastic. "Now, are you Amy or Lucy? Jessie just said red hair—"

"Amy," Jessie threw in, flat and unenthused. Like I'd just had a stroke and couldn't talk for myself. Renee got up, slid the venison onto my plate, gave me a look that at least tried to be friendly. Dammit, Lisa, get the hell out here before I go and drag you out of—

"Our chickens are laying!" the woman exclaimed. "At long last! We couldn't not share a few eggs." She flourished a little saucepan proudly, pulled from the depths of the basket, waiting her turn at the flame. "Plenty of fat for the pan. How many did you bring, Russell?"

"There were 'bout six," Russell said. His voice was reedy and thin, the faintest little whistle coming from his mouth like some of his crooked teeth were missing. "Rhody and Carla put in laying overtime. I brought three. Everyone can have a bite or two, anyway."

"Or three," Renee said. She went up to the deer's remains, pulled away a thick little gobbet of fat. "I don't like eggs. Amy, this is Tina and Russell, they're from the human settlement Jessie mentioned—"

"Cowleston," Tina said. She rubbed the fat all over the pan's insides, none of my hypocritical squeamishness; the pendant around her neck, a big cheap-looking cross, swung from side to side as she worked. “That’s what we’re calling it, anyway—very unimaginative but it gets the job done. Nice to meet you, Amy. I hope you like them fried.”

Clever, Jessie, bring along the humans from down the road, laden with treats, have them take us all off your hands in one go—Jessie wasn’t looking especially devious, though, more like my mother would when it was her turn to host my aunt and uncle for Christmas and she was counting the minutes until they left. Poking at the fire, muttering to herself like Tina hadn’t said a word.

The venison was good, a bigger piece than I could finish. “Fried is fine,” I said. “But they’re your eggs, you don’t have to—”

“*Amy*!”

My mother’s voice, high and anxious, from the doorway of our cabin. I motioned to her impatiently and she came stumbling up, still half-asleep, silent Nick padding along close at her heels. Jessie stayed bent over the fire, muttering some more.

“I woke up and you weren’t there,” my mother said softly. She glanced at the trees, the gutted deer carcass hanging from one of them, and quickly turned her head. “I thought maybe—I got worried.”

Ever since she’d found Lisa and me talking in the woods—eavesdropped on us, God knows what she heard, even though she kept insisting she’d barely heard anything—my mother had attached herself to me like a silent sentry, where’re you going, what’re you doing, how do I know you won’t go kill yourself in my absence? Plenty of time to do that before, Mom, plenty of years you weren’t there at all to stop me, but now you want to play catchup ‘cause *you’re* scared—the little flicker of anger that darted through me light and quick, it wouldn’t help anyone right now, so I pushed it to the side, offered her and then Nick the rest of my meat. No takers.

“Doesn’t he eat?” Jessie asked, as Nick settled down with his nose on his paws, staring transfixed into the flames. “Ever?”

Didn’t care if my mother did or not, that was clear. At least she was consistent. “Never,” I said.

Renee and Linc exchanged glances. Jessie just nodded like that didn't surprise her, reached over to stroke him without taking her own eyes from the fire. "Nice change, anyway," she said, as Tina fussed with her little frying pan. "I mean, if folks I've never met before are gonna just drop in from the sky like this is fucking Grand Central Station, at least one of you doesn't expect me to fuss and feed—"

Right on cue Stephen came stumbling up, blinking with sleep, and Lisa came from the last cabin carrying Naomi; introductions all around, Tina lighting up like she'd been waiting to meet us all her life and Russell standing back silent and solemn, not shy but not effusive, waiting for everyone else to seek him out. You could tell he'd be just fine if nobody ever did. Naomi kept staring at Tina, or actually at Tina's necklace: a full crucifix instead of just a cross, cheap metal painted to look like gold, but instead of the little Christ figure being nailed down in a loincloth, he was in full robes, unbound arms held out to the viewer, the cross at his back like a bird-perch from which he'd spread wings and fly unimpeded right up to heaven. Slowly, like she couldn't help herself, Naomi walked up with her eyes all on it, and as Tina smiled at her, she touched it with tentative fingertips.

"My mommy had a necklace like that," she said.

Tina's smile grew wider and happier, and she leaned down to Naomi with real pleasure in her eyes. "Your mother was churched? That's wonderful! I haven't met another believer since—well, in a very long time." She smoothed Naomi's hair, the little cowlick in the back springing up right on cue once her hand departed. "Gets a little lonely sometimes, to be honest."

I remembered then where I'd seen that peculiar sort of crucifix: Talitha Cumi Church, the little storefront ministry a few blocks from my house, the one that took the whole Lazarus story to mean zombies were God's creation too, that when Jesus and Mary went bodily into heaven, it meant they were also undead. Along with a whole lot of other weird ideas. It was all the same to me and my mother, we didn't believe in anything, but people called them necrophiles, Satanists, even Nazis, even though they didn't seem to have anything against Jews. Or anyone else. Naomi curled her fingers around the little floating Jesus, let the pendant go.

"We went every Sunday," Naomi told Tina. "Sometimes Saturday too."

"How old are you—six, seven?" Tina looked all excited now, like they were both conspirators in some grand wonderful cause nobody else knew about. Dean Sewell, this Baptist kid at my old middle school, he'd get that same look whenever he talked about how much he loved Jesus and it always made me nervous. "Have you been baptized yet?"

"I was going to be," Naomi said. Eager and swift, like she'd been waiting and waiting for the rest of us to ask her about it. "We had baptism practice, after regular Bible school, and I had a white dress and a flower-wreath for my hair. It kept falling off. I needed bobby pins."

Her face fell, grew pensive, the little light of that memory fading and going dark. "I never got my bracelet," she said.

"It was being engraved special, Mommy saved up the money just for that." She stared down at her feet, voice dropping to a whisper. "But then she got sick."

Churchers, part of their whole baptism ritual was that you got a special ID bracelet you had to wear night and day, with your name and family details carved on it so if you came back a zombie—I think they thought everyone did, sooner or later—there'd be a way for believers to find each other. Dog tags for the Lord. There was a churcher girl in my class and everyone made fun of her for it, trying to grab it and rip it right off her arm. Tina's eyes softened and she set her frying pan aside, holding out her own, bare-wristed hand.

"I lost mine," she confided. "I don't even know where or how, suddenly I just realized I didn't have it anymore. That was hard. But I think God understands these things happen. When we're blinded or crippled is when He best helps guide us. I mean, look what He's done right now, leading us both to each—"

"Did you want me to fry those up?" Lisa asked. I could see her wishing for a proper crucifix of her own, or a Virgin Mary statue to hit Tina over the head with. "I mean, if you're too busy with the homily."

Russell didn't smile, exactly, but his eyes, his face suffused with a sudden warmth, like the lines cut deep in the skin were rays; he'd been a handsome man, you could tell, a good long time ago. "Don't let her talk put you off," he said, giving Tina this easy look like her talk was part of the air, the water, he could tease about it because he'd never lose it. "It's like she said, been a year and a day, for real almost, since she found anyone who—"

"I'm Catholic," Lisa replied, stroking Naomi's hair as she talked. "So it all means nothing to me anyway."

"I don't expect it to," Tina said, picking up her frying pan. "We don't proselytize. I thought it might mean something to your little girl, though, that's all."

"Some food," Stephen said, "might mean a lot to the rest of us."

Renee's lips twitched, over where she and Jessie and Linc sat still steadily shoving morsels of meat in their mouths, licking fat from their fingers; she got up, the tarnished rings covering her hands gleaming with spit and grease, and wandered over to the carcass. "You're welcome," she said.

Nick got up from his place at the fire, settling himself right next to Stephen without bothering to turn round and round for a comfortable seat. He gazed up at Stephen, as heated and fixed a stare as he'd given the flames, then put his ears back and let out a low, rumbling growl.

"Stop that," Stephen muttered, half-hearted, as Renee's hands pinkened and reddened and the meat cooked for him, for my mother and Lisa and Naomi. "Just stop."

Stephen looked dreadful this morning, eyes bloodshot and puffy like he'd been drinking and shadows underneath them that made skull-like hollows of his face; he'd picked the stitches out of his throat sometime during the night, nothing left of our lab misadventures but the faint puckered suture-holes already healing over, and my own neck itched and twitched needing to do the same, afraid if I tried it I'd end up gaping open and gushing blood.

After his outburst yesterday, he'd just sat there on the beach with his knees drawn up nearly to his chin, rocking vaguely back and forth and staring at the sand in something close to misery. Nightmares? Night visions, something that—why couldn't we be alone, so we could talk about it? One night alone together, a few minutes here and there in the lab or Paradise City, that was the whole of whatever we'd had.

Stephen mumbled vague thanks to Renee when she handed him a plate, and he and my mother lowered their heads and attacked their meat, my leftover meat, the one oozing fried egg divided between her plate and his. Naomi, thanks to Lisa and Tina's silent, ecumenical flickers of agreement, got a whole egg for herself. As she ate, she pointedly ignored Stephen, angling her small self as far away from him as she could without actually turning her back. I made myself concentrate on the egg I was sharing with Lisa, deep rich-tasting orange yolk like they always said chickens gave if you let them scratch for grubs and run around (but nobody let animals just run around, back before, having an open farm was a flesh-invitation to the undead so they penned them up in factory farms, guarded with machine guns for their own protection), the faint gamey flavor from the cooking grease, because I knew Nick wasn't just barking at nothing. He'd seen something. We all knew Nick saw something. Stephen was scared and that made me scared and I didn't know what to do but keep pretending everything was good and friendly until I'd finished my meal. Just like every meal, back at my uncle's, when my mother was still missing.

"We saw you folks coming down the main road yesterday," Russell said, into the silence. "Thought we'd let you rest a night before we came over to visit. We're camped out in some of the old houses just down the way, what used to be Wakefield Dunes, plenty of supplies to share and beds and company if you—"

"Nick!" my mother shouted. "*No*! Stop it!"

Nick was growling louder now, then barking sharp and fast at Stephen as he sat huddled over his breakfast, and before I could stop him Nick leapt at Stephen's knee and knocked the plate right out of his hands. Dish and venison and fried egg went flying, thudding wrong-side down on the leaves at my feet, and instead of rushing to eat it, Nick darted around the trees, hurtled back toward us, thudded to a confused, noisy stop at Stephen's side once again. Naomi gasped, fork frozen halfway to her mouth, and Stephen sprang to his feet, a streak of dried yolk like paint smeared across his flushed cheek.

"Nick!" Naomi cried. Genuinely scandalized, she sounded. "*Bad* dog! Why did you do that?"

"Here," Lisa said with a swift glance at me, holding out her plate. "Take the rest of mine, I don't want it."

"I'm not hungry," Stephen said softly. He held the syllables thoughtfully in his mouth, like a fruit he wasn't quite sure was ripe enough to bite; his hand ran fretfully through his hair, his eyes darted from me to Lisa still holding out her plate to the underbrush where Nick crouched, barking and barking. "Amy? You got him to quiet down last night. Make him stop."

I couldn't, today. I just knew I couldn't, even though I didn't know why, any more than I could stop him following me back at Lepingville; there was something in the air all around us, a heavy restless miasma in the morning sky that I couldn't see but could almost taste, a gamey flavor like the venison weighting down my stomach but stronger, more sour, the first cousin of rot. I'd thought it was just the air in the cabins, but it was everywhere, its pounding staleness filling all our lungs; Nick's incessant barking, here and last night, it was like he was desperately trying to cough it all up.

I called Nick's name, almost crooning it, and he didn't quiet down. I knelt down in the ruined leaves, stretching out an arm to stroke him, and then without any warning a mass of fur and teeth and high howling canine panic was flying straight at me, a wild blindness in his eyes as he sent me sideways and sprawling on my back in the underbrush. His jaws were wide open inches from my face, drooling with heat and ready to snap, my mother came running toward us with a scream—but he didn't bite me, he didn't even try, just barreled over me where I lay and disappeared at double speed, running feverishly through the trees and out of sight.

It's all right, boy. It's all right, it wasn't me you were after, I was only the thing standing in your way—and they all knew it too, I could tell by their faces, as they ringed round me where I lay with mud caked down my shirt front and egg yolk drying in my hair. All except Stephen, almost shaking with anger as he helped brush me off and set me back on my feet.

"I'll go after him," I said. There was blood all over my jeans, I'd knocked my leg against a sharp rock, but I barely felt that or the bark-scrapes on my palms. "He's never been like this, not before, we need to figure out what he's seeing that's making him so—"

"He's not seeing anything!" Stephen shouted, an ugly spitting rasp in his voice, pacing feet twitching to kick anything in their path. "Other than easy targets, that's what he's seeing—first Naomi, now you, he's your own damned demon familiar and he goes and turns on you, too!"

"He didn't! He hasn't turned on anyone, you're just—"

"What, I'm seeing things? Like yesterday, on the beach? Like I just hallucinated him going straight for your face?" He swept an arm through the air, at the greenery around us, the sky. "The trees, the animals we saw coming here, the... whatever it is right now, that feeling in the air, it's following us wherever *he* goes—he's part of it! If he's not causing it, he knows damned well what is!"

"He wasn't going for my face! He was just trying to get away, everybody saw it! He's shit-scared, just like the rest of us!"

"Stephen," my mother said, and she'd never liked Nick, never wanted him, but she knew I was right this time, knew that whatever has seized hold of the air, the woods, the world had Nick as unmoored as we were. "Think about what you're saying. I know things have felt... not right, for a long time now—"

"Not right at all," Tina said, quietly. "Not where we are, either."

"Exactly! It's been everywhere!" My mother flung her hand in Tina's direction, *see there don't you see*, and Naomi's eyes were growing huge with fright and Jessie, Linc, the others were approaching closer, cautious, ready to try and break up an actual fight. "Stephen, think. You don't seriously believe Nick could be in eighty different places at—"

"Why not?" Stephen shouted. "Why couldn't he? Everything that's happened? The way Amy met him in the first place?" His eyes were on me now, the accused, the softhearted fool who'd dragged the blight into our midst and wouldn't see it for what it was. "Everything you keep saying you've seen, Amy, why couldn't—"

"*Saying* I've seen." I shook my head. "You still don't believe it, do you? I tell people over and over what happened and how he saved all our hides, including yours, but you never listen to a damned word I say!" I was shouting now too, hoarse and hurting and ready to hurl Tina's frying pan right at his head. "None of you do! Nobody! I thought you were different, that you understood what—you *saw it happen*, you saw him get us out of there, and you still don't listen!"

"Because you're not listening to me!" Yelling back, yelling like we were all alone and nobody else watching us mattered, the scars on his neck dark red and throbbing. "Because it happens right in front of everyone, plain as the fucking sunshine, and you don't *want* to see it! You don't want to listen to a goddamned thing except what you want to hear!"

My mother put a hand on his shoulder. "Stephen—"

He yanked himself free and stalked off toward the beach, not slowing down even when he stumbled and nearly fell over a thick protruding tree root, never looking back. Nick's infuriated echoes still reverberated from the woods; as we stood there listening they grew farther and farther away, still frantic, ever fainter, and then nothing.

Everything was quiet, for a moment, then Jessie shook her head and picked up a bucket sitting pitside. "Congratulations, ma'am," she said, without too much malice, as she doused the fire. "You certainly know how to pick 'em."

"So did you," Renee said, quite calmly, as she started stacking plates. "Once."

Jessie glanced at Renee like she wanted to yell, but there was sadness in her eyes, sadness and a peculiar embarrassment I knew didn't come from any of us hearing this. "Exactly," she said.

Linc reached out and rubbed her arm, casual little intimacy that made a pang go through me: *Stephen, goddammit, you fucking fool.* Didn't he realize that even though he was wrong about this, about Nick, that I still understood, that we both together felt how strange and wrong everything had become? Just like Nick, just now? Lisa and my mother both glanced at me, apologetic like this was somehow their fault.

"Don't ask me," I said, wiping my fingers on one of the bandannas Linc had been passing around for napkins. There was a quaver in my voice and that just made me feel angrier. "I mean, seriously, nobody ever ask me another—"

"Nick will get lost," Naomi said, tearful. "We have to go look for him."

"He'll be fine," Lisa soothed, wadding up another bandanna and dipping it in the bucket to scrub Naomi's face clean. "He'll come back, just let him run around alone for a while. Away from people." She glanced over at me, apprehensive, confused: she knew Nick hadn't tried to attack me, would never countenance his coming back if she thought he'd attack any of us, but he'd had still spooked her. Like he had since first she'd seen him. "It might be better that way."

"He got scared, that's why he ran away!" Naomi was now crying in earnest. "Just like Amy said! He's scared and all by himself and we have to find him!"

Nothing was going to dissuade her so Lisa sighed, took her hand and they went off together into the trees, following what they could of Nick's path. Russell, who'd been quietly sitting there taking all this in, gave me a sympathetic attempt at a smile.

"We're all spooked, too," he confirmed. "Can't put my finger on it. Last few days, especially, I keep waking up at night and even though I can feel the air going in and out of me, it's still like I ain't breathing anymore—"

"We don't know what to think," Tina said. Her stubborn good cheer wavered, faltered just a little bit, as she wiped out the frying pan and repacked her basket. "I just worry that maybe it's some new sickness, or—I'm trying to put my trust in the Lord, I really am. Though sometimes that's hard. But I don't know what to think."

Everybody was staring at me and I wished they'd stop. I edged closer to my mother's side. "Don't get mad at Lisa," I told Tina, though why I even cared about that I couldn't have said. Just sick of yelling, sick of sniping, never mind who or what set it off. "It's not the Catholic thing, she just gets jealous about Naomi—don't get pissed at her about it." I shrugged. "I mean, Naomi is all she'll have left."

It took me a moment to realize what I'd just said and they were all staring at me harder, Jessie, my mother, all their faces ranging from puzzlement to open alarm. *All she's got left*, I opened my mouth to say, *that's what I meant*, but the words seemed to stick and falter in my throat like a dry little wad of paper scrawled with lies and I couldn't say them, something inside me actually refused to say them. Because what I'd said the first time was right, and I knew it was right. Naomi was all Lisa *would* have left.

I didn't know why I said it. But I knew it was true. Feeling all through me like when Nick was first following me, that feeling of being truly seen for what I was for the first time in my nothing invisible life (though they were watching me all along, all that time I thought my mother and I had no friends, it turned out we had acquaintances and observers around us, everywhere). Everything in me, laid bare under the light.

"Amy," my mother said. The fear in her that I'd elicited without trying gave me an unwelcome surge of guilt. "What do you—"

"So where'd that come from?" Jessie cut in. "What you just said?"

Jessie, Lisa's sister, who saw things other people didn't, Lisa said. She was looking at me with sharp, matter-of-fact eyes, no surprise in her, and her ex friends were too.

"I don't know," I told her. "I really don't." I glanced at my mother. In for a penny. "It's like—something told me to say it, before I realized I hadn't thought of it myself, because it's true." I swallowed. That spotlit feeling, again, that feeling of being X-rayed in public and everyone seeing the plastered-over hollows where my bones should've been. And another feeling too, compulsion. "It's something that's going to happen, no matter what we do."

Birds called out overhead, the insistent exuberant cheeping of hungry chicks. I hoped their mother hadn't dropped to the ground, somewhere, falling in mid-flight for no reason whatsoever. Jessie nodded at me, then turned to Russell and Tina.

"Go back to Cowleston," she said. Sharp and commanding, but not angry. "Might be better that way."

"Might be needed there either way." Russell took up Tina's basket, glanced at her with a stubborn flash of habitual amusement. "If Reverend Kim here's gonna insist I'm the mayor—"

"We all picked you, didn't we?" Tina slid her arms into the jacket she'd spread on the ground as a seat-cushion. "I'm sorry we had to meet like this, but you're all welcome to come to us if you want to. We've got a sign out by the roadside. There's only about thirty of us and plenty of foraged supplies. Down around what used to be the Convent of St. Ignatius, you can't miss it." She glanced at Jessie. "Stay safe, all of you. Let us know what's going on when you can. And God bless."

They headed through the trees and toward the road without looking back. Jessie waited until they were out of sight or earshot, then turned to me.

"I don't know what's going on here," she said. Her eyes flared up, the last remnant of something predatory and merciless that'd once been all inside her, eating her alive, but now was just an ember, an echo. No less frightening for it. "If you do, you'd better spill it right now."

"Or what?" My mother's words were quiet but her face was

grim. "Or what then? Are you threatening—"

"She doesn't need to threaten," Linc said. That rumbling, almost guttural voice, a man's voice with all the wear and tear of age, though he looked no older than me. "We're all threatened—we might not know how, or why, but we are. That's the point." He turned to Jessie like of course she would know, like she'd known too much before this to let them down now. "So what do we do?"

I expected her to snap back at him but her shoulders sagged, she seemed to huddle into herself, and she was so small, so thin, a child swimming in a sea of grownup's clothes. She gazed at the ground, squeezed hard on a stone she'd pulled from her pocket, then looked up with a sort of weary, old-woman resignation.

"I don't have a fucking clue," she said. "But the kiddie, the one Lisa dragged in? I have a feeling she was right. We have to go find that dog."

NINE

STEPHEN

They were all just seeing what they wanted to see, hearing what they wanted to hear, and I was the rotten branch on the tree for trying to warn them. To keep us halfway safe. Didn't I try and look out for Naomi, back in Paradise City, when Billy and Mags would make her cry every day just for fun? And for poor crazy Janey, who even before she got to Paradise went through things nobody wanted to think about, who even when her "husband" Don scolded her still kept forgetting to eat? I know it didn't do us much good, all my looking-out. It didn't do Amy any good at all—dragged off to the lab, her throat cut, made one of us and I'd have let them do anything to me, I didn't care what more they did to me, if only they'd stayed away from her.

Did she understand that? That what happened to her—stolen away, throat slit, Billy and all the rest of them after her in the woods—that was *my fault* for not looking after her, and I wasn't going to fuck it up again? For her or anyone else? Nick, that thing just barely masquerading as a dog, it had Naomi out in the lake up to her waist, a fast rip current surging toward them both to drag her under. I *saw* it, right here, last night, from this same spot on the dune ridge where I was standing now. Standing right here, I saw Nick splash around the shoreline and then paddle further and further out. A long, thin, frothing plume of lake water approached them both from the side, moving faster than any wave should ever move, while Nick stared hard and long at it like he was pulling it in by invisible reins. Naomi laughed and waded after Nick happy as anything because she was just a kid and didn't understand, past the waist, up to the chest, as I tried to outrun the current and grab her before she was pulled in and drowned—

But then something happened and we weren't in the water, we were back on shore without my knowing how we got there, and Naomi couldn't have been out in the lake like I'd thought because everything but her sneakers was perfectly dry. Just like Nick's fur, not even a stray droplet of water to betray him. But I *saw him do it.* Just like I saw him knock Amy to the ground and sink his teeth into her cheek, ripping and tearing down to the bone, Lucy's screams just making him bite deeper—but then there wasn't any blood, and Nick was somehow gone, and everyone thought I'd gone crazy with hating him. I saw it! I saw him do it! Amy had been the only person alive who could see and hear Nick, once, before we ever even met, and that didn't make what she saw of him untrue—but now she thought I was crazy too, she thought I was just making up stories too. Why would I do that? Why couldn't anyone trust my own eyes... not even me?

I keep seeing things everyone else tells me didn't happen, and for a few minutes when I woke up this morning, I couldn't see anything at all. I stared into the darkness, waiting for my eyes to adjust and thinking it must still be the middle of the night, and then I realized that this was something else entirely. Nighttime had shapes, nebulous and disorienting but still visible in the shadows, and faint moonlight trickling through our cabin window that had no curtains. This, though, this was a formless colorless blank, an absence, not just a lack of light and vision but the impossibility of such things ever even existing. As if I had gone to sleep normal, and somehow woken up not merely blind, but with no eyes at all.

My hands flew to my face in a panic, seeking to assure myself my eyes were still in their sockets, and I blinked and blinked frantically but nothing happened, *nothing* was there at all, and I opened my mouth to shout for help—who could have helped me?—and then, all of a sudden, the world was there again. The light was deep gray and pale pink against the cabin wall, the first full light of sunrise. Lucy was curled into a ball next to me, an arm flung over her face, still fast asleep; Amy was already up and gone. Nick was there too, a coarse hot weight against my shoulder, gazing straight at me. His eyes just inches from mine, unblinking and expressionless. Blank. His teeth bared, ready to bite, ready to—

Except that he can't have been there, next to me, because even as I stared back at him I heard him outside the cabin, heard his barking and Amy's voice shushing him through the open window. I turned to the window, sitting upright looking for him and Amy outside, and when I turned back again there was no Nick beside me. Gone. Which had been the real him? Both of them? Did I dream him, dream the void and the blankness that preceded him, and only think I'd woken up?

I already have voids and absences, huge blank spots in my brain, thanks to what they did to me all those years in the lab over and over again. Memory holes, ridiculous trivial shit sometimes like what I used to eat for breakfast or how to get to places I'd already been dozens of times, but bigger ones too, whole months and years just wiped out. Gone. Maybe all this was another side effect, another way for my brain to misfire. I hoped to God not. Amnesia was embarrassing, but hallucinations—if that's what they were—were humiliating. Even Amy, the way she looked at me. I'd thought she would understand. Maybe she did, inside, but didn't want to. I knew that feeling.

I didn't imagine anything. I knew I'd seen it. I *had*. And that I'd... not seen, at all, this morning.

It was stupid to come down here, sit around sulking on the

sand like a kid Naomi's age when there were questions needing an answer. I had to find that so-called dog, if he hadn't already fled somewhere no human being—even one like us—could follow. I didn't want to hurt him, I didn't have fighting anywhere on my mind. I just needed to see him again, to try and work out what exactly I was seeing when I looked at him, and why. Maybe it wasn't even him at all, really. Maybe it was this beach itself, where we were, that was causing it.

I didn't ever want to hurt him. I swear. It's the truth.

I climbed back up the ridge and headed for the trees, veering far away from the cabins because I wasn't up to talking to anyone just then. Part of me was afraid they might laugh. The woods were still thick and green and if the ravages of... something else had set in, like we'd seen on the road, it wasn't spreading fast. I set off to the left, my feet slippery on slick mats of fallen leaves turning to muck, and as I circled around a huge old oak's tree trunk, nearly ran straight into Lisa's sister coming the other way. She jumped backward, glaring at me, all thin sharp angles like some stick figure drawing and her narrow face gone narrower with suspicion.

"So what the hell are you wandering around for?" she demanded. "If you changed your mind about breakfast, you're a little late."

I couldn't stand their voices, the exes, hard and super-staccato like high heels on a corrugated metal floor. Amy's voice was full human, soft and flowing like water, there wasn't anything harsh about it to my ears even when she was mad as hell. "I'm walking around," I said. "Is that allowed? I thought you were happy if we all just stayed out of your way."

She stood there with her arms folded, sizing me up and down. Her hair fell over her face, auburn hair in such long snarled clumps it looked like failed dreadlocks. "That dog," she said. "Does he talk to your little girlfriend, or something?"

I blinked. He made her nervous, too? I'd thought Nick was the only one of us she could stand. Lisa had warned us she always picked animals over people. "I doubt it," I said. "Why don't you ask her yourself, if you really want to be sure? Is it true what Lisa told us, that you can see things other people don't?"

Jessie's eyes actually went wide in surprise. Then she shrugged. "She said that? Well, anybody can see just about anything, when they're delirious sick. Don't listen to her."

Delirious sick. Maybe that was my problem—another fever, another plague. I hoped it would happen fast, if that's what it was, not make me some demented hallucinating thing before it finally killed me. Without bothering with goodbyes I turned away, heading past the big oak and deeper into the trees, and she surprised me again by following me, as if she were on the same goose-hunt I was but also didn't want to talk about it. We walked along in silence, side by side.

"Word of advice," she said, after a few moments. "Things you think you see, and nobody else does, don't bother trying to convince them they're there. It never works." She laughed, an explosive burst that sounded like a human doubled over coughing. "No matter what, *even if* it seems like they're listening to you, it just never fucking works. They just go along with it so they don't hurt your feelings or start a fight or some other equally shit-useless reason, and it just makes you feel crazier than you already worry you are."

I thought that over. Then I plucked a stick from the underbrush, fringed all down its length with tiny pale green leaves that would never mature, and poked at the leaf clumps below our feet. "You don't like us humans," I said. If that was what I still had a right to call myself, after what the lab did. Whatever I was, though, at least I wasn't like her. "So why don't you just chase Tina and the others away from that settlement they were talking about? Another favor to Lisa, like us?"

"They only got here after she left." She sounded irritable, like I'd just mentioned something any polite person would ignore, but then, she hadn't stopped sounding irritable since we arrived. "They just showed up here one day and kept coming. *I* can't stop them from setting up down the road if they want to—I'm not a fucking feudal duchess. The rest of them at least know to leave us alone. Tina, though, she always thinks she can make another fucking convert." She snorted. "And I mean, a convert that actually used to be dead for real? In that whackjob religion of hers? She'd shit herself with happiness."

She shook her head suddenly, thrust hands in her pockets as she pushed ahead of me through the cottonwoods. "Anyway. They're there, we're here. Not worth the trouble of getting rid of them." Her voice dropped, muttering almost, like she was talking to herself. "Not much of anything's worth the trouble lately, if you ask me—"

The sky went dark. The sun was gone.

We both stood there blinking into the sudden darkness, actual darkness and not a blank void because I could still make out the shape of her, the surrounding trees and bushes and rocks. And then the shapes, themselves, began to dissolve. The shadows were gone, my own hand in front of my face gone, everything—

And then as fast as it had vanished, the light was back, and the woods were back, and only a small, swift shadow was passing overhead, nowhere near big enough to block out the sun. We both looked up, watching the dark spot of a bird—a hawk of some sort, big-beaked and wide-winged—maneuver over the trees and out of sight, and then we stood there staring at each other, waiting for something to happen. For something horrible to happen. The sun kept on shining, and the world kept its shape.

"We're out here looking for the same thing," Jessie said. "You and me. Aren't we?"

"Are we?" I asked. I knew we were, somehow, I'd known it since she started following me. Somehow. "How do you know that?"

She pondered the question, hands in her pockets. "I don't have a fucking clue."

She took off, slip-sliding unevenly on the muddy leaves and sandy dirt, her head hanging down so her limp clumpy hair fluttered like torn strips of cloth as she threaded through the cottonwoods. Even at a laggard pace she was faster than me, fast enough I had to almost jog to keep up. Who the hell put her in charge of this snipe hunt, anyway? But exes were all alike, always grabbing charge of everything and everyone like they did you a favor—even Lisa, dragging us out here for no good reason I could yet figure out, though Amy wouldn't hear a word said against her.

But it happened to both of us, me and Jessie, that split second just like this morning when light and vision and everything else disappeared; this time it wasn't just me. It wasn't just my head, my memory, my craziness inventing it all. So I must not have just imagined Nick being beside me and not beside me, this morning, two places at once. Drowning Naomi, but not. Maiming Amy, but not.

A hallucination? Or a warning?

We *had* to find him.

A small, dark thing shot ahead of us, just yards from where we stood, zigzagging over the underbrush in a blur of feverish speed. Jessie let out a surprised sound, ran toward it—but as soon as we saw it, it'd vanished, lost among the trees. I couldn't even tell if it was dog-shaped or deer-shaped or what it was, it was going far too fast. Jessie banged a fist against a tree trunk in frustration, barely seeming to notice when the gnarled gray flutes of bark made her knuckles split and bleed.

"Nick!" she shouted, in the direction the thing had gone. "Here, boy! Nick!"

No answer. We kept walking. And walking.

"He's got to be nearby," I said. "He wouldn't just leave Amy."

"Keeps that close an eye on her, does he?" asked Jessie.

Answering that felt like disloyalty to Amy, like betraying a secret. So I didn't say anything. Even though the question made my stomach twist.

"This way," she said, and barreled over a hillock of interlaced tree roots and slippery rotten leaves without waiting for me. "Nick? Nick!" Nothing. "For fuck's sake, why doesn't your damned girlfriend come and help us find him, if he won't listen to—*Nick*!"

I cupped my hands over my mouth. "Nick!" Nothing. Then

I had an idea—a stupid idea, but I didn't care. "*Nick*! Amy wants you! *Amy's* looking for you!"

Nothing.

And then, like there'd been a test, and I'd finally passed it, the faint but not faraway sound of barking. We took off toward it, over a narrow dried-up ditch that might've once been a creek, past thick handfuls of mayapple and violets, into a tiny clearing bordered by butternut trees where Nick crouched down, his teeth bared and his eyes gone blank. Jessie crouched down beside him and made wordless sounds, soothing apologetic noises like we'd scared him, but he kept on barking like he couldn't even hear her, a guttural basso drowning out her, and the birds, and everything else—

And the woods and the world were gone again, vanished, blankness like the blank of Nick's eyes surrounding me and swallowing me alive. And nothing was in front of me and nothing behind me except a sharp hot whiteness, a dog's teeth fully bared and his mouth wide open to devour me where I stood, and through the void I saw him. Surging up through the blankness, leaping for me, for my throat.

And I raised up my arms, to stop him—

A high, outraged yelping and howling, the unmistakable noise of an animal in pain. I heard it as I came back to myself, as I felt someone with a grip that could break bones twisting my arms behind me—animal howling, and pounding footsteps. I opened my eyes that I'd squeezed shut against the nothingness, a mere split second of nothingness, and saw Amy running toward us, Lucy panting to keep up; as they reached the clearing they almost fell over each other, they'd skidded to a halt so fast. And Nick. Nick lay cringing at my feet with his ears flat back and rheumy eyes wide with fear, any dog anywhere trapped and afraid. A bloody streak ran along the length of his side. More blood on the top of his head, where the fur, and the skin, were split open.

I stood there over him, my breath uneven and loud like I'd worn myself out in just that split second, and as Jessie let me go I realized I was holding something, gripping it hard enough to break in my hand. A small, heavy piece of branch, the kind lying all over the woods, the bark on its business end smeared with blood. My fingers faltered and it dropped from my hand back to the ground.

Lucy gasped. A hot thick feeling of disbelief surged over me like nausea and I opened my mouth to say something, to try to explain, but there was nothing I could say. Nothing. Amy took a step toward me, another, her whole face pleading with me to explain she hadn't really seen this, it was all a mistake.

"What did you do?" she asked, very softly.

I kept trying to talk, to explain what I'd seen and how I hadn't even known what I'd done, no memory of striking him or even picking up the branch at all—but words wouldn't come, I'd forgotten how to talk. Nick cringed and whined and Jessie crouched beside him once again, gently touching the parts of him I hadn't beaten.

"He went crazy," she said. "Just grabbed a branch and went at him, I couldn't stop him before—"

"What the hell did you *do*?" Amy repeated.

I shook my head. I didn't do this, I *didn't*, but I did, but he'd come after me, even if yet again nobody else had seen it he'd come after me. Hadn't he? "I—"

Amy marched up to me and shoved me so hard I stumbled and nearly fell; her hand rose to slap, to punch until she left bruises, but her fingers shook and she dropped her arm again. "Did you enjoy that? Were you just waiting your chance to do that while my back was turned?" She was yelling, yelling herself hoarse, and I had to explain what had happened, that all this was some sort of mistake, but it wasn't, it wasn't. "How could you do that to him? To get him to *stop barking*?"

I was going from hot-sick to cold-sick, my teeth actually

chattering, and my head shook like I was some wind-up toy gone berserk. "Amy, I didn't know I did it, you have to—everything just went blank, Jessie saw it happen too not even half an hour ago, then it happened again and I don't—I didn't—"

But Jessie's voice sliced and cut right through mine. "Nothing *went blank*—some clouds passed overhead, that was all, nothing else happened. Okay? Nothing. Until you went crazy and beat a fucking dog." She kept stroking Nick, who'd grown calm and quiet; he'd already stopped bleeding, he wasn't as badly hurt as he'd looked, but I knew that didn't matter. That in the face of this, the little details didn't matter at all. "You proud of yourself? You a big strong man, now that you've found something a third your size to fuck with?" Her mouth was twisted on itself, each thick heavy word spat out in quiet rage. "You another fine upstanding human fucking being? One of the really good ones?"

I was growing hot again, from her words and her lies. Pretending nothing happened before this, that we hadn't talked at all, that all we saw getting here were some *clouds*. "There is no way," I said, not caring that Amy and Lucy were listening, "that I'm taking morality lectures from your kind. No way."

"My kind." Jessie laughed, a sound like a handful of gravel hurled at a closed window. "My kind, that stayed in the woods and minded its own damned business until *your* kind went out and fucked us up and fucked themselves into oblivion—"

"Is this what Natalie meant?" Amy was nose to nose with me, trembling with rage, Lucy's hands on our arms trying to calm us both, cool little islands lost in a boiling sea. "When she said you'd enjoy trying to get her to talk? Is this what she—"

"He was attacking me!" I shouted. Hadn't he been? Hadn't it been real? Then why didn't I remember hitting him? "I didn't mean to do it—he came after me!"

"Like he 'came after' Naomi? And me? Just say it, Stephen, you hate him, you've hated him ever since he—"

"He's part of all this!" Wasn't he? Was something else doing this to me, turning me against him? What was happening to me?

"I can feel it! It's him!"

"He's not part of anything! He got us out of the lab! He got me there in the first place, to try and rescue *you*!" She shoved Lucy's embracing arms away, the slick brownish-black leaf muck clinging to her sneakers as she paced back and forth, back and forth. "We wouldn't even be fucking standing here without him and Death gave him to me and Nick's trying to warn us! He's been warning us all along, he's been getting us where we need to go! We had to get here because everything's falling apart and we couldn't face it separately, it had to be all of us—even Death is coming apart at the seams and we're all going with him, all of us together, and we have to save what's left and Nick was trying to *warn* us, you fucking son of a bitch, that everything's going away! Everything! Everywhere! But you're so fucking selfish you can't even see it!"

Her words reverberated through the clearing, words making flesh everything we'd all been hoping, pretending was just our own ghosts. It wasn't just me. Not just me. Jessie and Lucy stared at her, astonishment and fear on their faces, and now Amy looked like the one who didn't know what was real, what wasn't, what she'd even done. It was true, what she'd said. The truth of it was deep in all of us, just starting to show itself, like something at once sunlit and shadowy rippling against the surface of a lake. As it all echoed in her ears, Amy shook her head, laughing in a way that scared me, and I reached out to her just like Lucy had, knowing she'd push me away. But she didn't even see me, not anymore.

"Don't ask me why I said that," she warned us, backing away like a robber on the getaway. "Don't ask me why I said that, or where I got it from, because I don't know. I don't have any damned idea."

"Amy!" Lucy shouted, as Amy ran. "Amy! Please!"

She didn't go after her. None of us did. We stood there in the clearing, all of us together but still miles apart, and Nick gazed silently up at me, his jaundiced eyes as clear and calm as ever I'd seen them. He wasn't cringing anymore. He wasn't afraid of me. Those eyes were clear and calm and full of... forgiveness.

Understanding, a dumb canine understanding, and forgiveness. I felt such shame seeing it that my head dropped down, as if someone were about to beat me in turn, and I looked away.

"It wasn't just clouds," Jessie said. "That we both saw." There was no apology in the words, just a simple, flat correction of fact. It had nothing to do with me. "But it has to be. It has to. Because otherwise..." She broke off. "It has to be just clouds."

We heard the sound of shouting, Amy's voice hurling fury and frustration at the universe, at us, at everything coming apart. We stood there, in the clearing.

TEN

NATALIE

"Where are we even going?" I said. "Are you sure you know—"

"Just shut up," Billy mumbled. His latest bout of half-silent weeping had passed and now he just kept stumbling forward, head hanging down, a drunk trying to walk a straight line miles long. "Just follow me and shut up and don't open your goddamned mouth ever again."

I shut up, not because crazy Billy said so but because I had bigger things to think about. Meeting him out in the open, I'd be, the Friendly Man, after all those years shut away in secret, and the thought of it was like I'd been stuck in a stifling stale-stinking room and a door I didn't even know about opened up wide, cool sweet air rushing through my nose and over my skin and the scent of spring just coming to—he knew we had him on the run. We had his secret, our lab could stop Death in his tracks, and that's why he was trying to scare us. Scare me. It wouldn't work. I pulled Sukie out of my pocket and hugged her tight, for strength.

Billy's chin was still down close to his chest but he turned his head, saw me and Sukie, shook his head and snorted as the thin creeping curl of a grin twisted up his mouth, a caterpillar crawling slow over a waxen leaf. "How fuckin' old are you?" he demanded. "Fourteen? Fifteen? Unbelievable. Dolls. Jessie was fifteen, sixteen, when she died, if she could see this—"

"Your Jessie's dead," I snapped, settling Sukie in the crook of my arm. When he wasn't crying or singing or muttering to himself, he kept throwing out names of people I'd never met, his fellow rotten things, jabbering how they were probably somewhere out there dead like they were supposed to be and eatin' fuckin' fresh deer liver right now and—boring, people who can't stop sobbing over what's dead and gone are so *boring*. "They're all dead. I don't care what she'd say anyway."

Billy just shook his head, laughed in a soft rumbling way that made me hate him, trudged forward and forward over the rain-damp dirt and unmown grass at the side of the road. I kissed the top of Sukie's head when he wasn't looking. She had her own secrets too, Sukie did. Deep inside. Billy was the last person who needed to know about those.

"Pierre Beach," Billy said, stopping in his dirt-smudged tracks, squinting at the road sign and frowning and saying it slowly like it'd been decades since he'd read a word. They'd all good as forgotten reading and writing, the ones who'd been dead long enough, of course some of the oldest ones born last century or whenever had never been taught how at all. "Indiana Dunes National Lakeshore. So how the hell far is this from Prairie Beach, anyway?" He turned his squint on me, eyes pale like how an icy lake is tinged with an afterthought of silver-gray. "We barely ever went up here, Mags and I. Don't remember the half of it."

"What difference does it make?" I asked. What was he asking me for? I'd never been outside Gary in my entire life. "We're not going back there anyway, it only matters where we're going. I want to know where we're going—"

"God, you're a fuckin' kiddie, dollie-babies and whining and when do we get there, when do we—you're worse than that

Naomi. I'll know it when we find it, shut your fucking squirrel-trap and I'll know it, I can listen for it—"

Pierre Beach, what was left of it, was a tiny little beach town set right at the bottom of the lake basin, at the shoreline we'd been following as Billy dragged us east; the warped bent remains of security fencing, the bright orange AUTHORIZED RESIDENTS ONLY signs and stickers on abandoned cars, the big sprawling houses behind high walls of their own. All that useless used-up fuss and bother told you who'd lived here, senior lab personnel and anyone else rich enough for a beachfront view and protection from the "elements." Once I heard some of the techs laughing about how they'd shot a couple kids trying to scale a beach-fence, without bothering to check they really were undead first, but they probably made it all up to scare me. But I hoped it was true, that the kids they'd shot really had been alive. It's what the unchanged humans all deserved, what they all got in the end one way or another.

The main street was long and pale and empty and if you were going to have a shootout, like in some old movie, this was a perfect place; was this it, was Death going to meet me here? I wasn't afraid, I had Sukie, and my knife, and secrets. As my steps slowed, waiting to see if anything came out to meet me, Billy realized he was trudging alone and turned back and grabbed my arm so hard I shouted.

"No," he muttered. "You gotta come with me, I don't know much but I know you gotta come with—"

"Don't you touch me!" I rubbed at my arm, throbbing where he'd dug in his fingertips. "How d'you know it's not here, anyway? How do you know anything?"

Billy's eyes went to narrow pinpoints like two little clear glass beads, the look that always made the humans at Paradise scramble for cover and speed up frantically to look busy. "Kid," he said softly, "you follow me. That's what I know. You follow me, we both go where we're supposed to go at the same time, or I get left behind, and if I get left behind? You're gonna be fucking sorry."

His face, the look on it made my stomach twist up hot and

sick and it wasn't fair, it wasn't fair he could do that to me when it was me Death really cared about and we could kill his kind, like Amy killed Mags dead right where she stood. Nobody ever remembers who they're talking to, when they talk to me. "You don't know anything," I said, and when he took a step closer so his breath was on me I clenched my teeth, like that could tamp down my racing heart. "Maybe I'm staying *here*, maybe—"

"Please don't fight. Please? You can't. We have so long to go before we're finished."

Billy and I both jumped. She'd emerged from one of the houses, a rambling mansion done in "rustic" gray shingling whose roof had nearly caved in from some storm, and her blonde hair had gone wild and unkempt and no more lipstick but there was no mistaking Janey. Her eyes that always looked half-dazed, so pleasant and friendly in the wrong sort of way, those hadn't changed.

"How the hell did *you* get here?" Billy demanded. I could tell he was as surprised as I was at her turning up, because he didn't yell right off or hit her. "Yeah, why am I even asking, of course that fucking Don would jump ship and get out before—"

"Don's dead," Janey said. A tiny little quaver in her soft voice, gentle convulsion of her features that soon subsided. "I don't know how it happened, we got out of Paradise City before the really big fires started, he said he knew someplace he could take me where I'd be safe, and then—he just fell." Her hands twisted around each other, wringing out an invisible washcloth. "He made me put on sensible shoes before we left, but I could have high heels again later on, he said. When we got there. He was right there, walking, talking, and then he wasn't anymore. East, all I know is he said we were going east. He didn't say where. I never needed to ask him things like that. I trusted him."

She raised her head and I saw the motion of her throat as she swallowed, gulping down a hard little stone. "But I can't stop just because he's dead, I—I need to look for something. I don't know what it is, but I have to look for it, I have to find it." Her hand fiddled at her throat, at a teardrop-shaped black pendant like onyx round her neck. Another of Don's useless gifts, like the lipstick. "There's somewhere we all need to go, Don too, and if I just find it I can—I keep thinking, I'm supposed to tell someone something, I don't think it's you, there's a message I'm supposed to give someone but... I don't know who they are." She shook her head sadly. "I don't know what it is."

I looked at Billy, as if he could explain this. He stared at her, pondering, then smiled at her all slow and bright like she were a stupid little child. Just like he thought I was. "Did Don say where the safe place was?" he asked, his whole mouth a bucket sloshing with sugar-water. "Did he tell you?"

"East," Janey said, and tugged at her necklace harder. There were bruises at the base of her throat; Don never hit her, I didn't rule out she'd put them there herself. "We have to go east. All of us. I still have to deliver my message."

Billy studied her a little longer, then he turned to me. "Y'see? I told you it wasn't here. I told you."

Maybe this was a trick of Death's, to test me. Maybe they were trying to lead me off track on purpose, both of them. "But—"

"We're going now." Billy had my arm again and was shoving me forward, and I was so confused by Janey showing up and everything else that'd happened that I just went ahead and let him. "All of us. We're going."

I can't believe I used to wish so wildly to get out of Prairie Beach, see the rest of the world, when the rest of the world all looks exactly the same. One tiny little beach town after another gone to plague and ruin, the same tall sharp grasses and cakey sand as back home, the same thick clustering clumps of trees and random daubs of foliage you could see anywhere but at least these were all green, all alive, Death had let off trying to scare us so easy when there was a bigger fight coming around the corner. When we came around the corner, when I finally fought him in earnest.

As we walked, Janey pressed fingertips to the bridge of her nose, winced like something had struck her; Billy had her other arm, he was dragging her along like he'd tried to drag me, but of course, she wasn't complaining. Janey was like that. At least she wasn't a snotty bitch like Amy, thinking she was better than everyone else. She was all right for company.

"My whole head hurts," Janey murmured, as we passed the remains of some kind of factory; what looked like big piles of steel girders still sat in the yard outside, higher than our heads, rust slowly overtaking them like a creeping orange moss. "It just won't stop."

Even with the old mills right there on Prairie Beach, shadowy bookends at the far corners of the lake, I kept being surprised at how you'd see an oil refinery, then right up against it huge untouched swathes of sand or forest or wildflowers. I wished she'd be quiet so I could look at them in peace. "There's probably rain coming," I said, pointing at the clouded-over sky. "I always get headaches right before it rains."

Janey just shook her hanging-down head, almost gritting her teeth at the sensation. "It's my whole skin," she said. Not the whiny way Grandma sometimes said I complained—*Natty, now do you really think one little girl's petty complaints should be such a universal concern?*—but all matter of fact, like these were things we just needed to know. "And my eyes," she said, closing them hard for a few moments, "it's like this weight is coming down on them, pressing—"

"Yeah, things are shit all over." Billy tugged her along, letting her stumble and trip. "Mags is dead, some fucking frail's got a tiddy-headache, my heart's breaking *will you two quit foot-dragging and move*!" He whipped his head around, glaring at me clench-toothed and feverish, angry waves of heat stirring up a lake of ice. "We ain't got all year to get there!"

Janey's sensible flat shoe I knew she hated hit a rock hard and her eyes snapped open from pain; she smiled in her old vacant far-seeing way, she didn't complain. I didn't like it, how Billy treated her, Janey was all right. It was like watching someone keep yanking a kitten's tail. Don would have killed him, if he'd seen it.

"He's right," she said, and something in her voice was so sad and it had nothing to do with Don or Billy or any of us, I could feel it. "He's right. Nothing's got all year left."

So she knew about it too, just like Billy: that the showdown was coming, that I had to face Death with just wits and science and Sukie as my weapons. She was literally sensing it in her bones, that's what was hurting her. I felt sorry for Janey, I'm not some psycho sadist like what Amy liked to think (too bad she never saw her precious Stephen's juvenile record, before the lab, before she ran off with him, if she thinks I'm so terrible), but at the same time knowing everyone could *feel* it and sense it inside themselves, it buoyed me up and made me happy inside. The same feeling as when Grandma brought me back from death and it turned out I'd been part of some hugely important new experiment, I'd just *proven* something in the very flesh about life and death, except better. Because I was in charge of all the proving now. The proving grounds. That's where we were headed.

"It's not long now," Janey said suddenly. Her eyes that were always far away, they were practically orbiting Pluto. "It's so soon, I didn't expect it nearly so soon, if only Don were—"

"Shut up." Billy grabbed a hank of her blonde hair, something I'd seen Don do when Janey got too far away to reach without a reminder, except Don just took a little bit of it and tugged careful but Billy jerked her whole head backwards with his fist and she shouted. "You keep walking and *you* keep walking and if I hear another word outta you, Janey, I'll send you right back to Don, I'll break your fucking neck. Shoulda broken all your necks." His laugh was a skittering perilous thing, a little boy flying along the ice knowing any moment he'd crash into a tree. "All the fucking hoos, everywhere. Back when we were dead and had a chance."

Janey put her tongue away. I kept my mouth shut sightseeing the mills and flowers and maybe a half mile later she turned around to look at me, the look on her face, there was such pity and sadness and it was all directed at me that I didn't even want to think how crazy she'd got. Why was she feeling sorry for me? I had important things ahead of me, I had the whole universe at my back and I was saving it from *him*. I wasn't upset about Amy anymore, things were so much bigger now than her. They always had been.

I stared back at Janey cool and calm and she nodded, a sorrowing nod like she'd just known I wouldn't understand whatever crazy thing she was thinking, and swiveled her head back to the path; US 12/20 kept inching forward and forward, everything on it new to me except so much of it looked all the same. She kept walking. Billy's shoulders were hunched forward; he'd started crying again.

The road ran parallel to a set of rusted-out railroad tracks for two or three miles, then it widened and went gravelly underfoot, then turned narrow again, the trees overhead curving together in a canopy. It would've been nice, I guess, all dark and green and cool inside with just little bits of sunlight glinting through like lighter panes of stained glass, except half the trees were bare gray branches and as we walked, Billy still with a grip on Janey's arm, little pencil-shavings of dry bark drifted onto our clothes, our hair. My feet were killing me, my stomach twisted up starving, I'd been so wild to leave I hadn't even thought of food, but now I couldn't think of anything else. My little hoard of chocolate bars, the really good expensive kind from the lab's emergency stores that I'd hidden during the plague, I could've been eating one of them right now. Up ahead, even though there was nothing around us but the woods and beaches I was already sick of looking at, Billy suddenly stopped.

"We're there," he said, a little thread of triumph snaking

through his voice like someone had tried tricking him out of the knowledge. "Almost there."

"I think so," Janey said. Just as mild and soft as if he hadn't left her arm ringed with bruises. "I just wish I could remember what I was supposed to tell—"

He yanked her forward. Another half-mile down, my feet hot and raw but if I complained it'd just set Billy off, there were the beginnings of another tiny abandoned town—not even a town, really, one of those little summertime beachfront hamlets that was a few houses thrown together, a couple of stores, police station with a group hazard-shelter underneath. People, though. As the trees opened up and gave way to grass and the road became pure white gravel, like back home, I saw the smallest little signs of life, like the faint wing-flutter of a bird that looked dead but was just stymied, half-paralyzed by the cold: bicycles propped neat and unrusted against a shed wall, the raked-up beginnings of vegetable gardens like Paradise City's in what had been a front yard. A silhouette, just visible in a house window, watching us approach. In the center of what had once been that whole town was a huge oak tree, living-leaved and trunk so thick even Stephen's long arms couldn't have circled it, and nailed to the tree was a hand-painted wooden sign with tall, thin, sprawling black letters: COWLESTON HUMAN SETTLEMENT. ALL ARE WELCOME. GO TO THE GRAY HOUSE WITH THE RED MAILBOX OUTSIDE.

Billy hunched forward, frowning his way through the sign, then snorted like that was just the funniest thing he'd seen in his life. "So cute," he muttered. "That's just so fuckin' cute—okay, then!" His voice rose to a shout, there in the middle of what had never quite been a town square. "All are welcome? Here I am! You frails hear me? I'm here to get what's mine!"

A gray-shingled house with a cardinal-red mailbox on a pole wasn't ten steps away, turn your head and there it was, but before we could go to it (was that where Death was waiting for me, was he luring in more humans in the guise of rest and welcome?), the door opened and a little group of people came swiftly through the yard, down to meet us. A skinny, sunken-eyed man with shaggy hair and beard, half gray and half redheaded just like Amy's mother; behind him a short stubby little woman, Chinese, Korean, with a Purdue T-shirt straining across her chest and a huge cross slung around her neck. The others, a girl maybe sixteen holding a baby, an ancient dry stick of a man who could barely stand upright, they fell back. Billy smirked, letting go of Janey as he folded his arms.

"Well, hello, folks," the red-haired man said. "I guess you've read the sign." His eyes flickered to the dark finger-shaped marks on Janey's arm, then back. "This is Cowleston, idea of it at least, I'm Russell and—"

"I don't give a shit who you are," Billy said, his harsh grating ex's syllables a short sharp shock after Russell's quiet solicitude. "I want something to eat, and then I want to know what you've done with my girl."

Russell, I'll give him credit, he didn't blink. If he were in charge here like it seemed, he'd probably already dealt with so many crazy people this was a drop in the Atlantic. "I don't know who your girl is, mister," he said, calm as anything. "But if you think she's come here, maybe I can help you out—"

"Does *she* want to see *you*?" the short woman asked. Fingering her cross, like that'd help her. Something in me liked how nervous she was. "Because you should know that humans are free agents here. We're not sending her back to you, if she doesn't want to go."

Billy just stared at her, and when his eyes, his mouth creased up smiling it was like his icy-lakeness broke out in soft, ominous cracks. "A human," he said, "thinks she can keep Mags from me. A human." He took a step forward. "A fucking hoocow bitch thinks that—"

"You leave her alone," the old man behind her shouted. Trembling, whether from fear or palsy or both I couldn't tell. "We don't want your kind here. Get out and leave us alone."

"Tina," Russell said, without turning around, "take them back into the house."

"Is that where you're hiding her?" Billy gave Russell a shove, just a tiny little tap on the shoulder, and that was enough to throw Russell off balance, make him stagger backwards. "Is that where you've got Mags? Because you're giving her back now. You and whoever that was behind the wall, that high wall I can't get over, this is where I'm supposed to be and you tell me what you know, tell me how to get her back before I—"

"Get out!" shouted the girl with the baby, it didn't cry but just stared at all of us with big wide fearful eyes, six months old at most and already it'd seen too much. "Leave us alone and get out!"

More people emerged from the other houses, the yards: a burly man with dirt-caked jeans clutching a trowel, two women with what looked like chicken feathers stuck to their shoes, a much older woman smart enough to linger near her front door. The man took one look and jerked his head at the women to stay back and that made Billy actually throw his head skyward and laugh, a snarling spit-soaked ugly sound.

"Go ahead," he said, to nobody in particular, "try and bash my head in with a garden hoe. Go on! You can't fucking do it. If you could, I'd be out of this shithole faster than—I want my girl back." He grabbed Russell by the shoulders, dug and gripped and twisted and Russell's knees buckled, his heels digging new divots in the dirt. Billy shook him, a dog shaking furious at a rabbit in his teeth. The short woman, Tina, tried to pull Russell from his grasp and Janey just stood there like always, wide-eyed, round-eyed with fear, dismayed fingers splayed over her mouth and I didn't like this anymore, *stop, stop—Billy let him go.* Russell swayed in Tina's arms like the palsied old man, gulped, straightened himself out inch by inch though I could tell it hurt like hell. The others just stood there, watching, just like we were. Because even a dozen armed humans against an ex was no fair fight, because there was nothing they could do.

"This is a human settlement," Russell said. "Just like the sign says." Still calm, still quiet because he was stubborn as hell, that's probably how he got here in the first place without dying. "There's nobody here named Maggie or Margaret—we keep a roster, we take attendance at Sunday town meeting. I'm sorry for your loss." There was an incipient tremor in his voice that diminished swiftly, swallowed down hard. "We've got nothing against your kind, but your kind disrupts things for us, so I'm afraid I have to ask you to leave. There's a good bit of beach, just about a mile down the road—there's a few like yourself out there and a lot of empty space if you want to be alone. Good woods for hunting. I'm sorry for your loss."

You sort of had to admire how he gave that speech, all steady and sensible like he wasn't talking to something that could gut him with one fist, tear away his face with nothing but bare hands. Talking like he really had any hope of keeping us out.

I didn't like this. I didn't like it and I couldn't make it stop. Billy smiled, and nodded, and then punched Russell in the face so he went flying and kicked him into a curled-up ball, kicked him again, and some of the other humans were running to try and pull him off and Tina, in the Purdue T-shirt, she marched up and kicked Billy, hard, over and over.

"Oh my God, don't!" I shouted before I could stop myself, Billy would kill her and I didn't want to see her die in front of me. Russell groaned out some warning from the ground but Tina just stood there, eyes blazing, until Billy stopped and looked up at her in amazement, at her fingers grabbing in vain at his arms.

"The fuck," he muttered.

"You get out," Tina said, and I could feel the heat coming off her, burning up with her own righteous wrath, fists forming at her sides. "You get out, go try and scare someone who actually gives a damn for your— "

Maybe she thought Billy wouldn't hit her, a woman. She bet wrong. She fell hard and rolled, like a toy tossed out of a crib, and the man with the trowel couldn't get a grip on Billy's arms and now that baby was screaming, it wasn't any fool, and the palsied old man and old woman on the porch, living ballast, were watching in helpless wide-eyed horror. Billy grabbed Tina's head by a fistful of her black hair and spit in her face where she lay, a long vile stream; she screamed, and Billy laughed when he pulled his hand away and it was still holding the hair, smears of blood on the severed ends. Janey who'd just been standing there shaking like the old folks let out a cry and kicked Billy just like Tina had, tried giving him a good shove, and she couldn't make him budge.

"You don't need to do this," she pleaded, so soft and quiet and Daddy-may-I-please-have-this-toy like Don had taught her and I was afraid for her, afraid but frozen where I stood. "You don't need to hurt anyone like this, when you'll see her again so soon. I know it. It's part of the weight pressing down on me, all that knowledge. I *know* it." Janey laughed, blonde hair all unkempt in her eyes and suddenly I saw a different person there, someone she might've been before all this, ready to bust up with the absurdity of what she was saying even knowing it was all true. "It's like he said, like Russell said, she's not here, you have to go further down the road—"

It was like I saw the blood before Billy's fists even before they landed, the stream of it sharp against Janey's skin as it ran from her nose, her mouth, and it was worse even than with Russell and she curled up and cried and I was screaming at him to stop, stop. Humans were running from out of nowhere now, from the houses, the gardens, the woods, a few dozen at the absolute most, they were dragging Russell and Tina away, they tried coming between Billy and Janey and got torn up in turn—I was on Billy's back now, leapt up piggybacking, fingers gouging at his eyes, trying to get around his neck. I could kill him. I could kill him like Amy killed his precious Mags, like they all killed those Scissor Men in the woods, an ambulating thing dead rotten inside was no match for *Homo novus*, just let it happen, feel the strength I had to have somewhere inside flow all through me—

My neck wrenched backward and I seemed to be sailing through the air, and when I opened my eyes I knew it wasn't right away, that minutes or hours had passed even though I hadn't felt it. My shoulders, my arms felt like something had wrenched them out of the sockets, popped them back in, yanked them back and forth over and over, and my whole face was tender, swollen, like a great stubbed toe. I couldn't move. Turning my head to the side made waves of sickness surge through me and I saw Janey lying there next to me, limp and bloodstained like an old rag tossed in the trash. Pairs of feet all around us, threadbare sneakers and dusty cracked boots and two bare, waxen-pale sets of toes, fringe of dirt all around their edges like a piecrust, planted flat and wide apart inches from my head. I looked up. Billy, his face twisted up smirking and more tears rolling incongruous down his cheeks, blotted out the sun above me.

"I'm done dragging you along, deadweight," he said, almost as soft as Janey herself. "Rot here with the rest of your kind." He glanced over where Janey lay, laughed. "Thing is, I think that little bitch was right. Think I know where to go now. And you, you don't know it but you ain't never leaving here."

The great barefooted cloud covering the sun lifted, floated back toward the road, and the light came flooding back in. It was too much for my eyes and I closed them again, and then couldn't open them for a long time.

ELEVEN

LISA

So, we got this far, all the way from Great River to the south, Gary to the north, Leyton to the west and Cowles here in the east—all of us, one route or another—and now we were falling apart fighting over a dog. Not even fighting, really—the lot of us weren't even that much on speaking terms to scream at each other. I'd given up searching for Nick and managed to calm Naomi down and coax her back to the cabins for a nap. Jessie pulled me aside as soon as she saw me, told me what happened in the woods with Stephen; she had the same hard-eyed, hard-nosed look in the telling of it that I'd wanted to slap off her face dozens of times before, while we both were still living. I never did. She would've, without a second thought, if the situation were reversed.

"Your kiddie can stay," she told me. "You wouldn't if she didn't, anyhow. Amy can stay for a while longer, too, her and her mother. Stephen, he's out. I want him gone by sunset tonight. And don't bother running to Renee to be your angel of mercy—if it were up to her, she'd kick all of you, including the dog, out of here right now."

"Jessie—"

"No." She shook her head, over-emphatic like she was trying to shake water from her hair. "Enough fighting. I've had enough fighting for ten lifetimes. All of us have. I need some peace and quiet, and there won't be any with that boy around. I know his type. I *was* his type." She laughed without mirth, crossed her arms so her fingers dug gently into her own sleeves. "Russell will take him in. Russell'd take Hitler in, if he asked nice enough. He's gone tonight."

She trudged off into the trees without a second glance. I heard the rise and fall of voices, her and Linc saying things it was probably good I couldn't hear, and then Naomi slipped out of our cabin, pressed her small head against the side of my leg. She'd heard everything, of course, though she'd been meant to be napping. Six years old, seven, and she didn't miss a trick, probably the only way she'd lived through that first winter.

"I hate him," she said. Her fingers crept to her mouth and her teeth tugged on a hangnail, biting down sharply.

"He's acting crazy now, all the time, and he hurt Nick. I'm glad he's leaving."

People used to like to go on about how different the world would be if children were running it, how much better, but kids are merciless when you've fucked up and Naomi's not got much reason, after having the likes of Billy as a stepfather, to forgive it. "Nick's all right," I said, and gently pulled her fingers away from her lips. "I don't know what happened, but Stephen would never just—"

"He did!" She stuck her hand back to her mouth, wrenching at the cuticles. "He did! He's—he's hoo chickencrap, that's what!"

She got that kind of talk from Billy, verbatim. Echo echo. It made me sad on her behalf. "Nick's like me, I think—nothing much can hurt him. And don't ever say 'hoo,' it's a nasty word for human beings and that's what you are. Or 'crap.' Do you want to walk around saying terrible things about yourself that aren't even true?"

Naomi hung her head, shook it. She had such thick hair, thick deep mahogany brown with glints of dark auburn in the right light; I liked looking at it, for its own sake, from gladness that chance had handed her at least one nice thing. "I was saying it about him," she muttered, "not me."

"Stephen's sorry for what he did." That wasn't a lie, I knew it wasn't, though Amy wouldn't hear it and Jessie wouldn't have let her, either. When I prayed she and Amy would get along, when I was holding my breath hoping Jessie wouldn't have one of her *moments* and kick us all out on sight, this wasn't the kind of mutual accord I had in mind. "He got scared, Naomi, and fear makes you do some terrible things without thinking." I brushed her bangs from her eyes, silky-thick hair so unlike my own drab scraggly flyaways. "You heard what Jessie said—he thought he saw something he didn't. He thought Nick was attacking him. Like last night, when he thought Nick was going to hurt you. He's sorry for it now, and we're all scared, aren't we, there's some pretty scary things happening that—"

"I'm not scared." Naomi scowled at me, baring her teeth like she must've seen Mags do in fights. "I'm not scared at all. I'm just glad he's leaving."

Bared teeth like a zombie itching for a fight, their version of a cat's hissing and bristling fur, but her eyes were shadowed with adult fatigue and full of doubt. *I'm not scared, right? Am I? Do I have to be?* And me, I itched inside to tell her she was right, to *make* things right with a finger-snap and a triumphant smile—that was the better part of my love for her. I couldn't give her birthday parties, I couldn't give her Karen's bedroom and toys and dolls, I couldn't give her anything, but *that* I should be able to give. But in this world, that was just like dreams of birthday cake. I couldn't give her dreams, just a few years' worth of hope. Please, God, if You really exist and I'm not just kidding myself, don't let her figure that out until years away, until she's already grown up and ready to leave.

"Go take a nap," I said. "For real, this time. And if I find you running around the woods playing when you're supposed to be in there—"

"I am sooooo dead," she sing-songed, "so soooo dead I'll be crying at my own funeral." And hurried back inside.

My lips twitched, wanting to laugh; already I've become predictable enough not to be intimidating. Would Karen have talked like that? Mouthed grownup words and looked up at me through the veil of them, scared, needing me to—the thought of all the things that could've happened to Karen, that first winter, made my skin hot and my stomach twist up with a sick scuttling panic. I marched away from the cabins, each step hard and arduous. Physical effort always made me feel better. Nothing from last winter ever happened to Karen. Karen was safe. I'd keep on keeping Naomi safe. I didn't see Jessie again, as I descended the ridge; she was God knew where and I was glad about it. I didn't want to talk to her.

Stephen was huddled near the shoreline, right up near where the tides came in; he stared out at the choppy gray water with arms wrapped around his knees, chin angled down, the sort of quiet wretchedness that isn't seeking sympathy or a chance to explain or anything else but a hole to crawl into, to be by itself with itself. He barely glanced at me when I sat down beside him.

"Funny, isn't it," I said, as the water rushed in, slapped the sand like dozens of tiny, sharp little tapping fingertips, then swiftly and quietly retreated. "The lake looks so different, depending on where you're standing. The water's bluer over at Prairie Beach... it looks bluer, at least. And the tide doesn't seem so strong."

"There's an undertow anywhere you go," he said. His chin was resting on his knees now, dark hair falling over his face so I could barely see his profile. My fingers itched to cut it. "Anybody can get pulled under. Any time."

"True enough," I said.

The tide came in. The tide went out. The faint, faraway shadow of what was left of Chicago was harder to see, this far east, not a smoky charcoal outline like in Gary but a half-dissolved gray mirage.

"I didn't mean to do it," he said. "I didn't even *know* I did it."

His fingers shook a little and he gripped his knees tighter. I've been there, I've been there plenty of times: if you don't hold yourself as still as possible, you really will dissolve into a thousand screaming pieces. Having Naomi isn't magic, but it helps.

"I believe you," I said.

"I didn't—I didn't know I was doing it, while I did it. I'm serious." He shook his head, somewhere between genuine remorse and bewilderment. "The whole world just went... blank, like the sun blacked out and everything disappeared, and then I saw Nick coming at me and I swear I don't remember ever picking that branch up off the ground but then Nick was just—lying there, and I was holding it—"

He uncurled a hand from his leg and gazed at it, as if it could tell him something, then squeezed it closed and tight again. "Every time I look at him I think he's about to do something terrible, or that he actually *is* doing it and I have to stop him, and then—I can *feel* how much he's part of all this, except, maybe he's not, maybe something's playing tricks on him too. Maybe something out there just wants me to think that about him."

I gazed at the water, the smooth wet strip of sand it flowed over, the lake stones embedded in the strip here and there like hurdles on a long flat track.

"Did Amy tell you my brother was a scientist?" I asked. I didn't say who he'd worked for, I couldn't think Stephen would ever want to hear their names again—but then, around here *scientist* and *worked for the lab* are pretty much one and the same, unless you're writing up studies for the oil refinery about how that on-site cancer cluster doesn't really exist. "It's like he always used to say, correlation isn't causation. Wherever *we've* gone, all of us, this has been happening. So maybe it's all of us." The thought of that being true made my stomach lurch, but on the other hand, what we all accidentally started we could deliberately finish. We didn't get this far to just sit down in the sand and cry. "Maybe it's that... entity, that was following us before, maybe it's angry we wouldn't play along and it's acting out. It could be any—"

"I think I used to be someone you didn't want to cross." Stephen was frowning at the water now, frowning like he didn't really know if this were confession or manifesto. "The kind of person who'd hurt an animal without thinking about it. I think I used to be, what's that word, sort of a sociopath? Before the lab ever got hold of—I don't know why I think that. But I'm good as sure, before all this, that I did something wrong." His heels dug into the sand. "Something a lot worse than—Natalie, at the lab, she said I'd probably enjoy hurting her. She said it like she knew something about me, and she might, if she ever saw the files. They kept files on all of us, you know—where we were from, who we really were. But I never saw mine, and I don't remember anything. I don't remember at all."

I thought about Amy, and her old teacher. The one she'd struck in the face with a shovel, again and again, until she died. Linc, who I was ready to hit with a shovel smashing his head in, because Jessie and I, traveling the roads when the plague was in full bloom inside us and out, were just that frenzied for any kind of meat. Jim, who died right in front of us both, his sisters.

All right, then. There was nothing to be done about any of that now, was there? We'd all done what we'd done, we'd all had our share of sickness and remorse, we all just had to keep moving. None of us were saints, but I wouldn't countenance Amy, or Stephen, or anyone else, giving themselves up as a demon. That was the death of hope, and hope was all we had left.

"We've all done really wrong things," I said. "It's hard to get through life without doing at least one really wrong thing, it's the nature of the—"

"You don't understand. I'm not talking about—I mean, I think I might've been someone who should've been in prison. Or an institution. Someone who can't be trusted around other people. I don't like other people, I never did—not until I met Amy. Sometimes—" He broke off and laughed, a bleak little sound. "A lot of times, I feel like I'm just play-acting a regular person, like I'm actually in a play and I never got my script, but I can sort of figure out my lines from watching everyone else act. I do what I know I'm supposed to do, but I can't even see the point of it, and other people, sometimes they just don't seem real at all. Amy understood that. So I could talk to her without a script, I could"—he laughed again—"improvise. I don't know why I'm like that, or what caused it. Or if I was born like that. And thanks to the lab, I never will."

Homo novus, Amy said they called them at the lab. New man. Maybe it was beyond just screwing with life and death, maybe they were trying to make people new and not themselves in more ways than—oh, God, Jim, Jim, goddamnit Jim, what did you do? What did you *know*? All that money you brought home. All those promises you made. Did you know about Stephen, about Amy's mother? Did you meet them? You always claimed you were just one step above the custodial staff, but you were always so cheerful when you said so; I should've known that meant you were lying. So much, so goddamned much went on in our house I can't ever tell Jessie. That can't ever be forgiven.

"You're sorry you hit Nick," I said. "Doesn't that count for something?"

His eyes, staring at me, were so dark and there was something merciless, perpetually unhappy, inside them. A complete lack of pity, turned on himself. "Does it?" he asked. "When I couldn't stop myself from doing it in the first place?"

"Lisa?" someone called from up on the ridge. "You down there?"

Amy. I got to my feet quickly, brushing away sand and bits of twig as I walked. What'd happened now? Amy and Lucy met me halfway down the ridge, Nick trotting by Amy's side; he was silent now, none of the barking frenzy of the woods, and they both looked perfectly calm. Behind me I could hear Stephen, panting to catch up.

"I just wanted to tell you we're going into the woods," Amy said. She glanced at her mother, who was holding a large tin bucket rusting at the seams. "I guess it's a little early for berries, but Renee said there's some wild strawberry plants, if you know where to look. Pass the afternoon."

She was staring at Stephen as she talked, and he at her, and her eyes were just as cold and indifferent as his were open and pleading; the real conversation here had nothing to do with me. Nick didn't growl or bark or cringe at the sight of Stephen. At least that was something. Lucy kept looking back and forth at both of them; she had plenty of sympathy for Stephen, I could see it, but if she had to choose sides here, then she already had.

"I'll be around here, then," I said. "Naomi's asleep in the cabins, or at least she's supposed to be. If you find her wandering in the woods, tell her she's in for it."

"Amy—" Stephen put out a hand.

"Okay," Amy said. She took the bucket from Lucy's hands, turned, and walked up the ridge without looking back. Nick followed close at her heels. Lucy hesitated.

"I'll catch up," she called to Amy. Who still didn't look back. Lucy shook her head at us both.

"You've done it, I think," she said to Stephen, without any condemnation. There were long columnar shadows beneath her eyes, ones I had a feeling would still be there even after twelve hours' sleep. "I can't get her to see things from—"

"You don't need to run interference," Stephen said. Weary, exhausted even, but also grateful. Something about Lucy's presence had a tonic effect on him—a maternal one, almost. Though I was sure he'd deny it up and down if I said so. "Just watch out for her. Okay? Because whatever happened, even if I made a mistake, just my mind playing tricks—that isn't a real dog. It just isn't."

"Stephen." Her eyes grew darker. It was like I wasn't even standing there. "You can't start this again."

"He isn't!" Stephen's voice cracked with frustration. "I'm not defending myself, okay? I know what I did but I don't change what he is, some sort of... harbinger, or—"

"You're wrong." Lucy shook her head. "Stephen, you're wrong."

"I'm not so sure about that," I said. I wasn't sure he was right, either, but then after everything that'd happened since last year, I wouldn't feel sure of a damned thing ever again. "Sometimes, when she's around him, she gets this sort of faraway look in her eyes"—Stephen was nodding in furious agreement now—"I can see it. It's like he takes her someplace she's not even—"

Lucy spun toward me, pivoting on her heel. "You know what," she said, "you really need to quit imagining you're some sort of expert on my daughter or what she thinks."

The sensation started as a heavy walnut-sized lump in my gut, then melted and traveled molten and swift up my back, my neck, the muscles at the back of my head tightening with a scorching heat. An old familiar feeling, even now in this strange new body only half mine. "I was expert enough to get us both from Leyton to Gary in one piece," I said. While you were still mucking around God knows where, while you were still letting her think you were dead. If you were my mother? I'd never have forgiven you. "I was *expert* enough to get her through Paradise City without her getting beaten or—"

"And then you just sit there, nice as you please, and listen while she as good as tells you she's going to kill herself." Lucy's words wavered and she was blinking back a shiny-brightness in her eyes, but the core of her was stone. My own molten heat cooled and congealed in the face of it. "Behind my back, sneaking away to whisper like it's got nothing to do with—"

"What do you mean, kill herself?" Stephen demanded. "When did she say that?"

"It *doesn't* have anything to do with you," I said. "It doesn't have a damned thing to do with you. It's her, and if she felt better talking about it to me than you, don't stand there blaming me. Ask yourself what she could ever have to say to you, after you ran off like—"

"I was ill." A confession full of remorse, but no useless apologies. "I wasn't in my right mind, not at all, and I have a feeling you know something about how that feels. So I'm asking you again, how dare you just let her say those things without telling me—"

"What did she *say*?" Stephen shouted. "She's going to kill herself? When? When did she say it?"

"She didn't say that!" I yanked at my hair in exasperation, the old tug and sting that brought tears to my eyes but it brought me down a bit, too, doing that, tears of fleeting pain like cool soothing water. "She didn't say—she's confused, all right? She doesn't know what she is anymore, she doesn't know if she's part of this life or, or—"

I didn't want to say it. I wasn't going to consider it, that other possibility, any more than I wanted to hear Jessie's constant stories about how much better off she'd been dead. Zombies were extinct now, deal with it. So whatever had happened to Amy, or Stephen—or Lucy—they couldn't be that. "She's confused," I said. "Anybody would be. She just wanted to talk it out."

Lucy considered this, gazing down at her feet. "But me, I wouldn't understand." She shook her head, laughing, and there was an edge to that sound that reached out and stung me deliberately, anew. "*I* wouldn't understand that feeling at all, no, it's just got to be you. You've already got one damned foster kid, all right, that you picked up from who knows where. So leave off mine once and for all."

"You *left*," I said. Just like I ran away from Jessie, that first time at the cemetery, screaming, sick. "Whatever reason you had, you left. For years. She had to grow up all by herself, and you can't control what she—"

"Jesus God." Stephen was laughing now, as he walked away from us. "She wants to kill herself, and we're all standing here fighting—I'm gonna go find her. *Goodbye*."

"She did not *grow up all by herself!*" Lucy's face had gone scarlet, as hot as mine felt. "How dare you? How dare you stand there on your fucking high horse and—"

The sound of screaming cut us off. Loud, tearing, panicked screams from the woods, the thickets of trees, where Amy had gone to hunt strawberries.

TWELVE

LUCY

Stephen froze where he stood at the sound, then darted into one of the cabins. I sprinted past the firepits and into the cottonwoods, desperate to keep up with Lisa. She hurtled past me with inhuman speed, our sneakers slapping the underbrush, vaulting over thick undulating roots toward—

"Jessie!" Lisa screamed, not slowing her steps. "*Jessie*! Where are you? Help!"

I heard more footsteps, the sound of shouting behind me, but I didn't turn around. Amy's screams had stopped. That sudden, abrupt silence was so terrible to contemplate that I kept on running, kept going so I wouldn't have to think—and there, in a big, open clearing fringed with oaks and maples, I saw it. Lisa, Jessie, and the others stood in a semicircle around a tall, pale, barefoot man with hair the color of ice, drawn and emaciated like someone in the final stages of the plague; his face was contorted with triumph and hate, one arm holding Amy pinned to his body and the other closed around her throat. He'd lost a shocking amount of weight in just a matter of days, but I still recognized him: the man from the lab, the one who'd barked orders at the Scissor Men and then dragged Amy away to kill her.

I screamed as loud and long as I could, crazy enough with fear to imagine that might scare him into letting her go. He didn't budge. I tried to throw myself at him, but Lisa had me by the arms, holding me back, barely even noticing when I fought and kicked and screamed some more for her to let me go. Across the semicircle from me Jessie's eyes widened, her own face twisting in what looked like silent laughter; she rose up on her toes, limbs poised with a dancer's precision, and nodded at the man like she wasn't at all surprised to see him. Like *she* knew him, too. Her lips curled in the semblance of a smile.

"Billy," she said. And took a step forward. "Long time, huh?"

Nick was nowhere to be seen. I didn't want to think what might've happened to him. Amy stood there, rigid, gazing back at me desperate and sick with fear. Let her go. Let her *go*. Someone please, please, show me how to make him let her go.

"I never knew what happened to you," Jessie said to him. She was circling them now, hands clasped casually behind her back, like a museum-goer studying an arcane piece of art from every possible angle. "You and Mags, taking off like that for Valparaiso, maybe 'cause you were afraid of me—" She laughed in earnest. "That's what Sam said, anyway. When you left. That you both went out Valpo way."

Billy's eyes were narrow and thoughtful and far beyond any of us. "Mags is dead," he told Jessie. "This bitch killed her."

Jessie nodded. So calm, how the hell did she dare to be so—I thrashed hard in Lisa's grasp and she held me even tighter, muttered desperate calming syllables that my ears wouldn't process into words.

"Well, that's how it is with us, isn't it, Billy," Jessie said. Getting closer to him, little by little, not too much at a time. Amy kept her eyes on me, trying not to struggle, the berry bucket on its side at her feet. "Fight breaks out, you stomp a few heads, every now and then it's someone you really liked who gets it, but that's our way, Billy, that's how it works. You know that. You've done it." She was trying to soften her voice, the softest grating, scraping harshness her post-plague vocal cords would allow. "We've all done it. Remember Lillian, when Teresa got her? Remember Old Mike from the South Bend gang, that their chief was so sweet on, when you tore him up? That's how fights work. That's how it goes. Their chief didn't hold a grudge." She reached out a hand, careful, still too far away to touch. "Neither should you."

Billy's arm tightened against my daughter's chest, the slow strangling grip of a snake, and she closed her eyes, awaiting the inevitable. I made a low, animal sound I couldn't hold back and Billy chuckled quietly, shook his head. "Sometimes, Jessie," he said, "you're still such a damned kiddie—not like that piece a'shit I left behind with the hoos, but you got your moments. Me, I don't wanna kill anyone." So calm. Sickeningly calm. "Ain't no point in that, not with what I see coming—and when it does, I want her to live through all of it. With no eyes. No fingers. No tongue, no teeth, no *face*."

He yanked hard enough on Amy that her head jerked back, eyes still tightly shut. "The bitty leftovers after a fight, nobody to show no mercy and just stomp her. She can live like that forever, she can live and live and live in the middle of all the nothing, just like they tried to make me do puttin' me in this filthy hoo-body—but it's okay, you see, 'cause Mags is past it all already. Mags just went on ahead early."

Tears leaked down his face, his words wobbling like a distressed little boy's. "She just... went on ahead. So it's all right. But for doing it? A fucking hoocow, thinking she can raise her hand to one of mine?" He bared his teeth, voice sinking to a hoarse, hissing whisper. "She's gotta learn her *place*."

"You can't do that, Billy." Renee stepped forward, bolder than Jessie, the bad cop. "We're all as strong as you are. And we won't allow it."

"You don't make the rules, 'maldie bitch." He pressed his fingertips to Amy's shoulders, wrenching them, and her eyes flew open and she gritted her teeth in pain. "You keep your mouth shut and you stay happy Jessie took a shine to you, 'cause you don't make any of the fucking *rules*—"

"The gang's over with, Billy," Linc said. "Over and done with. That world's over. The old hoo-world's over. Everything we knew, or thought we got used to, is—" He broke off. "Just be glad Mags is well out of it, one way or another, and leave the kid alone."

"You can't touch her anyway," another voice said, from right behind me.

Lisa whipped right around with me, both of us nearly tripping over each other's feet. "Naomi?" she said, not bothering to try and prettify her voice. "Go back to the cabins. Go back there *now*."

"You only think you can touch her." Naomi stood there, defiance beating back fear, small feet planted wide apart in the mucky ground. "You think you can. But you can't."

"I should've snapped your neck and eaten you when I had the chance," Billy whispered. "You know what stopped me? You wanna know? *Mags*!" His voice rose to a shout. "Only thing that stopped me! I told her, lady, it's a fuckin' piece of meat, you start getting all hoocow-sentimental on me and I'll—but it don't matter now. She's dead. She's dead and it's time to punish the—"

"Naomi!" I shouted. "Do what your mother says, now!"

Naomi just shook her head. "He can't touch her."

"The youngun's right."

That voice wasn't any of us. It was coming from *inside* the trees and as all of us, even Billy, stood there astonished, he came out from amid the branches: the man in black. The tall thin silent creature that had followed us from the lab down the road, night and day, and then vanished as abruptly as he'd appeared. There in the flesh, silent no longer, with waxen white hands folded against his coat-front and a black hood, a death's-hood, pulled up to obscure his face. Trotting along beside him was Nick, unharmed, as obedient as if he knew this stranger from long days past. And something told me he did.

"Billy." The man halted a few feet away, watching from under his hood. "You gotta let go."

Jessie and Renee both drew in startled breaths. Linc looked sharply from them to the man and back again. Did they know him? Were we all supposed to know him? Amy looked as confused as I felt. The stranger stepped forward, putting out a thin, pale, finely sculpted hand.

"Enough, Billy," he said. The faintest little trace of a drawl flavored his words, like a broth nearly boiled away in the pan. "That's enough."

Billy stared back at him, still clinging to my daughter like he was a little boy and she his big cheap stuffed-animal prize from the fair. I kicked and struggled against Lisa with renewed force, my foot slamming into her shin hard enough to make her gasp, and then suddenly I was staggering free while she, Renee, Linc, and Jessie were on Billy all at once. Naomi went running headlong to join the fray and I grabbed her, almost tackling her in the underbrush to keep her back; Naomi was screaming, I was screaming, the others surrounded Billy in a volley of feet and fists. Nick sat there, watching impassively, just like the stranger in black. Lisa was grabbing for Amy as Amy thrashed like a fish in Billy's grasp. Billy yanked Amy backwards, Amy howled in pain—

And then I saw a metallic flash from the corner of my eye, a head of dark tangled hair. Stephen had come the long way through the trees, to try and take Billy by surprise; he had the big hunting knife from Jessie's cabin, still rusty with animal blood. Billy sent Renee thudding onto the leaves and Stephen shoved his way into the breach, spitting and seething with hate, slicing at Billy's back, his shoulders, his gripping arms. The wounds were deep and bloody and completely useless, sealing themselves tight mere seconds after they opened up. I flew toward them, Naomi abandoned and forgotten, desperate to try and draw blood myself. Then I was in the middle of the fight, dead at the center, and I had Amy in my arms. Lisa and I both had both in our arms. Billy threw himself on us with a grunt of rage, and Stephen raised the knife once again—

There was blood everywhere, spattered all over my clothes

and hair, and Amy and I were both screaming at once. Screaming together, as the knife went in.

Jessie and Renee had Billy, panting in their grasp. Linc was sprawled beside them, out of breath. Amy was beside me, on her knees in the leaf-muck, clutching her side where the last knife-thrust had gone in. Where the knife stuck out of her flesh. Her shirt, jeans, groping palms all soaked in red.

"Oh, Jesus—" Stephen, his face chalky and drained, knelt beside us with horror and panic in his eyes. "I tried—I was aiming at—"

"*Don't pull it out*!" I shouted.

I was sobbing now, my sleeves and jacket front turning wet as I clutched Amy to my body, and Stephen was frantically pulling off his jacket to try and stanch the blood that wouldn't stop coming. "Don't pull it out, Stephen, it'll bleed even more—if—"

"I didn't mean it!" Through a blur I saw him pressing the wadded-up jacket to her side, trying to hold her like I was holding her; I shook with terror and that shook Amy's body in turn, and everything was hot and cold all at once. Stephen began to sob. "I was aiming for him! I thought I got his—Amy, I didn't see it was you! *I didn't mean it*!"

Billy chortled in glee at the sight of us, there on our knees in the mud and blood. Linc punched him hard in the gut, but he still wouldn't stop. Nick, that horrible *thing* Stephen had been right about all along, just sat there staring like it was a movie; I'd thought he loved Amy at least, I really had, but he just sat there, watching her die. Amy lolled against me, ashen-faced, dazed with surprise that something hard and sharp was sticking from her flesh. That she was bleeding all over us, all over me. That my baby was dying. Her muscles were going slack, limp and useless to outrun death—and then suddenly the man in black was there, Nick at his side, calm and easy as if Amy had all the time in the world. The man reached down, a long graceful bend from the waist, and before I could stop him, he slipped his thin fingers between our bodies, pulled the huge horrible hunting knife out of Amy's side, and let it drop like a great thick splinter into the leaves.

So he was here to kill her after all, just like I'd always feared. He was here to kill all of us. I didn't care. I didn't want to live, not without Amy. I was crying, ugly sounds forcing themselves in great hiccups from my chest; Stephen rocked back and forth where he sat with his head in his hands. But then, as the knife thudded to the ground, I saw the man put his palm to Amy's side. Her blood welled up rich and dark between his fingers, like flood water overwhelming a drain; then the horrible gushing flow became a thin, steady trickle, then a weak sporadic drip. Then, nothing. When he pulled his bloodstained hand away, there was no wound. Under the torn-up shirt, Amy's flesh was smooth and unmarked as if she were like Jessie or Lisa or Billy—an ex, a plague-dog made incorruptible by chance.

Please, please let me not just be seeing things, like Stephen. If the whole universe doesn't hate me and Amy and all our kind, and everything else that lives, please—

Amy clung to me like she was a baby all over again, taking a cautious breath, then another. Nick wagged his tail, nuzzled at her leg. Stephen stared at us in disbelief, one hand reaching out to Amy but not daring to touch her. Naomi squatted at the edge of the clearing, eyes closed tight and her hands pressed flat over her ears. Lisa, glassy-eyed with shock, went over to her, tugging gently at her raised wrists.

"It's all right now," she told Naomi. "It was an accident. Amy isn't hurt."

An accident. Just an accident. Nothing to get all worked up about. How is my baby not dead? Is this like the lab all over again?

Naomi slowly opened her eyes, clutching Lisa like Amy clutched me; Stephen had his head back in his hands, wretched and lost there in the leaves. The man in black knelt down beside him and he cringed, like Nick, like any dog knowing he was about to be beaten, but the man's bone-white hand patted Stephen's shoulder with soft, fluttery little beats. Beats like the wing-flaps of some tiny bird.

"It was an accident," the man agreed. "That kinda dustup, all them arms and legs, I'm just surprised you didn't manage to stab yourself."

"Who are you?" I asked. My voice was so steady, it amazed me. I reached out and laid my own hand on Stephen's arm, to let him know I didn't blame him, not for this or anything else; it was all a mistake. Disaster was averted. Somehow. "What are you?"

Billy laughed, a long sharp sound like a gunshot reverberating through the air. He thrashed in Jessie and Renee's grasp; Linc punched him again, hard and fast to the face, the gut, and he subsided.

"No," Billy shouted, not the least out of breath from the blows. "You ain't nothing like what I want. Where is it? Show it to me!" His face darkened, flushed the color of brick with rage. "Show it to me now!"

The man didn't seem to hear Billy. He stood up again and the hood slipped from his head, revealing a head of short-clipped hair as silvery pale as Billy's. This wasn't a young man's light blond, though, like Billy's; you knew, looking at him, that it was the true white of old age. His face was thin, intelligent, with long deep seams at the eyes and mouth that could've indicated a hard-living forty-five, a well-preserved seventy-five, or any point in between. His lips had a firm humorous twist; his eyes were a pale, clear blue that seemed to see into and through us like he knew everything we thought, everything we felt. Everything we were.

Death? But he couldn't be. He just seemed too... friendly, for that.

Linc opened his mouth like he wanted to say something, then closed it again; he stared at the stranger with an uncertainty, a disbelief that had an undercurrent of something else in it, something I didn't understand. He turned to Jessie, both of them silently seeking clarity from the other and not finding it. Lisa had no idea what all this meant, either. I could tell by her face.

Then Jessie let go of Billy, who lolled sullenly in Renee's half-hearted grasp, and went up to the stranger with slow, measured steps. Though I could hardly believe it, she looked afraid, but not of him: afraid, rather, that something she had guessed about him might be wrong. She touched his sleeve, brushing it tentatively with her fingertips, and as she looked up at him, I suddenly realized I was wrong. That wasn't fear in her eyes. It was hope.

"Florian?" she said.

BOOK TWO

SPIRITUS MUNDI

THIRTEEN
JESSIE

"Florian."

He just stood there, looking at me, like his sudden arrival out of nowhere was any old afternoon. His face was like it must've been in life, no longer bone-stripped but still thin and angular. He had the same eyes, too, water-pale blue, steady and gentle, and when they were on you, like they were on me right now, it was like he wasn't seeing anything else. I threw my arms around him and he chuckled, soft and low in his throat, just like before.

"Easy," he said. I could feel the words rumbling through his chest. "It ain't like you haven't seen me before this—"

"Shut up," I said, and hung on. Behind me all the others were muttering and murmuring, confusion, speculation, that awful boy repeating over and over he hadn't meant it with the knife and Amy going *I know, I know* like the call-response of two scruffy starving beach birds. It was the substance of all hoo-talk everywhere, ignorant surreptitious conference that never managed to find its way to the truth. When I pulled back, Florian was smiling. Even his widest smile now was nothing next to the death's-head grin he'd once had, that all our oldest ones had had. I missed it, that permanent skeletal dusty's grimace. I missed hearing the echo of him inside my head, his music, his part of all our music, as I woke and slept. I missed everything.

Linc went up to him, grinning too, able to believe it now as he clapped Florian on the shoulder. Renee still hung back, almost shy, but then she'd barely known Florian and when she had, he was dying. Next to her, Billy—what was left of Billy—sagged against a tree trunk with his head down, laughing quietly at nothing. Sam, poor Sam always did say that without Mags around, Billy'd be like a cardboard box in the rain. That was putting it kindly.

Was he here to take us all away? It was all right if he was, I wouldn't argue. Billy, he'd be so happy.

"What are you doing here?" I demanded. "Why now?"

Something sad flickered over Florian's face, but that was him; he got sad, everyone got sad. You couldn't trust someone who refused to let himself ever feel truly sad. He patted my shoulder and I reached up, clutched his fingers, still thin and bone-pale but strangely fat in my grasp from their layers of living-thing flesh.

"Can you stay?" Linc asked, still smiling and happy. He was the only person standing here who really understood what Florian was to me, and that thought gave me a fleeting lonely sadness of my own. "How did you get here, how—" Then Linc laughed, he was just so uncomplicatedly glad in a way he almost never was. "We're not all just seeing things..."

"Oh, you ain't just seeing things," Florian said. He patted Linc's arm in turn, fatherly, brotherly. "I'm here."

"Who are you?" the girl, Amy, was asking. Almost timid. Her dog, Nick, sniffed assiduously around Florian's bare feet.

"Florian was a friend of theirs," Lisa explained. Dutifully reciting what little I'd told her, gazing in astonishment at its appearance in the skin. "A fellow undead. Very old. He died—rotted away, I mean, crumbled into dust, before the plague ever hit."

"And now he's come back." Naomi, the kiddie, she looked the

least surprised of anyone, pressed like a growth against Lisa's shin. "Like all the zombies, all the dead people are going to as part of Tribulation, and Jesus will lead them to—"

"Tribulation is just a story," Lisa said. Her mouth had gone thin and tight and I could see her thoughts like they were written out, *that goddamned Tina and her goddamned storefront Jesus freaks.* "All the Rapture is just a story. Judgment Day isn't for a very long time and it won't look like that, it—"

"I haven't dreamed about you in forever," I told Florian. Where the hell had he been, anyway? Why had he just stepped out of my head when I needed thoughts of the old days, now more than ever, to get me through? To keep me even halfway tethered to Earth. "It's like you just left me. It's like you just wandered away while I wasn't looking."

A crash behind us made us collectively jump. A long, convoluted branch thicker than my arm and sprouting webs of tributary twigs all down its length, a network of nerves feeding a great curved spinal cord, had pulled loose from a healthy tree and plummeted to the underbrush; it was bare, gray, hollow at its core as though it'd been rotting for years still attached to its host. Bits of it crumbled into ash when I touched it. As we looked up into the tree, there was nothing but that same dry dead grayness, the outer layer of greenery looking glossy as plastic and just as false. That tree was fully alive yesterday, when Linc and I passed under it going hunting; when I'd looked up into its branches, just like now, I saw green and brown and only the smallest flashbulb-spots of sunlight able to penetrate between. There was a bird's nest next to the fallen branch, toppled as well, bottom edge facing upward like a little truck flung on its side in a tornado. I wasn't going to look at what was inside it. That, too, had died before it ever hit the ground.

I turned to Florian and the sorrow in him was deeper and stronger than anything I'd ever seen. "I didn't mean to leave," he said. "Didn't really want to. But here I am."

Stephen, the mighty dog-beater, was staring at Florian with eyes gone beady in suspicion and just try it, you little shit, just try getting in Florian's face and you won't have one of your own left anymore. I won't even bother, I'll just let Billy go to work. Florian, though, just turned to Stephen and smiled.

"It ain't out of your way to suspect me, no," he told Stephen. "It's just more complicated than that. I didn't make any of this happen—but I guess I'm part of it, in my own way. I never meant to be, I—"

"Are you how the lab can do what it did?"

It was Lucy, Amy's mother, who asked that. She reminded me of Renee, a skittish, shy core all wrapped up in an outer hide not nearly as thick as she thought it was, as thick as it needed to be. "They brought us back to life," she said, "again and again, after they killed us, and Amy—" She motioned shakily at Amy, who was standing, silent and gray-faced, with her mother and Stephen flanking her like bodyguards. Prison guards. "We never knew how they did it. We can't figure it out. Did you work there? Was it you?"

Billy snorted. Florian put a hand on Lucy's shoulder and she startled, then tried to look calm. "That lab," he said. "All that trouble. All them unnatural things they did. I had nothing to do with that, I never worked there. Never knew 'em. But." He sighed. "But that was my beach, that they did all their work in. My beach, that I left behind, and they go and do something like that in—"

"That's not *your* beach." Amy's voice was little, polite, but she shook her head like that settled it. "That's Death's beach, Death's house. Death's backyard. And… and I've met Death—I know you're not him, whatever you are."

"Death's backyard," Florian agreed. Mild and amenable as always. "I guess so, 'cause everything's Death's in the end—you, me, our bodies, our thoughts, everything we got that's us. Everything we leave behind. Except, Death ain't all there is. Something a lot bigger than him out there, even if he's carrying it around inside himself"—gazing at me, again, seeing into and through and past me—"and sometimes it's like he ain't no different than the rest of us, in that respect. Full of parts of his own self he can't ever understand."

I turned his words over in my mind; they were like smooth cool lake stones without a single crack in their surfaces, no way to get to what was really inside. I'd had a fucking bellyful of this kind of thing from him during the plague, during the horrible trek from Great River to Prairie Beach, sickening and dying and watching everything fall to pieces with nothing to guide me but vague visions of him still living, disconnected dreams where he urged me onward. Not this time. We weren't subtle artful people, we who'd not merely died but felt and lived all of death's realities firsthand, and I wasn't in any more mood to try and puzzle out poetry.

"Remember," I said, "when we were on watch or out hunting and it was all boring as hell, and you had all those stories to pass the time? The ones about when you were living back on Prairie Beach, or the Three Dead Queens, or all the ones you made up in your head? Prophecies. You always called them your prophecies." I plucked a handful of twigs from the dead fallen branch, watched them crumble to flakes there in my fingers. "Well, if you got one now, old man, that explains why you're here—or how—just tell it. All of it. I've got no belly for riddles."

Nick reared up, front paws pressed against Florian's leg. Florian patted him absently, soothed him, until Nick dropped back to the leaves and stared up at him just like all of us, dark and expectant.

"I ain't even supposed to be here," Florian said. "And I guess that's the whole damned prophecy."

"I couldn't talk face to face with living folks before all this. All this new change, I mean, that brought me back here in the flesh. That's why I couldn't explain who I was, when I followed you folks here—couldn't speak with a human tongue, couldn't say who I was. Don't know how that changed. Us full-dead folks, we're not meant to be able to talk to living folks at all. Not in any form. Not even in dreams."

Florian sat on a dead bit of log right up at the top of the big sand ridge, wrapped in his huge black coat like a strong winter wind threatened to knock him aside. Even though I'd only ever known him as a broken-down dusty skeleton, he looked so much frailer than that now, like a living old man, shivering even in the strongest sun. Amy's dog lay nose to paws at his feet, her dog that never needed to eat and came from nowhere into our world. Just like Florian had himself. Billy wandered around the periphery, not even glancing at Amy, all his killing and maiming fervor drained away. He and Mags should've just died back when the plague first hit, instead of hanging around to turn into this. Of course, you could say the same of all of us, sitting here, all except Lisa's little born-human, stayed-human kiddie. Of course, nobody ever talks about all that.

"Those dreams I had about you," I said, "back during the plague. You weren't supposed to be able to do that? Come and... talk to me?"

Renee and Linc swiveled their heads around to stare at me. I ignored them. The breeze blew a sporadic mist of sand against Florian's coat seams and pressed his thin pure-white hair flat against his face, each strand its own little down feather sticking to his skin, then lifted it up and let it flutter back again. "Don't look like I was, no," he said. "'Course, I didn't mind it. I'd missed you." He smiled a little. "And then, it was like the whole living world was coming back to me, stronger and stronger, while the place I'd gone to, after I died for the last time, was getting weaker and weaker."

He reached a hand into his coat pocket, took out one of the smooth matte stones that were scattered like the start of some great mosaic all over the sands; this one was dull green, with a few brown streaks like muddy rivers chugging through mossy, overgrown ground. As he sat there, he examined it thoughtfully from all angles, a new-minted phenomenon, as though he hadn't carried pocketfuls of them everywhere he went for centuries on end.

"The place you'd gone to," Amy repeated. Her voice shook with nerves, though her eyes were calm; she wore one of Renee's old shirts, her own torn to shreds by Stephen's knife, with a stiff black jacket with "LCS" stitched on the sleeve pulled over it. The jacket was torn up, too, but she wouldn't let it go. "When I... died, before, it wasn't like everything just disappearing. It wasn't just nothingness. It was like I went somewhere else, maybe only in my head, and then I came back. Like I sank to the bottom of the biggest lake there ever was, and then floated right back up again."

She glanced at her mother, like she expected her to back her up with *yep, big lake, dying is drowning, you're absolutely right*—but Lucy just kept quiet. Florian gazed down at his greenish-brown rock, like a tiny mossy riverbed in his hand. Then he placed it down in the sand by his feet.

"That don't sound familiar," he said. "Drowning and all that. But you got the rest of it right. It ain't just nothing, afterward, when you die. It's someplace. You can't say exactly where it is, what it is—but it's there, and you're in it, and it's too big for you ever to find the beginning or the end of it. And whatever it's made of, that place, that's what you're made of too. Like it's all a big giant beach, million times bigger than this one, and you're one little speck of sand on one particular dune. And no matter what, no matter how strong the wind gets, it can't ever shift you. You can't ever be blown away." He looked up at me. "Till now."

A warm, pleasant breeze snaked over the sands, but Florian burrowed down deeper in his coat like it was December. He pointed out beyond the ridge, his finger finding some precise, faraway spot none of the rest of us could see. "Remember I told you there was a huge sand dune, used to be out on one of these beaches? Hundreds of feet high? They carted it all away in train-loads, boxcars of sand, to melt down and make into glass. Guess they got as much as they wanted, 'cause they never came back again. Lately I feel like that dune, like something's breaking up and hauling bits of me away, melting me into something I ain't supposed to be—and whatever's doing it just keeps coming back for more, and more, and more. It's not just me, my particular dune, that's disappearing. It's the whole blessed beach, all around me."

There'd been a beach in one of those dreams I'd been having, the ones I didn't want to talk about: it looked like our beach but I knew, even as I dreamed, that it wasn't, and when I stood on the shore, the water suddenly rose up around me, suffocating me in blackness. It wasn't like drowning, though, not like that kid Amy insisted; it was more like a huge not-thing ate up all the water, and then it got even hungrier and devoured me. Another plague, a famine plague, like the one last year that left us all like this—except instead of just making you *want* to eat the whole world, this one actually went ahead and ate it. Except that was ridiculous. Because dreams were just dreams, they didn't mean shit.

Except they meant a lot, last year, when it was Florian talking to me in them. They meant almost everything. And without them, we wouldn't be here now.

"Like going blind," Stephen suddenly said. He'd been stone quiet, looking strictly at the sand instead of Amy sitting inches away from him covered in her own blood, but now his chin jerked up and he came alive like Florian had flicked a switch. "Like not just that you can't see, but there's nothing there *to* see anymore—"

"All eaten up," Florian agreed. "Big pieces of it, hauled away. All around me."

"I think I know what you mean," Stephen said softly. His eyes darted to Nick, still resting comfy at Florian's feet, and then away again. "It happened to me, when I woke up this morning. And—a few times before and after that." He grabbed a stick, speared the sand with it like he was trying to stab something underneath. "I couldn't see anything. Or I'd see something, I thought, but it was all wrong. Like with... Nick." He thrust the stick deeper into the ground, pressing his weight against it like it was a cane keeping him upright where he sat. "I saw things that didn't really exist, at least not in this—"

"Bullshit," Billy said. He'd been wandering round and round the ridge, shuffling quietly past murmuring nonsense to himself, but now he stopped in his tracks and glared at Florian, listing heavy to one side like he were deer's-blood drunk. "Talk and talk, old man, you never did do a goddamned thing but talk. Nothing's coming apart, it's all right there, waiting for me, but I'm stuck in this goddamned body and I can't get past the wall, to get to—"

"You've seen Death, too," Amy said to Florian. "Just like I have. Haven't you."

Florian lifted up his hands, examined with infinite interest their bony knuckles and sunken aged skin. "Just can't get used to havin' actual flesh and fat on—but anyway. Not in a good long time, I haven't. But when I was alive, alive for the first time, I was a young fella and I got into a fight—never mind how it started. We were both pretty drunk, I guess." His face closed up. "I got in a fight, and I killed the other fella. Got him good. And left him lyin' there. Spent the next coupla years looking over my shoulder, but they never caught me, maybe they never even cared who killed him—he weren't nothing, the other fella, wasn't rich, no family, and I wasn't nothing either. And nobody but us two saw me kill him."

He had Amy in his sights now. Staring at her so hard and intent it was like light, a harsh white beam of light, invading a softly darkened room. "Least, I thought no one else saw me."

Amy squeezed her hands together, slowly twisting them up, then down. Wringing them. Lucy's arm tightened around her shoulder.

"I'd got married," Florian continued. "Had a family. Bought a farm. I was walkin' along in the trees one day, tryin' to decide how much more land needed clearing, and there he was. Big as life, like they say. Big as night." His mouth quirked, a self-deprecating little twist. "I thought it was the devil come for my soul. He laughed at me when I begged him, said there weren't no devil and there weren't no hell but that didn't mean there was no kinda divine retribution. Told me all about the man I'd killed, stuff I'd never known about him startin' with his name, but I somehow knew it was all true. Told me how the man died, how I'd killed him, like he'd been watching it all. He told me—" Florian's hands went up again and he looked them over from all sides, flexing the fingers, flipping them slowly from palm to back to palm. "—that a person who takes someone else's life, for whatever reason, that person makes himself a special friend of Death. A sorta adopted child. And it's not like he does anything to ya, in particular, it's not the lake of fire... but you can still feel him all around you, everywhere, in all sorta ways you never did before. Dogs your steps, even when you don't see him or hear him and you're just goin' about your business. Like a weight on your chest, that you feel every time you breathe, or an itch that won't go away no matter how you scratch. And it stays that way. Waking and sleeping. Night and day. For the rest of your life."

Amy rocked back and forth where she sat, like she could somehow launch herself straight into the air and away from this whole conversation; then Lucy's arms reached out tighter, almost mercilessly steady, holding her still. So Amy had killed someone too, some fellow human? What the hell did if matter if she had? Hoos had done all sorts of shit to survive the plague-year—even Tina didn't claim dove-white sainthood, no matter how much she loved her holy talk—and in any case, why cry about it now? Whoever it was would probably have gotten sick and died anyway. Florian's wax-pale hands disappeared into his sleeves, like they were too cold in this near-summer to remain exposed.

"Remember what your brother said, back before everyone got sick?" he asked me. "That undeads seemed to rise up in cycles—lots of 'em at once, then for decades at a time almost none, then there they were all over again? He was the scientist and all that, at that big lab they went and built on my poor beach, I guess he'd know."

Florian had been dead, actually dead, by the time that talk with my brother Jim ever happened. But of course he knew about it anyway. Somehow that hardly surprised me. "Boom and bust," I said. "Dead folks tunneling up from the grave didn't just suddenly start happening, at some particular date and time—it'd been going on for thousands of years. That's part of why the Egyptians came up with embalming, thinking it'd keep them quiet in the tomb. And all that Samhain shit in Ireland." Anyone who'd gone past the third grade in school knew that much, but I still liked saying it, still liked thinking about how they'd tried and tried to hold us back and nothing they did, nothing, ever helped. Until the lab stole my undeath from me, without the slightest warning, and wiped out the better part of the living while they were at it. Proud of yourself, Jim? "But the scientists could never figure out *why* it happened. Or why some dead people rose up again, and some stayed put in the graves. Or why sometimes we rose up in masses, everywhere, and other times a hoo could go their whole life without ever seeing one of us. Or why it only ever happened to human beings, not any other animals. All that tax money, all that research, and they never figured out a damned thing."

Except, in the end, how to kill us dead, truly dead, for good. Except how to cut us few left off from each other like we were stranded on our own islands of exile, the brain-music that was our bridge and lifeline to each other silenced forever. Deafening silence. They managed *that*. The only justice was that almost none of the fuckers had survived to gloat about it.

"Only people," Florian agreed. "Not animals or any other living thing—and not all people. Here and there. Some and not others. Now and then. 'Cept in the boom times, so many of us were rising up we scared the hoos shitless. The Black Plague, so-called; the Detroit rise-up; the Pittsburgh Massacre—we showed them we could drive 'em into a corner. We scared them. So they retreated behind their gates."

The soft, quiet nostalgia it all stirred in me was a welcome pain. Without taking his eyes off Florian, Linc reached over and squeezed my hand; Renee pressed her cheek against my shoulder. They understood. Lisa sat there looking uncomfortable, removed, like she always had when she ran up against something only us three who'd been truly dead could understand. Naomi, her human kiddie, sat with her arms wrapped around her knees, leaning forward, frowning intently at Florian like he were a spymaster and she a field agent memorizing the secret codes.

"So things happened," Renee said, "like they were supposed to happen."

Florian laughed softly. His fingers emerged again out of his sleeves, grub-white insects tunneling slowly from dark folds of earth. "And just like Jessie's brother said, seemed like the more time passed meant more boom times for us, more bust times for humans, and they didn't rightly know what to think or do. These last few centuries, right before the plague? That's when we just started havin' boom after boom, hoos crowded into their little corners more and more, and that's when they really started gettin' scared. And nobody could figure out why it happened. They just didn't know what to do. Then, I guess, they finally decided they'd had enough and built all those damned labs."

The wind picked up, flinging fistfuls of fine-grained grit at our clothes, our hair; Billy stumbled past us, laughing at nothing in particular, and fell to his hands and knees in a bed of dead, splintered twigs. I turned my head away so I didn't have to see him crawl. Florian watched Billy's circuit impassively, a sort of pitying pitilessness lighting up his eyes as Billy laughed harder and louder, and shook his head.

"The way I see it, is this," he said. "Life's an arrow, a long flexible arrow, and however the shaft folds and bends and buckles, it always points toward death. That's the road. That's everybody's road—or it's supposed to be. Wouldn't you suppose, when the labs started tryin' to make a fork in the road away from him, take what was rightfully his, that Death'd get mad? Try to punish the folks who did it, shoot another arrow right through 'em? But he never did, not that I could see, all those years of all those labs doing what they did and he never went near 'em—he might be the most powerful thing there is, but I guess that don't make him fast or wise. He never went near 'em, and in the end, they did it to themselves. So it can't be down to them, whatever this is that's happenin' now." His palm ran lightly over his white hair, cupping his skull. "There's no good reason for it, that I can rightly see. No good reason at all."

From the corner of my eye, I saw Amy and Lucy exchange glances, Lucy put a hand to her mouth as if something had just occurred to her that should've been obvious long ago. She didn't say anything, though. They both kept dead quiet.

"I shouldn't be sitting here," Florian said. "I ain't supposed to be here, in the flesh. I ain't supposed to be able to open my mouth and talk to you, all you living folks, right now. This dog here—"

"Nick," Naomi corrected him.

"This Nick here." He smiled at Naomi, the absent grimace of a hoo so totteringly old he'd stopped remembering which kiddies were his own grandchildren and which were the neighbors' brats years before. "Nick, this fella, he ain't supposed to be here. Ain't supposed to be anywhere near here. There's a wall up between the living world and the dead"—here Billy halted in his pit-pony tracks, listening intently—"a great invisible wall so tall and so wide it's big as the afterlife itself, no way to cross it and no reason to try. Except now the wall's collapsing, bits and pieces comin' off to make holes, and I ended up crawlin' through one without ever meaning to or knowing how I did it. Just like this dog here, this Nick. That whole world's collapsing, it feels like, pieces crumblin' off it into slabs of pure nothing. And here, too." Florian tapped his chest, hard, his bone-white knuckles lingering and digging in. "Inside here, bits and pieces are comin' off too. There won't be anything left of me, soon. Nothing left of my world, over the other side of the wall. And if what that boy said's the truth, about things that shoulda stayed in my world—like me—comin' into his, seein' what he shouldn't and then bits of those things crumblin' off to make him go blind—then everything's comin' apart. Everything's turnin' to... nothing."

He was looking me straight in the face again. "So I decided, if I can't do nothing else, I can at least find my beach again, my beach I always missed. Find it and see it one last time, before it all crumbles into nothing. And find what's left of the old gang, you last ones left, and try and warn you what's coming."

Renee and Linc were staring at me. I pretended not to see them. Goddamn you, Renee. Goddamn you, Stephen the mighty dog-beater. Goddamn you, Billy, who should've died with Mags and stayed put with Florian wherever all the dead folks used to go. Goddamn all of you for being right.

FOURTEEN

LISA

"I knew it," Renee said softly. She was very nearly laughing. "I knew it."

There was a heavy burning weight in my stomach, like I'd swallowed one of the strange heated stones I'd experimented with as a makeshift oven, last winter. Linc shoved his fingers through his hair, a tangled-up snarl of black he could never tug a comb through for trying, and gazed at Jessie, who gazed stubbornly at the ground between her feet. This had to be some sort of mistake, some minor existential mishap, just like the whole erstwhile existence of zombies in the first place—of course we were all spooked. Of course we were all *tired.* Exhaustion did horrible things to your mind, your senses, hallucinations and delusions very much among them, and what chance had any of us had to sleep, truly sleep, just drop off and dreamlessly forget everything for eight or twelve or sixteen hours straight, since the first signs of illness had started? And if creatures already dead and bodiless, like Nick (I knew it, I always knew it) or Florian, could creep over to our side and back into the flesh without even meaning to, they had to have our same fleshly weaknesses and failings. Even if Nick never seemed to eat. Even if, on the road following us here, Florian had never seemed to sleep. This wasn't what Jessie's Florian said it was; he was just scared. Just tired. That's all. Now I just needed to convince my gut of that fact.

Amy looked up at Florian, her face so drawn and chalky she seemed like a browbeaten little old woman who'd slipped into a young girl's skin—just how much more shit would the universe throw at her, before it finally let up and let her sleep?—and swallowed, visibly, before she spoke.

"You said—you said you didn't see how the lab could have anything to do with it," she said. "Except there's someone still there, one of their experiments from the old days, and she's doing it. She's trying to bring the lab back at Prairie Beach, just like it was before. She already did it to me, she... killed me, and brought me back to life. Like I said about how I died, before. So I guess she knows what she's about, and I guess if Death wanted to, he could be plenty mad about it."

I was holding my breath, hearing all of this that Amy had already told me, and I didn't know why. What would Florian say, do, if he took this as some kind of defiance? Jessie had told me about him over and over last winter—she'd loved him like a grandfather—but he'd been a real proper zombie just like her and their kind had been cruel, predatory, their notion of a kiss a closed and driven fist. She'd told me about some of that, too, more than I'd ever wanted to hear.

Florian got up from his perch and sat down in front of Amy on the sand; his thin hands took hold of hers and he gave her a look of such weariness, such self-reproach that pity seized me without any warning. Amy shivered, as if the skin of his palms were cold. Back on his feet again, Billy shambled past, completely indifferent, wandering his useless circular path.

"'Cept it feels like *everything's* fallin' apart," he told her. "Even him, in a way, and why would he go and do that to the whole of existence? For no sound reason? When he could settle for killin' off the last little bit of humanity left—"

"What do you mean?" Stephen asked. His voice was flat, dull, like he'd already resigned himself to nothing that came out of Florian's mouth coming to any good: the false resignation of terror. "'Even him'? What does that even mean? What are you talking about?"

"It's like I told you," Florian said. "About Death always bein' there, when he decides you're one of his special pets, the weight you can't lift and the itch you can't scratch? That don't stop after you're dead, it never stops—'cept lately it's not just like he's gone from *me*, it's like he's nowhere at all that I could ever find him. You notice someone missin' like that, when they've been that deep a part a'you for long as you can remember, and I can't explain it better than that. D'you notice air? Not till you try to draw breath and suddenly, you can't breathe. Then you start gaspin' for air, and there don't seem to be any of it anywhere that you could ever find it—and you sure do notice that."

He studied Amy, his chin tilted thoughtfully. "Don't you?" he asked her.

Amy didn't answer. Lucy's arm tightened around her shoulders. Couldn't the universe just leave her the hell alone? Including that mother of hers, who showed herself only when she felt like it and seemed to think that warranted hosannas and applause? I was glad when Amy slid her hands from Florian's grasp; he resumed his seat, back on the log, and when I slipped my own hand into one of Amy's to squeeze it in reassurance, I almost gasped. It was, in fact, a little block of ice.

"Well, *everything* can't just not exist," Naomi declared, and the childish matter-of-factness—know-it-allness of her tone was strangely reassuring. Even if she was reciting things she couldn't possibly be old enough to understand, even if it was all wrong that this conversation was happening at all. "God created everything, and God's always existed even before He created everything, so something that isn't God can't—"

"It's true, isn't it," Stephen said. He was almost shaking. "It's true, all of it is true."

Billy stumbled to a stop right in front of Stephen, his former slave, one of his many slaves; he grinned open-mouthed and let a little river of drool snake down the side of jaw, his chin, into his collar in that way that Jessie's, Linc's, even Florian's rueful looks told me must've been a specialty of his in the old days. The hatred oozing from him was so strong it was like sweat drenching his filthy, torn-up gray suit.

"So you're back here to *warn* us, huh?" he said to Florian. "Mr. Piss-Poor Prophet, who don't know what's happening or why or which is his tailbone and which the skull—you don't fool me, you're here 'cause you're *scared*." The same sing-song sneer I'd heard him use to terrify Naomi, during our first nights in Paradise City, except now she sat watching him with hardened eyes and her small mouth set in a thin, contemptuous line. "Quaking in your boots, you sad fucking piece of shit, just like this spineless soft-headed little hoo"—he gave Stephen a mocking pat on the head, and Stephen jumped back with a snarl—"and even he's less of a coward than you'll ever be."

"Be quiet," Naomi told Billy, spitting the words through her teeth. She was clutching my hands for moral support, her whole body shaking in earnest, but she meant it. "I'm trying to listen to him. You don't know anything. He's an angel and God sent him and he's going to tell us what to do, so when Jesus comes back and all the graves empty out, and all the other dead bodies fly up as angels too—"

Enough. God was one thing, Tina and I could agree on that—I hoped, anyway, unless that cult of hers was even nuttier than rumor said—but the rest of this necrophiliac nonsense stopped right now. She was too young for it, no matter what had happened, too damned young for all of this. "Naomi? Things are bad right now, I know that, but this is not the 'Tribulation.'" I was trying to keep my voice calm, so she wouldn't think I was angry, but I'd had it. She was *my* daughter now, not that church's. "I don't care what anyone told you, there's no such thing as Tribulation and the Judgment Day isn't anything like—"

"Leave her alone." Lucy was sitting up straight and forward, like she was rocking in an imaginary chair. "She can believe whatever she wants. What makes you so sure she's wrong, anyway? Or that you're right? Six of one delusional self-satisfied fairy tale, half-dozen of another."

She smiled into the silence, a quiet little smile like she'd meant to draw blood and had just spotted that first, satisfying surge from the wound. She'd probably been waiting her chance to say that for days.

"Please don't tell me how to raise my daughter," I said, as quietly as I could manage.

"Then why don't you try returning the favor—"

"Mom," Amy said. "*Enough*."

"We're going to die, aren't we?" Stephen said. "All of us. Aren't we? We're going to become that... nothing, losing pieces of ourselves like—I don't want us all to die. I don't want to disintegrate into nothing."

"He's an angel," Naomi insisted. She was half in my lap now, scared too, all that cult-dogma they'd stuffed into her cold comfort when it counted. "God's warning us. So what do we do?" Her words skittered up a high, agitated octave. "Now that it's Tribulation for real, now we have the warning, what do we *do*?"

Florian glanced at her, gentle, any old man contemplating a grandchild. His deep-sunken, pale blue eyes were an old predatory bird's, so worn out and exhausted he just let his prey scuttle and fly right by.

"My God, pet," he said, "if I thought I knew, I'd have told you the moment I could talk."

"There has to be something," Stephen said, too slowly, too thoughtfully. There was a flavor and echo in his voice of Florian's down-country twang, too perfect an imitation to be mockery: an accent like my Bostonian ex-husband's, that only came out to play when he was angry or upset or tired. Just like with my ex, it felt like a warning sign. "There's gotta be something we can do, something we can give him, so he'll leave humanity alone. Isn't there." Silence. "Isn't there?!"

Florian seemed to think this over, just like Stephen had thought him over. His eyes were old and exhausted and resigned to anything that might come next. "Don't know," he said. "I don't rightly know, and I wish I did. I ain't special enough as all that, for Death to tell *me* personal just exactly what—but I passed on everything I do know, while I still have the body to tell it, before all those missin' bits and pieces make me collapse. And I got to see my beach, one last time, before it don't exist no more." He gazed at Jessie, Linc, Renee, Billy in turn. "And I got to say my goodbyes."

Stephen was on his feet and so was Jessie, so was I, both of us afraid Stephen might go after him—but Stephen just stood there, breathing hard, his face flushing deep and dark. "Don't fuck with us," he said softly, his teeth clenched.

"You know I ain't, son," Florian said. There was iron in his words. "You know it well as anyone sitting here. You *seen* it, especially when it strikes you blind. You know I ain't."

Nick laid his ears back and growled. Stephen barely noticed. "I'm not joking. Don't you fuck with me, don't you fuck with any of us—"

"Stephen," Lucy said, standing up in turn and slipping an arm around him. Her movements were quiet, contained, deliberately soothing, but her features were grim. "I agree with you. I absolutely agree. But you can't start panicking. Not now."

"Tell us what to do to stop this," Stephen said. "*Tell us.*"

"Enough." Jessie stood in front of Florian, as if shielding him from Stephen's nonexistent ambush, her teeth bared in a way that meant trouble. "I want you out of here. You can leave walking, or I can make it so you have to be carried out—"

"Don't you dare," Amy said, almost in a whisper.

Stephen laughed, a sound tottering and uneven with fright. "And that's any worse than what *he* says is coming? For all of us? Including you?" Nick started barking and Stephen's voice rose louder, sharper above the noise, little bursts of contained rage like dog-sounds of his own. "Because we haven't all been screwed with enough, have we, dead and alive and dead again whether we ever wanted to be or not? Half my fucking life, half of theirs"—he jerked a hand toward Lucy and Amy—"and everyone who got sick turning into—and now we're supposed to go, 'Oh, sure, absolutely, everything's coming apart and nothing will exist anymore, and we can't do a damned thing about it so I guess I'll just sit here and wait'? No! I've had it and they've had it and you're not fucking with us like that! Nobody's fucking with us ever again!"

"Stop yelling at him," Naomi shouted, and started to cry. "Why are you being so mean to him? It's not his fault! He's an angel, he's *going* to help us—"

"*He's not a fucking angel*!"

"Keep your damned voice down when you talk to her," I snarled as Naomi buried her face in my hip and sobbed. "This has been half her life, too, all of this, you don't ever treat her like—"

"So you don't care, that this'll happen to her?" Stephen was laughing now, hard, his teeth bared like Jessie's and every muscle in him tensed to leap. "We should all just sit here and wait to be eaten away into nothing? What if you have to *watch* while it happens to her first? Or Amy? You want that to happen?"

"Stephen." Amy was tugging on his arm. "She's not saying that. He's not. I know he wasn't. Listen to him."

"You don't understand." Stephen wrenched his arm free and there was a wet sound to his laughter now, like he would have cried with frustration if he were all alone. "You don't want to understand, all you want is to make me out to be the—"

"And you don't know what the hell you're seeing from one second to the next!" Amy yelled back. "You don't have a clue what's real and what isn't! You even said so! So stop thinking you talk for anyone else, especially when thanks to you, I'd be dead right now if it weren't for *him*!"

Stephen turned pale. So did Amy. "Okay," Linc said. "Enough. Everybody just—"

"Just say it," Stephen told Amy. "You think I hurt Nick on

purpose. Just say it."

"I—"

"That I hurt *you* on purpose? Is that what you think?"

"I didn't—" Amy grabbed at her hair in frustration. "Now you're just making shit up and pretending I said it! Is that what you did before? Was that your real excuse to go after Nick?"

"I told you what happened! I *told* you!"

"And *I don't believe you*!"

Renee laughed and shook her head. "I'm not listening to this," she said. "Jessie, Linc, *we'll* talk later."

She vanished swiftly into the trees, leaving the rest of us there with Naomi sobbing, Billy laughing in peals of lunacy, Nick running around the perimeter madly barking and barking while all the rest of us retreated into our own little columns of silence. Jessie put an arm around Florian, to help him to his feet like any old man, and her sharp intake of breath made me and Linc hurry over to them.

Florian stood there straight-backed and upright, nearly a head taller than Jessie, but his waxen white hands were gone, his arms were gone—his black coat sleeves flapped useless and empty, their contents eaten away before our eyes without any of us ever seeing it happen. Part of his face was gone as well; the dark hollow where that eye and cheekbone and ear had been wasn't an open sore, wasn't maiming, but simply a blank space where it seemed nothing, really, had ever been at all. As if we'd all only imagined his face had ever been whole. With what mouth he had left to him, Florian gave us a pitiless smile. Nick's barking went abruptly silent.

"It keeps comin' and goin'," he said. "Just like I told you. Don't know what happens next, don't know if—"

"Sit down," Jessie said, fear making her sound almost reverent as she pushed him back down on the log. "Rest. Don't try to talk. Don't move."

Nick padded up to them both, resting his head against Florian's shin; we waited, we kept waiting, but nothing else happened. Florian didn't speak, and he didn't move. Naomi ran toward him, choking back the last remnants of her crying, but when she had nearly reached him, her steps slowed, hesitated, and she stopped. Florian watched, no anger in his remaining eye, as she quietly walked back to me.

"I meant what I said before," Jessie told Stephen. Her mouth tightened as she spoke and she held Florian quite gently, carefully, as if she thought she needed to shield him from Stephen. "I want you gone. Every time you open your mouth or take a step around here, something goes to shit, and I'm not putting up with it. So get out." She glanced at Amy, at Lucy. "Any of you wanna argue with me about it, now's the time."

Lucy opened her mouth to speak, then Amy tugged on her mother's sleeve, shaking her head. Stephen took a step backwards, another, staring at Amy like he could have kissed, hurt, pleaded with her at all once; the air between them was thick and oppressive with indecision, tingling with countless unseen needles pricking their flesh, their nerves.

Lucy said nothing. Amy said nothing. I didn't know what to say, what good it could possibly do, so I said nothing.

"All right," Stephen said. He sagged in his clothes as he stood there, slump-shouldered, hollowed out and defeated like Billy. "I'm leaving. I'm going to Tina and Russell's town down the road. If I figure out anything about—anything, I'll send a message. Or something. That's where I'll be, if anyone's looking for me."

A few days, I thought, I'd give it a few days to blow over, then go and get him—we had to have at least a few days, all of us, to work through all this. We'd be all right for that long. Just a few more days.

Amy nodded at Stephen. "Okay," she said. Her voice was small and miserable.

Stephen nodded back. He turned to Lucy and me. "Thanks for trying to help me out," he said, and headed up the ridge toward the shortcut to the road.

Amy watched his retreating back until the trees had swallowed him. Then her face contorted, and Lucy grabbed her; Amy hung on fiercely, but she didn't cry. Naomi, tear-stained and mute, clung to me. Nick, all the noise and agitation gone out of him, nuzzled at Florian's shin some more, then lay down calmly at his feet.

"Good riddance," Linc said.

Amy shook her head, still buried against Lucy's shoulder, but didn't speak. Billy was ensconced higher up the ridge now, leaning against the trunk of a still-living maple; he wriggled his shoulder blades against the bark as though they itched, then folded his arms and narrowed his eyes in contemplation of all of us left. Then he grinned.

"He's right," he called down to us. "Florian, the incredible shrinking man? The fucking coward who shows up for nothing and can't say shit? He's right. He can't stop what's coming. You can't. Nobody can. It's heading straight for us, coming right down the road."

He laughed aloud, a sound of genuine, almost sweet-natured joy. "And I can't wait."

FIFTEEN

NATALIE

Head hurt. Back hurt. Everything hurt.

I was in the gray house with the red mailbox, me and Janey who was in a bed beside me, curled up and quiet. The palsied old man, the one who'd shouted at Billy, he was in the bedroom across the hall; the girl with the baby kept going in and out, talking to him, from the faint bits I'd heard I'd guessed he was her grandfather and he was dying. His heart, they couldn't find any more medication for it even though Russell and the others went looking. He seemed calm and resigned to it all and his granddaughter wasn't wailing or carrying on either—she was smart enough to realize he was lucky. That she was lucky too, whether she wanted to admit it or not, only one dependent mouth left for her to feed.

What would it be like, having family that looked like you and sounded like you, that was always just there? Who were all part of each other because part of their mutual flesh was one and the same, shared, divided? The thought of it was like longing, but gave way just as fast to a shiver of true disgust. Flesh shared, split, a lot of walking talking groups of amoebas—our way, creating our own new species one by one from a clean undivided source, that was better.

Head hurt. Back hurt. I pulled myself upright in bed and then that Tina came in, tray in her hands and a bruise ringing one eye, and went over to where Janey lay awake, bruised up herself, not talking.

"It's just canned soup," she was saying to Janey, as the scent reached my nose. "But it's good. Chicken vegetable. Have some."

Janey rolled slowly from her side to her back, used her heels to push at the mattress and raise her head. Without that red lipstick she used to smear on in a puddle of wet, her whole face was washed out and fading, skin pale and muddy all at once, dull dirty blonde hair falling dejected into her eyes. I could tell from watching her how much effort it took to move, after how Billy worked her over. She sniffed the soup and looked up at Tina, all polite anxiety.

"I'm not sure Don would want me to have this," she explained.

Tina had probably heard crazier than that, plenty of times, because she just nodded. That ridiculous cross, slung on its chain so it looked poised to dive off one of her big breasts, bobbed and shook with the gesture. "Just a little bit," she urged Janey. "A few spoonfuls."

"Oh, that's how it starts," Janey said. Dark and knowing. "That's how it always starts."

But she ate the soup anyway and when Tina put the spoon down, Janey picked it up herself, working her way steadily to the bottom of the bowl. All this time neither of them had said a word to me, not so much as glanced in my direction: I was the blight on the town, the troublemaker, the one who'd brought Billy in their midst even if he did beat my ass just as bad as theirs. Janey, they just assumed he'd dragged her along with him, but I was the one even Ms. Super-Christian couldn't stomach. I hate humans, ordinary unchanged human beings. I seriously hate them.

"Are you hungry?" Tina asked me. Her voice was even and

steady like that'd make me think she didn't hate me, like she could trick me just that easily. "There's some more of this, or canned pork and beans—"

She looked like she could use a lot less pork and beans. I swung my legs over the side of the bed, pushing through the little jolts of pain it sent up my back, and found my sneakers she'd lined up at the foot. Sukie my doll had sat beside me on the pillow, she was the first thing I'd looked for when I woke up, and I stuffed her back in my jacket pocket, shuffled out the bedroom door without talking.

The front room, what must've been the living room once, there were stacked-up cartons, a desk with papers on it and another bed in the corner, someone else huddled in it under a nest of blankets and coughing nonstop. Battered spiral notebook on the desktop and when I picked it up and leafed through, it was like Stephen's from Paradise City, lists of names, food and medicine inventories, a subdivided page marked "Special Needs": Medical, Religious, Psychological. Food Allergies. I couldn't find my name or Janey's, they must not have had time to write them down. The coughing was congested and wet and made me shudder to hear it so I dropped the notebook, went in stocking feet out the front door and sat to do up my laces on the porch.

It was still sunny outside, but a veiled-over sunny, light shining through a thin gray scrim of clouds; I wasn't sure if it was the same day we'd arrived here or not. Soft breeze, pretty view of all the gardens, that big oak in the middle of town—this must've been a nice place to live, before. Maybe once I had the lab really up and running we could move some operations out here, get rid of the humans and then this could be my house. I knotted up the left laces and then the right in hard little buds, they'd have to slice them off my feet if they wanted to take them, and when I looked up again someone was standing not a yard away staring at the red mailbox, and at the elephant ears of chard growing where there'd once been a lawn, and at me.

Stephen. I played it cool, staring back and waiting for Amy and that crybaby mother of hers to come up behind him and start acting like they owned the place, but it was just him. By himself.

He looked down at me and laughed. "Figures," he said.

"So where's Amy?" I asked.

He sat on the edge of the porch step, as far away from me as he could get, and huddled up so furious and wretched I could've felt sorry for him, he was one of us after all, but after how he and Miss Mystic left me in the dirt I couldn't care less. All alone. Trouble in paradise? What a joke. He wasn't even looking at me anyway, just like nobody ever did. He lifted his head and took in the houses, the haphazard gardens with only a very few patches of dry dead amid the green, the thick-trunked looming living oak.

"Things look okay here," he said. Not really to me, just aloud. "Maybe that was all a mistake, it's not everything and everybody that's—it's sort of okay here."

"It wasn't half okay getting here." I didn't want to talk to him, he certainly wasn't inviting me to, but he looked too pleased with himself and I didn't mind messing that up with the truth. Just like I did with Amy. "Dead plants. Dead animals. People, someone I knew at the lab, dropping dead right in front of me. You can ask Janey, she's here too—I think the same thing happened to Don." I reached down to my laces again, tugging them smooth, tightening them so I'd have something to do. "And him—you know. *Him*. The one I've been waiting for. He came. He was angry at me."

When was he going to show up here anyway, long last, now that Billy had done his job and got me here and thank God he was gone to go cry over Mags for eternity? He was supposed to be here. I was supposed to be feeling as acute and as *now* as I could, just like how all the living things left were supposed to be upended and flung into chaos by his coming: leaves swelling up with moisture until they burst, stones rumbling and cracking from the inside as their lava stirred back to boiling life, flowers killing themselves in the rush to offer him that single, perfect culminating bloom. People screaming, crying, screwing, fighting, knowing that this was the last chance, the last they'd ever have, just like how things were back at the height of the plague—and instead everything was just limp and drab and sad, the living things creeping away almost apologetically departing this life while my back was turned. Even when it happened right next to me. It wasn't a fitting tribute. Life should be sacrificing itself to Death in the open all around me, proudly, happily, knowing that after this last time it'd never have to fight again. Because I was going to win. I'd fight him and use all the lab's secrets against him and I would save everyone, everything, all the life left. It had to happen now, I had to fight him *now*—

But all I had was the porch and the oak and Stephen, useless Stephen, for company. He was looking at me now, at least, gracious of him. The way he looked at everything, like he were an artist, a painter, wandering around his own first big exhibition and realizing too late he couldn't draw for crap.

"The one you've been waiting for," he repeated. "And who'd that be?"

Oh, God. "Don't act like you don't already know." I laughed, because the truth of it just came to me. "Because if you didn't, and you weren't freaking out about it, you wouldn't even be here. You ran away from the rest of them because they can't see it, and you can—or maybe because they can see it, and since they do, you can't pretend you don't anymore. So you ran away. Didn't you."

Stephen gazed at me in silence, big dark eyes not the least caught-out uncomfortable like I'd wanted, and then looked away. He wasn't handsome but he had nice eyes, a lot of dark hair, I'd seen Amy looking at him back at Paradise when she thought nobody noticed. Always has to have everything for herself. The other one, why wasn't he here? Why wasn't he *here*. If he were off behind my back with her, again, I wouldn't be kind about it.

"Back at the lab," Stephen said, out of nowhere so I jumped. "You said, when I threatened to hurt you to try and get something about the experiments out of you—you said I'd probably enjoy that. You made it sound like I'd done things like that before." He ran a hand through his hair and it stood halfway on end, bristly and snarled. "Is it true? Or did you just say that to try and throw me off?"

Each of us had our own file, back at the lab, all the particulars anyone knew of our former lives, and if someone was a feeder from the juvie hall—the lab used a lot of them—his criminal records were included, the only fabrication in them the part about how he'd killed himself or run away from custody. Medical, Psychological, Special Needs, Allergies. The lab paid upfront for a lot of kids from juvie and psychiatric facilities, they needed them, but they didn't care what any of them had actually done—it could be anything at all, from armed robbery to shoplifting. Trespass on protected research areas. Vandalizing buildings. Kid stuff. Nobody wanted to put up with it, not when they were pouring all that tax money into making sure the right towns and cities were safe and guarded and nothing dangerous anywhere could sneak through the cracks. But the lab didn't care. I'd seen Stephen's record, I read the whole thing. It didn't take long. He stole a candy bar and a lighter, and mouthed off to the security guard who grabbed him. That's it.

"You were in juvie," I said. "I saw the file, I read it. I read everybody's file who was left. They were in a special room, I found the key." I laughed. "You don't want to know what Amy's mother did."

Prostitution, that's all Amy's mother did. A few "solicitation" arrests. But he wouldn't know that. Amy's file, nothing criminal in it at all. Little Miss Saintly. "You attacked another kid," I continued. "He was blasting his car radio too loud, or something like that, and you dragged him straight out of his car and nearly killed him. All because he made too much noise. He had to have surgery on his eye. And you hurt animals too. For fun." I pulled the knots on my righthand laces as tight as I could. "And you stole things. It's all right there, in your file."

I bet he would've done stuff like that, for real, if he'd ever had the chance. And he *did* steal something, so it wasn't a total lie. I sat there waiting, hoping for him to sag in cut-string shame and defeat, like Billy, for his face to distort and drag itself down in the knowledge of what he thought he really was. Instead he just sat there, almost delicately contemplative with chin on hand

and hair falling into his eyes to veil them, gazing at the oak tree with its big welcoming sign. There was a creak of wood behind us and when I looked around, there was Janey, still bruised and unsteady but out of bed, her face lighting up with incongruous pleasure when she realized who was sitting beside me. Stephen didn't bother turning to see.

"Oh, good," Janey said. She sat down between us, in the empty space filled with tension and dislike. "Now everyone's coming back again. I was sure that would happen but not just when."

"That old man," said Stephen. I couldn't tell if he were talking to me, Janey, himself. "Ghostly old man following us. He told us this whole story about the world breaking up and disappearing, how we'd all—like there was nothing we could do about it, just sit and wait. I don't believe that. It's not true." His free hand, by his side, slowly contracted to a fist. "None of that is true."

There was movement on another of the front porches: a woman, the bent-over elderly one who'd watched us arrive, she was out there again staring at us from the other side of the oak. I guess that's something that never changes either, how old people have nothing better to do ever than stare at everyone else living their lives. Janey rubbed her forehead, angled her chin toward Stephen with a fond look like you give a little kid, a baby brother.

"He has a dark coat," she said. Her old Janey-voice, so pat and cheerful like she'd gotten it pre-packaged from a box, but there was an undercurrent of real longing beneath, a wind just barely rustling a tree's thinnest, lowest branches. "And white hair, and pale blue eyes that look at you like they see everything inside, but even if you have a terrible secret you think you're hiding, it's all right. Because he killed somebody. Once."

That got Stephen to look at her, astonished. She smiled at him, wide happy smile even without her red lipstick. "You've seen him," Stephen said.

Janey shook her head. "But I dreamed about him. Sometimes, lately, ever since Don—" She gnawed at her lip. "Lately, it's like there's this weight on my eyes, my chest, and it pushes down so hard I can't think. Or breathe. But when I think about him, I feel a little better. I don't know how I know he's real, when I only had him in my head, but I do." She reached over and patted Stephen's hand, slow thought-out pat like she was rehearsing choreography. The Dance of the Big Sister. "So you can talk about him as much as you want."

I bit my own lip to keep from laughing. Another thing that never changes, Janey being completely insane. Stephen was always nice to her back at Paradise, more patient with all that than I ever felt, and now he just nodded and patted her hand back and sat there not talking anymore. The old woman across the way was walking toward us now, slow and hesitant, stopping to rest when she reached the oak tree.

"Janey?" Tina's voice, calling from inside before she poked her head out the doorway. "There you are. Do you want some cheese crackers?"

Janey smiled up at Tina and shook her head. Tina came shuffling onto the porch, her big stupid cross still bouncing on her big stupid chest, and offered the little plastic-wrapped cracker pack to Stephen in silence, like a consolation prize; he took them, split the wrapping down the seam, stuck the tiny red plastic paddle in the cheese tub with the same frowning concentration he gave everything. Cheese crackers to dog fights.

Of course, nobody even thought to offer me any.

"Russell said you came here by yourself," Tina said to him. All casual, like she didn't already have his name written down in one of her notebooks. Miss Social Worker. "Are you okay?"

Stephen shook his head.

Of course, nobody thought to ask after me.

The old woman by the oak tree was coming toward us again, stumbling a little on the uneven ground; Russell, the man with the red hair nearly gone gray, he'd come walking across the green and now he was helping her cross like it were a busy city street. Shouldn't they be shunning me, like the rest of them were? Because somehow Billy was all my fault? I reached into my pocket and pulled out the lake stones I'd carried with me, their weight and flat smoothness in my hand and the memories they carried with them an instant comfort; they felt hot, like they sometimes did, hot and almost humming like something inside them vibrated but maybe it was just me, just that nervous, flushed skin and tremors in my hands. Even Sukie where she was pressed secret against my side felt warm through the jacket cloth, like she was a real baby.

"Are you sure you don't want any lunch?" Tina was saying. "At least some cheese crackers?"

It took me a second to realize Tina was talking to me. So I existed all of a sudden? Don't do me any favors.

Russell and the old lady came and sat on the lower step and I ignored Tina just like everyone else ignored me, toying with the stones hand to hand, gripping one hard and still in my fist to try and see if it really were it trembling from inside, and not me.

"You can't be angry with us forever, you know," Tina said. Never shut up, just like the shiny overenthused new lab recruits, you could tell the woman just never shut up. "I'm sorry about the circumstances of how you got here, but—"

"Leave her be," Russell said. "She's not hurting anyone." He looked up at Janey. "You all right? Get something to eat?"

Janey nodded. "I'm not sure it's what Don would have wanted me to eat," she said, "but he always said, Jeanette Isabella, starvation is simply not permitted. So I tried my best." A little cloud crossed her face and she sighed. "I just wish I knew when I was going to see him again."

Stephen glanced at her and his eyes were troubled, almost fearful even, but he didn't say anything. Just shoved the empty cracker pack into his pocket.

The stones in my hands were growing hotter. I could feel the old woman looking at me but I ignored her, we had nothing to say to each other and she looked ready to keel over in two hours anyway. The old man in the back room, maybe she was his wife. Maybe Russell had brought her for a hospital visit.

Tina kept watching me too, like she was waiting for me to cry and hug her and make friends forever. "The stones will sing," she mused aloud. "That Bible verse, do you know it?"

"I'm not a Christian," I said. I just knew she'd be trying that next. "So forget it."

"My church's founder, a hundred and... forty-seven years ago? Forty-eight?" Off to the races. Billy should've hit her harder when he had the chance. "Now that's just sad, I was on the board's sesquicentennial committee at one point and now I don't even remember—Mother Anne Brown, our first prophet, she said, that verse wasn't just poetics, that stones have life inside them, they pulse, they sing—"

"Like bones," Janey said.

We all looked at her, surprised, because she actually sounded like she was right here and not somewhere planets removed. "A skeleton's a symbol of death," she said. "Bones look like white stones, or dead branches, like they prop you up inside and that's all. But they have marrow inside them, blood vessels. While we're alive, they're living too." She stuck out her forearm, examined the bumps and divots of elbow, wristbones, knuckles. "Like a piece of those rocks, inside us. Or like the rocks are living tissue too. We just haven't gotten to their marrow."

Was she trying to tell us something? Trying to say she'd always known more than she ever let on? I stared at her hard, trying the silent intimidation that sometimes worked with her back in Paradise, I couldn't say right out what I was thinking because there were too many humans here to hear it, but those others buoyed her up and circled her protectively without realizing they did it, their presence guarded her and gave her ammunition against me. Like Stephen, Lucy, Lisa kept me away from Amy, if it'd been just the two of us it would've been so different. Tina was smiling and smiling at Janey like she'd just found some extra Jesus behind the pickles in the pantry.

"You've read her work!" Tina said. "*Meditations Upon the Illusion We Call Death*. You never said."

Janey shook her head. "But I haven't. Don always said— "

"The stones sing," Tina kept on, oblivious, excited, "when they start to show their life, when they grow hot as human skin and tremble in a person's hand. When you can start feeling the presence of that marrow." Two little spots of color showed on her cheeks, beneath the long streaking bruise Billy had left behind. "But the true song is only sung when they split open, when they spill their marrow onto the— "

"Ow! Dammit!"

It was like the stones in my palm had been listening to Tina, like everything everywhere was in on its own joke and ignoring me—they'd grown hot as my blood while Tina jabbered and babbled, and then hotter, until I was holding live coals and my fingers flew open of their own accord, the stones clattering to the ground beneath all our feet. Stephen reached down and snatched one up before I could stop him, dropped it again swearing, and I dove into the dirt—neck hurt, back hurt, even my bones felt spongy and horrible—and snatched them both back up before I could think about it, before I could hesitate because my nerves remembered pain. I wasn't afraid of pain, not after all the times they'd given it to me. My fingers, my whole hand curled up tense and tight with the effort of not dropping them again, sweat broke out on my forehead and just as I couldn't stand it anymore, as I was shaking and feeling like I'd be sick or scream, both the lake stones split open there in my palm.

The stone pieces were cool again, as though great gusts of steam building up inside them had been released, and something sticky and sugary was oozing from them, a warm little stream of ink or tar. The color turned to molasses as it hit the air, blackstrap, then sorghum, and then it dried up and went grainy within seconds so I was holding a handful of brown sugar, gritty yet soft. Brown sugar, or sand. It almost seemed to hum to itself, the stuff in my hand, and the skin it touched was soothed, cooled, quietly humming too.

The singing sand streamed from between my fingers, like

it were water flowing through the cracks, and scattered on the ground. The hollow stone shells were all I had left.

The old woman, the one I wouldn't look in the eye because I was sure she was just here to spy for the neighbors, maybe check on the old man who might be her husband if she could spare five seconds, she put a hand to her mouth and made a sound full of dismay, but not surprise. Maybe she was in Tina's crazy cult too. Stephen and Russell, they just looked confused, but Tina's eyes were hard and suspicious in a way I'd never seen before, that made me want to laugh. Didn't take much for you to drop the mask, did it, Sister Superior? I know your kind. Everybody knows your kind.

"Is this a joke?" she demanded.

Janey and the old woman kept staring, staring at me, until I could've slapped them both, and Russell reached over and patted Tina's shoulder with a calm I could tell he didn't feel. "Let it go, Tina," he said. "This isn't the worst stunt by far anyone who's come here ever pulled—"

"I don't think this is funny." Tina had recovered herself, a little, she'd jammed that mask of willful good cheer firmly back in place, but the flush-spots were back on her cheeks and her mouth kept giving her away, twisting and curling into angrier shapes. "I don't expect you to share my beliefs, we've never proselytized—Russell's an atheist, you can ask him—but a little simple respect isn't too much to—"

"*Is* it a trick?" Stephen had left his perch and was squatting in the dirt, fascinated, a chicken trying to scratch up some elusive, marvelous species of grub. His fingers sifted through the earth, prospecting, but he couldn't retrieve any of the stony singing sand. He looked up at Tina, frowning, like she'd been holding out on us all. "So if you're me and you never believed any of that, and just saw it happen anyway, what does it mean?"

"It's not a trick." The old woman was on her feet, painfully, struggling upright with the help of a splintering porch pillar and waving off Russell as he jumped up to help. "It's not a trick, or a joke. Is it, Natalie?"

I hadn't told her my name. Someone else, Russell, he must've, but I somehow felt like he hadn't and nobody had and the old woman's voice was such a ruined thing, rasping and ill, like it was a delicate rare metal and just to be vicious someone had pounded it thin, twisted it into an ugly shape, left it out in the heat and rain to corrode. And it was familiar. Familiar like the parody, the shell of something that had worked itself into every corner of my childhood and—was this a joke? I glared at her, her ruined face, her sad thin sunken curve of a mouth.

"Like you would know," I said. A stranger. That's all she was. I was seeing things, like Tina and her pathetic angel-wing stardust fantasy she called religion. "Like any human being anywhere, knows anything—"

"No," said another voice. A woman's. One single, fragile word, a china egg cracked along its side. "You don't."

She hadn't been there in front of us, she hadn't been anywhere at all, but then she was: swaying barefoot back and forth in the dirt, a thin dark-haired woman in a torn yellow nightgown stained with long streaks of dirt and blood. The blood, the dirt were caked on her pipe-cleaner legs, her mouth was drawn up in a too-sweet, too-friendly television smile, her eyes were so big and dark and deep that they were like pits, twin wells in the ground, oozing the sad amiability of madness. Except behind all that, behind the bright-eyed crazy that had eaten up whoever this woman was when she was alive, you could see the glint and gleam of something else. Someone else, living inside her, using her hurt little legs to walk around on like he could use the body of anything dead. It smiled at me. He smiled at me. He'd come.

Tina, beside me, drew in her breath. Stephen made a wordless sound that told me all along he hadn't believed it, hadn't really believed Amy at all when she told him what she'd seen and how she'd got to the lab, and now here it was in front of him and Mr. Cool almost moaning in fear and I should've laughed in his face, I wanted to, but I couldn't laugh. I couldn't move. This was the moment, and I couldn't move. She, he, in that filthy yellow nightgown, stood there looking at the ground beneath its feet, the little bits of rock I still clutched in my hand.

"That won't help you," he said. "Nothing will."

It, he, glanced toward the sky. There was a long drawn-out sound, like Stephen's throat magnified, like something huge and heavy being slowly pulled apart, and then the sun vanished and the sky went out.

SIXTEEN

AMY

The waves go in. The waves go out. Not like ocean waves, great crashing cresting things I saw for myself when I was little, but quiet-strong currents that slip in more softly, rush instead of crash, and pull you under before you even realize they've got you. Their strength all contained in a sort of internal weight, no big white-capped heights, holding itself close like the fingers of a grim, bruised fist. The fingers straighten out, and the water streams over the sand. They draw back toward the palm, the water heads out.

This had all been happening since before any of us were born. And still was, now that we were all almost gone. The lake didn't need us, the seagulls, the trees, I felt like that should be all the real hint anyone needed. We weren't the center of anything, except in our own heads. Except the problem was that inside our own heads was where everyone was trapped. Including me.

After Stephen left, Florian—the remnants of Florian—just curled up quietly on his log, withering in slow degrees where he sat. Jessie cradled him in her arms with a ferocious expression, like she could somehow shield him from whatever was pulling him to pieces; Linc and Renee paced around them both, a team of doctors confronted with some bewildering new disease. Naomi cried and cried at the sight of her angel falling apart and Lisa finally had to pick her up, carry her bodily back to the cabins, Naomi screaming and donkey-kicking in the first genuine tantrum I'd ever seen her throw.

I was so glad my mother raised me agnostic. And that I didn't have any kids, or foster kids, of my own. It wouldn't work out anyway, if I did. I wasn't any good with people, including the ones I loved.

As I watched the water, I reached into my jacket pocket and took out a lake stone, the greenish-brown one Florian had relinquished back in the woods. Back when he'd still had hands. I'd picked it up, from where it lay on the ground at his feet, and he didn't protest, nobody tried to stop me: I couldn't explain why, but I wanted it, wanted it badly, more than any of the other stones scattered around and embedded in the sands even though many of them were bigger, smoother, prettier. It felt weird in my grasp, almost hot and twitchy as I passed it from palm to palm, and finally I put it away again. It seemed to press itself into my side, a whole pincushion of heated needles poking and prodding, but I didn't want to throw it away.

People have drowned here, from the undertow, storms. Folks heard "lake" and thought of a placid smear of blue crayon in a drawing. They had no idea.

I missed Stephen. But what good did that do either of us?

Nick who'd reattached himself to my side after Stephen left pressed his muzzle against my leg, stared lamplike at the water. After Stephen left, and after Florian started fading away, drawing away from the old ghostly man as if he really were diseased, contagious... was he? He said right out, Florian did, that Nick wasn't supposed to be here in the flesh any more than he was—was Nick going to come apart next? Fade back into oblivion, into the here-now-gone-again specter he'd been when I first knew him? I reached out in fright and hugged Nick to my chest, feeling good hard solid muscle and cold wet nose and warm thick shaggy fur. All four paws, all accounted for. And forget Florian, forget everything he said, it was Nick I really trusted to tell me the truth, but he still hadn't explained what was happening, the dead things, the blind spots, he still hadn't shown me—

Sometimes, and I wouldn't have told anyone this if they tortured me, I felt like Nick always knew what I was thinking, like he was thinking over my exact same thoughts at the very same time and mulling them and then I could almost hear him inside my head going *But I can't. Not yet.* I didn't actually hear anything but myself, it's just, I felt like I *should* be hearing him. Not like we could speak to each other—whatever his thoughts were, they seemed just as wordless and nebulous as any ordinary dog's—but we still reflected and mirrored each other so perfectly that I knew what those wordless nebulous floating things translated to.

I knew what he was thinking, really thinking, because it was always what I was thinking. Nick hadn't shown me what was really happening because, just like Florian, he couldn't. He didn't know. I knew that before he "told" me, but his telling me was my telling myself.

Or maybe I was just crazy. How would I know how any animal thinks, anyway? Presumption. Didn't even know my own mind.

Soft sounds behind me, the faint *swoosh* noises of sand displaced by human feet, then firmer louder sounds as the sand became more solid near the shoreline and I knew without looking that it wasn't Lisa, she couldn't ever manage to be this quiet when she was nervous. My mother sat down beside me, on the opposite side from Nick, and stared out with me at the choppy gray-tinged waters.

"How is Naomi?" I asked.

"Better." My mother reached over and worked her fingertips against Nick's forehead, a little massage. He suffered it in silence. "Part of it's that she's flat worn out. We all are. Lisa finally got her to take a nap."

Right after Naomi got done crying over that Florian, she started crying all over again because Nick still wouldn't be her best friend. Couldn't he humor her a little bit, at least? Dogs were supposed to love little kids. "I'm glad you didn't raise me to believe in all that stuff," I told my mother. "That church of hers. Or in any of Lisa's."

My mother made a little noise that wasn't quite a laugh. "No comment," she said.

None of that growing up, but now I saw things that weren't real, weren't solid, then suddenly became real, everywhere I went. Like Nick. And now, things that seemed solid but melted into air, into nothing, everywhere I went. Like the man in black. Like the man he used to answer to, that we all answer to in the end. The boss of us. Just like that Jessie does, apparently, except right now she's trying to pretend we're not even here.

"Do you remember when I was little," I said, "five or six, and you had that conference or whatever it was and we flew to Massachusetts? And saw the ocean at Cape Cod?"

My mother smiled. "You were seven. You kept asking, but what if the plane crashes? It was my first time on an airplane, too, but I could hardly look scared about it, not in front of you—"

"And when I ate the seaweed?"

She laughed. "The look on your face, I wish I'd had a camera. But when I tried some myself, I almost saw the point—it was foul, but something about the texture, it was this thick rubbery bright green stuff, it never quite broke down under your teeth so there was something satisfying about chewing it. Like how a rawhide bone must feel, right, Nick?" Nick who'd never chewed a bone in his life—this life, anyway—looked politely up at her. "Remember that little restaurant you liked, the clam shack?"

Plump little fried clams, still with their bellies attached like they didn't make them out here, and thin crumbly onion rings, thick airy vanilla soft-serve. I remembered. That was my favorite thing about the trip, but that's how you think when you're seven. That and the ocean.

"I wish we'd stayed out there," I said.

"There wasn't any way to do that."

"I know."

Because the lab kept drawing her back. Because the lab was her true birthplace, whatever her birth certificate—wherever that was—said otherwise. Her true home, Natalie's, Stephen's. And now mine.

My mother reached out to the thick wet streak of shore-sand just past us, smooth and even as a tile, and pressed her fingers to its surface. Dug in. "In a couple of days," she said, "when everyone's calmed down, I'll go talk to Stephen. See what we all want to— "

"I don't think we have a couple of days," I said. "Not if Jessie's friend is right."

My mother didn't answer. A seagull strutted, contemptuous, inches from her digging fingers, daring her to send him fluttering back over the waters.

"And I think Stephen is right," she said at last. A muscle at the side of her jaw drew tense. "Whatever's happening to the world—if it's really true—we can't just sit here waiting around for our own doomsday like a lot of— "

"And what the hell kind of magic trick are we supposed to pull to make it stop?"

My mother's profile, as she sat there resolutely not looking at me, was sharp and obstinate and why was there so much gray in her hair? In the two years she'd been away, it was like she'd aged twenty. "Because we're in it already, Mom, and you know it. We're in over our heads. And that Natalie's in over her head too, I can feel it, and now, whatever we do, the whole world is about to... I don't know what, something that might kill us, might kill lots of things, but— "

"We don't know that. We don't know there's *nothing* we can do."

"And if there is something, how the hell are we supposed to figure it out?" I wanted to grab her, shake the truth into her, it was staring her in the face and sitting cold-nosed and quiet by her side. "I'm not kidding, how exactly would we do that? And why would it be *us* who did? Something's happening that's way beyond us stopping it, it's happening and I don't think Natalie knows what it is either, just like the lab didn't know why everyone starting getting sick back last—" I shook my head, on the verge of saying something truly reckless, and then I said it anyway. "And seriously, why do you care anyway? You and Stephen? The whole world ending is just what you should want, right, since you're so sick of living? Like I guess it's just an accident, that when you left me you didn't kill yourself after all?"

My throat was tight and hot, saying it out loud. The thing I really feared. My mother turned her head toward me, her eyes still young like they were supposed to be but when my mother had been young like me, that's when she'd been saddest of all.

"Don't hold against me," she said without anger, "what I did when I was sick in the head. I realize that's asking a lot, maybe, but it's not fair."

I laughed. I couldn't help it. "You think I'm holding things against you," I said. "Me. You think I think *you're* the one sick in the head. You just don't get it, do you? Or do you think I was lying about what I—"

"Of course I don't," she said, sharp and sorrowful. "After all this? Don't be stupid. Of course I don't. And it's on my own conscience forever, that woman's death. Just as much as yours."

But I didn't have to do it, Mom. Your going away so we couldn't try and survive together, it's got nothing to do with what I chose to do to Ms. Acosta. But at least she was taking her own advice, refusing to go after someone sick in the head. She sighed.

"If I'd raised you with some sort of faith," she said, "even just the outlines of one, maybe you'd feel like there was more hope. Like Tina does. I can tell she's lived through all this by barreling through everything, shoveling through one pile of shit after another, she's so convinced that if she keeps going long enough she'll find a pony in her stable. Jesus in the manger. If I'd—"

"That's got nothing to do with anything," I said. Short and sharp.

"Amy—"

"I didn't tell all that stuff to Lisa instead of you because you left. Okay?" Gnats, sand flies veered toward my face and I brushed them away hard and brusque, hand slashing at the air. "The stuff about feeling caught between things, like I don't really belong in either of—I told her all that because it would've scared you. It *did* scare you, I could tell, you started thinking I wanted to kill myself or something—"

"Lisa thought so too. I could see it. Can you blame her?"

"Jesus, don't you think if I wanted to kill myself, I'd just do it? That I wouldn't have done it already? I've got good reason to, believe me. There's plenty of folks who'd look at what I did and think I should be dead." My eyes were hot and stinging and full like tears would well up any second but they stayed dry, I'd killed someone and soaked myself in their blood but my eyes stayed dry, good a proof as any of a hardened heart. You can't get blood from a stone, or salt water either. "But I don't want to die. I really don't. It's just—"

There were no good words, not to say this. But they were the ones I had. "It's just I don't feel like I'm really alive, either."

Another gull strutted past us, all bobbing head and gulping throat and sharp, indignant bird-eyes, going about its business like it would long after we were gone. The wounds in my own neck, where Natalie had slashed it, where we'd picked out the sutures last night one by one after it all healed with an inhuman speed, the itching there surged up and as I tilted my chin to scratch it, I could feel the skin, darker pink scar tissue, straining itself to stretch. A shiny little canopy tugged dangerously taut. My mother put her hand on mine, pulled my fingers down.

"You'll open it all up again," she said.

Our fingers twined together, resting on Nick's broad rough back. He gazed indifferently at the waters.

"Even when I'm here," I said, "even when I'm right here, with the clouds, and the lake, and the birds, and all of it, I feel like I'm not. It's like how my skin itches, where it's grown back. You always said that when I was little and hurt myself: 'Don't scratch. Itching means healing.' There's sand in my shoes, a little gritty. My socks are flat on the bottom from sweat, they need to be washed. The breeze is almost cool enough, but not quite. I can smell the water in the air. I feel all those things, all at once, like anyone would, except part of me thinks I really don't. I just *remember* those feelings, in the aggregate, I just know that in a situation like this I'm supposed to feel them. And both those things are true, all at once. I'm here, I really am, and I'm also really not."

Her hand in mine, though—that was unambiguous, that was real. I could feel it and remember how it felt beforehand all at once, without having to decide if it were really happening or not. She thought my words over, lending them weight.

"Maybe you've just had enough," she said. "Like everyone has. Detachment, dissociation, are perfectly normal human reactions to—I'm wrong, aren't I? Completely wrong. Just like that psychiatrist I saw was wrong, because I could never tell her the actual truth of what had happened to me. About my actual life." She laughed, and as she rocked back and forth where she sat, my hand in hers rocked too. "I'm wrong. Aren't I wrong?"

"I don't know," I said. It sounded right, didn't it? Detachment. Depression. Disassociation. All explained by: disaster. Perfectly nice and neat, all very textbook. Just what you'd expect. From someone who'd lived through this, done what I'd done.

She was looking straight at me.

"You do know," she said.

Dread. There's another word. But it wasn't the thing itself that I dreaded, it was saying it aloud all wrong. How did I tell her? Why was I so sure she already knew what I'd say?

"Maybe," I said, as the wind picked up and wrapped strands of hair around my face, "maybe it's because it was mostly just you and me, growing up, but I always felt, before this, like, how can you even trust anyone you haven't known all your life? How can you even start to tell them things, and—I guess that's why I never really had any friends. I mean, any best friends." I didn't need people, I'd thought, I had my dreams of music instead, though how I was ever going to get a band together with that attitude, God only knew. Dissociation. Distrust. "So, I mean, that's something I've found out, since all this happened. That you can realize you know somebody, really—hate them, or love them, or both at once, when you've barely even really met them. Like Lisa. Or how Lisa feels about Naomi. Or Stephen."

Get to the point. Stop dancing around it and get to the point. "I know you don't like her, okay, I know that, but I love Lisa. I mean, as a friend. A sister even. And I love Stephen." His name faltered in my mouth, like the sound of it had cut my tongue. "No matter what happened. But if something happened to him, if he died in earnest or just didn't want anything to do with me, with us, anymore, things would keep happening. They'd hurt, but I'd get used to it, and they'd keep happening." That I learned firsthand, after you left. "But—the other one. Not the man in black, not Jessie's Florian—"

"Natalie's friend," said my mother. Mockery, and sympathy—both for Natalie—all at once. "The other one."

"The other one. I—" How I ran away from him. It, her, them. How I ran from Nick, when Nick only wanted to introduce us properly, to stop my being afraid. I was afraid now, but only of the effect of my own words. I pulled my hand free, reached down and put my arms around Nick once again; he let me hug him like he never let Naomi, shaking her off so politely but not caring if she cried. I drew strength from the feel of his fur and muscular barrel-chest and the cool, silent hollow where he should've had, where I knew he wouldn't have, a living beating heart.

"I love Stephen," I said. "But... the other one. Him. It. Even before Natalie, and the lab, before I ever killed anyone—I didn't know before I saw him, it, face to face, that that's what I was feeling, but what I think is that he's what I've been waiting for, my entire life."

I pressed my cheek to Nick's back. His tail thumped against my leg. He was all good strong flesh shielding the curve of his backbone, without his ever needing to eat. Goddammit, I sounded like Natalie. I sounded like Natalie and that wasn't what I'd meant at all, not *romance*, not Death as some fantasy boyfriend or daddy-figure or—at least I'd said it out loud.

I felt the touch of fingers against my hair, and when they persisted I finally looked up. My mother's face, her eyes, I couldn't read them for trying.

"So I guess now you think I really do want to kill myself," I said. "Or that I don't really care what happens to the world, or that I'm so guilty about what I did, I think I deserve—"

"No," she said. An emphatic shake of her head. "That's the thing, Amy, I know—I think—what you meant. You're here, alive, but you're not. You're in his world, its world, but also in ours. Your outside self, it's flesh and blood"—she glanced down at Nick, gave a brief quick touch to his nose—"but inside you, it feels all clean and empty, like a house that's been cleared out. Space. And the reason it's empty is because nothing actually needs to be there."

Maybe I'd said it better than I'd thought, after all. I was embarrassed all over again that she'd seen inside me, that anyone but Stephen, one of my fellow hollow men, had—but she was one too, my mother. Not knowing which world she belonged in—that was really why she'd run away. I pressed my forehead to Nick's side. Protect me. Help me, even as you condemn me, just like you were sent to me to do.

"Death," I said. Out loud. "It's what I've been waiting for, without knowing it, my whole life. Not to die. I don't want to die. But—to meet Death, to see it, him, face to face. Because he's in there, in the hollow spaces inside. He's part of me. Before I ever... before everything I did, he was part of me. A house, where everyone's moved out? That's good. That's what it's like. And this is like, I'm in the cellar of that empty house, and the plaster of the walls is starting to crumble so you can see just how much hollow space there always was in there, all along, and I'm on the steps next to some old jam jars and canned things nobody took with them, all caked with dust, probably not fit to eat... and he's in there. Living. He didn't cause the emptiness, he isn't filling it up—he's just part of it, and always was. He's just there. Telling me everything he knows, everything he keeps from everyone else until they die."

I sat up, still embracing Nick around the neck like he'd only tolerate from Naomi in short bursts. I hoped she never saw us like this, it'd make her sad. "And all the times before this," I said, "when I would go down the cellar stairs, I'd sense something was down there with me but I didn't want to see it, I was scared of it like a little kid, so I made sure only to look straight ahead, grab my jar of tomatoes or whatever, get back up the stairs fast as I could without turning back—but now, I look around. I wait. And then I see him, in the shadows. Living inside me. Just like that Florian said. Just like that. And he's, it's, they've been there all along. And—it fits. It's *right* that he's there. It's all right. And he's never going to leave, and that's all right too. Wherever I go, he'll be there and however long I live, and we're part and parcel of each other, forever."

Just like that Florian said. But it'd left him now, that's what else Florian said, that eternal unspoken presence had left him and he had no idea where it had gone or why it had faded away. What did it mean? Did it mean anything? Was Death just growing sick of us all—us so-called special children, the despised orphans like Natalie, every last one of us—and cutting us loose, going so far away we'd never hear from him again? Maybe that's what Stephen meant, when he talked about feeling blind: something that he'd grown so used to seeing from the corner of his eye he barely registered its presence anymore, suddenly really truly wasn't there. But without Death—without that place beyond this one, Death's own house—what was there waiting for any of us, if the living world was dying? If Florian's world was collapsing, disappearing?

Nothing, that's what. Nothing at all. And you couldn't fight nothing, no matter how much something you had. The biggest number in the universe, times zero, equaled... zero.

But that couldn't be true. The things I'd seen that I'd thought weren't there, turned out to be real and true. The things Florian and Stephen thought they *didn't* see—the things we all thought we didn't see, like Florian's old-man limbs suddenly not there anymore—they were surely hidden behind some ever-shifting blind spot to taunt us, remind us who was really in charge. That no matter what we did or where we went, he, it, was still in charge of what we saw of *him*. Of dead people, of the world of the dead. That wasn't the same as nothingness. The presence of Death inside me—still, this very second—that was the opposite of nothingness. That was the whole point. Maybe everything we thought we thought we could *see* wasn't there, was actually safe and sound and solid. Maybe that sensation we all felt and pretended we didn't, growing stronger and stronger as the hours crawled by—that slow, creeping, unshakable premonition of disaster—was all just in our own heads. Maybe it wasn't only Billy, but all of us who were delusional bugfuck crazy.

He wasn't just leaving all of us behind, like he had Natalie in his anger. Was he?

Was I really just giving up too soon?

High, angry squawking sounds broke out nearby, the whooshing flutter-flap of wings, then suddenly silence once more. Some territorial fight over an insect, a shiny pull-tab, a bit of dead flesh from right after the plague when the lake shores were clogged with bodies. My mother, who understood everything and didn't want to, laid her palm down flat in the sand and patted thoughtfully at the soft, crumbly little ridges until they collapsed. Patty cake.

"I think we need to leave," she said. "We should leave here, as soon as we can. I'll talk to Stephen myself if you don't want to."

I dug my own fingertips into the patted-down mound, rucking up ridges and furrows all over again. "This isn't about Stephen, and you know it."

"I don't like this. I don't like this at all, it—" She looked up at me with desperate eyes, the eyes of someone who needs an older, wiser, better person to confide everything because they're so weary of being that person to someone else, but they only have themselves. It must've been fun as hell, sometimes, having children. "Something's going to happen to you, I can feel it inside that if we stay here, something will happen to you. We have to leave."

"We can't leave now," I said. "Not with what's about to happen. What might be about to—do you think there's anything we can do? Do you think everything he warned us about is true? That anything Stephen said he saw was true?"

My mother laughed, threw a hand skyward. "Ask Nick, maybe? You've been seeing these kinds of things all along, haven't you?"

"But it doesn't make any sense. It still doesn't make any sense."

I thought of when I'd finally run away from Paradise, away from Billy and his pals and smack into the path of those men, those boys who had their fists and an armory of guns and one poor, piteous woman they were holding captive. Who they shot in front of me when she tried to run away—who needs her anyway, now we've got a new one—but before anything could happen, something that looked like that woman's ghost, but wasn't any paltry ghost, came back and killed them all. And spared me. Collapsing like a teetering tower of building blocks there where they stood in the street, chain reaction of instantaneous death, while he, she, it stood there and smiled and worked its will on all their bodies—I could feel a heaviness inside me as we spoke, a weight of waiting like the thick ponderousness of air right before rain. If he, it really wanted to destroy everything, why wait? Why hadn't he done it already, all at once? What was the point of being so elusive and scattershot, keeping everyone torturously on their toes? Either do it, or don't. Or maybe it was like I was starting to fear: we were all just collectively crazy.

I wasn't afraid of him. Apprehensive, yes. Confused. Impatient. But not afraid. Dying did that to you, maybe. I bet Jessie knew all about it.

"I don't know what's the truth," I said. I shoved my fingers hard into the sand, past the first knuckle, wincing as the wet grains drove themselves past the quick of my nails. "I don't know what to do, or what to think."

"Then I guess we're all in the same boat," Jessie said behind us.

SEVENTEEN

LUCY

As Jessie spoke, I caught the faint smell of ash from the morning's breakfast fires. We turned without rising and saw her standing with her hands shoved in her pockets—God knew how long she'd been there, listening, and it felt weirdly familiar—her snarl of auburn hair tangling itself into new shapes with the wind and her mouth set in a tight, tense line.

"There's lunch," she said. She wasn't the least bit conciliatory, just announcing what was so. "If you want it."

We shook our heads. She came up beside us, tilting her head so she was squinting straight into the veiled afternoon sunlight. "Breakfast, lunch, dinner," she said. "Like living little squares on the calendar you mark off to know you're through another day. And another, and another, and another. Except it never quits, does it? You never don't need to eat—well, we can't really starve ourselves, our kind, but hunger'd still drive us up a wall if we didn't eat. I had a calendar, Linc brought me one a while ago. But we couldn't figure out just where we were on it—Renee didn't know the date and Linc and I had good as forgotten how to use one, and all those empty squares on that empty paper going on and on and on, it depressed me. It was depressing as hell. So we used it for kindling. Like we could just tear out and burn up all these days that keep going and keep going and never, ever end."

She laughed, shaking her head. "It never felt like this, back when we were all properly dead. Even when we spent ninety percent of our time eating or hunting to eat. It never felt like this at all."

Her voice unspooled evenly and steadily, like the tape machine on some old cop show where the killer finally gives her confession. I had the strange, distinct feeling we were being offered some sort of apology.

"Time does drag, sometimes," I finally said. "That's the truth."

Nick pulled away from Amy, padding over to sniff at Jessie's feet. She petted him, smiling—her soft spot for animals was obvious, deer kill or no deer kill—and he planted his front paws on her calf, wagging his tail hard as her nails raked his head.

"Florian," she said, still giving Nick an energetic scratch. "He—I kept seeing him, dreaming about him, all through the plague, that's how I know I was delirious. He helped get me where I was going, but—" She laughed again, the sound verging on a snort. "You don't want to take much of what he says literally. I mean, he's never lied, I don't think he could lie to anyone if he wanted to—except Teresa, maybe, but Teresa was the most bone-stripped bitch who ever walked the planet so that hardly counts—but he gets to the truth in pretty roundabout ways. So all that talk of his, about... it doesn't necessarily mean what it sounded like he said." She patted Nick, who obligingly set his paws back on solid sand. "It could mean a thousand and one things you won't figure out and he won't *tell* you until you're really in the shit, feeling like you've got nothing to go on, and then suddenly the light will go on."

She turned to look toward the ridge, at the dry gray latticework of dead trees that had spread so far, so fast, it was like the ridge was a hem and the trees, the standing kindling, a long strip of dingy lace trim. She didn't believe what she was saying, I could see she didn't; it was just what she had to tell herself, she was so afraid of what it might mean if she were wrong. I knew the feeling. Amy, though, she didn't look the least afraid as she sat there, quiet, listening to Jessie ramble on. As usual, and even after everything she'd told me, I had no real idea just what Amy was thinking. What were we doing here? Why, even after everything that had happened, was it so hard to convince her to just get up and leave? I felt a selfish nostalgia for the days when she'd been Naomi-sized, or smaller, when I could just pick her up and *go* and ignore any fireworks and operatics. *Tonight*, I thought. *I'll talk to her again tonight.*

Even though I was starting to suspect that Jessie, much against her will, didn't really want us to leave, and that she couldn't have said why.

"Florian," Amy said. "Is he still... here?"

Jessie gave Nick another thoughtful pat. "He asked us to let him just go into the woods, all alone, while we went about our business. Leave him be. I don't think he wanted us to—we saw him die before, you know, back when we were all proper undeads. Maybe he thought it'd be déjà-vu all over again, if we saw the rest of him disintegrate. Haven't seen him since. But I'm still *feeling* him"—she thumped herself on the breastbone, so hard I winced—"in here, and then suddenly gone again, and then back so I think it's like he said, he just keeps fading in and out of the flesh. So I don't know where the fuck he is. But I feel like he's still... around. Billy keeps yelling at him like he's there, anyway. 'You rotten fucking coward! Stick around in this misery if you want but the rest of us ain't afraid to fucking die!'"

Her voice was such a perfect raspy, spitting imitation of Billy's that I felt an instant, involuntary unease. Amy, her jeans and my old civil defense jacket stained with great splotches of her own blood, stayed silent. Jessie shook her head, measured and slow, and as she scratched under Nick's chin, she laughed.

"You're so quiet *now*," she told him. "So quiet, and the air's so heavy. Does that mean something? You're not going to tell me what it means, are you?"

Nick rolled on his back in the sand, caught up in the canine ecstasy of petting, silent as the grave. She looked up at Amy, her eyes unyielding.

"What does it mean?" she asked.

Amy shook her head. "I don't know," she said, almost in a whisper. "And he doesn't say."

The air felt hot, suddenly, hot as July: an oppressive heat that bore down on our skin and lungs and eyelids in a way not at all like an approaching summer storm. I saw Renee and Linc hurrying down from the ridge, one blonde-haired stick figure and one black-haired, panting slightly as they ski-slid through the sands to reach us. Jessie went half-running up to meet them, panting too like the heaviness of the air was sapping her strength.

"What now?" she asked them. She sounded afraid. Just like all the rest of us were afraid. Amy wrapped her arms around herself, as if gathering strength from inside for the next big blow. Her breath, like mine, was starting to come in short, almost painful-sounding bursts.

Like a weight on your chest. That's what Florian had said of Death. *That you feel every time you breathe.*

"Nothing," Renee said. She looked harassed and strung out, like she'd been chasing for hours after an out-of-control toddler. "Just, we've got to do something about Billy. He's broken all the hunting snares, Linc's gardening tools—"

"And there he is!" Linc jerked his chin toward the top of the ridge, scowling in disgust. "Following us everywhere, like a goddamned—and we can't even stomp him."

"And he'd be thrilled if we could," Renee said.

There he was, with that peculiar side-to-side toddler's walk of his as he made his way down the sand: the thing that tried killing my daughter two times over. I stood up fast, cursing myself for not retrieving that hunting knife when I'd had the chance, and Jessie actually patted my arm. "There's no more fight left in him," she said. "Trust me, I can smell it on our kind—he's hollowed out inside. All he can do is rip snares and break flowerpots."

Why was I supposed to believe that, when just hours ago he'd been ready to gut Amy with his bare fists? And all the rest of us, for good measure? Amy was back on her feet too, both of us steeling ourselves for round two. The air, burning and leaden, was sore in my lungs. Billy's torn gray suit had sand caked in every fold and seam; dirt and twigs festooned his pale hair. His shoulders sagged, his hands dangled low, and he smiled at nothing, nobody, spots beyond all our sight, as tears leaked like some slow, perpetual fountain from the corners of his eyes. I could've felt such pity for him, for anyone who looked like this, if I hadn't known better. Nick came up beside Amy, poised and alert, as Billy came closer.

"Snares," he said, still grinning as he twisted his head to Linc, not bothering to wipe his eyes. "Little pointed sticks, trapping pits—you'll be fucking around with guns next, won't you, 'cause you can't kill nothing anymore with proper bare hands? Won't you?" He thrust his face into Renee's, disgust creasing his features. "You ain't real hunters anymore, not like we were. Didn't need any fucking *toys* to bring our meat down. So I broke all that shit, everything you shouldn't need. But it don't matter anyway." He grinned at Jessie now, barely noticing me or Amy, happy in the way a man broken by torture is happy to see the executioner. "Soon enough, none of us'll have anything left to hunt ever again."

"You gotta stop, Billy." Jessie was calm and quiet, running a hand along his arm and pretending not to notice how her touch made him shiver and twitch in disgust. "You gotta stop. I told you, fights happen and folks get stomped and that's our way too, you can't demand one part of it and cry over another one. Mags got stomped, farewell Mags. The rest of us gotta keep going."

"Going." Billy held the word in his mouth like it were strange and foreign, then grinned wider and peeled Jessie's fingers, one by one, off his arm. "Going and going and going and—hey! You two! The fucking mutant and the cry-babby hoo-calf that thinks it sees angels!" He was bellowing that at the ridge, where Lisa descended, Naomi slung heavily on her hip. "Come join us!

Come one, come all, you gotta see this new sideshow, the woman who shits from her mouth instead of her—"

Linc punched him, swiftly and casually like that was a long-understood shorthand of their speech, and Billy grunted and staggered backwards; he kept right on laughing, unfazed, and the salt water kept trickling down his cheeks. "We're leaving," I said to Amy. "We're taking Nick and leaving, tonight."

"He has to go," Lisa said, jerking her head toward Billy as Naomi rubbed her eyes, glaring down at him in cold childish contempt. "He was wandering right outside our windows, saying filthy things, while we were trying to sleep. Right after he got into Renee's cabin and tossed half of it into the woods. We can't have a living poltergeist wandering around the—"

"Did I ask him here?" Jessie demanded. She turned on her heel, glaring at Amy. "It's not us he followed here."

"It's you that're his people," I snapped. The air was like fingertips, pressing down hard and painful against my skin. "He's your family, whether you like it or not, so don't you start in on mine!"

"Billy," Linc said, appealing wearily for calm, "Jessie's right, there's too much going on right now for us to deal with your shit. We can't kill you, but we can blind you if you don't leave us be. You know we can." That gravelly, old man's voice was so incongruous, ominous, from such a young, thin throat. "You know we would."

The way he said it so offhandedly, the way Jessie and Renee barely reacted, it was clear he meant it. Amy made a sharp sound, stepped back like it was about to happen right there in front of us, but Billy just mopped his eyes on his sleeve and chortled into the cheap, shine-worn cloth. Naomi's eyes were wide with fright.

"You'd never do it," Billy told Linc. "Not when we were dead, not now, you *could* but you won't. I know you. Don't you forget I know you. You couldn't live with yourself, and living and living with ourselves is all we got left—ain't that the shit, Jessie?" He sneered at her, the sharp corners of his eyes and mouth drawn up in mean-spirited mirth, but somewhere in his expression was a flash of sympathy, a sudden hint of regard that almost shocked me. "I know it's fucking you up inside, all three of you, just like it is me. I can see it. I can see it in all your little *pastimes*—" The sneer was back again, a thick blunt shadow blotting out the light of any past feeling. "—in your precious gardening and your hoo-books and drawing pictures of each other because you can't just be here and now, part of everything like you were before, you just watch everything and report on it from behind a little screen. I tore 'em all up, y'know. All those drawings I found."

His reddened eyes almost twinkled with triumph, as he shoved his chin right in Jessie's face. "Tore every one of 'em up, made 'em rotten pulp-paper just like they oughta be, 'cause you and me, Jessie? What we really are, were, before your brother went and fucked us all up? We don't lurk and watch and tell tales from behind a fucking screen."

Jessie kept her composure—clearly, not without a struggle. Renee shoved Billy away from her, snarling as he laughed.

"Get out," she said. "Get out or I'll do it, instead of Linc, and I won't lose a second's sleep."

Billy threw his head back in actual glee. It was the best joke in the world. We were all the biggest fools in the world. "Guess what?" he said, when he'd recovered himself, reduced to a congested whisper. "Wanna know what? You ain't *got* a second's sleep to lose. You ain't got a minute to tear me blind. You ain't got an hour to celebrate afterwards. It's done. It's all done." He gazed around him at the water, the ridge, the trees and cabins above and the seagulls strutting merrily below, and shook his head in indulgent dismissal. "All this shit, all this nothing, it's going away. Everything, everywhere—"

"It's all coming to an end."

It was a soft, insinuating voice, speaking straight into my ear, making a ticklish twitch run down the side of my neck. Only Amy was close enough to whisper into my ear, but it wasn't her, it wasn't Billy, it wasn't any voice I recognized at all. It was the voice of a man who wasn't there. And everyone else around me, I could tell from their faces, was hearing it right when I did, right then. Jessie turned ashen.

"Jim," she whispered, and then her eyes cleared and she shook her head. Naomi bit her lip, stifling a whimper of fear. Nick put his ears back and whined, and then growled. Billy's eyes were squeezed shut and he was muttering something under his breath, something whose words I couldn't make out but the tone was loud and clear: a prayer, I thought, a prayer. Of hope.

"*Of course*," the voice continued, teasing and playful and merciless, "*that means everyone, and everything. Here, there and everywhere. Even I can't hope to escape it*." The air around us contracted, tightened, swollen unbearably heavy with the weight of his words. "*But what does that matter? What that exists—here, there or anywhere—doesn't ultimately dissolve into nothing?*"

Jessie was staring out toward the water. A noise left her throat and we all turned at once, we all saw him: a tiny, silhouetted figure, a man-shaped shadow out on the horizon, outlined inky dark against the pearlescent clouds. He walked toward us, over the lake, and every step he took from horizon to shore covered miles in a single moment. He, it, was a gray-haired man in jeans and workshirt, with a heavy rucksack slung over one shoulder; his face was so bland and ordinary you forgot it as soon as you saw it but his smile, his smile split his face open from ear to ear, like a cut throat. Like Amy's or Stephen's cut throats, never closed up. Never, in an eternity, could you ever forget that smile. He took another step, and was a translucent giant; he moved swift and calm over the face of the waters, and his form blotted out the clouds, the sun, the sky. You could lose yourself forever, in a single part of him: a patch of a shirtsleeve; a magnified bootlace; one great, lamplit, night-dark eye.

And I knew who it was. The second we'd heard his voice, seen this chosen face, we'd all known who he really was.

Nick howled to split the sky open, but it was too late. The sky was a gaping wound. We were swallowed. We were all consumed.

Death found the sands, and we were all caught up inside him. He passed through us and inside us as he set feet upon the earth, and all the world around us went darker than blindness.

Air. There's no air left. I can't breathe, I can't—the sun was just a shriveled wizened match barely holding a flicker of flame, then Death blew it out and it was gone. The clouds melted before us, moon and stars and every last light in the universe were laid bare before our eyes and then all snuffed out, all at once—or maybe they were still there and he'd just blinded us all once more, left us blinded and stumbling in an endless, asphyxiating darkness. There was no air left. My chest convulsed frantically, trying to draw in the oxygen that wasn't there, and I flung my arms out in the black and touched nothingness, no breath left to scream for Amy, Lisa, Stephen, anyone—

I was on my knees in the sand, gasping, agonized, almost sobbing in relief and terror because now I could breathe. I could just make out Amy crawling choking through the sand trying to reach me, I held out my arms—

Darkness, again. No air. No light. A great invisible switch was being flicked off, on, off on a whim, and as I sank down and slowly suffocated I could hear him, it, chatting with merry mirthfulness right into my ear. Right into all our ears. Death was such a very friendly man.

"Imagine aging," he said. He was genial as a traveling salesman, taking some marvelous new gadget from his briefcase. "As fast or slow as you wanted to."

The air was back. The light switched on. Through a haze I saw Linc and Jessie, hanging onto each other as they retched for breath. I saw thin rows of sticks propped in dry dust that had been trees, oaks and elms and ashes once in the full flower of spring, toppling and falling to the bare gray dust of ground. They crumbled to powder, more thin gray grit blowing away with what had been their underbrush, and then everything was dark once again.

"Think if they could bring you back," Death said. His voice was so full of wonder, he almost drew me in: yes, imagine that. Just imagine it. "Bring you back just like you were before you died. You could choose when you age, how you age. Choose when you die. Tomorrow, or a thousand years from now."

Natalie's words, back in the lab, when she dared and taunted Death to come and get us all. Then I was choking again, panicked for air, and her words died away in the darkness, a roar filling my ears like the buzzing of a thousand flies.

"Taking away what's rightfully mine," he whispered. "But then, haven't all of you on this miserable little patch of sand done that, whether you meant to or not? Haven't all of you snatched life back from my jaws? Death, the only master of everything that ever lived, for all of mankind's existence—but now? Now, he's to be humanity's servant."

A dry chuckle sounded from the blackness.

"Think again," he said.

I was hurled back into air and light like something had flung me there on my face, and maybe it had. Facedown in the sand, I clutched handfuls of it and gulped mouthfuls of air, tears running down my cheeks. Renee lay next to me, half-fainted; Lisa and Naomi were both quietly sobbing and where were the others, I couldn't find the others for—Amy. She was right next to me, she must have been right there all along. We grabbed each other's hands and held on agonizingly tight, determined that the next time, when we went back under, we wouldn't both drown alone. Our fingers were dead bones, dead tree roots, knotted round each other in rigor mortis, petrifaction.

The sands and stones still stood—for now—but there was nothing on the landscape, nothing anywhere, but the fallen kindling of dead trees; the sky, or what had been the sky, was gray, not the variegated gray of overcast and clouds but a thin dim paint-layer of nothingness, the farthest horizon of the land of the blind.

The lake basin was empty, its waters drained dry, and an endless, sunken desert stretched as far as we could see. We were too scared and weak to move, but we saw it, we all saw it: the basin sands stirring and moving, a thousand little earthquakes roiling the surface of the desert like undeads crawling up from a great mass grave. The sands didn't shift, though, the ground around them didn't break open; instead, they just floated up from beneath the lake basin, floated from underground like the ghosts they were.

The lake bed was full of people. The lake bed was a teaming city of specters, thousands of them, crowding shoulder to shoulder where they once might have drowned. As they jostled one another, shoved right and left for a better look at the ruined landscape, shouted and called and reached out their arms, it was another great roar and crash of lake waves, an enormous undertow come to pull us all away. Their inchoate voices were deafening, a great rushing sea of sound, and over it I could just barely make out another, more familiar cry.

"Come and get me!" Billy. As he stood there on the shore he was almost wailing, his arms stretched out in hope and expectation and a near-transcendent joy. "No more light, goddammit! No more!"

Waves of the dead were washing up from the lake bed like an invading army, pushing past us and through us to claim their kingdom: the earth, the blighted ruined beach and forest and roadside and city, all the land of the living Death had seized back for his own. But that was disappearing, too. Whole patches of denuded forest and blighted sand suddenly weren't *there* anymore at all, even as I looked straight at them, eaten instantaneously away like poor Florian's face and body. Not emptiness, but nothingness. We all saw it, Stephen started seeing it before any of us—why hadn't we *listened* to him, why? Why hadn't I defended him, stopped him from leaving, when I had the chance? Amy and I crouched where the waves had once landed, and we heard it: a deep, low, relentless growling. A sound like the rumble of the strongest summer thunder that makes you wait, tense with expectation, for the jump-from-your-bed crash.

"They're everywhere," she whispered to me, her face drawn and white. "Everywhere."

And they *were* everywhere, running from the lake basin, hot on dead humanity's heels; they spilled over the sand in countless shades of black fur and brown and white, their eyes sulfur-yellow and full of sharp, penetrating light. Nick's cousins, his grandparents, Death's thousand billion ghost-dog familiars. Their bodies were solid muscle, their faces were lean and feral, and all their teeth were long and gleaming and bared to rip the living apart.

EIGHTEEN

STEPHEN

The air and the light were gone, and back, and gone again. Breath rushed into my throat in spasms and then, just as swiftly, I asphyxiated all over again. The sky went out and the world was dark as blindness, then it came on harsh and punishing as surgical lights, unbearable fluorescence, over and over as I coughed and retched for air and thought, *Amy, Amy's mother, Naomi, I have to get out of here and find—*

I couldn't see. I couldn't see at all. There was a great groaning sound like the earth itself was splitting open from pain, and a crash I felt shuddering through my legs, my chest, as something huge hit the ground. I was on hands and knees, groping through the dark, and as I crawled, my palms that had been on solid dirt suddenly hit a void, a blank, my arms dangling over a great cliff into nothingness. And then they were gone. My hands were *gone*, just like Florian's, eaten up by the thing that ate up the ground and I shouted, dog-wild with panic, and no sound came out because I had no more throat. No more face. I couldn't see. I couldn't hear. Sense and thought themselves were fading away. I was that great ravenous blank. I was nothing, I was not-being, nonexistent—

"Oh, Jesus!" someone screamed, as light and air and physical form rushed back in. It was me. I was lying on the rickety porch slats, lying there with a throat that could make sounds of terror, arms and hands that could touch my restored face. Everywhere around me people were running in panic and the great oak tree in the middle of the square had crushed someone to death, falling on its side as if a huge tornado had uprooted it. They were trapped beneath the mass of the trunk until nothingness ate the whole tree away, and all I could see of them was an arm, small bit of a sleeve, stuck under tons of powdery gray deadwood that had been a full-flower tree minutes, seconds before.

Every inch of ground was bare, flaking, lifeless bark, twigs and broken branches strewn far as anyone could see. He'd come back, at long last, Natalie's Friendly Man was back. I'd never wanted to believe Amy when she talked about him, even after Nick went from hallucination to flesh, never wanted to even though I *knew* she told the truth. Death. Death had us all, he was crushing all living things to powder in the palm of his hand—

But Florian, that crazy old man who was supposed to be a ghost, he was being eaten up and spat out, too. His own world, Death's world, was torn down and blown away, too. And that meant our worst most horrible fear was true, and Death was devouring not just everything living, but *everything* everywhere—and then what became of Death? What became of anything, ever, at all?

A voice that wasn't mine let out a soft, derisive chuckle, right between my ears.

"*Death was alive once, too,*" it whispered. "*Didn't you know that? Didn't you understand? But everything ends, in the end. Everything. Ever. At all.*"

The world went out. My breath was stolen. I toppled and teetered like that tree as my legs disappeared from beneath me; then, just as I hit the porch boards, the world came back. No time to gasp and retch for oxygen, no time to—I crawled across the boards, crawled on my elbows like an amputee even though my legs had returned. Janey was struggling to get to her feet, poor fucked-up Janey quiet as death, while goddamned fucked-up Natalie thrashed in Janey's arms and wasted what breath she had screaming in panic.

"What do we do?" Natalie wrenched away from Janey, eyes wild, like Janey were something diseased. "*What do we do?*"

"Road," I managed, addressing Janey, while we all coughed and wheezed for more air. I pointed in the direction of the beach. "The others, Amy, her—"

"You can't do this!" Natalie kept screaming at nothing. At the nothing she'd helped bring on us all. "You can't!"

I shoved her away and grabbed Janey's hand. Janey would follow me where I told her to. I pulled us both off the porch in case the house was the next thing to collapse. Every yard and open space around us was gray and dead and empty, what had been grass coming away in clumps of dust and horrible blind-spot holes beneath our feet; we stumbled and hit the ground on our knees, sure we were next. Those others left living stumbled in circles, disoriented, no warning. I'd been warned, I'd been warned and nobody listened to me, or maybe they had and I'd been too busy not listening to Amy, to Florian, to Nick, too busy feeling sorry for myself to—

Tina staggered toward me, her hair wild with bits of twig, and she clutched us hugging and then pulled back like she knew where we were going. Russell lay on the dirt behind her, silent and still.

"Go," she said, no wasted breaths, "We'll—" She looked around her, touched the cross at her neck, crouched beside Russell to take him in her arms. "—take care of—"

"You can't leave me here." Natalie grabbed my sleeve, tugging. I wrenched my arm away so hard she staggered backward, but she wouldn't budge. "You can't, he'll kill me, you can't—"

"Look over there," Janey said. As mild and sweet as always. Just pointing out a fact. "Look what's coming."

The square and the road and the whole ruin of Cowleston, everywhere I could see, was filling with the faces of people who were there but weren't there. There was bewildered disorientation in their eyes, a terror mirroring that of the living, and around their legs there surged fur and teeth and claws and watery-luminous eyes. Wild packs of dogs, dozens or hundreds of them in one seething mass, there and not there all at once. Above the deafening barks and howls I heard Natalie scream and then a whole group of the living, crouched by the remains of the oak tree, were pulled in before they could make a sound. They were smothered, extinguished, in that mass of fur, and I watched as the dogs devoured them without ghostly teeth or claws leaving a single mark. They just collapsed, and melted like burnt camera film in great spreading spots of nothing, and were gone.

I grabbed Janey's hand and we were running, running across the town square and past the houses and back on the short, less than a mile, endless impassable road heading straight down to the beach. The dogs were breathing down our necks, a hot moist canine breath that was a clean chill illusion at the very same time, and then there was no sound but Natalie and some other voice crying out, panting to keep up as we ran with our hands linked pretending she wasn't even there. Then the world went dark again, and there was no sound at all.

We were down, Janey and me, still clutching hands there in the airless dark. Then the air rushed back into our lungs and we gasped, overwhelmed to the point of sickness, dug nails into each other's flesh, stumbled far as we could manage down the road before the horrible darkness decided to return. Natalie was still right behind us, squandering breath sobbing, shouting at someone else to keep up or go lie by the roadside and die, but no time to tell her to do the same thing, no breath, no time, no air, no light—

Hurdles. It was a game, an obstacle course, and each time I

went blind and a fist squeezed my chest until the breastbone could snap and break it was just a hurdle, a passable hurdle, less than a mile and I needed to find Amy, Naomi, Lucy. I needed to find them and I wouldn't leave Janey behind. I wasn't afraid. I couldn't be afraid. I'd died before, more times than heaven allows—but I'd never been nothing before, I'd never before disintegrated and simply never been. I couldn't be afraid.

Oxygen. Light. Not sunlight, though, just a bleak watery gray gleam like a blindness all its own. The sun, moon, clouds were gone. There was nothing left in the sky.

Janey dropped to her knees, gasping even harder, her breath seizing, trying to apologize as I pulled her back to her feet. The lights went out. Just as swiftly, they came back on. In that instant, the dense walls of trees lining our path had all fallen without a sound, acres of forest gone to dry crumbling piles of wood. Janey yanked at my arm, scrambling over a logger's cluster of dead maples, actual hurdles thrown across our path. Not a living thing was left anywhere, not in the sky nor on the ground. Not a single living thing but us, leaping the hurdles on our way to hell.

It was almost a mercy, a kindness, when the lights went back out.

"Not now," Janey whispered, leaning over me, shaking me so hard my teeth clicked together. "We're almost there. I can feel it. We have to keep going."

"Get up!" Natalie shouted. "You have to— "

I'd passed out. The light was back and the ghost-dogs were running at us from every direction, slit-eyed and growling like the guard dogs in the old days at the lab, and we felt and yet didn't feel their teeth snapping at our flesh. Natalie screamed. The old woman who'd come with her helped me back on my feet. We ran until the rawness seared our throats and lungs. Not enough air, never enough air, in the dark or in the light. I saw a landmark I remembered, road signage lying flat on the dead dusty ground, that told me we were getting closer, I forced back nausea to sprint ahead, pulling Janey with me as we barreled over another ruin of elms, running headlong and smack into—

I stood there, panting, poor Janey almost doubled over but her fingers still wrapped around mine, and the man I hadn't seen standing in our path gazed down at us both with a happy little smile. Pale hair, pale skin, sharp colorless eyes, thin twisting lips that mocked himself and us and all of existence. A rucksack with a large wet stain slung over one shoulder, and jeans smeared with mud, workboots smeared with blood. Natalie and her old woman were behind us, hiding, no shame—Natalie knew who he was. But of course, we all did.

"I guess you wish you'd listened," he told me, and I didn't hear his words so much as feel them somewhere inside me, insinuating themselves deep in my head. He, it, shook his head, laughing softly. "I bet they wish they'd listened to *you*. I bet you all wish you hadn't wanted to know what Nick saw that you didn't." He chuckled, a sound dry and dead as the ruined wood. "So easy to turn you against Nick, all of you against each other—because human beings never listen anyway, not ever. All mouth. No ears. Now, those are freaks of nature worth the study."

I knew him. My memory was eaten down to nothing by what happened at the lab but I knew him, I knew that face; he'd worked there and he'd probably died there and now Death stood there grinning at me with that face as his mask. Like he'd chosen it on purpose, to try and scare me further. Janey made a hissing sound, and I turned and saw her staring at him in clench-jawed rage like she knew that face too. Like she had reason to hate it too. Her free hand rose up like she was gripping a knife.

"Get out of our way," she whispered, soft and searingly sweet, Don's compliant crazy little pet gone away and vanished. Another mask, dropped. "Get out of our way right now."

"So you can *run* and rescue all your little loved ones!" His feet shuffled in the ruins, a near-dance of gloating delight. "Scamper after them, when you tossed them over the side like so much ballast the second you fought! It never gets old, you know, watching the lot of you run run *run* like scared little rabbits, trying to keep me from your best beloveds—run into burning buildings, run through intensive care units, run across battlefields and over oceans and into back bedrooms four dozen times a night and none of it ever does any good at all." His grin was wide and unnatural on that human mask of a face, but the death's-head smile beneath it felt like the most horribly natural thing in the world. "None of it. But you crazy kids, God bless ya, you make Daddy proud and just keep right on trying! Right up to the *very end*!"

Janey listened to him with her brow knotted up and then she frowned—a frown like confusion, like disapproval—and when she suddenly let go of my hand, I was scared. It was like she'd slipped far beyond me into that sea of fur and teeth and nothingness, even though she was right there, even though we stood just inches apart. She was squatting down, beside one of the ruined woodpiles that had been standing trees, taking a great heavy branch in her arms like her own beloved child.

"You be quiet," she whispered, and there was fury in her eyes: fury like a candle flame that looked so pale and flickering and frail as its taper melted away, but that weak sister, that little flame could burn down a whole building. "You get out of our way, or I'll make you get out—"

"Janey!" Natalie screamed it for me. "No!"

But Janey had the branch in her arms, a huge dead dragging branch weighted down by so many offshoots she had to lift it two-handed, and with a scream of exertion and anger she heaved it at him. It went airborne, that huge heavy thing, and hit him in the skull. Death flung his arms out, grabbing at the thickest part of the branch like a child clutching a new birthday present, and out of the mesh of sharp twigs that would've sliced up any human face, I heard him laugh in delight.

"You never stop!" he cried. "All of you just never, ever stop!"

He lifted the branch up, tossed it hand to hand like it were a great light piece of honeycomb, and with a force no human could ever have managed, flung it right back at Janey. I jumped in front of her, my own hands raised to take the blow, but it was too late, it had already happened, and I was dragging the mass of twigs and branch off her body as she lay there, unconscious, on the ground.

Something was leaking from Janey's chest, from the side of her head where the branch had split it open. As she lay there. Not unconscious. Dead.

I looked up at Death and he looked back at me. Candle-flame eyes just like Nick's, flickering guttering flames that consumed everything in their path. Behind us, Natalie and the old woman screamed and wailed and cried, but I could barely hear them; there was nobody else there just then but the two of us. Us and Janey, down at our feet, who didn't rise up again.

A buzzing sound filled the air around us, the sound of ten thousand flies. Janey's body bloomed in patches of blindness and blankness, invisible insects eagerly gnawing her into oblivion, and as I watched, one of her hands disappeared. A foot. Part of her startled, distorted face.

"Thieves," Death whispered. "Thieves, all of you, thinking that when it's time for me to have you, time to claim what's rightfully mine, you can just grab your lives right back." His hand snatched at the air between us, bare inches from my face. "No more. I would have let you live, I would've let your sad little excuse for a world keep spinning, if that one"—he gave Natalie a horrible smile, and Natalie cringed and wept—"if *that* one hadn't spat in my face, hadn't started stealing and thieving and boasting how she'd bested me all over again, just like those filthy little labs tried to before—but no more. You understand me? You should. You and your dear best beloveds, back at the beach, you're every bit the thieves she is, whether you know it or not!"

His voice grew louder and louder, rising in an exultant echo. "Humanity's had its chance, *life* has had its chance—now this is the end. No more life for you to steal, no more death for you to cheat, nowhere to go when your worthless day's done—no more anything!" He was almost howling in triumph, in joy. "Ever again!"

And then, he was gone. As if I'd dreamed him, the dream melting from my ruined memory seconds after I awoke. As if he'd never really been there at all.

Natalie sobbed in great panting gasps. The old woman was stone silent. Some of Janey's body was still there beneath the deadwood, bits and pieces of disjointed, doll-part flesh the flies of blindness hadn't yet devoured. I pulled the branch away, picked bits of twig from her pretty blonde hair that never did her any good, put a shoe that had slipped half off back on her remaining foot. Janey hated being barefoot. She'd have slept in shoes if Don let her. The whole ashen landscape around us, the invisible starving flies, time itself, seemed to stop for just a few moments, to let me to do this. Just like Death, that had so kindly stopped for us.

"I never exist for him," Natalie spat out. The words were hard and congested full of rage but she couldn't stop crying, so broken and crying. "I'm always there for him. He's never there for me. He's not having it! He can kill any of us he wants, it doesn't matter, he's never having it!"

Most of Janey's face was gone, but there was still one wide-open eye, a fish-eye lens staring pitilessly at the nothingness of the sky. I closed it. Untwisted the necklace that lay in the spot where her throat had once been, a thin gold chain that was one of the last of Don's gifts.

"I know how to defeat Death," Natalie said. If grief and slyness had a child, its birth-cries would sound like her voice. "I know how to fight him, and win. You hear me? And I'm not telling you! I'm never, ever telling any of you!"

Most of Janey's hair was still there, fanned over the dirt like a discarded wig. It was sticky on one side, sticky and stiff where her head had come open. I ignored that. I smoothed it down as well as I could, gave her lone eyelid a brotherly kiss. Godspeed, Tina would probably say. I had nothing to say.

"You're never going to find out." Natalie was right there beside me where I squatted by Janey's remains, when I pulled myself back on my feet. "You hear me? You are *never* finding out." Her eyes shied away from where Janey lay and stayed fixed on my face, tearful and scheming. "I'm making sure of that. I'm going to fight him, and win! Just me, nobody else! Because it's our fight, his and mine, and I'm going to win!"

I did something terrible, back when I was first alive. Before the lab got to me. Something so awful, even Natalie didn't want to repeat it. She'd seen the files. All my records, right there in the lab. I was a bad person. Maybe an outright terrible person, straight from the start. She said as much herself. So it didn't really matter if I did another terrible thing now.

"I won't tell you." Her voice dropped back down to a whisper. "No matter what, I'll make sure you never find out."

It wasn't like with Nick, this time. This time, I knew what I was looking at. I knew I wasn't defending myself, or anyone else. I knew just what I did, and I did it anyway.

My fists flew out and I struck her, again and again. The old woman screamed, tried to pull me off her, but I shook her off and kept hitting until Natalie fell to the ground like Janey had, until she didn't move. Then I turned my back on them both and went on down the road, hellhounds on my trail, the sky's light once more guttering and dying out.

NINETEEN

JESSIE

The sky, the woods, the beach, the lake, all of it was gone. Everything was gone but us, crouched together on a sweep of ash that had once been sand, and the swarms of human and canine ghosts thronging everywhere around us. Nick, Amy's dog, had been carried off somewhere without our seeing it, swallowed up. Florian was gone, somewhere in what had once been the woods, eaten away. Just like we'd all be soon. We lay there, gasping and thrashing like fish, and I pressed my cheek to the ash, cursing everything and everyone that ever lived, and thought, *Just get it over with, fucking get it over with and let all of us die, dissolve, disintegrate—*

I took in a deep wasteful breath, sure I'd never have the chance to let it out again, but when I opened my eyes we were all still there. Amy held Lucy, and Lisa held Naomi; Linc and Renee and I were a tangle of limbs whose ownership hardly mattered anymore. The dead surged all around us, teeming lost and crying in the drained lake bed; why weren't we among them? Why wasn't I one of them? What the hell was keeping all of us alive? Billy lay curled with his back to us, face in his hands, and when I grabbed his arm, he hissed, bared his teeth like the old days come back.

"Why am I still alive?" he shouted, wild with frustration, at me, the lake bed, the sky. "Why the fuck am I still *alive*? It's done! I'm here! Just fuckin' do it and take me back!"

The sky went black again and I was blind, deaf, limbless, yet sinking under my own weight. My lungs were wet tissue paper, falling to shreds, disintegrating—and then I was whole again, retching, my face buried in the ash. And something was stumbling toward us, something human, crawling the last few feet on hands and knees. Amy didn't have the oxygen to waste on shouting, but she mouthed something like *Stephen* and they were hugging ferociously, Lucy almost crying with relief. I heard barking by my ear and there was Nick, emerging from the sea of tooth and claw. He'd come back, snapping and snarling at the death teeming around us like he could actually make it stop. One last reunion, one small mercy, before the end. Stephen was sucking in air now like a kiddie gobbling candy, flinging words back out between every stolen breath.

"Everything," he gasped, his eyes urgent and wild like Nick's; Nick circled us all, barking, letting Naomi grab joyously at his fur like he never had when the world was whole. "That man, Florian, what he said—everything eaten up—it's all true. Everything everywhere. Natalie thinks she can beat Death. She's wrong. She's so wrong." He laughed, dog-eyed and wild with the sheer absurdity of it, and held hard to Amy like she could keep him from withering away. "He said—Death said—no more life, no death, no nothing—because of—what the lab did—and that we're thieves that stole from him, just like Natalie, we're all—"

The sky went out. We fell and fell together in the blind darkness, and then I was rolling with terrible gentleness down a long, steady chute: just like when I was sick, like when the plague ate us all alive and spat us back out as something else. No light. No substance. No nothing.

That used to be my home, my good home. Lightless. Peaceful.

Then I had another home, a home above ground but still with darkness to spare, with the heat of hunting, with all of our collective inward music reverberating through me, through all of us, as our life's blood. That was taken from me too. Death said I was a thief, like that little lab bitch? How was *I* the thief, me who'd had my death, my afterlife, my everything ripped from my own flesh, my eardrums torn open and ruined so eternity no longer sang inside me? When did we get back what the plague had stolen from us all?

"Help us!" Amy, or Lucy, was screaming, stolen breath rising in a sob. "Someone—"

Florian. Florian tried to warn us that what fed on him was coming for us, Death was a ravenous new rotter and all of us were deer... but he said no more life, *and* no more death. No more anything or anywhere. Death would feed on himself in the end, like the worst-afflicted humans in the plague, so ripped apart by famine they attacked themselves and consumed pieces of their very own flesh—

The air rushing back into my lungs seared and burned like lye. The emptiness and silence deeper inside, though, that had started long before this, and oxygen couldn't cure it, and it never, ever went away. The lab. Always, always the lab. We weren't goddamned thieves like them—they'd stolen everything from us! Everything!

"We hate them just as much as you do!" I screamed, certain Death heard me, just as certain he didn't give a damn. "Just as fucking much! And we can't undo anything they did!"

Something laughed, a thick deep noise hovering overhead like a cloud, and Naomi moaned in fear.

"*The hell you can't,*" a voice said, somewhere inside me far beyond my ears. "*The hell you haven't. If you didn't steal back what was mine, you wouldn't be sitting here right now.*"

The air was going again. The most horrible part was, it always came back—

The beachfront was black, brown, gold, white: the fur of the ghost-dogs that leapt for us, snapped furiously around our island of ash, their eyes a searing torchlight as blinding as the dark.

There was nowhere to run from them, no coaxing them into calm; they were feral, starving, and all of us who'd lived on and on when we shouldn't have were the rightful food they'd been deprived of. Their teeth snapped at what seemed like the empty air and our flesh was intact, unbleeding, but their teeth still somehow crunched down on our bones. Crunched right down to the marrow. Something was howling in agony and it was me, it was Linc and Renee and all of us. This was hell. This was—

Lisa's arms were empty and she wailed with a sound beyond herself because the dogs had Naomi, they were dragging her into their sea of fur to drown. Dead humans all around them stared, cried out like Lisa, wept. Naomi's thin little arms flapped, like a chicken's wings when it senses the axe—and then Nick was there, everywhere at once, teeth snapping out right and left against that devouring mass. Naomi fell heavily back to the ash, Lisa snatching her up sobbing, and Nick was surrounded on all sides by fur, teeth, eyes. Swept away. Drowned.

The dogs receded. They had food now.

"Nick," Naomi cried, her eyes squeezed closed. "Come back—"

"You came back!" Billy was screaming. He was on his feet, swaying like a tree praying to snap in a summer storm, eyes wide and white-rimmed in horrible ecstasy. "You're back, you came back, I always knew those fuckers couldn't keep you from coming back—"

Dead folk pressed in all around us, hundreds of them or maybe thousands, their faces full of confusion and hunger and terror. Mags was there among them, shoving through the throng with her hard eyes and hard smile, but she didn't see me, or Renee, or Linc. She didn't see anything but Billy, just like when she was alive and her living flesh sang out only for him. Billy was running now, stumbling over that tiny stretch of ground not seething with ghosts, and reaching her, he fell with a thud down to his knees. He collapsed then and there, crumpled up at her feet with his face still twisted, deranged with joy. He died. And Mags had her arms around his body, pulling him into the ash-dark sea, and then they both disintegrated, turned to nothing, and were gone.

The sound was all around us, rushing waves of dead voices too numerous, too scared, to shape proper words. They all shoved and pushed now, just like Mags. The dead, too, were frantic for space and breath, like a penned-up crowd of concert-goers ready to crush and stampede in panic. Someone wailed, close to my ear; I saw Lucy, Stephen, and Amy holding Lisa back by force, holding her back from a dead little ghost-girl not three feet away. Even if Lisa hadn't been screaming her name, I'd have known it: Karen. Lisa's Karen, the niece I'd never met, dead of leukemia before the plague ever started. Lisa thrashed and bit and fought to get to her. We held her back, shouting at her not to be such a fool, such a fucking fool, and then Karen's face sank back into the crowd and was lost.

Lisa tried to claw and bite at my face, but we all hung on, Renee lying across her to hold her down. Lisa pushed her own face into the ash, breathed it in, trying so hard to suffocate.

"Hold me back," Lucy said, and even her steady voice was trembling. "Hold me back, if I see Mike, my husband—hold me back—"

We reached out, all of us, and we lashed her to the mast. We clutched tighter still when a hollow-cheeked man rising from the swell made her shake and hold out her arms. She didn't fight us, though. Her head dropped, and her arms, and tears rolled down her cheeks. And then, just as quickly as he'd appeared, he was gone. She said his name again, under her breath, and sat next to Lisa as we released her, sinking down there on the ash.

Mags. I'd seen Mags but nobody else there waiting for me in the multitude of ghosts: no Sam, no Annie, no Joe. I couldn't have borne Joe. No mother. No father. No brother. Thank God, no brother. Amy stroked her mother's hair, staring at me over Lucy's head. Her eyes were wide and pale, like a terrified horse's just before the runaway coach plunges over a cliff, but everything else about her was so still and calm. Just like me.

"I kept... disappearing, on the way here," Stephen said, and shook with hysteria-edged laughter. "Just like Florian, losing his hands, his face—those dogs had no teeth in me, but it didn't matter. It didn't matter. There's nothing we can do."

"I didn't see him," Amy said. "My father. Mom, I know you saw him, but I didn't see anything where you were looking—"

"Because he's gone now." Stephen wasn't laughing anymore. His voice had dropped, gone quiet with the realization. "Because while you were looking, while both of you were looking, he suddenly didn't exist anymore."

And if he didn't exist, not anymore, wouldn't their last memories of him start to go next? And my memories of Florian, of Billy, of everyone else would start to go too, and everyone else's of me... and if our memory of each other was the only real world beyond this one, then not only would we no longer exist, we might as well never have lived at all. And it didn't matter, because there was nothing we could do. Lisa rocked silently back and forth where she sat, Naomi in her lap, with a face that told me she'd never forgive any of us this last betrayal, not ever. Naomi was mumbling something I couldn't hear, maybe a prayer. Lisa was far beyond that comfort.

The sounds of the dead rose louder and higher around us as we crouched in the diminishing eye of the storm. They were screaming now, like the sound of a tornado rising up, like dogs howling in useless aggression and pain. Their world was eaten up and gone, just like this one soon would be, and all they knew was that they were supposed to be somewhere that wasn't here but they couldn't go back, there was nowhere left to run. Their hands clawed at the ash, missing us by mere inches, and some of them actually cried with fright.

Enough of Death. Enough of his shit. I'd had some small, meager semblance of a life, here on Florian's beach, and Death took it away and he was taking the next life beyond away from Billy, Mags, all the rest of us, and I'd fucking had *enough*.

"Florian!" I screamed into the maelstrom, as if that could really summon him. But he didn't come. If he even existed anymore, to make that choice. If oblivion hadn't consumed what remained.

But *I* remained. All of us remained. This whole so-called den of thieves. And if we went looking for our slanderer, our tormentor—if we demanded some *actual answers*, once and for all—and our punishment was that we'd no longer exist... how the hell was that any different than this? I didn't even care anymore. Because I'd had enough.

"Stephen's right, isn't he?" a voice shouted, straight in my ear. "There isn't anything we can do."

I reached into my pocket, letting my fingers close around the hot little coal that was one of Florian's lake stones, from his first beloved beach. The one the hoos ruined with their fucking lab. I'd hurl that stone in Death's face, if I had a chance, while I still had an arm to throw it. He thought some sorry piss-ant little *scientists* were hot to fuck him up? Seriously? He had no idea. The stone vibrated in my hand. It sang. I could hear it, above the cacophony of the dead, deep in the emptiness inside me where once all our voices had echoed.

"There isn't," Amy repeated. I could feel her eyes on me. "Is there?"

I turned, and just stared at her. And then she laughed, a wild sound thrown in the face of the storm. In her hoocow face I saw my own thoughts, my own reckless anger and spinning bewilderment; a germ of certainty untwisted from a split seed inside me, shoving toward the sunlight, and I knew, I'd known all along, what I'd do. What *we'd* do. What I should've let Lisa just go ahead and do.

Why was the thought of oblivion, the thought of simply not existing in any way, any form, at all, so much more frightening than death *or* life? Maybe I'd just had too much of those last two, too many times, to feel any fear. Maybe that bitch Teresa had been right, in the old days, and my ego really was just that fucking huge. Maybe it was that it was one thing if it were only me, or anyone I loved—but everything everywhere never being and never really having been, never ever, was just too much to bear. But that would happen anyway, no matter what, if I did nothing. And there was one thing left I could do. That we could all do, right now.

The roar of death and the panicked lost grew higher, and louder. It didn't matter. The singing of the stone still drowned it out. I took Amy's hand, her hand that she'd slid from her mother's grasp. Lisa sat up straighter and stared at us, a dawning suspicion in her eyes. "What are you doing?" she demanded, and when neither of us answered, she was up on her feet. "What are you doing?!"

I laughed. I couldn't help it. "I'm sorry," I told her, shouting over the roar of the displaced dead. "I'm sorry I held you back—but you can't pull a Billy and just run off by yourself. We should all go together, when we go."

Lucy's mouth dropped open and she shook her head in disbelief. "No," she said. "Stop talking like that. Stop it right—"

"What else can we do?" Stephen asked. Now that it seemed we were finally bowing to the inevitable, all his fear, all his hilarity had vanished; he looked almost serene, like Sam from the old gang in his last hours of dying. "This is it." He kissed Amy, knelt down to kiss Naomi, gave Lucy and Lisa a solemn embrace. "Goodbye."

"This isn't how Tribulation's supposed to work," Naomi cried. "The angels didn't come! I said the Last Days prayer and they didn't come! Believers are supposed to *win*!"

Hang in there, kid, I thought, *it ain't over yet.* Even if Lisa was right about her whole weird-ass religion being even crazier than most. Linc kissed me. Renee kissed us both. Lisa hoisted Naomi up against her hip, long since ready, her eyes and mouth gone grim. Lucy was still shaking her head, like she could somehow talk us out of it. Like Stephen wasn't right, and there was nothing else we could do.

Like it wasn't clear to anyone with eyes that now that she had Amy back, no matter what happened, she'd follow her daughter to death and beyond.

"You're going to look for him," Renee said, her face drawn and pale. "Aren't you?"

"I should have listened to you," I told her. "When you asked me to do it before. I should've listened. But I was never was much good at listening."

"It won't work," Linc said. "Just like I told Renee, before. It won't."

"No. It probably won't." I shrugged. "*Nothing* left to lose."

"Amy!" Lucy was shouting. Panicked with the knowledge that she couldn't stop us, that she couldn't stop herself from following. "*No!*"

Too late. Time to all hang together, and my feet and Amy's were already swinging in midair. We walked forward, Lucy right along with all of us, into the endless ocean of the forever dead, and the undertow of their limbs and joints and formless disoriented terror pulled us out to sea, swept the eternal wave over our heads.

And so we drowned.

BOOK THREE

CASTLES MADE OF SAND

TWENTY
LUCY

Quiet. Everything was so still and quiet.

We were alone, together—Jessie and her friends, Lisa and Naomi, my daughter and Stephen and me—in a blighted wood on the edge of a lake whose horizon seemed to recede forever and ever into the distance. Bare, chalky gray ground, like soil destroyed by decades of drought, stretched in every direction; sparse handfuls of thin, unhealthy saplings broke it up, taking shallow root in the ruination of beach and forest. The last teeth left in an old man's mouth. The lake looked cold and gelatinous and still. Between the trees, in spots that seemed to shift and crawl away every time I tried to focus on them, blank spots of nothing nibbled slowly, quietly, relentlessly at everything they saw.

Were we dead? Was this all that was left of that other world, that afterlife Jessie's old grandfather-ghost had assured us was real and true? *Mike, my poor sweetie, do you hate me now because I followed these folks here, but not you? Because I put you here, some version of here, in the first place?*

But he hadn't hated me for putting him here, back when it was still what it was meant to be; I'd hated myself instead, because I hadn't understood, I hadn't seen. But now that I was standing here in this monstrosity of blight I knew, without having to be told, that these empty, miserable remnants were the wreck of something once unfathomably beautiful. The terrible, overpowering once-was-ness of it all hit me so abruptly, so brutally, that I nearly doubled over; my body cried out for the loss of a limb I only now knew had been severed, my insides contracting with a sadness that could never be assuaged. Because it meant that something, the something that contained *everything*, was going. Gone.

Was this what it felt like, to be Jessie and her friends? Was this what it had meant, to have been a true part of Death and his—its—endless unknowable world, and then to be thrown by force, by the plague, by the lab's arrogant incompetent gameplaying, back into dreary, ignorant, eternally purposeless life? I hadn't known. However many times the lab made me die, I guess I'd never been dead long enough to be here, to have *this*. I wept, suddenly and silently, at the thought of it, the knowledge of just how badly and how often we'd all been cheated, and I wasn't the only one wiping my eyes. Next to me, Naomi stared around her in disbelief and then, like the rest of us, started to cry.

"If this is heaven," she whimpered, "I don't *like* it."

Renee and Linc turned slowly round and round where they stood, blinking back their own tears and craning their necks in a way that, another time and place, might've almost been comic. Stephen squatted down, taking a cautious pinch of dirt in his fingertips, then let it trickle away.

"I keep feeling like I hear something," he said, not rising to his feet. Leaning back on his haunches, his dark hair a shaggy tangled mess, one ear unconsciously tilted in the direction of some elusive unknown sound, he suddenly put me so much and so strongly in mind of Nick that I almost jumped to see it. "But there's nothing. Is there?"

I knew what he meant. There was a ringing in my ears and the feeling of something lurking just unseen in the corner of my eye, something that would vanish anew every time I turned to try and see it full face. Just like those spots of nothingness, eating up the world. Jessie, gazing out at the immobile lake with a hand shielding her eyes—even though there was no sun—snorted at his words.

"I think I know exactly what you're hearing," she said. She dropped her arm and reached that hand into her pocket, as if reassuring herself something was still there, and then, satisfied, turned back to the lake. "No worry."

Lisa knelt down beside Naomi, hugging her, murmuring reassurance. It wasn't helping. "So maybe you could tell the rest of us?" she demanded, hoarse and worn down by sorrow.

Jessie didn't answer. Amy, standing beside Linc with her arms wrapped tight around her middle, shook her head, as if settling some sort of private argument with herself, but she didn't speak either. Something, if only the instinct of having lived with my own daughter all—most of—her life, told me she knew what we were hearing too.

"I want to leave," Naomi said. Then, louder, "I want to go home! I don't like it here! Miss Jessie, figure out how to take us back home!"

"Miss" Jessie, "Miss" Lucy—they'd trained them that way at that strange little church of hers, the kids, to be preternaturally polite to any adult they saw. *Excuse me, ma'am*, a trio of them had nervously asked me back when Amy was still a toddler, when they found me behind the house weeding the tomato patch, *but may we please cut across your yard? We want to get to the park but we're not supposed to cross Lombard Avenue, there's too many trucks*. Yes, of course they could. They scuttled swiftly across and away, treading on as tiny a scrap of grass as they could manage, and a few days later—I couldn't believe it—I got a *thank-you note*. It read like a parent had dictated it, but still. I was almost relieved when I discovered one of them, in the great migration, had grabbed a clumsy fistful of raspberries off the canes I'd planted near the easement: not all the alien seed pods under their beds had opened up. Still, they didn't beat the shit out of their kids like some of the Baptists did, so there was that.

They were right after all, Naomi's strange little church. Didn't they always say that the dead would return in the flesh to the living world, just like Jesus had allegedly walked from the tomb, and lead us all bodily to some great judgment? That the trees, the rocks, the whole world would rise up and sing when that happened, and their song would start as a great endless wail of Tribulation? That's what it said, anyway, in the church pamphlet one of those kids "accidentally" dropped in my yard. And, more or less, they'd been right. What a happy mistake.

Jessie glanced over at Naomi, at all the rest of us. Her expression said it all: we weren't her concern right now, we never had been. We were all just along for the ride. She didn't look half as sad as I felt, but that didn't fool me. She and her friends were merely resigned by necessity to what for me, for all the rest of us, was an acid-bath shock of grief.

"What are we hearing?" Lisa repeated. More quietly, but with an edge presaging anger. "Tell us."

Jessie dropped down onto the shore, cross-legged, her back curved like she were shielding something cherished in her empty lap. "I don't know."

"You just said—"

"Because," Jessie said, "it *could* be what I want it to be, what I keep thinking I hear. It could be this." She slipped her hand back in her pocket and retrieved a flat dull-colored stone, one of the dozens scattered over every sand dune on every part of the Lake Michigan shore. She held it up, as if it were significant somehow, then put it away. "Or, it could be the sound of everything coming apart."

That ringing in our ears, a buzzing that rose and fell like the sound of great swarms of faraway flies, but sometimes when it fell there were seconds, endless seconds, of a silence so great it went beyond mere deafness. Just like those blank spots were no ordinary blindness. That was what she meant, and none of us needed it better explained. Stephen, on seeing the stone, rose slowly to his feet.

"What does that mean?" he demanded. "Does it mean something? Back at Cowleston, Natalie had some, and then they split open—"

"They did?" Jessie turned sharply toward him, not trying to hide her surprise. "When? What happened?"

Stephen shrugged. "Right before... all of this, before all it started. Just before. She was holding them in her hand, and then it was like they'd grown hot, like they burned her, and then they split open right in her hand and this sort of sand came out—was it a trick? Did it mean something?" He stood over Jessie, as if waiting for her to produce the stone from her pocket again, but she didn't. His eyes were swollen and puffy, ringed with exhausted shadows. "Tina got angry when she saw it, she thought it was some kind of ugly joke—but I don't get the punchline. What did it mean that that happened?"

Hearing that, Jessie suddenly looked as sad and lost and confused as all the rest of us.

"I never knew," she said. "I never really figured that out, except... that sometimes, somehow, it made some things better. Fixed some things, maybe. Cured them." She laughed, a tubercular spitting sound. "But it sure as hell isn't fixing this."

Stephen sat down next to Jessie and he looked so overwhelmed I could've hugged him, but he wasn't that sort and except with Amy, neither was I. Linc and Renee exchanged glances, looking like parents suddenly saddled with the care of someone else's children, and it was a relief to want to laugh. Silence interrupted the ringing in my ears once again, an ominous split second, and Naomi rubbed fretfully at her own ear as though it hurt.

"I want to go home," she whimpered. "I don't like it here, I want—"

"Used to be a hell of a lot nicer than this," another voice said. "But I can tell I don't have to tell ya that."

From somewhere between the blank spaces, he'd emerged: Florian, walking toward us with pale blue eyes full of kindness and melancholy. Amy, Stephen, and Jessie drew in sharp breaths of surprise, and before Lisa could stop her, Naomi ran to him and, sobbing, flung her arms around his legs. Florian smiled at her, then reached down and gently unhooked her grasp.

"Easy now," he said. "I can't say if I'm here or there or am or ain't any given second, and if I go again, I don't wanna drag you with me—"

"I want to go with you!" Naomi cried, and sobbed harder. "I want to get out of here, you can take us out, I want to go home—"

"Child," Florian said softly, "when I ain't here, I ain't nowhere, and I ain't never been. And every time I end up nowhere, I leave part of myself I can't ever get back, and… you don't want that. That's what you're tryin' to fix, bein' here in the first place, ain't it?" He patted her on the head, gingerly, as though he feared his touch were diseased. "So you gotta stay and try, like it or not. You gotta stay and try, for as long as what's left of this place stands—Lord, pets, I never thought I'd find you again, I'd just be eaten up for good and that'd be that, but I never was gladder to be wrong. Never gladder."

When he looked at the rest of us, his smile faded and his shoulders sagged and he looked like the sad old man he must once have been, the gaunt skeletal undead thing Jessie had once loved like a grandfather. He gazed up at the ruin of the sky, back down at the ruin of the ground, his eyes shining full and bleak like he were too far gone to weep. Renee and Linc, ignoring his hesitation, went and took his hands; Jessie stayed where she was, but nodded like she understood him better than any of us. And, of course, she did. Stephen took a few steps toward him, then faltered and stopped in his tracks.

"So this really is it," he asked Florian, "it's where you go when you die?" He kicked at the ground, releasing a small ashen puff of dry dust. "I've died a lot, I mean, more than most people. I don't remember anything like this... I mean, like what it must've been. Once."

"Neither do I," I said. Of course, I didn't remember any of it, at all. A side effect that always suited the lab right down to the ground.

"You weren't dead long enough, any a'them times, to see

this," Florian said. "Just like us, when we were proper undeads—we didn't hang around the grave long enough to cross over to this side. If we had, we'd never have been able to come back."

And never have wanted to. He didn't need to add that part, we were all thinking it. We'd all been so badly cheated.

"So we're meant to be stuck here," Amy said, "forever." She trembled suddenly, contemplating it, and I went and put an arm around her. "Except that like you said, everything's falling down—"

"—and so things that should be here, ain't." Florian rested a sunken, hollow cheek against Renee's blonde hair, just for a second, then raised his head again. "And things that *ain't* meant to be here—well, here I am, talkin' to you."

A strange look crossed Amy's face, like she wanted to argue with that, but she didn't answer.

"Those stones," Stephen demanded. "What are they? Do they do something... magic?"

"Never knew," Florian said. "Never rightly knew. All I know is that when I had 'em with me, in my pocket, I felt worlds better—"

"They helped us," Renee said. "Me and Linc and Lisa—and Jessie—during the plague. Just having them seemed to help. I'm not sure how. But they did."

"But they're not helping any of this," Stephen pointed out. "Just like Jessie said."

Florian shrugged. "And they didn't stop my dyin' either. So like I said, I can't rightly explain 'em."

He flickered and faded, standing there before us, like a reel of film running out and emptying off the spool. His face twisted in alarm and he flung his arms up, like he could somehow push away the great furious force bearing down to devour him, and then where he had stood was a man-shaped blind spot as painful to the eye as a sudden flood of fluorescent light. I blinked hard, saw Amy and Stephen involuntarily jerk their heads away, and when we recovered ourselves, he was there again but not there, all at once. The fear on his face was more frightening than any of the desolation around us, and the sight of it made fresh tears run down Naomi's cheeks.

"It's all going," Florian said. The outline of his white head, his black clothes, had melted together and faded; his voice wavered, echoed, and we had to strain to hear him. "No afterwards. No memories. No consciousness. Nothing. Everything that is, was, ever would be, vanished forever in a—"

And where he had stood, there was nothing. Nothingness. And no sound either, but the soft monotonous buzz of a thousand unseen, starving flies.

Lisa and Naomi were both crying again, almost decorously silent as their faces went wet. The fly-buzzing tickled my ears, my insides like a maddening little itch, and I felt myself twitching in the effort to dispel it. Linc shuddered with the sensation, gritting his teeth. Jessie, though, she was calm and still, her eyes darting from the stagnant lake to the dead flat land and back again as if trying to decide something. Then she glanced at the not-there spot where Florian had been, where now the ashen ground and sky had almost vanished in turn, and squinted with the effort to focus on it. Then she smiled.

"Later days, Florian," she said.

Then, without hesitation, she walked down the shoreline and straight into the pewter slick of water. Lisa, Linc, and Renee stared in disbelief, then started running.

"What the hell are you doing?!" Lisa shouted. "How can—"

"Fuck, it's cold!" Jessie shouted back. She was in it now up to her knees, the water not flowing aside in her wake but forming tiny hillocks, thick and solid, as if her legs were a shovel pushing through mud. She halted and turned to us, motioning impatiently. "Come on!" We didn't move. "For God's sake—what're you afraid of?" She started to laugh. "That we'll drown and die? *Here*? Seriously?"

Lisa looked embarrassed and defiant and bewildered all at once. "*Yes*!"

Jessie shook her head in disgust, kept pushing forward. She was up to her thighs. "The woods are eaten up," she pointed out. "Like the termites got to a house so bad, the walls are about to go. But we can still see the whole lake, can't we? See?" Her hand swept the air, reaching toward the horizon that kept receding faster every second. "There's still something here. There's still something that *exists* here, and it's not fading away, so I'm going toward it. Only an idiot would go where there's nothing, so you all be fucking idiots if you want, but I'm going."

"Going where?" Linc shouted. He looked less frightened than the rest of us—if only because love can make you trust the good judgment of someone who's clearly out of their mind—but every bit as confused. "You seriously think you can find—"

"Him? It? Yes!"

"And what?" Renee demanded. "Talk him out of it? How the hell are you going to do that?"

"So why'd you come with me, if you didn't even want to try?"

Jessie was in up to her waist now, the water—the mud, the mire—not splashing but oozing as she turned toward us once more. She wasn't shivering, didn't look cold, but then her kind, the exes, were nearly impervious to the elements; what would happen to one of us, in that expanse? Would we be pulled under immediately, suffocate before we could be eaten up? She was laughing, at us or herself or the absurdity of it all I couldn't say, but the edge of recklessness, of desperation, in her voice shouldn't have been perversely reassuring. But it was. All of us, in over our heads.

"I did it before," she said. "Talked him out of... some shit he wanted to do, sort of. Maybe. It's hard to explain. But I did it, anyway. I didn't just give him everything he wanted. I didn't just give in!" She was up to her chest. "So are you coming, or not?"

Slowly, Amy walked up to the very edge of the shore. I didn't try to stop her. I couldn't move. She was shaking. "What if we drown?" she called.

Jessie shrugged. "Didn't you say you already did? Before? So if it happens, it won't be anything new."

She ducked underwater, and didn't emerge. Lisa let out an awful sound, and as she was rushing toward the water with Naomi at her heels, Jessie's head and shoulders rose above the surface. She took a long breath, then another, and I noticed that her hair, her clothes, were still dry.

"We won't drown," she said. "Not right off, anyway."

Renee's lips twitched, like she was long since used to this kind of thing from Jessie. She probably was. "What's it like out there, soldier?"

"Cold," said Jessie. "Freezing." She cupped her hand, took a handful of the liquid around her, then opened her fingers to let it trickle away. It hit the lake surface in slow, fat clumps. "But it's still *here*."

Amy went in past the shoreline, up to her ankles. I didn't try to stop her. The lake lapped around her shoes and she started shivering, so violently that one of her feet jerked back toward the shore, but she put it firmly back down in the current and stayed where she was, and the horrible chill must have passed. Stephen waded in next to her, taking her hand, and also flinched with cold, and also recovered himself. Linc and Renee followed, wading in right up to their knees without any apparent shock.

"I think you're kidding yourself," Stephen told Jessie. "I don't think we'll ever find him. Not this time."

"Because you would know," Jessie said.

"Look, he's already said his piece. We all heard him." Stephen lifted up a leg, slow and careful, like he worried the droplets surrounding it might be little weights to drag it under. "He even said to me, he said, 'Death was alive once too.' He said that. So if this is all... Death deciding to die, somehow, to not be anymore, what the hell are we supposed to do about that? Why would he ever want to be found? He'll just hide until we're not there anymore to seek."

"So sit there and cry some more. Why do I care?" Jessie tilted her chin back, gazing overhead, then squinted and winced and dropped her eyes. "But it's the only thing left to do, and we're here, and the trees behind you are mostly gone and now the sky's starting to disappear. So either we at least try for the last word, or..." She folded her arms across her chest, elbows poking up from the lake surface as her hands disappeared beneath it. "Or nothing."

I looked up into the sky, like Jessie had, and what I saw—or rather, what I didn't and couldn't see at all—made me shudder and look away. Amy was in up to her knees, Stephen letting her lead him in turn. Linc and Renee were already two more bobbing heads in a dry, formless, iron-colored sea.

I took a deep breath, and a running start, and waded in behind them. The cold filled my mouth and lungs with fistfuls of crushed ice, and I almost screamed at the shock of it, and the strange silken weight of whatever I'd walked into made nasty little prickles break out all over my skin, but then it passed. With astonishing speed, it passed. Lisa was still on the shoreline, Naomi standing beside her.

"Well," I said, feeling incredibly foolish. "Goodbye."

I was already in up to my waist when I heard two more shouts of pained surprise, a woman's and a child's, then silence as we all pushed forward. I was afraid to look back, afraid even to listen lest it be Naomi crying out in distress and Lisa shouting for help we couldn't give, but the soft, thudding swish of whatever it was that surrounded us, pulsating with a strange quiet tide all its own, was the only sound anywhere around us. The fly-buzzing noise that had maddened me back on the ashen ground, down my back and in my ears and everywhere inside my head, had disappeared. There was nothing to do but go forward, Jessie's unkempt auburn head and Renee's sleek blonde one our only beacons, our path leading us deeper and deeper in, and yet we never lost the feel of a lake bed beneath our feet. None of us, not even Naomi, went fully under. I kept my eyes on Amy, just a few yards ahead of me, unable otherwise to trust she was still really there.

For a second—just a split second—as I followed her, my vision blurred and there seemed to be nothing in front of me, no Amy, no nothing. But as soon as it came, it was gone. I blinked and gave my head a vigorous shake, in pure relief that it had passed—and for just a split second, when I looked a few yards ahead of me, I realized I didn't know who I was looking at anymore. That person with the auburn hair and the ripped-up, too-big navy blue jacket hanging off her shoulders, the girl with the dark-haired boy briefly pressing his cheek to the top of her head, I had no idea who she was or what she was to me or why we were both together, in this strange little expedition whose purpose I no longer knew.

But as soon as it came, it was gone, and I followed without hesitation where Amy led. Amy, and the others whose names I now couldn't quite remember.

TWENTY-ONE

AMY

Drowning the second time, it wasn't like the first. I had been all alone before, when Natalie killed me and I slipped into death, my fingers fanning out like coral fronds as I sought rescue and touching only the emptiness of water. But we'd all held hands this time and Stephen's fingers, as we waded, were like seaweed, those thick pliable greenmeat clumps I'd bitten into and made my mother laugh, all those years ago when we visited the ocean; they wrapped around my own fingers and tugged hard, keeping me upright, helping me stand instead of lie on the bottom of that heavy, freezing, bone-dry lake.

We were in up to our necks, all of us, the currents of what wasn't water or ice or fog or any substance I recognized now no longer fighting against our steps, but acting as cold fingertips to push us forward, gently but relentlessly forward. Forward to what? There'd been a horizon, of sorts, a long thin pencil-mark just barely separating the dull tin color of the lake from what remained of the sky, but it had disappeared entirely once all of us had stepped offshore. I counted heads swiftly and we were all there, all pushing our way through, everyone else's mouths firm with concentration and their eyes fixed straight ahead; our limbs made soft swishing thuds, the sound of oars dipping into and drawing aside actual water, but otherwise, all was silent.

None of this bothered me, I suddenly realized: not the astonishing vastness of this place, not its silence, not its strangeness or its plasticity or its all-encompassing cold. I wasn't afraid. I was just doing my best to get the lay of the land, for as long as that land might last.

But how could we possibly find what Jessie wanted—find *him*, who clearly didn't want to be found? Not ever again? And what would we do if we did?

Did it matter? At least, did it matter to me?

Part of me, I realized, just appreciated being here. Part of me was just glad I'd had a chance to see what lay beyond life, to *know*, even seeing it in such decay and neglect and willful spreading rot. Even knowing that soon, no matter what we said or thought or did, it and me and everything else wouldn't exist anymore—

Forward. It didn't matter what I wanted, not after everything I'd seen before we slipped away—we *had* to keep moving forward, pushing ahead, trying to find him who had no intention of being found. We had to. On the nothing-to-nonexistent chance that we might bring back what had already been devoured, that we might save all this, that we might soothe away the terror of thinking that in the end, the very end, we all amounted to nothing. Forward. I closed my eyes, renewed my hold on Stephen's hand, and gave each leg stern, implacable orders. Left. And right. And left again. Rinse. Repeat.

And it was then that I realized it was this world, the one we traversed now, that was the one that I truly wanted to save. An overpowering sensation was coursing slowly, relentlessly through me, like the currents of that strange lake, like the quiet pulse of my own blood, and as I gazed all around me at the half-eaten sky and the ruined shore and the ceaseless rush of un-waters, that sensation just kept getting stronger, seeking out every hollow space inside of me to fill to overflowing.

It was love. I loved this place, this awful unimaginable place, and it was for *that* that I went forward: I loved it, and I couldn't stand to lose it.

This place. Not the one we had left behind.

The lake that had us up to our necks suddenly rose, higher and higher, and one by one we were all pulled under. Naomi and Lisa vanished first, not even a chance to cry out, and then Jessie and her friends, and then my mother. When Stephen and I went under and the freezing gray seemed to stop my eyes and ears and mouth, I felt no fear, no urge to fight for breath; somewhere, in those desperately loving spaces inside me, I knew what had happened. Somehow, not knowing how, we had found the other shore.

"Look!" Naomi shouted, not in fear or pain but almost with delight, as if she'd just seen something she'd never again expected in her lifetime. "Look! Is it for us? Can we watch?"

We were all together, dry and breathing, in a room that was dark and quiet and had a strange but familiar smell: a sort of waxen rancidity like something pretending to be butter gone bad, mustiness of old cloth and close air, oversweet fruitiness like spilled soda. Mouse droppings. There were chairs all around us, their vinyl seats worn thin and sometimes split open, oozing cushion foam; we were in an aisle, a thin-carpeted aisle with tiny guide-lights glowing red along the border. Dormant little beetles, with luminescent shells. Up ahead, a rectangle like a windowshade except too big and laid the wrong away across. Silvery-white, and blank.

Naomi was already running for a seat, settling in for a show that might never start. Lisa followed her with slow, cautious steps, hanging onto the tops of the seats for guidance down the aisle like a far older woman afraid of falling; her face, in the screen's dim light, looked creased with confusion, as if she couldn't quite remember who this little girl was, calling to her, or why it should matter, but knew she was meant to be dutiful to her, supposed to follow. Like a far older woman, whose memory was slipping her mind's harness and cantering away. As she passed me, she stopped and turned.

"Do you know that little girl?" she asked me, in a fearful whisper.

My stomach dropped and kept on falling. The eaten-up sky. Florian's ruined face. My poor Nick, who wild foolish hope had made me sure would be waiting there, here, somewhere to guide us through. And now our minds, our memories—it wasn't fair, it wasn't *fair*. I loved this place. I loved it. How could he—it—let it betray us, feed on us and itself and everything else, without even giving us a chance? My mother came up the aisle, her hand almost timidly touching my shoulder. I turned urgently toward her and saw Lisa's same expression, and my heart stopped. I made myself smile anyway, the corners of my mouth pushing up and out with the same force of effort I'd used fighting through the lake.

"Go find us a seat," I whispered, before she could ask who I was and make me cry.

She nodded back, knowingly, like she still understood that in such places as this we were both meant to sit together. She still knew that much. She drifted silently into the nearest row of seats, Stephen following suit, and they both stared straight ahead at the blank rectangle of screen, just like they'd stared right before them on our trip to this shore. In the front row, I saw one blonde head, one black one, that had already seated themselves, and in the aisle, Jessie still standing there next to me looking as stricken as I felt.

"I guess it was inevitable," she said, her voice so casual and calm but betrayed by the barest tremor. "I mean, you can't remember what doesn't exist—and even if it does exist, when you're coming apart yourself, naturally your brain starts going to shit. Eaten up."

"We still remember Florian," I said. "And Billy, he got eaten up too, right in front of us, but I still— ”

“And I still remember what Florian said, about how it didn't just happen all at once but parts of him kept getting ripped away. Little by little. He's eaten up, all right. I guess it's just that he's not yet... digested.”

I shuddered. Her, she just looked happy to have figured something out about all this.

All we were to each other, eaten up, just like a hand or foot or face at the worst of the plague. So stupidly, I'd thought nothing could be worse than that. Lisa sat a few seats away from Naomi, never glancing at her, the blank screen commanding all her attention—I should have been ready, I should have *known*, but I wasn't, I wasn't. He was probably laughing at me right now, laughing at us all. Naomi didn't seem to notice Lisa's indifference, if she even knew who Lisa was anymore. Stephen, my mother, they didn't call to me to come sit down. They didn't turn around.

“But with everyone else forgetting,” I asked Jessie, “how do you and I still know each other? And ourselves?”

She shrugged. “Give it time,” she said.

There was a faint click and whirring and we both turned around, staring up, but there was no little square of light at the back of the theater, no projection booth.

“I loved movie theaters,” I said. “I wanted to just stay in one forever, after everything became so awful.”

“So why didn't you?” she asked. She frowned at the movie screen, at the dilapidated seats, like I had done this to us on purpose. “It sounds better than that place Lisa said you both got stuck in, Heavenly Acres or— ”

“After I killed someone, I wasn't thinking straight,” I said. “I had to leave in a hurry.”

It was so easy to say that here, it slipped out like nothing; probably because there were no secrets here, I knew that from the first time. I drowned and sank to the very bottom and the memory of Ms. Acosta was right there, waiting for me, both times.

But now, nothing. Where was Nick? I'd been so stupidly

certain I'd see him, so cocksure, and he would have known me, nothing and nobody could've kept him from knowing me. But Nick didn't exist anymore. And when Jessie finally forgot me, and I her, neither of us would either.

Jessie thought over what I'd said. "I've killed plenty of someones," she said. "I didn't act like that."

"You haven't killed as many as you say," I said. Because I knew she hadn't, because there were no secrets here. She glared at me.

"One's more than enough," she said. "You should know."

The screen flickered to life in glorious, spotty-faded black and white and it was me, small me maybe two or three years old—my younger face from pictures—and my young mother who looked so much like I did now. She was holding me upright and waving, smiling silently at the camera like the way people always pose in old home movies: *Look, Amy, look, there's Daddy behind the camcorder. There's somebody. Look! Wave!* We'd never done home movies, either that or there'd been some from before my father died and then she got rid of them all. Look. Wave.

Maybe there were clues here, in the home movie, things to tell us where Death was or how to find him. Maybe he was cutting us a break. Maybe badgers lay eggs. But I never could resist a movie theater. They were still the best places to curl up and sleep. Little-me toddled and young-Mom waved and then the picture changed and it was all close-clustered banks of trees, spindly and thick and lacey trunks and branches just starting to get their spring leaves back; in the foreground there were maybe ten or twelve people, men and women alike, but they were walking strangely, all stiff-legged with a hitching, hesitant gait somewhere between lurch and limp. Zombies. Actual undead, of the kind the plague had all wiped out.

"Was that it for all of you?" I asked. "The plague? Or are there still some real zombies—"

"Undead," she said. "We never liked that other word."

"Are there still real undead? Somewhere out there?"

The sudden longing in her eyes startled me.

"If there are," she said, "they're nowhere I am. You humans, you're just endangered. It seems like we're extinct."

The zombies, undead, onscreen were all sorts of rotten and covered in things I was glad I couldn't see clearly, seething crawling things, but it wasn't awful when it was just a movie and you couldn't smell them. They were doing something strange now, some of them had taken each other's hands and started tottering in slow, awkward circles around and around, no seeming destiny in mind and the most aimless and random shifting of partners—sometimes three or four, sometimes two, some joining hands in a little ring. Two of them, one small and skinny, the other tall and broad and so infested it made me shudder, they broke away a bit from the others and began moving in a recognizable rhythm: step-two-three, step-two-three. A waltz. They were waltzing, these dead things, as the others danced in shuffle-step or circles or all by their lonesome, all around them.

The others, curled up in their seats, watched in utter silence; they looked half-asleep, heads tilting gently forward and then back, eyes closing and then opening again, like cats on sunny windowsills pondering whether to tip into a full nap. Did they see what we were seeing? Did they see anything at all?

I turned to Jessie. She stared up at the screen, watching the tall broad seething thing waltzing its little partner round and round, watching with too-wide eyes and a pained set to her mouth. "You bastard," she muttered, eyes pinned to the screen. "You goddamned bastard."

Whether she meant Death who'd put us here to watch this, or the seething thing, I couldn't rightly tell. Maybe both. The dancing was atomized and piecemeal and there was no rhyme to their rhythms and yet somehow I could see it, all their ceremonial stumbling around becoming a flowing, easy harmony in time with music I couldn't hear. Somehow no matter what their actual steps, all of them were waltzing, waltzing perfectly, step-two-three around the forest clearing; a peculiar sort of energy seemed to flow from thing to thing, drawing all their particular movements into one. It was like watching the revealed inner workings of some great ticking clock.

"I can't explain it," Jessie said before I could ask. Eyes still fixed on the screen. "And I wouldn't, not to a human. But it was—you got this feeling inside you, this need to move, to dance, and—it was something that connected all of us, all of us could hear the music of it, simultaneously, inside our heads. Whenever it happened. You couldn't make it happen, sometimes it just did. Then we were all like, I don't know, limbs or cells or something in one big body." Her teeth caught her lower lip for a moment, pressing into the soft flesh uncannily like Lisa always did, then unlike Lisa, releasing it before it became raw. "I could hear music inside my head, once. Music that couldn't be written down. But I don't hear anything anymore."

The dance continued. I wondered what they were all hearing, whether it sounded like an actual waltz or some other, alien melody only they would find beautiful. I wondered which one was Jessie, of the smaller things dancing, because they were all so rotten I just couldn't tell.

"You wouldn't explain it to a human," I said. "But you just did."

"For the deaf among us," she muttered. "No. I wouldn't. If you think I just explained anything to you, you're even dumber than you look."

She wasn't fooling me. We barely knew each other but it wasn't hard to see how every time she told someone something important, something she thought they might use against her, she went running backwards fast as she could; she didn't trust anyone, except maybe that Linc and Renee who didn't even know her anymore, but sometimes she still couldn't help talking. Kind of like Stephen, who didn't even know me anymore. No wonder they detested each other on sight.

"I don't think I'm human," I said.

It just slipped out. This place did that to you.

"Not just since Natalie killed me. Maybe not even since I was born. My mother died and was brought back and died again a good dozen times before she got pregnant—can a dead woman have a living baby? The lab wasn't very sure, that's why they were so excited about me, Natalie said. That's why they let her go when she ran away—my mother, I mean—so they could watch us both. See how we integrated." My hands, thrust in my pockets, curled slowly into fists. "See what kind of human beings we made, if we really could pass as the real thing."

Jessie shook her head and laughed. "All that time, they were terrified we undead would start breeding—never mind we never had sex, or wanted it, and couldn't have had it if we *did* want it. Just the idea spooked them. And then they turn right around and deliberately make an experiment of it anyway. They were that stupid." Her voice was a harsh, scratchy chuckle. "That relentlessly stupid. Every damned time, hoos manage to surprise me."

I didn't say anything. I didn't care about whether zombies had ever had sex, any more than I cared about the dodo's zoology.

"So," Jessie asked, "how did you 'integrate'?"

I thought about it. I'd had no friends. My mother had no friends. But human beings, we—they—liked to go on about loneliness being our, their, given condition, so that couldn't be the measure. Anyway, my dad had loved her and she him. Other than blowing off school sometimes, I never caused any trouble, not until everything fell apart and I killed someone else. Human beings feel lonely and they feel isolated and they feel alienated, but the sensation inside me that I was thinking about was far beyond that; I didn't need anyone to tell me it was, because I just *knew* it since I was a child. Hollow walls all inside me, their plaster so thin any random fist could punch right through them, that's all I'd ever been and all I knew of myself and what was behind those walls, waiting to reveal itself, it unnerved me so much to imagine that it was best I'd never tried. I'd never thought anyone else felt this way, not even my mother, because we never talked about it and I never knew the reasons she might feel the same. Stephen, he was the very first who knew what that feeling was. Who knew it with me.

And if it wasn't as strange a feeling as I'd thought, if there were thousands of people secretly walking around feeling just like me, maybe that just meant the lab had been our wonder-working providence for longer, more often, than anyone ever imagined.

And now this place, this weakened decayed place disappearing all around us, was seeping into those hollow spaces like a winter wind whistling through the gaps around a windowframe, filling them with a harsh, bracing, shockingly newfound love. I couldn't stand it. I couldn't stand the thought that that was what really sustained me, and that soon it wouldn't exist anymore.

The figures onscreen were slowing, winding down, still in rhythm yet somehow I sensed a collective exhaustion overtaking them. Dance night was nearly at an end. I wished it wouldn't stop. I wished I could see pictures of my young mother again. Of her with my dad, who loved her and me but I barely remembered him now.

"I'm sorry you went deaf," I said.

She didn't say anything.

The movie was going spotty, big white patches eating up the picture like the film had started to melt. Without planning it or really thinking about it, we joined hands, she and I, and we headed down the thin-carpeted aisle as dusty and grimy and faintly lit as any real movie theater's and we kept on going, squinting into that brighter and brighter projected white light. She wouldn't have stopped, not even for a moment, if I hadn't tugged on her hand and made her.

"Come with us," I called, to Stephen, my mother, Lisa, everyone still in their seats. "You have to come with us. Please."

Were they supposed to stay here? Was it wrong of me to want them? I couldn't leave them behind, I couldn't leave everything and everyone behind like it didn't even matter if it all got taken away. It wasn't fair. I expected them to stay curled up comfortably in their seats, to nod off and fall asleep and break my heart in earnest. But they got up, they all got up right away and filed through the rows like they remembered just enough to know I was someone they listened to—sometimes, when they felt like it—and as he came closer, Stephen smiled at me like he almost knew who I was. Almost. My mother stayed close to him and me, sensing somehow that she should. Lisa hovered at the periphery, bewildered and lost.

We walked right through the screen. It yielded to us like the surface of a jelly, that faint sensation of a cool wobbliness as you press a finger straight down, and then we were where we really had been all along, in the realm of those things that weren't alive anymore but could still run, skip, waltz in film, in pictures, in memory. On the other side of the great white screen.

TWENTY-TWO

NATALIE

I didn't really know where I was. Not that it mattered. Stephen left us here to die and there weren't any woods anymore, just every now and then remnants of grass or dead bush twigs sticking straight up from the ground like broken fingernails, and the sun was gone, wetly smothered, like someone had spilled a huge bowl of oatmeal all over where there once had been a sky. The damp that wasn't clouds had all the weak failing light that was left, contained inside itself, and soon enough that would fade away, too.

Stephen left. The other one, he left too. Everyone always left me, in the end. It wasn't fair. Janey had even left me; her body lying there with one arm flung out wide and her pale hair coated and tarnished, dim with what looked like dust in the horrible oatmeal light, that had vanished too. It happened right in front of me, inches from my nose while I lay right there watching, but somehow I never actually *saw* it. Left me behind without even trying to say goodbye. Just like everyone else. Everyone.

The old woman, the one who'd invited herself along with us, she was crouching over me where I lay on the ground but I shoved her away, dug my heels into the dry dust, used the leverage to slowly raise up my knees and press my palms to the dead dirt and pull myself up sitting. Inch by inch. Every punch and kick from Billy, from Stephen, roared and echoed burning hot through me and I wanted to cry but I just gritted my teeth, made myself be as tough and indifferent as any good lab rat. When I was finally able to sit up, we were face to face, right up close.

"At least that awful darkness is gone," she said.

Then she looked around for a second, scared like she'd just tempted fate, and that made me think even less of her so I looked away. The problem was there was nothing left to look at, everything so desolate I really could've cried. We could breathe but the air was burning, unpleasant, like catching constant lungfuls of someone else's stale cigarette. I decided to keep looking at my shoes instead.

"Are you all right?" she asked.

Her voice shook and quavered like someone much older, she couldn't have been more than seventy or even that, and that somehow made me dislike her even more. "Do I look all right?" I spat. "Seriously? And if you are, with all this, you're completely crazy. Of course, everyone is, lately. Including that stupid Amy. So I guess you've got an excuse."

Janey's dead foot only half-inside her shoe had been curved and pretty, the line of her toes snaking at just the right angle from the arch. Stephen, when I'd seen him wheeled in from experiments robed and barefoot, he had strange feet, like someone had snuck in during the night and moved all his toes a half-inch upward for a joke. Bad shoes, Grandma once explained to me, malforming his feet when he was young and the bones were more pliable. Babies should never wear hard shoes. My feet, as I studied them, just looked like plain old feet. Plain old shoes.

Something popped and crackled in me, a memory. "You look like her," I said slowly. "A little bit like her. You have her eyes, and her voice except it's cracked and too old and awful, and it should be her face except it's so old and worn out it can't be hers.

Grandma wasn't half as old as you: You're her." I looked up then because I couldn't help it, I couldn't help but feel wild hope now that everything else had gone. "It is you, isn't it?"

She flung her arms around me and I smelled dirt, sweat, horrible bone-breaking weariness and I almost cried a little, I couldn't help it because I'd thought I'd never see her again. But only almost. She still had that lab smell just like I did somewhere deep in her pores, that lingering not quite medicinal something that got in your skin and even now wouldn't get out, nothing could ever scrub it away. I closed my eyes and took in breaths of it, for familiarity, but I didn't hug her back.

She pulled away and I was glad of it, even though I didn't want her to leave. "I'm not surprised you didn't know me," she said. In that quavering, all-wrong old woman's voice. "At first. The last year's been..." She broke off, something flitting across her face like terror, then caught herself. "I'm not what I was. I've paid for all this as much or more than anyone, Natalie, you have to believe me."

"What happened to you? Where did you even go?"

"I don't want to talk about it."

The big things were all hers and not mine, same as always. Same as when she was director-in-chief of the whole entire lab, even though she was nothing now but a dried-up stick thing crouching in the dust. But that would all change, I had it in me to change all of it. I clutched Sukie where she was curled up safe in my jacket and smiled. It was disgusting, what happened to people when they'd stopped being young and there was nothing keeping them from drying up and blowing away just like everything around us, every flowering thing, and nothing convinced me of how right the lab's work had been like the sight of her. Her hair gone dust-gray, strands all uneven and broken off and great salmon ribbons of scalp, dry scaly scalp, showing through. Lines all over her face that hadn't been there at all, just a year ago. Shaking in her hands. Shaking in her throat. I had it in me to change all that. And everything else.

"I didn't leave you there on purpose," she was saying. Nattering, chattering, like old people do, about stuff far in the past that didn't matter a damn. "I—you don't want to know what it's been like for me, Natalie, since all this happened, I wouldn't want you to know. I'm here now, anyway." She gave me one of those smiles, those awful determined smiles people only paint on their faces when they're neck-deep in crap and need to believe they can sing and dance their way out of it. "We're here."

We were there, all right. What did that have to do with anything? She used to be so efficient, Grandma was, all brisk and no-nonsense and she told you right out what she was going to do to you, why she was doing it, you understood when you were in her hands that you were part of something big and important. *I* understood, anyway, Stephen just screamed and screamed but that was his lookout. He didn't even remember it now, I bet. Grandma had places to go. None of that arms-around-you nonsense either, a little pat on the cheek if she were happy with you but that one touch was like a scent, it lingered with you for days.

I didn't like this woman. I wanted Grandma back.

"I never told you my name," she was saying. Rocking back and forth where she sat, like stupid Lisa in one of her hair-pulling moods, what *happened* to her? Why did I need to know her name? "Ellen. I'm Ellen." She laughed, a cracked crooning sound. "Of course, that used to be classified information too. But what wasn't. What wasn't? Call me Ellen, Natalie. Doctor, Grandma, after what we've made of the world, honorifics are a little beside the point, don't you think?"

It was just way things were right then that was making her sound crazy, the horrible air and the drifting, disintegrating specters of dead people. So many of them, pushed so tightly into such little bits of space that they were more like solid blocky columns of air than people; you might see one little hand reaching out from the mass, a lonely reproachful pair of eyes staring back at you from the nothingness, but they were all just *there* and so you didn't really see them. And then, even as you were looking at them, there was nothing left to look at anymore. It was probably too late for me to save them, by the time I got things right side up again they'd probably all be gone. First, though, to get Grandma back to her old self. I was pretty smart and she'd taught me a lot, but I could only do what I could do. I needed her. The *old* her, not whoever this was.

"I know something that was Death's secret," I said.

I felt a little jump and skitter inside me, saying that out loud without a whisper, and that bit of cowardice irritated me so I spoke louder. "I know how to get around Death, how the lab used to defeat him all those times. All those times with me and all the others. And none of... this... matters, because the secret's out and there's nothing he can do about it."

There were only a few stones still left in my jacket pocket but it didn't matter, right down the road from us there were more and you couldn't kill rocks, not like you could trees and birds and people. I pulled one out, a plain gray one I held out in my palm for Grandma to see. Vibrating at my touch, shuddering, growing hotter and hotter there in my palm until I cried out between my teeth, I couldn't help it, and then just like before it split open. Tarry blackness inside, spilling out, turning sugar-brown and sandy when it mixed with the oxygen in the air—except in this air it took longer, slower, not such a pretty candy-sandy color but the tarnished brown of a bad apple. It didn't matter. I could still feel it inside me, a wonderful ache inside my own bones as the tarry stuff changed and turned dry. Growing pains. I cupped my hands so the sand wouldn't spill, and smiled at Grandma.

"It's a rare thing," she said. Putting a fingertip to the sand. "When this happens spontaneously. Extremely rare. But hardly unprecedented."

That didn't bother me because for a moment she actually looked like her old self, quizzical and knowing and impossible to please. She still thought I had to please her. But that was all right, because when I explained it all to her she'd realize *she* had to please *me*.

"It doesn't just *happen*," I said. "I make it happen. I can make them break open. It's because of me."

"It happened spontaneously at the lab, once or twice—not with experimental participants like you, just random workers who were handling them and got a surprise. As I recall, we could never work out just why it happened, or how, without our having to break them open mechanically..." Her face grew thoughtful. "They meant to try and run studies but we could never get the funding, too much outlay for too little potential result. Always, the fights for funding. If they had only understood what we were trying to do, so much would've been different."

One or two others at the lab. Whatever. "Well, I don't see your 'random workers' here now," I said. I studied the bad-apple-colored stuff cradled in my palm. It wasn't painfully hot anymore, but holding it was still like having a tiny little flame all my own, flickering stubbornly against the bleakness around us; it made me feel better, it reminded me who was really in charge of things now. All of this could be fixed. The clustering ghosts seemed to draw back when they saw me split the stone open, clearing a space, watching to see what could possibly happen next. Good. They were Death's and already I had what was his on the run.

"You're right, of course," Grandma said. Ellen. I just can't think of her as "Ellen" but that's what you called a working colleague, their first name, that was how you showed you were equals. Ellen. "That stuff you've got, right there, the stones—that was how we did it. That was what we used in our experiments, to bring the dead back. We were trying to replicate its chemical properties, create a serum or—"

"I know what it's for," I said. Airy and casual, just to show her she wasn't the only one who knew things. Had she forgotten just how much she'd taught me, on purpose, before the sickness came? "I've used it. I used it to bring two people back, two people I killed myself, I—" I bent my head down and before she could stop me, blew the bad-apple powder gently from one palm to another. Some got scattered and lost, but not all of it. "Into their mouths, their nostrils. Breath of life. It worked. Both times, it worked."

"Then you were lucky," Ellen said.

She didn't look nearly as impressed as she should've, just drew her knees closer up to her chest and folded her arms in their huge flapping men's sweatshirt even tighter. "First, you were lucky the stones opened up at all. Even with our best equipment, no matter what we tried, sometimes nothing could make them crack, it drove us— "

"It's got nothing to do with luck," I snapped. Lectures, always the lectures, she never just talked like an ordinary person—she did realize I didn't work *for* her anymore, right? Didn't she? We worked together now. "It's control. It's power. It's being the *right* person, trying to open them. It's never not worked, for me. Ever. It just took me a while to realize what that meant."

She kept shaking her head but she liked that idea, she liked thinking it was all control and power and will and I could see that in her eyes. Too bad for her that it was me who had all that, not her, she'd have to treat me differently now. "Well, *we* couldn't always do it, and couldn't work out why. There seemed to be no rhyme or reason to the process—we found the substance by accident, we found out what it could do by accident. Whether or not we could make it do that seemed entirely arbitrary, and not really up to us. And even when we could, and we used it—it didn't always do what it was supposed to do. It didn't always bring the dead back. Or bring them back as themselves."

Still shaking her head, dry flyaway cotton-wool hair floating away from her cheeks, like a palsy or nervous tic. "So many experimental participants brought back damaged, useless, all the neurological—we were always so careful never to say research *subjects*, that word was forbidden. Subject to. Subjection. Not good. You were participants." She stared me with eyes suddenly fierce, piercing, like I'd sneered at her, demanded she justify herself. "And you were. Weren't you? Didn't I start teaching you what I knew, before... all this? You would've risen very high, Natalie. You were one of our most significant successes and you would've been one of our best scientists, when you were older. I'd have personally seen to it."

She didn't get it, did she? I didn't need her seeing to anything. I had what I'd sought. Almost. Almost there. "I know it works," I said. "You know it works. But why does it work? What's in here, in these stones, that does this? I looked for the files, the studies, but everything was such a mess for a while and then I think some pipes burst in the winter, a lot of printouts got lost—"

"That's just it," she said, smacking a palm against a fallen branch. "That's just it. We could never figure out a *consistent* method for opening the rocks, extracting what was inside, and whenever we tried running tests, it actually vanished. I'm not joking—it would just dissolve right in front of our eyes, or if we did manage to salvage any, minutes later the vial, the slide would be empty. Not even the most microscopic traces left. It was like it had a mind of its own, like it could sense whenever we wanted to learn its secrets, and so it ran away."

That scowl, that was a flash of the old Grandma: not hot anger, but cold frustration that the universe wouldn't bend all the ways she needed it. "So you see, we were stuck with always judging our moment, when the stones graciously decided to open up, and—"

"Janey," I said. God. Why had it only *now* even occurred to me, why the hell had I just sat there all this time, like an idiot, when I could've been doing this for her? She'd been well within her time to revive, I could have saved her before her body somehow slipped beyond my—Janey. She'd tried to defend us back at Paradise City, me too, not just Stephen. I wished I'd had some lipstick to give her, a pair of high heels. She loved high heels, Don would raid closets in empty houses to find them for her. Her pretty blonde hair I'd always envied had turned dark and crusted on one side of her head, her skull was split open but that wouldn't have mattered, I knew I could have—desperately I scanned the flotsam of dead faces drifting past, huddled shoulder to shoulder like they were cold and wandering lost, bewildered, all around us, but she wasn't there.

Poor Janey, gone, and it was all my fault. But I was still here. Death was too scared to get rid of me and that's how I knew, despite everything, that I was going to win.

"I have what Death wants," I told Grandma. Ellen. "I have the stones." I tossed a few of the emptied, split-open fragments of the gray one carelessly away. There were always more. "I have the knowledge of what's inside, and the gift to use it. Stephen ran off on a wild goose chase for his precious Amy, when he can't even save his own behind for trying—but I've got what saved them both right here, and nobody else gets their hands on it. Nobody."

I could smile about that again, savor the quiet well-earned glee smoldering like a coal inside my chest; I'd stood Death down twice now, and I was still standing while everyone around me fell. That meant something. It meant something good. "I'm the last one left with the gift. The last one. I'll learn how it works, I'll coax it into showing me its secrets—you saw, it didn't disappear in *my* hands. I'll learn what it's all about. You watch me. What the lab started, I'm going to finish." I swept an arm through the thin filthy air, sweeping the ruin of earth out of my vision like crumbs off a table. Temporary. All temporary. "And all of this, I'm going to bring back."

Grandma, Ellen, her head jerked up and she stared at me with amazement in her eyes, dismayed disbelief and also this wary look like someone who'd been expecting a fight. Was spoiling for one. "You've only ever managed to revive two people," she said, "and that out of sheer luck. And that's all. Just like no matter what we tried, we failed a hundred times as often as we succeeded. And now—"

"*Two people*!"

Who the hell did she think she was, sitting there talking like that? Saying only *luck* had managed what I'd done? She'd just got through telling me I'd have been one of them, if the plague hadn't happened, she'd have trained me up to be part of her team. She'd just *told* me. Except I didn't need a team, and I didn't need her. Not anymore. "I brought two people back, days ago I did that, and one of them was a lot colder than you ever let me get when you—I did that. I have the secret. If you think you can stop me, you just try."

"Me? Stop you?" Laughing softly now, rocking back and forth, forth and back like the crazy old bat she'd become and if Janey were only here, she'd have understood and not laughed. Janey would've been sweet and docile and helped me whenever I needed her to and I would find out where Death had taken her, I'd bring her back, I'd bring everyone back. This fight, this grand duel with Death, it wasn't over yet. I would win.

"Me, stop you," she repeated. "The *world's* stopped you, Natalie, in case you haven't noticed. We started by wiping out humanity dead and living, because we just couldn't stand the idea of sharing the planet with our own deceased kind, and then we finished by bringing on this. All in the name of progress, which is to say our own need to be secular messiahs. All to get more research grants. Money. Egotism and money. That's our legacy. Pride and greed." Laughing harder. Louder. "We destroyed the world in order to save it."

She chortled and choked and there was actual spit forming at the corners of her mouth, white and ropy even as she doubled over with laughter gone to dust-dry coughs. Janey'd been just a little bit crazy but Ellen, Grandma, was out of her mind. Why was everyone I used to look up, care about, such a disappointment in the end? I'd have to talk to her like a child.

"We haven't destroyed the world," I said, slow and patient. "Death's tried to, because he can't stand we have his secret. The genie's out of the bottle. As for humanity, before—"

Well, what about it, before? I wasn't one of them, almost nobody who'd survived was one of them and they never did me any favors, none at all. Grandma certainly never did, whatever she said now. "Dinosaurs. They had their time, they're nearly extinct, *so what*. We're here now. *Homo novus*, the new humanity, and as I bring us back, there'll be more and more of us and we'll take our rightful place on the planet. We'll bring the plants and animals back, the whole ecosystem back, Death's secrets are in the palms of our hands, we've literally breathed them in—"

“Two people!” She gasped for breath, still laughing, her voice going up and down like a rocking chair seesawing on its runners. “Two people you managed, just two, by sheer blind luck, and you look at all this and actually think you can—”

“We can have children,” I said. The thought of what the world would look like with just us in it, no Death to rule over us and no her to ruin the fun, it made me smile in her face and not care about her laughter, her spittle, her senile foolery. “We're not like zombies, sterile remnants, revenants—we can breed, we can have children. Like Amy. You were all so excited about Amy, I remember that, because you thought it was impossible.” Wonderful perfect Amy you probably always loved more than me, probably just waiting for your moment to bring her back to the lab and introduce her to everyone, everyone who celebrated *her* birthday and not mine while she wasn't even there. To make her your right-hand assistant and not me, even though she knew less than nothing. Turned her back on me. Ignorant traitor. But I'd have to forgive her, for our species' sake. For now.

“I'm going to find all the secrets of the stones,” I said, “all the ones you couldn't—new ones, that neither of us know are in there. I'm going to find all of them. And when I do, *Homo novus* won't owe anybody *anything*.” Not Death, not you either, Grandma. Ellen. Whoever she really was now. I couldn't help smiling, thinking of the future. “We won't owe anything to Death, or to age, or to illness—and so we won't owe anything to life, either. All that we'll ever be beholden to is ourselves.”

Poor Janey. She vanished before I could save her but I'd figure it all out very soon—even if I couldn't save the others, all the others now swarming sadly around us, I'd bring *her* back and it wouldn't happen ever again. I'd find a way to make her one of us. She was always nice to me, she wouldn't act like Amy and Stephen did when I brought them back. She'd be so happy. She wouldn't have to worry anymore about what Don or Billy or anyone else said. She'd be beholden to nobody but herself.

There was so much to fix. I had to get started *soon*.

"No more teachers," Grandma said. Tempered and subdued, none of the old briskness, the syllables turning over in her mouth painfully and slow. "No more books. The holidays have begun, and they'll never ever end."

"This isn't holidays," I said. Good and sharp, like how she was always sharper than she needed to be with me. "This is work. I'm ready to get to work. We're going to rebuild all of this, all ourselves, and we won't owe any of it to anyone else."

"You could," she said, and she was nodding now like she finally understood it, like I'd passed some sort of secret test. "If you were a grown woman, the world what it was, all the resources there at your—you might have done it. I really think so. Just enough knowledge on your side, just enough human disorganization and panic for you to exploit, in the name of your own kind—you have it in you, Natalie. You really do."

Could have. If. Not *can*. She still didn't get it and that was making me angry. "*Could* have done it? Are you even listening to me? I'm *doing* it. It's happening. It starts right now." I clenched the last bits of stone in my hand, the jagged candy-shell remnants emptied of their filling; they prodded my palm soft and insistent like another set of fingers and that vague pain where they dug in felt good, like a little reminder of who and what was really relevant here. They were living things too, these lake stones, they understood me and life and death like Grandma and all her lab flunkies never had. "If Death wants a war, fine, he's got one. He declared it. And we're declaring our independence. And we're going to win."

Grandma, Ellen, thought that over, her ruined chin resting on one knotted-up, trembling fist. She nodded some more. "And in that case," she said, "I finally know why I survived all this. Why my life was spared. I thought it was punishment. But it was something more."

She uncoiled her clenched fingers. Stroked my face right along the hairline, old gesture from the old days. "My life was saved," she said, "so that I could stop you."

TWENTY-THREE

STEPHEN

Where was I, and what was I doing there?

I was almost certain I'd known, once, not long ago. But that had faded away and I couldn't remember. I really couldn't remember. We'd been watching a movie. There was a little boy on the screen, with dark hair and hesitant swaying toddler's steps, carrying a toy he kept frowning at and examining like some factory inspector as he cradled it in his arms. A stuffed dog, with floppy felt ears that looked frayed and chewed to pieces. Nothing else seemed to happen in the movie, though, just him walking around da-ba-da'ing to himself and his toy dog, but I still liked watching it. It felt like happiness would've been just sitting there and watching that kid forever.

"You have to come with us," someone was calling. "Please."

I didn't want the movie to be over, ever, but then it was and all of us were getting up to leave. The usher, or whoever she was who was kicking us out, I knew her. I knew I knew her. I liked her, her quiet voice and anxious eyes and tangled red hair whose texture I felt like I knew, like once very long ago I had touched it. Maybe I could talk her into letting us stay? But almost before I realized it, we were all leaving, me and the pretty worried girl and the few other moviegoers, all strangers, and we walked like it was nothing right through the blank white screen. It yielded to us like a curtain, soft and heavy, and I shivered as we pushed through it because it was so cold—

Water. Except it hadn't been water, it had just collected in the lake basin in a semblance of waves and currents. We'd left the shore, all of us together, wading through it to the other side, and then without knowing how, we were in the movie theater. But why had we done that, and who were all these people? We were looking for... something, someone? But how? Why? What was this funny spot over my vision, growing slowly bigger and bigger the more I turned my head, like I was going blind on one side? I didn't want to go blind. I needed my eyes, now more than ever, but I had no idea why.

I shook my head and rubbed my eyes, frustrated, scared, and that red-headed girl looked terribly sad. She said something I forgot as soon as it left her lips, fading like I was losing hearing along with sight, and she hugged me. That felt good, but I still didn't know who she was. Another red-haired woman, older, hugged her back, but that just seemed to make the younger one sadder. I couldn't quite see where we were anymore, but something familiar insinuated itself into my socks as I walked, the soft, faintly scratching grit of sand; when I deliberately shoved one sneaker into it, the ground yielded, sank down over my foot and ankle like a great collapsed anthill. Definitely sand. Someone would be happy about this. Someone had told me how much he wanted to see his beach one more time, a long time ago, but I couldn't remember—I couldn't—

I couldn't see anything now. I was blind. Somehow that didn't upset me anymore, even knowing I had needed my sight, my eyes, for something terribly important. Whatever had mattered, once, was now dissolving all around me in a way that felt, at first, almost sweet. Like sugar in hot tea. I couldn't see anything, and I fell. Someone—I hoped it was the red-headed girl—was cradling me on the sand, and voices were shouting and calling around me, but I couldn't tell one from another. They were as musical and indistinguishable as the cries of birds.

Whatever "birds" were.

I fell because I no longer had feet. They just disappeared from under me, an empty space where once something had borne my weight, and so I collapsed. Had I ever had feet? Was I something that was supposed to have feet, arms, eyes?

I still had hands. I put them to my face, at the place where I was almost certain I was meant to have eyes. They were gone. No sight, no more sounds either. Had there ever been anything to hear, to see? Had I always just imagined it?

Some small, stubbornly solid part of me was screaming, deep down inside. It gagged and choked on the sickly sweetness, as my limbs, face, memory melted away like sugar in hot tea, and even without ears I kept hearing it, somehow, far within: *No! I don't want this, I don't want to be nothing! I don't want everything to go away! Stay here!* But there wasn't any "here." There wasn't anything. There wasn't anything left of me.

I was something, once. A thing that was. That existed. Wasn't I? I couldn't remember. I couldn't.

Memory. I didn't know what that was. Not anymore.

Existence. That was—

Nothing.

TWENTY-FOUR

LISA

"Stop it!" someone kept shouting at me. "You have to stay here, you have to remember who you are! Goddammit, this can't happen now, you have to—"

"Jessie," someone else said, pleading with the woman shouting at me. It was a red-haired girl with tears running down her cheeks, staring in a way that puzzled me at an empty space on the ground. "She can't help it, for God's sake, Florian and Stephen couldn't—let go of her. That won't help. Let her go."

The angry girl, Jessie, had my shoulders in a death grip and was shaking me back and forth, making my teeth rattle, but the funny part was I couldn't actually feel her touch at all—not even a sensation of pressure, like when a drill bears down on a numbed tooth. I trembled in her grasp and yet it was as if she never really had me, as if she held nothing. She let go, looking miserable and lost, and the red-haired girl reached up and tucked a lock of my hair behind an ear. I didn't feel that either.

"She's still here now, at least. That's something, isn't it?" The red-haired girl, the nice girl, turned to Jessie, then to me. "You're still here," she told me.

Was that important? I nodded and smiled, in case it was. *Be here now.* The ground beneath my feet was pale and grainy and once had a name, a name particular to itself—not "dirt," not "grass," if I gave it a few minutes I was sure it'd come to me—but the thought drifted away as soon as it appeared, drifted out and upward into the great bright blueness overhead. That, too, had once also had a name. Wandering over that strange ground were three little receding dots: a black-haired boy, a blonde girl, a woman whose hair was the same bright shade as the nice girl's where it wasn't wide ribbons of silvery white. There was a child there, too, not more than maybe five or six, but instead of walking around, she was just lying there, curled up in the shifting hillocks. A nap, that might be nice. Lying down. Standing here, however important that apparently was, was exhausting.

I would have asked what things were named, who everyone was, but I didn't seem able to speak. I wasn't upset or afraid, because it wasn't like I'd lost my voice: it was more like I'd just been confused, before, and made a mistake thinking I'd ever had a voice at all. I still had eyes, though. So I watched. Jessie had me by the arm again, an encircling proprietary touch I couldn't feel, and she glared at the nice girl like whatever was bothering them both was all her fault.

"Naomi's going too," Jessie said, jerking her head toward the sleeping little girl. "You see?"

"Then it's better for Lisa, this way," the nice girl said. She was wiping her eyes. "Because that would just kill her."

What was going on? I felt almost relieved that I couldn't ask. I couldn't speak for this Lisa person, but I had almost died once, almost died of grief and loss for a little girl who wasn't called Naomi, a long time ago. I couldn't remember any more than that, but I still felt it inside, stabbing me with a pain Jessie's dug-in nails could never have managed. I stretched out my free hand to stay the nice girl's tears—that might be her child, lying there, possibly dying—and she smiled at me like she was in pain, gently pushed my fingers away.

"Amy," Jessie said to the nice girl, quietly. She was staring at the others, who were wandering farther away. "Your mom."

Amy didn't turn to look. She just shook her head. "It's too late for her," she said. "I could see it back in the movie theater, or... whatever that was. It was already too late then. She didn't know me." Her eyes were leaking again. "She didn't know me."

"Then pull yourself together," Jessie said. "If it already was too late, then that's that and it's done. We can't lie around crying now."

Her eyes, though, weren't nearly as hard and sharp as her voice.

Amy didn't answer. She squatted down, running a palm almost tenderly over the empty spot at our feet, and then stood up again with a handful of that oddly crumbled-up ground. She put some of it in her pocket, letting the rest drift back through her fingers and fall.

"It doesn't hurt, anyway," she said. "At least, it didn't look like Stephen was in pain, or Florian—for God's sake, why isn't it happening to us, you and me? Why aren't we forgetting everything, like the others..."

She trailed off all of a sudden and her eyes widened, full of a newfound apprehension I couldn't understand, and she slipped her hand back into her pocket. The same one where she'd put that bit of pale earth.

"Jessie," she said. In a low, urgent voice. Then she pulled from that pocket a slim, flat, hard thing, a dull greenish color with striations of brown. A stone.

Jessie let me go, and reached into her own pocket, and pulled out another stone, a different color. A color whose name wouldn't come to me. She and Amy stared at each other, like something had just happened they couldn't believe for even a minute, and then they were laughing, hard and helplessly, like they might never stop.

"I took it from Florian," Amy managed, when she got her breath back. "He left it on the ground, back in the woods at your beach, and I took it. I just wanted it. I didn't steal it, or at least I didn't mean to, he never—"

"I should have known," Jessie said, eyes still shining from all that laughing, like she hadn't heard a word from Amy's mouth. She was pacing back and forth, agitated, delighted discovery and fearful confusion lighting up and darkening her expression all at once. "I bet that's why we can still remember Florian too, and all the ones who don't exist anymore—I should've *known.* I'm a fucking fool, of all people in the whole goddamned world I should've—did your mother ever pick up any of the lake stones? Or Lisa? Lisa, these things. Do you have any of them?" She was shouting again, so slowly and loudly that I grimaced, her hand with the stone in it shoved in my face. "Do you? Just nod or shake your head!"

I didn't understand what she was asking me, so I didn't do anything. She made an impatient sound and grabbed my hand, prying it open; she stuck the stone on my palm and curled my fingers back around it, around that hard thing that had pressure and yet at the same time, no weight. It dropped straight through the flesh and bones of my closed-up hand, and onto the ground at my feet.

Jessie's face, her eyes, clouded over. Then she picked up the stone and turned back to Amy.

"That answers that question," she said, much more softly. "They're keeping us together, somehow. And I should've known it. After everything that happened during the plague, I should've known."

She put the stone back in her... clothes. The place in clothes where you keep things. All at once the word wouldn't come to me. "That's what he meant," she said. "When he called us all thieves. It has to be."

Amy frowned.

"It has to be," Jessie kept saying, walking around so fast now that the ground was spitting excited little puffs of itself all around her feet. She ignored me now, avoided looking at me, like just the sight of me somehow hurt. "Remember what I said, about the stones helping us when we got sick? Me and Linc and Renee, and Lisa too? We were supposed to die, but because we had these, we didn't. We lived. You and Stephen, your mother, *you* were supposed to be dead, but you lived. You came back. That lunatic kid you told me about from the lab, she fucked with all this stuff and— "

"But we didn't mean to come back!" Amy was clutching her own stone two-handed, like she was scared it would grow legs and leap away. "Me and my mom and Stephen—and Natalie too, when they were still experimenting on her—none of us did it on purpose."

"And I didn't know what the hell I was doing either, with the stones. It was all just an accident. And I only ever knew the lab was trying to get rid of us, of undeads—I had no clue they were gunning for life everlasting." Jessie stomped her feet and laughed. "Doesn't matter, obviously. We all fucked up, so we all need punishing."

She grabbed a stick, a lumpy uneven thing, from where it lay and trailed it over the ground. It crumbled and fell apart right there in her hand, and as she dropped the stick again, its soft little fragments disintegrated completely, not leaving even a trace of dust. Or that other stuff, the kind of dust that happened when something burned in a fire. It had a name. Fire and things burning, did that feel hot, or cold? I couldn't remember.

The two girls, Jessie and the other one whose name had escaped me again, had stopped marching around and stood staring at each other. Maybe they'd forgotten what came next, like me. The quiet was heavy, thick, like air before... that thing that sometimes happened, with flashing light and water pouring from overhead.

"But we didn't mean it," the red-haired girl kept saying. "We weren't trying to steal anything. Natalie even invited us to join her, in more experiments, and we said— "

"I bet you didn't mean to kill someone," the other girl spat. "Did you? But that doesn't matter, either. Too late. You did it. And believe me, if I'd known what I was doing myself, if I'd known what it was like being..." Her voice faltered. "If I'd understood what it would be like, walking around in a human body again, barely feeling anything like I did before, not *hearing* anything at all like—I'd never have done it." She tilted her head back, shouting at nothing. "Did you hear me? I'd never have done it, I promise! I didn't wanna cause trouble! I'd have just let us all die!" Silence. "That crazy old fucker Billy was right, I admit it! We should've all just been good little boys and girls, and laid down and died!"

Her words echoed around us. Nobody answered.

The shouting girl shook her head. "See?" she said. "It doesn't matter, and it never will. Regret never matters for shit."

Beyond us, I saw the light-haired one wandering around and around in ever-widening circles, drifting slowly out of our sight. The dark-haired one now lay motionless in the sand, beside the little girl. The third one was missing. One. Two. Three. What comes after that?

"Stephen," the bright-haired girl said. "Before he... Stephen said Death told him that he was once alive too. Death was, I mean. Alive. And he, Death, said he couldn't escape all this either. You remember? We all heard that. So is Death just, I mean is he—"

"Dying?" the other girl said. "You mean, is even Death just another undead, a cranky old dusty crumbling into ash?" She was starting to laugh again. "And so he decided fuck it, all living things ever did was bitch and complain about him anyway, so if he's gotta go, he's gonna take us all with him? Yeah, that sounds like him, all right." She dug a heel into the ground, turning slowly on her foot. "I guess maybe that means this was all gonna happen anyway, sooner or later? Maybe. And even with all that power, all that everything, he just can't help it. He can't stick around forever either, he just let us think he could. Kind of humiliating when you think about it, huh?"

I couldn't stand anymore. I fell down, and landed on my side. On the thing that lay below. Looking into the thing that lay above. The voices were still talking, but it was harder to hear them.

"Then why not just end things *fast*?" the first one asked. "Why bother with all of this? Why make us watch?"

"Because it's like I said," answered the other. "All of this is just like him. Because Death's a sadistic son of a bitch."

The sounds drifted over me where I lay. They made no sense. But inside, in the last part of me still left, I knew it didn't matter. Because nothing, not since the second I was born, had ever really made any sense. It never did, not for anyone, ever. We just liked to pretend that it did.

"She's going," someone said. "So are the others."

"Hey, Lisa," someone else said. A soft voice. Sad. "You annoyed the shit out of me, but you were a good sister. Most of the time. So thanks."

"I don't want this," said the first voice. It was stretched and thin, like it wanted to tear in two and let a scream come out. "I don't—"

"Well, we're both still here," said the second. "At least, we are now. Nothing to do but keep going."

Nothing to do but keep going. Those words, those sounds, made no sense. And yet they did, somehow, inside, in the last disappearing part of me I still had left.

Another sound rose up, a great loud buzz. It swelled up and grew bigger and louder, pushing its way into what was still left of me, and broke me all apart.

TWENTY-FIVE

AMY

"Keep going?" I asked. I was laughing and I couldn't seem to stop, because now my mother and Lisa and Stephen were gone for good, and only the lake stones were letting me remember they'd ever been, and the only other option was to scream. "Keep going? Aren't you the one who just said you might as well have just laid down and—"

"Too damned late for that, isn't it?" Jessie shook the sand from her shoes. "It's always too late, no matter what—I told you, regret means shit. This is all we've got left, and he hasn't done us in yet, so I want to find him before he does. I want to find him. We need to have... words." Her voice rose up into the sky, the bright blue beautiful unreal sky that wasn't anything but another mockery, shrill and raucous as a gull. "We've got *words*!"

Renee was gone too, and Linc, and poor Naomi who withered away and vanished all alone. And Nick, who I'd so blindly thought would be here, he was my guide and my friend and just the thought of his reproachful eyes and quietly thumping tail made me want to start crying again, I wanted Stephen and Nick and Lisa and my mother—words. They were every bit as shit as regret, and

Jessie knew it. And they were all we had left, them and a false sky and sea and sand into which we too would surely soon disappear. And our feet, to let us walk in endless circles seeking the biggest of big nothings until we fell apart, fell down, disappeared.

As we all went through the false movie screen, the floor beneath our feet had softened and shifted and before we had time to lose our balance, it became sand. The fragrant cool air became heavier and thicker, full of the constant possibility of rain, but instead of blankness and blindness there was sunlight, everywhere, and blueness overhead diminishing to grays and violets at the edge of the horizon. Far off at the bottom of the dune where we now stood was a great expanse of choppy dark blue water and out on the horizon itself, its perfectly straight ruler-line separating dark blue from light, the faint shadowy outline of something that looked like what had once been Chicago. The way it always looked from across Lake Michigan and the Illinois state line, like a far-off, overbuilt island smoldering with smoke.

All false. All delusion, just like that movie theater spinning random reels of a few final, happy memories before we all waved bye-bye. Like everyone but Jessie and me had begun to do, bare seconds after our feet found the sands, eaten up and blown away. Like the terrible shoreline from where we'd all started. I loved this place, this place I had so suddenly and desperately wanted to save, but that was just more mockery too, more delusion. More sadism, a little taste of everything I'd missed. What I loved, all of it, was already lost.

I'd never meant to steal anything. I'd never meant to reject Death's gift: my own inevitable death, the ticket to this place that, before the lab's meddling, before the strange interceding mercy of these lake stones, I could never have refunded. That little seed of himself that he offered to, pressed on, everything that lived. Without ever intending it, I'd thrown that in his face. Which was the greater unknowing crime—the theft of life, or the ingratitude for life beyond? Both of them, now, lost.

There was deceptive calm and quiet here and cool spring

breezes, but mostly there was light, deep strong light ubiquitous as the air. Everything was so fresh, so clean, and beside me I saw Jessie craning her neck to take in the china-blue sky, pulling in long, savoring breaths. She pivoted on one foot, a single slow revolution, and shook her head.

"Always seems to come back to this," she said quietly. "This beach. Real or imaginary. Every single time."

"He's making fun of us," I said. Was he? Or was this some little hint, a single dropped stone on the pathway to find him, and we'd just lost our sense of direction? The last good place. The last place that *was* anything. If Death himself were... dying, somehow, was where we stood now his own final rallying surge of vitality, his last gasp?

"Any time you think you know where to go next," I told Jessie, "just yell. Any idea."

No answer. She took in another long, audible breath, savoring the clean sweetness of the air.

"I never thought I'd actually be happy to *breathe*," she said softly.

So matter-of-fact. So pacific. I remembered how people with the plague, sometimes, could become so angelically peaceful right before the end, the fight drained from them altogether. It was creeping over me now too, that same sudden yielding lassitude, the same yearning to give in and give up. She'd said we had to keep going, it was all we had left to do, but weren't we just kidding ourselves? Wasn't all that was really left to us just standing still, standing right there? Saying another goodbye? It was so beautiful, like Lake Michigan but also like all the memories I had from when I was little, that time we went to Cape Cod; if I went down to the shoreline, I was sure I'd find that same salty rubbery seaweed floating in the water. I was scared to go down there and I didn't know why.

Because maybe he, it, was waiting out there, on the horizon, just like before when he came to greet us and love us and swallow us whole. Because maybe all this wasn't just mockery after all, not just a random bit of fruit casually tossed just out of Tantalus's reach. Maybe he was lulling us, distracting us, with sunshine and sweet memories and our own long goodbyes, so he could slip away somewhere like an animal and quietly, finally cease.

We had to get out of here, before I decided to forget why we ever came.

"We have to go." I tugged on Jessie's sleeve, insistent like a child. My younger self, at Cape Cod. *Can we go to that Clams-'N'-Cones on the highway, for fried clams? Can I have soft-serve?* "Over that next ridge, or... somewhere. Now. We have to keep moving. We have to. You said so. You said it yourself."

Jessie said nothing.

"We can't just stay here," I said. "Waiting. It's selfish. Horribly selfish. We have to try. That's all that's left to do. You *said* so."

Jessie folded her arms across her chest, gazing out at the water. Staring as if she awaited something, someone, to rise up and flood us with his own all-consuming light. Just like me. Just like before. I didn't like her and I didn't understand her and I knew she felt all that doubly for me, and I couldn't, I wouldn't, go on without her: I'd been alone before, all alone, after Ms. Acosta and before poor lost Nick, and I couldn't do it again. I wouldn't. I held my breath, standing there in the clean sweet illusion of air.

Then she shook her head hard, like wrenching herself from a daydream, and as if *I'd* been the sorry lingerer, she jerked her head impatiently toward the sands.

"Up that way, I guess," she said, already starting to walk. "Over the next ridge. Better than just standing around here doing nothing."

Her eyes flickered back toward the water, the tiny shadowy outline on the horizon of a phantom city always out of reach. Her steps faltered, hesitated.

"I guess it is, anyway," she said.

Then she turned her back on the water and we headed up the ridge. A seagull flew overhead calling and crying out and even though I heard its long cloud-trail of a caw, felt its shadow fall on me and then swiftly depart, I never saw an actual bird at all.

TWENTY-SIX

NATALIE

"My life was saved," she said, "so that I could stop you."

Grandma. You could be so stupid sometimes, about the most obvious things, when you were actually so *smart*. But I'd heard scientists were like that, sometimes, and artists too. They didn't live in the same reality as everyone else. But that hardly meant reality didn't exist.

"I'm not stopping for anything," I said, "and if anything did stop me, it won't be you." I hugged Sukie my doll where she sat safe in my jacket, warm and lumpy inside where I'd stuffed her gut full of all the extra lake stones she could carry. "Just because you failed, that's no reason I should give up—"

"One had to be careful at the lab, working with young children." Grandma shook her head of ruined, broken-off hair, hunched forward like an ape as she talked. "When they were the participants, in the experiments, it was so easy for them to get attached to you, start thinking they cared for you, and you for them—a terrible mistake." She smiled again, like she thought I just couldn't get enough of seeing her missing teeth. "That could be fatal. To do what we had to do, every day, you had to cultivate and nurture a certain sense of ruthlessness."

"You were plenty ruthless," I said. "When you had to be."

"Jonathan, the one you called 'Daddy' when you were little—we never did figure out just why you got so attached to him in particular. He barely saw you half the time." She laughed in reminiscence, not hearing me, not hearing anything but her old-person memories unwinding like a spell to invoke them in the flesh. "But I suppose it flattered him, your trying to toddle around after him everywhere he went, so the Daddy part stuck. You really had to be careful with the younger children."

She pressed her fingers to her temples like her head were killing her, but there wasn't any pain in her face. "I got a visit," she said. "I was dying. Or thought I was. Not of the plague—like you, like a trifling percentage of people, perhaps I was immune. For whatever good it did me. I got the flu last winter, some horrible strain. I couldn't breathe. I lay there in an abandoned house, all alone, curled up on a filthy mattress piled with filthy blankets and coats and dozens of them couldn't get me warm. I could feel my lungs filling up like I was drowning. And then, I saw him." She laughed, and it was like hearing the grinding wheeze of a car trying to start in the winter. "First he looked like Jonathan. Then... his face changed, somehow, right there in front of me, and he became this skinny dark-haired boy. I knew that face too, it was one of our hardier experimental subjects—but it wasn't him. It *looked* like him, but it wasn't him. Just like it hadn't been Jonathan, before."

Her head bobbed and her neck curved down, imitating the motions inside her throat as she swallowed. "He said—he said that I was finished, that everything everywhere was finished, in ways I couldn't even start to imagine. Because of the lab. Because of everything we'd done. I knew he wasn't lying. That he wasn't... human, he was something far beyond that. I just knew, just like I knew that he meant every word and that he truly could do it. He could end everything, everywhere, in ways that made our poor accidental plague look like a day at the races. I—I screamed, I was so frightened. Because he was standing there, knowing who I was, wearing that false face he'd stolen God knows when or how, and I knew it was true. Every word. And he laughed."

The Friendly Man. Again. Friendly to everyone but me, always everyone but me. "I've met him," I said, trying to sound bored and scornful. "He's no big—"

"He said I'd live through the flu, just like I'd lived through everything else that was done to—happened to me, before that. Not because I deserved to live, but because I didn't deserve the peace, the surcease, of death... and that nobody would ever have that again, nobody would have *anything* ever again, unless I made sure the lab ended its work forever. That wasn't just humanity's last chance—it was everything's last chance. I had to stop it, me personally. Or know that when everything finally ended, it was all because of me. All of it. Me. And I knew he meant it. Every word."

Her eyes dulled suddenly, their feverish glassiness filming over with dust. "Then he laughed again. And he said, 'Well, you wanted to be God, didn't you? So how's it feel?' And then... and then, he was gone."

She sat there, silent now, stewing in her own misery like something half-melted and sodden in its puddle: a dropped ice cream cone, a filthy boot-stomped chunk of slush dissolving in a March thaw. I folded my arms around me, pressing the spot where Sukie nestled safe against me, and smiled.

"You certainly took your time getting *back* to the lab," I said. "If you ever did. I never saw you there." Although, in fairness, I hadn't been back there very long, it took me ages to get out of Paradise. Although, also in fairness, I'd accomplished all by myself in weeks, days, hours, what had taken her years. Let her talk. Let her scream and faint and piss herself at the thought of him, my dueling partner. *My* enemy. He didn't scare me, and I didn't need her anymore.

"You don't know what I've been through," Grandma said. "I don't wish to discuss it. I'm just lucky to be alive. But I finally got away from... all that. I got here. And I found *you*." She started laughing again, that nasty wheezing sound I'd already grown to despise. "When he told me my fate, I knew he meant every word, but I also never dreamed the lab could possibly return again, in any form, after the plague and the utter destruction of—I never dreamed it. Never." She shook her head, amazed at her own obstinacy. Her own idiocy. "But then—but now—I've found you. And heard all your plans."

I smiled. I couldn't help it. Scrape away the thick patina of all that crazy, and maybe she still had half a working brain left after all. Enough to see that she was too late to stop me, and he was too weak. No matter all this, no matter what anybody said. He was always so willing to sit and talk with anyone who wasn't me.

"I walk my own roads," I said. I lifted my head to prove the point, gazing down the twisting forest road that led to the beach, but it was all so bleak and terrible I had to turn away. The ghosts, the faded wisps of them dissolving all around us like bits of grimy tissue paper in a great brackish puddle, even they couldn't stand what they saw around them, couldn't believe we'd been brought to this. By a jealous, vindictive, rotten, greedy little demigod who mistakenly thought he should have charge of everything. "You don't have anything to say about that, not anymore—and he certainly doesn't, either. Times have changed. I'm grown up."

No answer. Just like the old days, when she'd just turn her head on her long, curving neck and glide away if you said anything she didn't have time to, didn't care to hear. She must have realized, crazy or not, that her little stories weren't getting her anywhere.

"This is between me and him now," I said. "Just us. Not you. You're not part of this anymore."

"You can't continue this," she replied. Her chin rose up high and haughty like it still mattered if someone offended her, denigrated the position, the dignity that nobody had anymore. "You absolutely cannot. However abortive your attempted experiments have actually— "

"*Two people*," I whispered from between my teeth. "That's two more than you ever thought possible now, you just got through saying so. All by myself. I don't need him, and I've decided, I definitely don't need you."

I could tell I was getting tired, drained from the anger of having to waste my time with her, because the sky and the light seemed to be growing even dimmer, big malformed dark spots floating just at the edge of my vision and then vanishing. Just a trick. Another of his stupid useless tricks. Grandma's eyes had gone big and bright, like a hawk's spotting a rabbit.

"Do you know who your real father was, Natalie?" she suddenly said. "Never mind Jonathan or any other happy surrogate figure, do you know who he really was? Well, I don't. Nobody did, including your own mother. She was quite young, barely out of her teens, and found herself pregnant—amazed that sex with random men could somehow result in that, typical of her sort—we paid her a very comfortable amount of money to see the pregnancy through, and to give you to us for safekeeping. And after all the care and attention we gave her, all the money, she changed her mind at the end. She thought she was really the one in charge of everything, and not me. She actually tried to *threaten* me. I had to take care of that. And I did." She nodded, at nothing and nobody in particular. "I see you haven't fallen far from the tree."

Was this supposed to mean something to me? Was it seriously supposed to hurt my feelings? A human mother was nothing but genetic material, long since donated to a better cause, and it meant nothing to what I was now. "She was trying to *stop* you, right? Stop you from your experiments, from making me what I am? Well, you didn't listen to her pathetic little threats, and I'm not listening to yours. The work goes on. That's what you always told me. The work goes *on*."

"A selfish, irresponsible, smirking little brat who thought growing a baby made her some sort of—all we had to do was wave a few thousand dollars in front of her face and she signed you away without a second thought. Just like she conceived you, without a second thought. Just like you're condemning all of us, everywhere, without a second thought." Her breath came harshly now, spots flaring on the grayish, ruined skin of her cheeks. "So many of our subjects were just like her, drug addicts, drinkers, party girls, their lives one long moronic trek through impulse after impulse—I thought our work gave their lives actual meaning. Actual purpose. But we were just as bad. We were every bit as bad."

Somehow, my hands were in hers now and the skin of her fingers was dry and cold, as broken and torn up as her hair, but she held on and squeezed and I couldn't pull away. "All we did was chase after our own infantile impulses, our most selfish self-serving instincts—why must we age? Why must we die? Why can't *we* have the final say in all of that, because we're so pathetically frightened of the alternative? And we could make so much money, earn so much acclaim doing it, too! What an unbelievable return on a few irresponsible, smirking little investments! Well, I suppose thanks to our work, and especially thanks to you, we all finally know that you can't remake reality by whim and impulse, and there's so much out there that's worse than death. So much worse than death could ever be." Again, she rocked back and forth, forth and back, hands wrapped around mine like a bicycle chain wound around a pole. "Two people? That's two too many. It stops now, Natalie. It stops *now*."

So weak. So damned weak. But I kept forgetting, she wasn't *Homo novus*, she wasn't one of us. Frail, just like Billy and the rest of them always said. I was laughing. I couldn't help it.

"No," I said.

"You can't continue. You can't. Look at what's become of us, Natalie, *look* at us—"

"I don't need you now, Grandma. *Ellen*. You taught me not to need you. Human beings like you are finished and it doesn't matter how much he tries to scare me, Death doesn't run this place anymore." I twisted my hands hard, wrenching them away. "And no matter what you used to think, you never did."

Her breath was deeper now, slower, like each exhalation unwound itself from some great soft ball. Her eyes were heated and crazy and saw nothing but me.

"You have other lake stones, don't you?" she said. "There in your pockets. Clever girl, taking them with you, you never missed a trick. You can't do any more meddling without them, you were right about that. Give them to me."

The world was shifting and melting into pools of bleakness and congealing that way, like dirty wax. The ghosts were vanishing, dissolving so slowly and yet so swiftly I could barely recall where I'd once seen a hand, a bowed head, reproachful unhappy eyes. There was a sound somewhere far off, a weak piteous animal cry.

"No," I said.

"You can't be trusted with them. Either throw them away, get rid of them right now, or give them to me."

The animal sound grew louder, a wailing rumble like some sort of infant thunderstorm. I just looked at her.

"No," I said.

The rumbling noise grew louder and then it happened, she leapt on me and we were fighting, furious, desperate, her fingers scrabbling for my pockets and me kicking, shoving, biting any part of her in reach. She pushed me, trying to hurl me on my back, and I stumbled and staggered and my jacket flew open and she fell, Sukie tumbled from her safe secret pocket and landed headfirst on the ground. Grandma—Ellen—stared at Sukie, at her grimy yarn hair and tousled rag skirts, and at all the uneven lumps and protrusions studding her cloth torso, her face, her fat little stuffed arms. The rocks in her head. Then we were both scrabbling for poor Sukie in the dust, all clawing nails and shoving palms and it was like fighting Amy's horrible dog all over again, and my teeth found thin paper-dry flesh thin hanging off the bone and I sank them in, deeper and deeper, and she screamed.

"Give them to me!" she howled. Grabbing for poor Sukie, kicking me in the side so I gasped and folded up like a school chair, her breath and her eyes hot and wild and this was her last chance, she knew it and I knew it, I was taking away her last delusion that she mattered at all. "You'll destroy us all with those, you'll destroy everything that's left, hand them over before I—"

"No!" I shoved back, furious at the strength in her, at her refusal to lie back and die already because it was my world now, the third species' world, I'd kill her here and now and never bring her back— "No more listening to you or him or anyone else—I don't need you! I know everything you did, and more—"

"Give them to me!"

"I know everything! Everything!"

"Give them to me now!"

She grabbed Sukie's arm and I heard the rip of cloth, seams straining and splitting along Sukie's stitched-tight side, and something swarming and red pulsed through me faster than blood and I hit her in the face, again, again. She was still moving and that enraged me so I grabbed for a thick heavy broken-off branch and the side of her head was horrible wet now just like Janey's had been, dark dampness soaking her broken-straw hair, and I kept striking her over and over and I couldn't stop.

"You don't run anything!" I was screaming, and she couldn't hear me and it didn't matter because I wasn't talking to her anymore, all this time I'd been telling it to someone else, to the someone making that animal noise like the howling of dogs coming closer and closer to where I stood. "I don't need you! I know all your secrets, I can make anything live or die! It's my world! It's my world, so come and get me!" Deafening, howling dog-cries all in my ears, making my skin pulsate and shiver, dark mass of them covering what had once been forest and beachland and they were everywhere now, everywhere, I wanted to scream again in happiness because I wasn't afraid of anything. "Come and get me! Come on! Come and meet who's in charge of you now!"

Everything was the wails of ghost-dogs running toward me and I couldn't hear myself talk. I couldn't hear myself and I couldn't see anything but pale teeth and dark fur and lamplight-yellow eyes and they were closer now, my dogs, my servants, they were everywhere, I—

TWENTY-SEVEN

AMY

We marched in circles. It was impossible to see just where we were or where we'd been; everything was the same and the nothingness had no signs or landmarks, just gritty-soft sand paler and cleaner than anything up above and the wild cries of phantom gulls in the clear sweet air and somewhere out there, always just out of our reach, the shoreline and the water stretching on to the horizon. It wasn't so bad, this wandering through nothing on our way to nowhere. It was peaceful. The feeling of seeking something we both were certain we'd never find, somehow that was a good clean feeling just like the sand and sky around us: boredom was banished, frustration impossible, because the looking itself was all we needed and someday, maybe, we just might reach the shore. Except that the shore wasn't real, nor the water, nor the sand, none of it truly part of life or of death. An illusion, to distract us and make us forever lost on our way to him—or perhaps Death's last feverish gasp as he, himself, lay dying.

But how could Death ever die, whether through our own human breed of decay and decline or in a fit of self-destructive rage? It had to be a lie, another fool's trick, when he claimed even he couldn't escape it. It had to be, because of that other thing he'd said, that—

That someone else had told me he'd heard Death say, someone I loved, someone who had just disappeared into the nothingness consuming all. Not Lisa. Not that little girl of Lisa's... not my mother... it was coming to me...

I still had him in my head, dark hair, off-kilter smile, a face that was engaging without being handsome, but not his name. Lake stones or no lake stones, it wasn't coming to me. There'd been an old man, too, who'd told us something important, but his memory was already lost. Just like Jessie had said would happen. *Give it time.*

"We can't stay here," I said to Jessie, to myself, there in the middle of the vast endless beach. I meant to sound sharp and loud like something neither of us could ignore but my voice was blunted by the quiet breezes and the far-off, close-up sound of the tides, the swell and strike of lake water against the sand like a fist punching out slow rhythms on a beanbag. "We have to find a path, a road, some way out—I'm starting to forget the others, just like you said. I'm starting to forget. Soon we might not remember why we're here at all."

Jessie turned to me slowly. She motioned around us at the sand, the sky, the vastness where we could both spin forever with our arms touching nothing, and in her face I saw the same urgent, thoughtful confusion I felt. "Remember Death," she said. "Forget everyone else, they never existed now anyway—it's a waste of energy, a waste of time. Remember Death. Remember him. Never let him go."

Because if he, too, were sliding slowly into a big nothing of his own devising, then even him we would forget. He, too, would be digested. The thought twisted my gut into a noose. Jessie stopped still in the sand and gazed into my eyes.

"I know you met him too," she said. "Met *him*. Face to face. Remember that." Trying to convince herself, as well as me, that this was our right road. I could see it in her eyes. "You can't find someone when you don't even know what they look like."

An artist's rendering. Have You Seen This... Thing? Entity? Angry God? But she was right, I had seen him, I truly had: that horrible day when our flight from Paradise City had gone so terribly wrong, when the others were captured or dead and I was all by myself, all alone. He stood there before me in a deserted street wearing his real face, none of the guises of our gone loved ones he liked to use to taunt us all, and as I tried to flee him and ended up right back where I started and almost pissed myself in raw uncontrolled fear, I saw, in him I saw—

Endless light. Endless night. Not two roads diverging, but the same constant, eternal path. Just as this beautiful miserable vanishing afterworld and the drab living one I'd left behind were really one and the same, a great half-discovered country, our own individual lives and deaths nothing but mile markers and signposts. All of us, all us humans, we'd been fighting the world's longest and most idiotic sectarian war because life and death were *the very same thing*. I saw it. It stood right there, staring me in the face just like Jessie did now, and I had been too distraught, too frightened, too all-alone to even try to understand what I saw. Only here, in this endless nowhere, was there the space to breathe and stand back and say out loud what some deep hidden part of me, seeing him, had instantly known as truth.

"There was light in him," I said.

That sounded so flat, so insufficient, spoken aloud, it didn't even begin to encompass what I meant. What I'd seen. But Jessie didn't mock me, she didn't snort and turn her back and resume her directionless plod over the sand. Instead, she smiled.

"Light," she said. "And night." She tilted her head back, savoring the semblance of a pungent lake breeze, exposing her throat like a cat wanting to be petted. Like a captive, awaiting the blade of her assassin's knife. "They're both inside him, all of it is inside him, and life and death put together are... this. Eternity. Right here." She squatted down suddenly on the sand, sliding it through her fingers, watching it stream slowly, inexorably back onto the dune. "This thing that's dying. Which means, since he *is* all of that, that he really is dying. He really can't escape it either."

She glanced up at me, and the naked need I saw in her for reassurance, for comfort was almost astonishing; she'd never have let that slip in the living world, never in front of a mere human pulled off that mask for a moment, but here it all came out so easily, here you couldn't and wouldn't hide anything. She needed me to tell her she hadn't just made it all up, that Death's true face had been more than a dream.

"But that can't be true," I said. "Something that *is* life, just as much as it's death—that thing can't die. It can't. It's impossible."

"Why?" she demanded. Sharper, contrary, more like her old self. "We've all got a little life and death in ourselves, right, don't we—we're born, we die, we have a tiny little stake in all of that too? Travel the same road? Everything living dies. Nearly anything living can *decide* to die. If it's got the will to decide anything at all. Why couldn't Death just... decline, like some old dusty, and crumble into nothing? Why is that so impossible?"

Because he's everything, I wanted to argue. *Because look all around you, and see that becoming* nonexistent *is so different, so very different than dying. Because it's one thing for what's living to choose to die, when really living and dying are just one and the same, but this is* everything *becoming* nothing, *everything can't just up and decide it wants to be nothing*—but I was no philosopher, and it wouldn't sound half as logical said out loud as it did in my own mind. And she was probably right, that I was probably all wrong.

And because since there were no secrets here, none at all, I somehow knew she could hear me without my even having to say it.

Death's true face, that awful blinding darkness and midnight sunrise spilling from behind the remnants of his human masks, swallowing up the moon and sun and all parts of the sky—I mourned the sight of it, the feel of his presence, that all-encompassing everything and suffocating womb. I mourned it like a lost lover. I wanted him back. I wanted it all back. I didn't have to say that aloud either, to know how deeply she shared in it.

"Say it," she said. "Out loud. Just say it."

"Why should I?" I asked. The cries of the gulls were growing louder. "Why would he ever care? If he is... dying, how do we know he could even hear it?"

"Because that's part of remembering him," she said. "That's part of never letting go. So just say it."

Because I can't say it. Because I'm too afraid that if I do, all I'll hear is laughter, or silence. She didn't have to say that aloud, for me to know she felt it. All right, then.

"I love this place," I said. To the sky, the sand, the birds who weren't really there. "I love what made it." My voice caught, cracked. I swallowed, waited until I could control it again. "I want all of it back."

The ground shifted beneath us and the sand took the look of soil, damp yet pearlescent and deep black like a field of crushed coal. Flowers, indiscriminate clusters of daisies and roses and lilac and hibiscus and blossoming clumps of roadside weeds—flowers that had nothing to do with each other in life, now thrown together by a higher hand like all those vanishing human ghosts—stuck pale tendrils and fist-thick shoots up from the dark wet ground. They grew up to our knees in seconds, burst out blooming and overpowered me with color, then curled up, withered, rotted too fast for me to take in that little glimpse of pure scarlet, those tantalizing flashes of yellow-pink-white-blue-living breathing green. They went limp like dirty string, the wan brown color of rotten apple. They fell. Then they rose again, over and over, bursts of frothy pink like apple trees in spring.

There was a sound, up above my head just like the phantom gulls, of a baby crying. It stopped, suddenly, just as the flowers all withered and died, and then as their rotten brown stems went green and straightened toward the sky, it started up again, the wailing rise-fall-rise of any healthy child, newborn child, that sky frightened me so much I dropped once more to my knees in the deep dark soil, gritty yet gleaming like someone had sifted pearls into mud. Inside my head, as it wept, I heard her voice, *Amy, Amy!* pleading and furious as I raised the shovel over our heads, as I kept bringing and bringing and bringing it down but after the first blow all speech was gone—and then fearless, beyond fear, merely wanting to know. *Amy? Amy. Where are you? I know you're here. But where are you?*

Why should I have been surprised that even after everyone else had gone, everything else was disappearing, she was still with me? Why should that have scared me? She'd be with me all the rest of my life, no matter what happened to me or where I went, and that was my doing, just like Kristin's baby she killed to spare it a worse death would always be with her. No, I wasn't surprised. But I was so scared. Because I was so sorry, but that didn't mean anything—no matter what Lisa's priests or anybody else said, being heartily sorry changed nothing forever.

But at least we had flowers. They bloomed and rotted and bloomed again and they weren't just chimeras, their petals were soft and bruised at the touch and their scents mingled and clashed and went sweetly unpleasant as they decayed, living things here where there was meant to be nothing, and when I looked up at Jessie, I saw she was crying, too. No phantom. I reached up a hand to her and without taking it she sat down heavily beside me, right there on the dirt.

"What is it?" I asked. But I think I already knew.

"Goddammit," she said, and sounded like her old self as she scrubbed furiously at her streaming eyes, rocking back and forth where she sat. "Why couldn't we have all just died? When does it *stop*?"

I laughed. It was a cruel sound but I wasn't trying to be cruel. "It never stops," I said. "Ever. At least, it was never supposed to, ever, before we all interfered. Isn't that the whole point?"

She wasn't listening to me. Instead she'd scooped up a handful of the dirt, touching it there and here like probing for bruises on a piece of fruit; I saw dandelion spores mixed in with the blackness, brown seeds and bits of leaf and smears of pollen from the rotting blooming things around us, but they just threw the soil's blackness into sharper relief, the gritty black whose sheen wasn't from shards of pearl but something inside itself, in each bit that was a grain of tarry sand. I touched it and felt tiny pinpricks on my fingers, each clump and grain a sharp little rock.

Jessie looked back up at me, red-eyed, infinitely tired. Then she smiled.

"'Death ain't all there is.' That's what... that man said to me. That old man I liked. Before he disappeared." She stirred the mixture in her palm with one slow fingertip. "He said, the old man said, that even Death has parts of himself he can't understand, just like a human being. Just like us. And that even though he's carrying something much bigger inside himself—the light in him, and the dark, just like we both saw—it's like he's really no different than the rest of us, deep down inside. Or maybe not deep down inside. The other way around. He's no different than us... on the outside."

The gulls were still calling, or a baby still crying, up overhead and that distracted me so I couldn't get at the kernel of what she meant. The deep-down-insideness of what she meant. I sat down beside her, taking up my own clod of earth. It was a handful of freshly whetted needles, burrowing into every pad and fold of flesh, but I didn't care. Seeds mixed with rot. Grains of lake-stone sand, which brought things back to life in ways nobody had ever been able to properly work out, part and parcel with the detritus of death.

People used to claim a meteor had landed on the site of Lake Michigan, thousands of years ago, creating in an instant the lake basin that scientists insisted was the slow work of an Ice Age glacier. That traces of the exploded meteor got into the sand and lake stones, infinitesimal particles, and that was what originally made the dead start coming back to life. Stupid myth, stupid story, though less poisonous than the ones that claimed it was the CIA, NASA, Jews, Communists, the Pope, secret nuclear testing, God's Eleventh Plague, a Potawatomi curse, why not just go all out and claim it was a Venus space probe or something—but somewhere, inside that whole ridiculous story, there was a plain observation of fact long suffocated in a swaddling-cloth of fairy tale. Something forever alive was contained *inside* something temporary, something mortal—like a carapace of rock, that could be broken, shattered, split open, or could wear away slowly, under the quiet onslaught of water and wind and infinite time.

"Death contains everything," I said. I squeezed my fingers shut around the clump of earth, my eyes prickling with the same burning harshness as my hand. I welcomed it. I relished it. "Everything that is, was, ever could have been. Life. Death. Eternity. He is the *container* of everything." I was very afraid to say aloud what came next. Fear, of any sort, was beside the point. "But the actual container, itself..."

"Old wine in new bottles," Jessie said. Then she laughed. She looked scared too. No hiding anything here. "And bottles, they crack and break."

The flowers around us withered and fell and died, and this time they didn't spring up again.

Death was alive once, too. That was what he'd said, the boy I had loved and forgotten. That was what he said Death told him. But how could that be true? Living things had always decayed and died, it was their nature, our nature; unless zombies had been some sort of last surviving, diminished remnant of a past human immortality, there had never been a time without Death. There had never been a world without Death...

...but maybe Death—and life, and eternity, for Death was everything and all—had never had any sort of *contained* form at all, and decided it desired one, required one, to walk the earth. Maybe Death, life, eternity, everything and all, were a sort of contagion, an all-encompassing one, just like the plague had been. A virus in need of a host. Viruses, I remembered from biology class an eternity ago, consumed their hosts in the process of replication. Death entered a host, lived inside them for as long as the host—or Death—could stand it, and then...

"Death," I said, scarcely able to credit my own words, "really was a human being, once. Or rather, what contains him once was human. He carries everything, eternity, all of it, like Atlas or something, but not on his back, it's all inside of him, hiding inside, just like we saw—" I was babbling now, giddy beneath the painfully blue sky filled with shrill skittering cries, but I didn't care, I couldn't care, it was all spilling out as if somewhere, deep in the parts of me I'd thought hollow and empty, the wellspring of this knowledge had been hiding all along. "Not the same person, necessarily, maybe Death keeps changing hosts or something, maybe it's like a sickness jumping from person to person—"

"And now what contains him really *is* dying," Jessie said. She was leaning forward where she sat, our foreheads nearly touching: putting our heads together. Were we right? Would it even matter if we were? "Just like I said, just like an old dusty slowing drying up and blowing away—or maybe he's just sick and tired of carrying around eternity. Maybe hoos pissed him off so much that he's giving it up. Not giving it up to another person—"

"But giving it *all* up." I shivered. I felt hot with excitement, sick with fear. "Refusing to pass on the burden. The illness. The..."

What was the word? What was it? I'd learned it when I was little, from the children's collection of Greek and Roman myths someone now lost from my memory had given me for a birthday, handwritten love scribbled on the flyleaf and a lot of words inside that I had to sound out carefully, put aside my reading to look up and scribble down in turn. Helot. Hoplite. Vestal. Stele. Stoic. Hubris.

"Apotheosis," I said.

The dead flowers were black with rot, drying into deep carbonized grit, softly shedding bits and pieces of themselves until they were indistinguishable parts of the dirt. The sands. The sobbing child-sounds overhead became the cries of gulls once more and we were back on the beach, back where we'd come from, but this time grasses swayed in clumps scattered over the surface, and every inch of sand, every last little wind-made divot and mound, was dotted with soil-dark stones like raisins in a loaf. Too many to collect, too many too count. Jessie and I were standing in beach grass up to our knees, feeling it sway and brush our pant legs like an insistent, half-hearted little caress, and someone else was standing further down on the beach, there on the shoreline that'd once seemed miles away. They were holding something in their arms. They were—

They *were*. She was. Overhead, underfoot, all around me, calling my name. Inside my head, my heart, where I'd placed her, in a moment of murderous rage, for as long as ever I might live. Jessie stiffened, drew in her breath, so I knew she saw her, too. We walked toward her in silence, and when Jessie tripped over a rock, cursing under her breath and her footsteps lagging, I didn't slow down.

I don't know what made me so certain, what gave me such absolute sureness what would happen next. Maybe it was this place, this soon-gone eternity, that did it. Maybe because I'd somehow known something like this would happen all my life, that I was empty and so I needed someone else to inhabit me and that someone, who I'd forced to live inside me whether she wanted to or not, was standing down there on the beach. Holding the one who lived inside her, and always would. That made it okay. That made it more of a fair fight.

I walked down the beachfront and the gulls cried overhead, real gulls now or at least they seemed more real, I saw flashes of white when I looked up and not just small escaping shadows. As I came closer, Ms. Acosta didn't move from where she stood. The lake water rolled in behind her, licking the very backs of her ankles in their sensible awful-looking white sneakers like nurse's shoes; her hair was full gray just like last winter, a furzy areole that the shore winds made stand almost straight up around her head. She smiled at me, shifting the baby more comfortably against her chest.

"Shhh," she said. "She's sleeping."

I looked closer into her cradle-folded arms and saw the minute, unmistakable rise and fall of the baby's chest, her shoulders as she dreamed an eternal dream. Infant shoulders I could've spanned with my one hand, that soft pulsing spot at the top of her head where the dark hair was thinnest, a tonsure. I wanted to touch her as she slept but I was afraid.

"Where's her mother?" I said.

"Dissolved to powder just like the rest of them."

Ms. Acosta's voice was quiet and calm. Big clear eyes stared at me, washed out and faded but still with a soft, quiet luminosity, watercolor streaks against the colorless parchment of her face and hair: just like when she was alive. There wasn't any blood on her. I'd been afraid there would be. Jessie had come down the sand-slope leading to the shore and stood there now, halfway between me and the safety of the ridge, watching without knowing what to do next. I didn't either.

"Dissolved to powder," I said. "Her mother. So why hasn't she?"

Ms. Acosta smiled, a little crook of one corner of her mouth. "Because she and I will always have unfinished business between us," she said. "Just like you and me. I can't put her down that easily."

No. She certainly couldn't. I should know. It wasn't such a bad burden, though, not when it came to meet you halfway.

"We can't be the only ones with unfinished business," I said. "There must have been billions of them, trillions. So why are we the only ones left?"

Ms. Acosta laughed, the sneezelike nasal honk we used to make fun of back in school, ten thousand years ago. "Why does one exact leaf fall off one exact tree, onto the roof of one exact passing car? Why does one raindrop splash into one exact gutter? Why does one atom, in one breath of air, find its way into any one set of lungs?" She shifted the baby up towards her shoulder, shook the frowsy hair from her eyes with the old stern, Amy-you've-done-it-again look. "Why was your mother—by the way, it was her who gave you that book—in the wrong place at the wrong time, to let the lab first take notice of her? Why did you never die in the plague? Why did your friend over there"—she nodded toward Jessie—"live too, when every part of her wishes she hadn't? Everything, everywhere, it's all just so eternally random."

Her voice—his voice, its voice—was thin and reedy and every syllable seemed to vanish on the wind, rising up toward the endlessly wheeling gulls who never descended to feed. I put my hand to the back of the baby's head, felt the same heat and steady pulsations as I had in the lake stone still resting, undisturbed, in my pocket. I willed that sensation to strengthen me. To dispel terror.

"You're dying," I said. "The shell of you, I mean."

"I'm *tired*," she said. "I'm weary. I'm sick unto myself of all of you. I have had enough."

I gazed into the semblance of Ms. Acosta's gray eyes, their washed-out watercolor. "I didn't mean to take anything from you," I said. "I'm sorry."

She pressed her cheek to the baby's skull. "You and your friend," she said, "know what that all counts for."

Nothing. Less than nothing. It was still the truth and I was still glad to have said it.

"It can't have always been you," I said. "Can it? I mean, whoever you were, once, back when you were just an ordinary human being—you can't have been the only one in all of history who ever... contained all this."

She smiled. "Incubated this contagion."

Jessie, unable to contain herself, crept closer.

I stroked the baby's hair, sparse and soft. Its flesh was as real as mine. Its bones as solid as mine. I got it wrong, I thought, believing Death's appearing before me as Ms. Acosta, as myself, as anyone else was some mere disguise: Death *was* everyone else, was all of us together, and we burst out of it, him, in ways and at times, perhaps, even he scarcely could control. Brimming over with everything, with the sum of all existence. What would that feel like? If I was right, if Jessie was right, if this angry god that contained all and everything was also and at the very same time encased in flesh just as real, bones just as solid, breath just as vital as ours...

"What happened?" I asked as Jessie came up beside me. "Were you forced? Tricked? Did you… inherit having to do it, or something?" My face flushed, my own thickheaded toddler questions embarrassed me, but we'd found Death and we'd found so much more and I couldn't stop now, I couldn't stop even knowing the next stop would surely be nowhere and nothing. "Or is it just like you were saying before, about everything being eternally random?"

No answer.

"So are we both crazy?" Jessie demanded. "Or is it true? Is any of it true?"

The words burst from her, she couldn't contain them, but she sounded a way I'd never heard her before: humble, that was what she seemed. Awed. Almost timid. As perhaps she'd been the very first time she met Death, saw what we had been calling his true face—not understanding, any more than I had, that *all* of it was his true face. All sides of him were just as real. All was all.

"Is it true?" Jessie repeated. "Is she right?"

Ms. Acosta's smile deepened. It was far too broad, far too wide, for any mere human face to contain, but in that unnatural mouth and those washed-out, colorless eyes there was no anger, no wrathful rapacity, only a sort of weird delight. She ran a finger over the baby's tiny ear, its full round cheek, as it ignored us all and slept the deep, profound sleep of oblivion.

"I can't help it," she said. "I mean, it's absurd of me, I know that, but I like a good laugh as much as anyone. Even if it's on myself. So I always get such a kick out of accidentally tipping my hand."

A small dark shape was running over the sands, running like he'd never be out of breath and like the sharp hurting stones were just more padding for his paws. A speck, near the shoreline. Over the ridge. Up the duneface toward the grasses and trees and us. A sound came out of my throat like joy and I went running to meet him midway, and as Nick jumped at my legs and I wrapped my arms around his good solid weight, the beach itself dissolved, vanished as suddenly as had my ghosts; vanished with the calling gulls, the sunlight, as we emerged into a somewhere that was all dark, milky-thick fog. Then sunlit, and green.

TWENTY-EIGHT

STEPHEN

"Amy?"

I could hear. I couldn't see, but I could hear a woman's voice, a woman I knew, rising in disbelief. Sobbing laughter. "Amy? Jessie! How did you—Stephen? Oh, Christ!"

A weight, something both soft and sharp, flung itself on me and I shouted, then was shocked to realize that meant I had a voice. Then shocked all over again that I had arms to held onto the weight, fingers to clutch it, a memory to know once again who it was. Lisa. That was who spoke.

Lisa. Amy. Jessie. I'd forgotten them all, I'd forgotten everything, I'd felt my own body falling into nothingness but somehow, now, I existed again. This wasn't like what had happened all those years at the lab, being shoved headfirst into death over and over again and then frogmarched back into some parody of life—I was reborn, in earnest. I was nothing become something. I was life and death surging together in a single exuberant high tide, the waters bottled up and contained and crashing inside my own flesh. My pulse thudded so hard and fast and out of control that I should've been scared, I should've felt like I was dying, but wasn't it all the same, in the end? Wasn't it? Dead or living, I *existed.* I *was.* I was *here.*

I started to laugh, and it was with joy. I was blind, I was seized up with a heart attack, I had no idea where I was or who was with me but dammit, I was here!

Then my heart slowed down, and joy gave way to simple relief, and by slow degrees my vision came back. Lisa was still holding onto me, grinning and with eyes so shiny I knew she felt just what I'd been feeling, that the waters were crashing inside her too. Inside all of us. Renee was laughing and crying and kissing Lucy, Naomi, any and all of us in reach. Linc grabbed hold of Jessie and held on tight, his arms trembling and eyes wide as a cat's who'd pounced on a rabbit, then just as quickly, he released her. Nick trotted in a circle around us, sniffing, taking his canine notes on what had become of us. I grabbed Amy and didn't let go.

"I remember forgetting everything," I said, and laughed with the last remnants of my weird reborn bliss. And disbelief. "And then, I... something happened, and I was gone. And then I was back."

"We—" Amy trembled from head to foot. I tried to steady her, even though I still didn't know what had happened or what would happen now. "Jessie and me. We didn't fade away when you did, before. Those lake stones, they—we saw—"

She could barely speak. Jessie, buffeted like an old newspaper in a windstorm from Lisa to Linc to Renee and back again, couldn't either. Had they found Death, faced him down somehow like Jessie had been crazy to do? Was all this, right here, some sort of unexpected reprieve? It couldn't be, I knew it couldn't. Nothing was ever that easy.

"Where are we?" I asked. "Are we still... dead? Do you know this place?"

It was some sort of park, it looked like, not a tiny contained city park but somewhere big and wild and overgrown: a nature preserve, with picnic tables. Except the tables were nestled in grass so tall and thick, the blades were like long, thin, decaying teeth eagerly chewing and swallowing them up. A handkerchief-sized parking lot, its asphalt cracked and spitting up weeds, lay behind us; up head, beyond the picnic tables, was a riverbank almost hidden by clusters of trees in full summer leaf, a crumbling wooden watermill, a white-painted hexagonal gazebo on the summit of a small, gently sloping hill. The front of the gazebo was open, two or three nearly rotted-out steps leading inside; an angled plank bench lined the other five sides. Someone was sitting inside it, watching us, a skinny little woman I was certain I didn't remember from this or any lifetime. She had black hair even wilder and more snarled than Linc's, sallow skin, and, I saw when she raised a hand in mock greeting, fingers covered nearly to the knuckle in jangling gold and silver rings. Just like the ones Renee had on her own hands.

Nick walked up closer to me, wagging his tail; I petted him, a silent apology, and felt a heavy, quiet sort of relief when he stayed at my side.

"Do *you* know this place?" I asked him.

"We do," Jessie said softly. She, and Linc, and Renee, stared fixedly at the black-haired woman without waving back. "We did. Before she took it away from all of us."

The black-haired woman rose from her bench and came toward us, smiling.

TWENTY-NINE

JESSIE

Well, heigh-ho, Teresa, long time no see and fuck you forever! And there was Teresa's gazebo, the simulacrum of it, her own ash maybe still swirling around its rafters like an angry cluster of bees. It was the first thing you saw in Great River Park once you passed the red brick visitors' center, the parking lot, the water mill that had still been operational until we undead took over the place. Home, a year ago, a thousand years ago. Ours. Except not.

Why the hell did he, it, have to decide to show up as Teresa? I wanted to see Sam again, Sam who'd killed himself and then found himself right back on earth undead. Or Sam's poor Ben, who hated hoos with such poison I was Our Lady of All Flesh in comparison. Or Mags, poor Mags, or Annie, our peacemaker, who we'd had to kill for her own sake when she lost her eyes. Anyone else. Anyone at all.

The part of Death that was Teresa—the part I'd once thought no more than an outward disguise, a shell, but really and truly was her—stopped before me, the innumerable grave-robbed rings I now thought of as Renee's clinking and clicking on her emaciated fingers. She shoved her wind-chime hands into her pockets.

"Didn't you ever once curse this undead life?" she asked me. Still smiling.

Joe's words, the last time we ever saw each other. Poor Joe, who I used to love like the crazy kid I was back then, even after he turned his back on me and all of us, even after he gave up. Linc stared past Teresa, fixing his eyes on the gazebo's peeling white wood, and I saw a muscle tense and tighten along his jaw, something in his eyes between weariness and longing. The others were huddled behind Renee, holding their collective breath, waiting on some sort of signal I wasn't going to deliver. Amy came running up, then her steps faltered and she stopped.

"So we did it," she said to Teresa, but soft and tentative like she were in someone else's church or temple, afraid of offending. "We found you."

"Why you?" I demanded. "Why couldn't you have come as someone else? Anyone else?"

Death, Teresa, the part of Death that was Teresa, just shrugged. "Aren't you glad it wasn't that worthless brother of yours, yet again? Maybe I have less say than you think, over what part of me shows up, and when, and how." She cocked her head to the side, like she always had alive whenever she thought she'd just said something flat-out clever, and grinned. "Anyway, this part of me was a loudmouthed braggart, wasn't she, when she was living? Wasn't that part of why you hated her so much? So it makes sense for her to show up in me now, when I went and shot off my big mouth and gave myself away—"

"Then we were right," Amy said, and then louder when nobody answered: "We were right. Weren't we?"

Teresa reached out, as if nobody had spoken, and clapped me on the shoulder. Behind me I heard Lisa draw a sharp breath.

"Let's go for a walk," Teresa said. She tilted her chin up, calling to everyone. "You crazy kids too? Just a short little stroll, how about it?"

Shoulder to shoulder with Teresa I walked toward the gazebo, the others beside and behind me, easy familiarity guiding my steps, Linc's, Renee's. Our feet, they knew these hillocks and ridges and sloping crests of ground we'd walked hundreds, thousands of times, in our time of endless dying; we knew it like hands know a lover's body in the dark. We followed the curve and bend of the river, crossed in a line over the old footbridge, took a gentle left to where open fields lay to one side, the beginnings of the woodlands the other. I surprised a deer here once, a stag so unexpected and big and beautiful I let it go, sated as I was on possum and raccoon, watched it bound back into the trees and toward the water knowing he and I couldn't want for anything else. A thousand years ago, give or take a few centuries. Gone, and gone.

"Where are we going?" Amy's mother asked aloud. "Are we still in..."

Her voice died away, and we kept on walking. Florian had had a tree deep in the woods where he'd hidden his lake stones, the last part of his unspoken past he couldn't bring himself to give up, circling the trunk like a crude new-laid mosaic. Linc and I, though, we'd buried the remnants of his remains deeper in the woods, under an older, bigger tree that struck us more worthy of him than that sapling-stone. Whether or not Death had intended it, or anyone else liked it, that was where I was going, one last time.

I could remember Florian again. Did that mean he was back like the others were back, Linc, Renee, Nick, all of Amy's people? And what did it mean, their return?

We passed the weather-stripped sign marking the Sulky Trail turnoff. That first deep bend in the river, with a tiny wooden observation deck hidden in a cluster of bushes. The old playground, farther in the woods near the river's second footbridge, where Joe and I had met for the last time and—enough. I closed my eyes and walked with him, imagining him beside me, the both of us wandering just like the old days over the trail and out to the underpass and the far side where nobody would bother us.

That little hillock here, at the start of the trail—watch those hoof-hollows, good for nothing but catching muddy rainwater—then that tiny clearing where the deer liked to feed, poor stupid deer never figuring out how easy they made it for us to snap their necks and pick them off, and then, and then—

I closed my eyes again. I imagined them all right beside me, all of us walking like the old days in a fractious, but easy group: Teresa striding ahead, in search of places none of us wanted to go; Ben and Sam joking about God knows what, Sam's face seam-splitting in a rare outright grin; Billy strutting and waddling alongside, Mags never a moment out of his sight. Me and Joe in the center, letting everyone else do the talking. Renee, still shy, bringing up the rear, with Linc wandering aimless from person to person, never lingering long at anyone's side. And last of all, Florian, our eldest, our heart, nothing ever the same after he died and left us. Our unspoken flesh and bone.

"Here," Linc said, startling me from my thoughts. "Right here."

A clearing, small but still more than big enough for the lot of us, bordered by clusters of beech, maples, ash. A big oak tree almost at its center, old and thick-trunked and with deep-fissured bark perfect to give undead, itchily infested flesh a good satisfying scratch. Florian's tree, with his last few surviving bones and the soft crumbly top part of his skull buried in its roots at our feet. One last sight of it all. One last time.

Amy, the hoo-kiddy who couldn't have had any idea what this place meant to me, she looked at the tree and looked at me and all of a sudden, she smiled. And I smiled back because there was such a strange lightness in that deafeningly silent air, a lightness and ease I saw on all our faces and that feeling had a name: relief. Whatever happened next, whatever became of existence and us, soon all of this would be over. We had found Death and emerged from oblivion and that had to mean, it *had* to, that at long last we were getting out. I wanted out. I was so tired of all of this. Living, dying, living-in-dying, I wanted off the merry-go-round. I'd had enough candy and rides. I wanted to go home to where it was dark and quiet and sleep and sleep forever. As much sleep as I should've had before I first woke up from the dirt, back when I was newly made and newly buried. Please, please, let me the hell out. I didn't want anything, didn't need anything but to be there in the stillness forever.

A gentle bony hand, *all* bones, rested on my shoulder and when I turned, Florian was there. He took me in his arms and when he let me go, as he embraced Linc and Renee, and Amy, and an eager Naomi, his expression was grave. Teresa just stood there, watching.

"I ain't meant to be here," he said. "You weren't never meant to see me again, or talk to me again. You know that. It always meant that things wasn't right."

And that memories were all I was meant to have of him, or anyone else I'd lost. And that any talking we were meant to do would have been just another memory, an endlessly repeating retread of what we'd already said to, done with, thought of each other long before he'd gone. That was all you got. That was all they needed. It was all just the nature of the universe.

"I know," I said.

"So, I gotta leave now." His pale blue eyes blinked fast, hard. "I gotta leave now forever."

I nodded. Florian looked almost sad, just on the far edge of sad, but stronger than that in his face was that same relief I was allowing myself to feel, allowing to leak prematurely into my bones. Because I wanted out that strongly, that badly. Naomi, still hovering around his heels, tugged urgently at his sleeve.

"Don't go," she pleaded. "Please?"

Gently, he detached her little hand, pushed her back to Lisa's waiting arms. Urgency made his eyes heated and fierce but there was a quiet at the bottom of them, an underlying kindness that nothing could alter or diminish. Just as he'd been in life. My memory of him hadn't failed me. It hadn't lied.

"You ain't *gotta*," he said, to me, to Amy in turn. "Remember that. You ain't gotta." He put a hand on my arm. His fingers just barely curled around it, but his grip was iron-strong. “Both of you, either of you. All of you. Before you say yes, you gotta be sure.”

“Sure of what?” Lisa frowned, looking from him to us and back with unease curdling her words. “Sure of what?”

“It’s time,” Teresa said softly.

“It is,” Florian agreed. “Long past time.”

Then what had been him flew back inside me, inside all of us, and was gone from my sight forever.

THIRTY

AMY

Years ago on my birthday my mother gave me a book, a secondhand Bulfinch's Greek and Roman myths full of illustrations so beautiful, they made me wish I knew how to draw. As I stood there, face to face with Death once again, surrounded by the only people left to me in a place that was someone else's longed-for home, the stories from that book kept coming to me stronger and stronger and I couldn't get them out of my head. Iphigenia, sacrificed by her father Agamemnon to ensure safe passage for his ships battling the Trojans—I always rooted for the Trojans, Aeneas escaping the ruins with his aging father clinging to his back. There were some versions where Iphigenia offered herself willingly, a good Greek virgin obeying the behest of the gods, and of war. And ones where Artemis wrapped a cloud around the sacrificial altar, carried the real Iphigenia off in safety to some distant island while a double, a dummy, a ghost was "slain" in her place. The letter of the law obeyed, the spirit hardly mattered. Not all sacrifice was what it looked like—

Old stories in lost books, stories nobody would ever tell again because there was no one left to hear them. We had summoned Death back from oblivion barely knowing how we'd done it, but all I could think about was Iphigenia, movie theaters, the smell of fake butter and the sugary tastes-like-real-maple-syrup my mother and I had every Friday night, our weekly pancakes and bacon dinner. The dry shuddery feel of Mrs. Acosta's flyaway gray hair and her nubbly cotton sweater pressing against my skin as she gave me a hug, the strawberry cake my mother bought from a tiny Polish bakery every birthday, the faintest scent-memory of motor oil on my father's skin, the wild stomach-drop of my first time on a swing set, the big roller coaster at Prospect Fun Park (1,892 Days Without An Environmental Incident). The feel of my own hair against my hand, thick and a little coarse and begging to be washed. The steel wool of Nick's fur. The waxen sweet of candy-corn pumpkins at Halloween. The lethal apple-cider smell of Dave's diabetic dying breath. The unyielding discomfort of unbroken Doc Martens, the only gift my aunt ever gave me that I'd liked. The strange lit-up quiet after a heavy snowfall. The first lilacs of spring. Florian's face, as he told us all goodbye.

Every memory, every gathered-up impression, every interior scrap and souvenir of what it had been to be alive, and all of it was killing me. It was killing me because as the memories of life rushed through me at quintuple speed, I also felt for the first time, swelling up so hard and fast in me that it shoved aside the air, all the death around me, all the death I'd caused: Ms. Acosta, Mags, Billy, Phoebe even though I hadn't meant it, Stephen's final trip to the lab and a slit throat. Probably Natalie, whom I'd deliberately turned my back on and forgotten. And so much more than that, so many more, all the death, the dying, the remnant-ghosts everywhere in the universe. And I felt all the life, too, all the life in everything and myself, swelling up full of air a buoyant balloon and there simply wasn't one without the other, life and death were a single body and trying to conquer either one only maimed, disfigured, blinded, stifled the heartbeat of all the universe. Without one, there wasn't the other.

Ever.

That was just how it was. That was how it always had to be.

"Precisely," Death said to me, nodding with a satisfied, press-lipped smile. "Exactly."

You gotta be sure. Sure of what? What was I sure of? Not anything much, just a few things. A very few things. I loved my mother, and Lisa, and Stephen. I was a killer and I was sorry about it, but I couldn't change it. I wasn't human, not really, not any more than Jessie or her friends were. Maybe since before Natalie ever touched me, maybe ever since I was born. Maybe that meant something. Maybe it always did. I loved this world, this afterlife, the hidden viscera and lungs of the body that encompassed life, and death, and all. I loved it, and I had to save it from nothingness because I never wanted to leave it. But even now, that wasn't up to me.

Was that surety? Was that certitude? It was all I had. It was all I would ever have to offer.

"Come over here, Amy," Lisa said quietly. "Jessie. Come and stand with us."

We ignored her, our only regard for Death. She, he, it looked different now: a white-haired, dark-skinned, arthritically pinched old man, wrapped in a dirty terrycloth robe exposing sharp shaggy shins and bare callused feet, his expression the baleful glare of someone long used to snapping his fingers and getting his own way. King Lear. I always liked Greek plays better than Shakespeare. Nick left Stephen's side and padded up to me, the feel of his fur offering comfort, sustenance, in the face of whatever was about to happen.

"This is what you wanted, isn't it?" the old man said to Jessie, his voice querulous and creaky and nobody's we recognized. "To see the old stomping grounds, one last time? See your kindly blue-eyed Grandfather Maggot one last time? Well, here he was, and here you are. A little reward, for all that hard work trying to get to me. Enjoy it."

Jessie reached up to the oak tree, pulling down a branch and contemplating its leaves like she'd never seen such strange, verdant, tissue-thin things before. Then she let the branch spring back.

"We know you now," she said. She was calm, calm and so overwhelmingly tired. "You said it yourself, you tipped your hand. We know you."

Death sat down right there on the ground, near a cluster of bushes covered in sprigs of tiny white flowers. The oak leaves were full summer-sized, but nearer the ground, the buttercups, the goldenrod, the violets bloomed in all their color, an endless spring. His heels stuck in the ground like twin trowels, bare brown toes pointing skyward.

"You were just like us, once," I said. I wanted to sit down too, to savor the scents of the flowers and the dark soft earth, but part of me insisted on remaining standing even though there was no place to flee, nowhere to run. "You were alive, and human. Then you became something else. You became everything, living and dead."

Behind me, Stephen made a startled sound. "That was really true?" he demanded. "I thought... maybe it was a riddle or something. A puzzle we had to solve. It couldn't be that simple."

Death grinned at us, a mouthful of yellowing half-broken teeth. His eyes flared up, very briefly, with the lively pleasure of a far younger thing.

"It's just that simple," he said. "I told you so! I gave myself away. I do that, sometimes. A lot of the time." The smile faded, his face going calm and serene. "But of course, nothing's ever really that simple. As you already know full well."

I moved to sit down next to him. He shook his head, and I stayed on my feet.

"Don't ask me who I was," he said. "Don't ask me what I was, what I looked like, how I thought or felt or what I believed about anything, when I was just another human among humans. Don't ask me what made me into this." He rested his palms on his cloth-covered knees. "Not that those are taboo questions. It's just been so long, and I've since become so many things at once, that I don't remember. I don't remember what I was, or how I became otherwise. Not at all."

"I barely remember being human either," Jessie said. Her words were slower, more careful than I'd yet heard from her: smooth pebbles, each held on her tongue and dropped steadily from her lips, as if she feared the wrong one would explode the world. As well it might. "And it was only... ten years ago, fifteen, that that's all I was. And I've still only ever been one person, the same person, even since. I've never held every living thing inside me, every dead thing. I've never *been* all of existence."

Death thought that over. "I'm not all-knowing," he said. "I'm not all-seeing. *Being* everything doesn't mean you *understand* everything, any more than being human means you comprehend every last aspect of humanity. You lot never do stop surprising me, usually in unpleasant ways."

"Like now," Jessie said. "With the labs."

"Like now," he agreed.

He slipped a hand into his bathrobe pocket, taking out a dull green lake stone broken up with a few mud-colored, zigzagging streaks. It looked exactly like the one Florian had left in the woods, exactly like the one I'd slipped into my own pocket; I didn't need to check now, to know that pocket was empty.

"The thing is," he said, the soul of calm, the very voice of reason, "the earth, poor thing, it's been out of balance for so very long, so impossibly long—nearly as long as humanity's been around, to make the place worse and worse and worse with your meddling, your industrial filth, your insane conviction that you alone among any living thing are special, chosen, important enough to slip the bonds of your own mortality." He shook his head, soft ominous laughter rising from his sunken throat. "And not just immortal, but eternally strong, eternally young, eternally rich and powerful and alluring—the greed. The insane, sickening *greed*!"

He clenched his fingers tight and I heard a sudden snapping sound, so much like bones being broken that I jumped. His hand unfurled again and the lake stone was just so much ash, inky ash spilling from his palm and spinning on the wind. My mouth felt suddenly dry-caked with grit, a tormenting need to cough, but I knew that'd give no relief.

"Greed," he repeated. "Let's face it, I think we all realize you're entirely beyond help, you lot of humanity. Nothing to be done. You certainly can't police yourselves, you never leave anything well enough alone—" He looked up at me and laughed, an avuncular little chuckle that made the skin at the back of my neck tighten up. "It's like I said to you before, I'm sick and tired of it. I'm *sick*. I'm *tired*." He reached over and pulled a buttercup from its stem, examining it, his thumb caressing the soft yellow petals like they were the only thing in existence that had never let him down. "I am, as our dear Jessica phrased it, 'dusty.' In other words, I have decided—I have realized—that I am simply too damned old for all of this."

The elderly man in the bathrobe wavered, faded, and in his place came the man I'd seen back at Jessie's beach, blue-jeaned and work-shirted, with a head of barely graying hair and a broad, self-satisfied smile. Jessie shook her head in disgust.

"Why," she asked, "do you always have to come back as Jim? Of every living thing that ever was, why?"

Death laughed again. "C'mon now, sis, I know you've always had a hopeless temper—just like Dad, and I bet you can't even see it—but you don't have to be so *petty*! After all, we owe so much of what's happened to good old Jim."

He flickered again. Changed again. "And to me," said Natalie, with unmistakable pride. "Especially to me."

My stomach soured. I knew that Natalie wouldn't live through this, somehow I just knew back when we all left her there in the ruins of her own lab. And I left her there anyway. No matter that she'd killed me, no matter what else she'd tried to do to all of us. Another death at my feet. Like he could hear what I was thinking, Nick snuffled and whined and pressed paws against my leg as if trying to coax me away from the clearing. Nowhere to run. Nowhere to hide. No wish to do either one. I patted him, and swallowed.

"I meant what I said, before," I told Death. "That I was sorry

I ever stole anything from you, accidentally or not. That I was sorry about everything. You could..." I glanced at my mother, who watched me with fearful eyes and clenched fists but made no move to stop me, and leapt into the breach. "Natalie was right, wasn't she, that we're sort of... unique? All of us made this way by the lab? You could have me as a sort of... a sacrifice. Something to... that could maybe expiate what happened, or something." This had all sounded a lot more eloquent in my head, and in my head I hadn't stammered and stumbled through it with a dust-dry tongue and acid creeping toward my throat, but then Iphigenia and Polyxena had had the best talent in Athens for speechwriters while I only had myself. I stretched my arms out wide. "I mean, here I am. You can have me."

"And me," my mother said immediately. She was by my side before I'd ever heard her steps. "I'm no different than she is. I'm made as differently as she is. You can have me too. You can have me instead."

"And me," said Stephen.

"No," Lisa said. Her arms were wrapped around Naomi, roping the little girl to her body. "*No*."

But nobody was listening to her.

Death, still in Natalie's form, stared at us each in turn. Then Natalie was Jim once again and Jim slowly, mockingly, shook his head, a familiar malice dancing in his eyes.

"For Amy so loved being-ness that she gave her one and only self, that whatever exists et cetera, et cetera..." He flicked dismissive fingers at me, stretching his legs out more comfortably on the earth. "We've all heard that old chestnut before, and it means nothing—other than that, predictably, you still don't understand. You can't *sacrifice* to someone what's already theirs, and like all human beings since the dawn of humanity, you just can't accept that the second you're conceived, that very second, you're mine. Everything everywhere is mine."

His face flushed, darkened with a breathless anger, then just as suddenly he was composed and smiling, methodically pulverizing the buttercup's petals between his fingertips. "There's death and life in everything, everywhere. They're one and the same. They're all simply *being*. As you already figured out for yourself—and if you hadn't, I wouldn't be bothering with you right now."

Linc and Renee exchanged glances. Then Linc walked up to where Death sat among his flowers. "So you really are dying," he said. You're crumbling away, just like— "

"Am I?" Death mused. "Is that what this feeling is? I really don't know. I don't know if this was always going to happen. I don't know if this is the long-delayed old age of the human being I was... whoever that was, whenever that was. Or simply the vessel of existence—namely me—cracking down the middle and snapping, what with how humanity keeps gleefully flinging me to the floor. I do not know." He shrugged. "But I do know that whatever the truth is, I *feel* so old. I feel as though I've been as I am forever, and that it never comes to anything. I feel as though I could lie down forever." His voice was so soft now, insinuating, a dangerously tempting lull. "And that feeling of falling, that you humans have sometimes when you're losing yourselves to sleep? I could fall myself, fall and fall through a dark chasm of nothingness and never stop. Never land." A barely audible whisper of longing. "Because there will be nowhere left to land, and nothing left that falls."

We'd failed. He'd never really meant us even to try to succeed. I was shaking. Stephen stroked my arm, a quick nervous touch of reassurance. His fingers were trembling too.

"You can't," he told Death. "You were a living mortal thing once, too, you said so, and you never asked to be born. You can't just take existence away from everything, just because you're angry, or tired, when you only ever contained it, you never *created*—that's worse than anything Natalie or anyone else ever tried to do."

Death contemplated Stephen's words. His face crinkled up in a bemused frown.

"Please," he told Stephen, "do not tell me that was somehow

meant to shame me."

Stephen glanced fearfully around at us, as though we were all going to ambush him, force him to stop talking. We couldn't. We wouldn't. "What's beyond you?" he asked Death. "What... lies beyond you? You're existence, but did something else bring existence itself into— "

"Yes." Death nodded. "Don't ask me what, or how, or why, because I don't know. I don't know, any more than anything else that exists has ever known its first cause. But the answer is yes. And that is the last you ever get from me."

"Which means," Stephen said, barely hearing him, pushing doggedly onward, "that you never *created* life itself. Or any of this, right here, anything beyond life. You said it yourself. You're just a vessel. You simply embody." Death shrugged, just a little lift of the shoulders. "You only ever contained it. You wouldn't even be destroying your own work. It'd be the worst crime, the worst— "

"Sin," Lisa said. Very quietly.

"Fine. If you want. The worst *sin*, that there ever was."

Death smiled. "And such," he said, "is the nature of oblivion, that once the crime is committed, it never really happened at all. After all, its victim never was."

Stephen sputtered, lost for words. My mother opened her mouth to speak. "I— "

"I think we're through now," Death said. "In fact, I think everything, everywhere, is finally and forever through."

He stretched out on the ground, lying on his side, an arm cradling his head. "Go along now, pets," he said, still with Jim's body and face but Florian's hoarse, reedy timbre coming from his mouth. "Go along. I'm tired."

I had lost my peripheral vision without realizing it, all my sights telescoping down to him as the sky, the trees, the ground lost their form and dissolved. It wasn't him doing that to me, or to the chimera of woods around us, it was my own fear. I felt something cold and wet nudge my palm once more and could have cried with relief because Nick was still there, Nick would be there beside me no matter what, I couldn't do this all alone. Even if I was sure. Even if I was absolutely sure.

Was I sure? Would I ever really know? Would I ever even remember?

"You're old," I said. "You're tired. You're wearing out."

A hand rested gently, fleetingly on my shoulder. I turned, expecting to see Stephen, my mother, but it was Jessie. She knew, she knew what was about to happen. Maybe she had all along. What had she said? *Old wine in new bottles*. Exactly. She knew.

"You don't remember what you were, or when you became what you are now." I rocked from foot to foot where I stood, to keep myself from turning tail and running away. There was nowhere else to go. There never had been. He showed me that, back when I first saw him face to face. "But you didn't begin that way, you *became* it. You know that much. Which means... you took someone else's place. Someone else who had this burden, this everything, and grew old, or disgusted, or tired, and gave it all up."

He turned his head where he lay and his eyes, fixed on me, were wide and dark and fathomless. We could all fall and fall through them and never stop. Never land.

"Someone else could take it from you," I said. "Couldn't they. Someone else could become what you— "

"Stop," Lisa said. She looked around at Stephen, at my mother, in disbelief that nobody else tried to stop me. That they knew they couldn't stop me. "Amy, Jessie? Do not say another word."

But I wasn't listening to her, because there was no time left. We had no time left. Death's black chasms of eyes had turned to a hard pounding light that overwhelmed, blinded, a spotlight shone straight on our faces. Jessie and I turned to each other and she looked so wretched, every inch of her outlined in sorrow and remorse, that I smiled and touched her face the way a mother might touch her child because there was no call for that, absolutely no call at all. I knew what I was going to do and I had for such a long time now and it was all right, it was all truly all right. We could have been friends, maybe, she and I, in another kind of life. Maybe, just now, we'd turned out the best friends each other ever had.

"I can't," she whispered to me, quietly, a broken sound. "I'm sorry. I just can't. I want off this merry-go-round, I can't stand it, I—"

"You 'ain't gotta,'" I said. "It's all right. It's going to be all right."

She couldn't do it, and I understood why. I always had. Finally, I thought, I almost started to understand myself. This had been coming, slowly, gaining on me moment by moment, my entire life. One way or another. And I knew, I was sure, what were to be my last words.

"Don't say anything," Lisa insisted, louder, defiant. She knew what was happening, she knew and I wouldn't let her stop it. "Nobody say another damned word, don't, please—"

Death was losing his physical form, turning taller, lighter, darker, as he prepared to consume this whole earth, the skies, the stars, his own self. Everything that was and would be. This was the end. This was our final chance.

"I'll take it all from you," I said. "I'll take your place, I'll be what you are now."

My mother made a sound, a wordless animal sound like a mother might make when she loses her child. But she didn't try to stop me. I wouldn't be stopped. "You can die. You can sleep. You can sleep forever. I'll take it all from you, everything that is, everything that—"

"*Amy*!" Lisa cried, frozen where she stood, a paralysis of panic. "Amy! *Stop*!"

"Eternity!" I shouted. "Eternity! I choose eternity!"

All that was left of his skies, his stars, his kingdom was his face, swollen to Earth-size and then Jupiter and then something for which Jupiter was only one of hundreds of fleck-tiny, barren moons. He was the earth and the heavens and the day and the dark, one eye a blinding beam of perpetual sun, endless light, and the other a chasm, a miles-long well choked at the very bottom with drowned bodies. An endless night. His smile was the earth opening up to swallow us all, a smile splitting his immense face open ear to ear, like a cut throat. Everything was overpowering light, everything overwhelming darkness.

He stretched out a hand to me, a huge enveloping hand. I was right, I was sure, I'd never take back what I'd given him but we would all cease to exist anyway, that was just how it was, at long last it was all over—

Blue.

The blueness all around was soothing and cool, a clean, medicinal stream bathing a wound. But it was nothing but the blue of an ordinary sky, an ordinary sky on an ordinary day in late spring heading into early summer. The sand, ordinary sand the color of an unfrosted cake just out of the oven, sank and settled beneath my body and sloped gently downward, from a ridge punctuated with tall grasses and stubby scrub trees to a long stretch of choppy gray water. Out there on the horizon, plainly visible on a sunny clear day like this was, was the smoke-colored outline from the lake's other shoreline, the standing remains of what had been the skyline of Chicago. There was a faint echo inside my skull, a memory of a profound and fatal vertigo long since subsided. I lay there on my side and slowly, carefully, raised myself on an elbow, as if from sleep, like the sand were the tangled sheets of the bed I'd left behind, back home, a lifetime ago—

"Amy!" voices called out. "Are you there? Amy!"

I didn't feel any different, not really, other than that tiny, insistent echo that wouldn't leave my head. Was I supposed to feel different? Had it all really happened?

Something cold and wet gently prodded my arm and that

made tears stream down my cheeks, tears I quickly mopped away: good boy, good Nick. I knew he'd never really left me, ever. I threw my arms around his neck and he wagged his tail, licked my face like he might've done back in his first flesh-and-blood life. I rose to my feet and called out, even though I could see them plain from where I was, I called out as if I'd gotten lost in a thick expanse of woods.

"Here!" I shouted as they came running, stumbling. "Over here!"

And then I was running too, stumbling toward them: Jessie, Linc, Renee, Stephen, my mother, Lisa, Naomi, unable to believe we were really here, all of us on Cowles Beach—no. Not Cowles. Up there on the ridge was the familiar outline of the erstwhile lab, our old ancestral home. Empty, forever. They all ran to me and I ran to them but then just inches away from me they all stopped short, not knowing what they were looking at, not sure who or what I was anymore. My voice, though, it had still been mine. My hands raised up to my eyes—they looked like they always had. Had what I thought happened, really happened? Were we dreaming, were we dying, were we even here—

And then I heard it.

The music in my head was strange and lonely and wild and like nothing I'd ever heard before but it was everything I'd ever wanted out of music in my whole life, everything I'd ever dreamed of sounding like when I had my band, my imaginary band that was going to play amazing frightening things no pop-addled kid could understand and tour Europe and go everywhere, everywhere making hostages of the world with our rhythm. It was the saddest and most beautiful thing I'd ever heard, it was just a few ragged, uneven, tentative notes flying through my mind but it was perfect, perfect madness, perfect melancholy, perfect beauty—

Calliope music, like something at an old-time carnival. The ghost of a carnival. Wild and mad and *perfect*.

I stood there listening and when I turned to Stephen, when I saw the look on his face, I knew that he heard it too, that that raggedy free-floating waltz was filling up every hollow space he'd ever possessed, we'd ever possessed. He heard it. He took my hand, not knowing yet what it meant, just knowing that whatever it meant there was no stopping our ears to it, no turning back. My mother slipped her arm around me, looking scared, exhausted, but the music despite its sadness and her fatigue made her smile.

"Do you hear it?" she murmured. "Do you?"

What a question. What a question to ask when I could see us all hearing it, the sound pulsing between us and among us like electricity singing flesh—flowing from me, to her, to Stephen, to Linc and Renee standing there with wonder on their faces and hope in their eyes. To Jessie. Who heard it in her own mind, heard it in disbelief, and then when she realized she hadn't imagined it and it wasn't going away, she started to cry, silent tears of relief coursing down her cheeks as she grabbed Linc and Renee, as she kissed them, as they smiled and each put up a hand to wipe her face dry.

"It's over," Jessie whispered, and the happiness in her face gave me such a sudden overwhelming sense of sorrow that for a moment, it was hard to breathe. But only for a moment. "Finally. It's all over."

Was it over? Was I, now, what I thought I had become?

"Do you hear it?" My mother touched her ear, carefully, like she were afraid to shatter an eardrum, and then she turned to Lisa standing there with Naomi close in her arms. "Where does it come from? Can you hear it?"

She smiled again, smiled so wide and happy I grinned back and couldn't stop myself from hugging her. "Do you hear it, Lisa? Do you hear the music?"

Lisa gazed at all of us, each to each, and I saw the beginning of a terrible suspicion dawning on her face.

"I can hear you," she said. So calm, so quiet. "But I can't hear any music."

Naomi glanced up at her, confused. Scared. "I can't, either."

The music spiraled upward and outward and everywhere around us, anarchic and beautiful, warming our skin and easing into our bones like the soft steady overhead sun. Jessie kept on quietly crying, Renee and Linc drying her eyes for her in silence. Stephen and my mother held tightly to me and I held back; I stretched an arm out to Lisa but she stood where she was, not wanting to believe it. Not wanting to believe that through no fault of hers, no fault of Naomi's, there was a new and unassailable wall that divided us, the hearing and the deaf.

THIRTY-ONE

LISA

Were we dead? Was this just another illusion, like the parkland and the woods?

There was sky and sun overhead, and sand underfoot; the lab building sat empty and quiet up at the summit of the dunes. Prairie Beach, again, as it had been ever since the plague roared through it and past it and burned itself out. Jessie, Amy, everyone was back, everyone—

I could feel the grit of sand in my sneakers, that little ache between my shoulder blades I sometimes got when I was tired, the flyaway twitchiness of hair strands brushing my face. Maybe this was heaven but I still felt like I needed a bath. I felt funny, too, in another way: like there'd been something small but weighty and oppressive lodged inside me, a stone, a growth, a cherry pit stuck in the back of my throat, and without my noticing it had quietly dissolved and vanished. Naomi was crouching on the sand, her hands clamped over her ears and eyes squeezed shut bracing herself for another terrible surprise. I gently touched her hair and she jumped, her eyes flying open, and then reached down, pressing a hand to the sand. She looked up at me, not rising from her knees.

"Are we dead?" she asked. Very softly, as if she were afraid one errant word might shatter the sky. "Is this heaven for real?"

The grit of the sand, the dry twitch of my hair was what decided me. "I don't think so," I said. "I think—I think we're back. I think this is the world."

The world. The living world, where my feet itched and my neck ached and where ever since the illness, since my transformation into what Amy called an ex, every word I spoke was a sharp hissing jackhammer thing, every consonant cut slices from the air; sometimes, as I talked, I actually felt my tongue snapping painfully as a rubber band against my tense-jawed mouth. That was still there. That hadn't gone away. If this really had been heaven, I'd have sounded like a human being again. I'd have been one, instead of... whatever I now was. Whatever Mags and Billy had been.

But I was alive. *We* were alive, all of us here and shouting for each other and running at double speed to find each other again, and the world was back! The whole world was actually alive! Wasn't that something? Wasn't that something absolutely wonderful? How had it ever happened, how had it—

And then I was remembering how it happened, remembering it like the way some dreams only return in their own good time after sleep retreats. I knew what had happened, what Amy had said, but I also knew, I was certain, that it couldn't have been real. It couldn't have. It was a dream, as much a delusion as that parkland, those woods—

"Do you hear it, Lisa?" Amy asked me. "Do you hear the music?"

No. I didn't. Not like them. I heard their voices, and the calls of the gulls, and the soft rolling rush of the waves, but I heard no music at all.

Jessie pushed Linc's hand away, wiped her eyes, and that's when I realized she had been crying. Jessie was crying, and there was music playing that I couldn't hear, and something was wrong, someone needed to tell me what was wrong. It couldn't have been what I thought had happened, back in the world of the dead, nothing to do with what Amy had said. It couldn't have.

"I think..." Jessie glanced at Amy, her breath audible like she'd been running a race. "I think this means he said yes." She glanced at Amy, panting now, her voice faltering. "I think, I think this means—that Death brought us back—from oblivion—that he's passing existence on to—I feel funny, Lisa. I feel—"

Amy threw her arms out to Jessie, as if she were about to faint, but instead Jessie sat down hard in the sand, relief and pain cutting creases in her face. As I ran over to her, Renee and Linc sank to the sand in turn, drained and played out, all their unnaturally youthful faces so suddenly sick and old. No. They were just exhausted. We were all exhausted. Everything would be all right now, everything. What I thought this might mean, it wasn't true.

Amy was looking at me as if she could hear my thoughts, as if my thoughts scared her because she didn't know how to tell me I was wrong. Nick, her dog, sat calmly beside her as she stood there, watching Jessie fall to the sand, and there was something different about her too. There was something in her eyes that hadn't been there before, at once distant and removed but yet as close-feeling as skin on skin. So intimate, even without touching, that it was like she could see right through me and into me and—no. Something was wrong. I needed someone to tell me what was wrong. I left Jessie's side to go to Amy, and she took my hands in hers. She turned her head toward the ridge, gazing at what had been the lab.

"It's true," she said. Quietly. Gently. The same meditative way Florian had talked. "It really happened."

Lucy, standing there beside her, turned pale and nodded and then, I didn't want to, I *refused* to, but I understood. Death, and life, and all of existence, had taken hold of her, poured into her small skinny human body as if she were now a bottle that could somehow contain oceans, her flesh and blood only a shell surrounding—no. *No*. I shook my head and looked to Lucy and when I saw she understood as well, when I saw even in Naomi's eyes a kind of childish understanding and awe, I wrenched my hands away like they'd been burned.

"No," I said aloud. "No."

"It happened," Amy said. She was already beyond me. Standing there, not two feet away, she was already beyond us all. "Death, and life, and all of it, passed from the person who used to carry it—he got tired, he couldn't stand the burden anymore, and now it's passed to me. I took it." For a moment she looked on the verge of laughing, as if she couldn't truly believe it herself, but it had changed her already. Already, she was something not like us. "And it's inside me now. I can feel it, I swear it really is like being a glass or a pitcher or something filling up, I can feel all of it pouring inside—"

"No!"

"I chose it," she said. So calm, so sure, so beyond us all. "Maybe someday I'll give it up, just like he did, I won't be able to stand it anymore—but I chose it." She glanced again toward the lab. "I never even thought about it before, you know, but this means I'll be everywhere—I'll see the whole world, I'll *be* the whole world. Remember, Mom, how much I always wanted to just get out of here and travel?" She wrapped a tendril of hair, bright strawberry-auburn hair, around her fingers and laughed. A happy laugh. "There'll be almost nowhere I can't go—"

"No."

"That's what I always wanted when I was—what I always wanted before. I won't know everything, though, he said so. He said he wasn't all-knowing, not ever. Or all-seeing. So there'll always be something to learn, something I haven't seen. Things to surprise me. I hope some of the surprises are good."

She reached out a hand for me, let it fall again unsure what to do. "So don't be sad for me. Please? I'm not going to die. At least, not for a long time."

But Jessie was. I knew it. I could see it. I had Amy on one side of me and Jessie on the other and devil and deep blue sea had me so confused I didn't know what to do, who to—

"You can't go," I said. Flat, final, childish, and which of them I meant it for, both, neither, everything, I didn't know. "You can't. You can't go."

"She has to," Jessie said. Quiet, calm, just like Amy. "And we have to."

"I can't—"

"I'll be all right," Amy said. "And so will they."

She ran over to them suddenly, to where Linc and Renee and my sister sat exhausted and draining on the sands, and threw her arms around Jessie, who suffered the embrace for just a few seconds and then briskly pushed her away. At least that much hadn't changed, even now that she really was finally—she pushed Amy away but her eyes were solemn, almost sorrowful, someone saying goodbye to a friend. Amy reached down and embraced Linc for a moment, then Renee, and then she turned to me looking just for an instant as scared, as lost, as when I'd first rescued her from that poor feral dog.

"Were those my first?" she asked. Her voice shaking. "I didn't mean to. I didn't try to. Were they the first living things that I..."

Her words trailed off. No. I couldn't lose my sister again, not again, and Amy, it's like I told her, I have *three* daughters and I can't lose the second just like I did the first—my heart cracked and split open and released a geyser of tears, Naomi grabbing me and hugging me as I sank in shame to the sand. Was she next? Would I lose her next? Jessie slid over to me, half-crawling, and for just a precious few seconds, her head was in my lap.

"It's what I want," she whispered. "It's what I want and I'm not afraid. This has been like torture. Everything since I came back alive, it all—Joe was right, in the end, I didn't want to believe him when he first said it, but he was right. This has to end. All along, I was supposed to be dead. Now I can get off the merry-go-round. Now I can stop being so dizzy from all the spinning—life and death and—and I can rest. Okay?" Her head jerked up and she was pleading, pleading with me who she couldn't help but leave behind, to be all right. "Please?"

"Lisa," Naomi whispered. "Don't cry."

"I don't want you to go!" I was the child now, surrounded by maddeningly sure and decided adults, and I was horribly ashamed of myself and I couldn't help it. I looked over at Linc and Renee as if they could somehow stop this, knowing they couldn't, and for one mercifully brief second I hated them for it. "I don't want any of you to go!"

"We'll be all right," Linc said. Gentle but unyielding, as he took Jessie back from me. Holding my sister, his wife, in his arms. "Don't forget, we've seen it all before."

The tears wouldn't stop. "Amy." I was back on my feet now, desperate, as if I could bargain with this, as if exactly that perpetual human failing hadn't nearly destroyed everything and everyone. "I can't let you. I can't let you go again, I can't let you be all alone—"

"She won't," Lucy said. Scared, so scared-looking, and so firmly decided. "Because I'm going with her."

"And so am I," said Stephen. "Just like we said we would, before—*he* can't stop us, the other one. He can't. We're going." His eyes blazed up fiercely for a moment, as if he actually longed for someone to just try and stop him, and then his face turned pensive. "I don't think we were meant for regular living life anyway," he said, "any more than dead people—we've died too, like they have. Over and over again, just like them, except in a different way. We're used to going back and forth."

Lucy nodded. "Never felt like one of the living, not really," she said. "Even before they—even before. Never."

Stephen reached over and kissed Amy on the temple. "So that's how it is. We're going too."

Nick, all this storm and fury surrounding him, he just sat there calm as anything with his rheumy eyes gazing around him and his tail resting still against the sand. There beside Amy, his mistress, his protegée, no doubt at all that he was going too. Everyone going, except Naomi. Everyone leaving.

"You can't do this," I shouted. I knew how infantile I sounded, and I didn't give a damn. "You can't, this goddamned—suicide pact—you can't—"

I was sobbing again, too hard to talk, and Naomi was crying too and I couldn't have that but I couldn't stop, I just couldn't. Lucy came up to me and before anyone could stop me, I shoved her away, putting every ounce of inhuman strength I had into the push, watching in a fury as she flew backward and landed square on her ass.

"Are you happy?" I demanded, standing over here where she lay sprawled in the sand, spitting out the words almost in a scream. "Happy now? All that 'get away from *my daughter*, don't tell *me* how to talk to *my daughter*, how to protect her, how to'—her own mother, and you didn't even try to stop her! You didn't even try! Now it's too late and you get to drag her along while you cut your own throat and you must be *fucking thrilled to death*!"

Stephen and Amy leapt in front of Lucy like they were afraid I'd kick her, hit her, but all I could do was disgrace myself as I stood there and cried. Lucy waved them away, then slowly pulled herself back to her feet. She looked me without rancor, tears brimming in her eyes, but she blinked them back before they could roll down her cheeks.

"I'm not happy," she said. "And I'm not unhappy, either. I've just never been so scared in my life. But I'm not leaving Amy behind, not ever again. No matter how scared I am. No matter what." She pushed the back of her hand over her eyes, rough and abrupt like she was squeegeeing a dirty window. "And like Stephen said, that's just how it is."

Amy put her arms around her for a moment. Steadying her, like Naomi was still trying through her own sobs to steady me. I had to pull myself together, for shit's sake, *right now*. I mopped my own face and squatted down, held Naomi close to me lest someone try to take her next, but the salt water wouldn't quit leaking from me. How did I stop Amy, stop Jessie—I didn't know what to do.

There wasn't anything I could do. There wasn't anything they *wanted* me to do. Amy, so shy, so certain, ran a hand over my hair.

"You're not alone," she said. So sweet, so sad, so merciless. "Naomi needs you. And you need her. And—and exes *can* die, look what I—look what happened to Mags." She swallowed. "Your daughter Karen, you'll have her again, and Jessie, and... and everyone. Not right away, but you will."

She was smiling again, happy for me. Genuinely happy, and already so far beyond her own fleeting personhood, as if it were just a memory from decades, centuries back. "You'll grow old and die, a long time from now, and then you'll have everyone you lost again."

"And if I don't?" I demanded. "If what happened to Mags was just an accident, a freak accident, what then? What if I'm stuck like this... forever?"

What if I had to watch Naomi grow old and die, watch everyone grow old and die, nothing but decades and centuries of long goodbyes just like this one and no Karen, no Amy, nobody else ever again? Amy shook her head, but whether that was certainty or mere reassurance I didn't know. Maybe I didn't want to know.

"Nothing," she said, "anywhere, stays what it is forever. That's what the lab thought they could do, and they failed. They failed at it and failed and failed, until nobody was left to try." She looked back over the ridge, as if she were waiting for someone to arrive. Someone who should have been here long since. "Even Death isn't what he—and someday I won't be this anymore, someone else will take my place, and then I'll be there with you. We all will. Just like Florian lives inside us, and somewhere else too, in death. It's a good place, death. The afterlife. You know that. We've seen it."

She hesitated, then gave me a tentative, one-armed hug. "It's—it's part of Death, and Death can travel back and forth from it like living things can't, but even Death can't say exactly what it is or where it comes from, if it really is underground or in the sky or just all in living people's minds. But wherever it is, some good part of you goes there, and stays there, and feels itself there and everyone it knew and lost around it. And it's a happy place. You have to believe me, Lisa. It truly is."

She had raised her voice because Jessie was listening to her, craning her neck there on the sand. Linc and Renee and everyone else were listening too, anxious, needing the truth from the source. Treating Amy like that truth, already, without any questions, this couldn't be happening—I grabbed Amy, hugged her fiercely to me, and she hugged back and made a little shuddering sound against my shoulder, the cloth of my T-shirt there suddenly turning damp.

"I'm scared," she murmured into my ear. "But it's okay. It really is. Please be okay. I need you to be okay."

I wasn't okay, I wasn't at all—but what choice did I have? What choice did anybody ever have? What choice was there, that night the police came to our house, Jim's and mine, cherry lights revolving wild outside and voices saying *There's been an accident, a very bad mother father sister so sorry, so very sorry*—

I'd had another year with Jessie, another year I would never have had. Now she was ready to go. I had Amy, who I would never have met. And she was ready to go. They needed me to be okay, because I'd already been given so much more than I would've had and now, now it was time, now it was their time. I would never have had Naomi. And she wasn't going anywhere. I would never have had any of this, if it weren't for the whole world spinning so horribly out of balance. If it weren't for Amy, Jessie, all of us in our own small ways, reaching out hands to yank it into orbit and grab it all back.

But what you've had, once you've had it, however you got it, it was so damned hard to just quietly give it up—

"Look," Lucy said, pointing.

We all looked, up at the crest of the ridge. Wandering out of the trees near the aquatorium we saw the nebulous, unmistakable outline of a deer, nibbling idly on the long uncut swathes of grasses now lining the white gravel road cutting across the ridge. And a few yards away, walking toward us, the outline of a man whose face never stayed the same, but we still always knew.

As if he'd been waiting to see him all this time, as if the sight of him were the key to his own release, Linc made a gasping, choking sound, rocking back and forth where he sat as if he were in pain. Then he toppled very quietly to his side and his breaths became easier, longer, drawn out, but there were fewer of them than there should have been, and dead spaces between them. I could almost feel it inside myself: his heart running down, his lungs giving out, his accidentally stolen life draining from his body. He lay there on the sand with his eyes closed and then without our seeing it happen, Renee was lying next to him, sunk against his shoulder, with Jessie's cheek rested in his curved palm. They were ashen, shadows guttering blue beneath their eyes and their eyes closed against the punishing weight of the sunlight. We ran to them, we all ran to them but they weren't dead yet, not yet; they were fading away, instead of burning up. We would all be allowed to say goodbye.

The man came closer, and closer.

THIRTY-TWO

AMY

All it took was one word. *Eternity.*

I could feel it inside me, rising up full and fast, the nourishing sustaining thing rushing into all the hollow spaces like water released from a jar. Like a libation, a slaking libation poured lovingly on dry untended grave-ground. A feeling of life. I had been alive for seventeen years without ever feeling alive and only now, now that I would never again be living as I'd known it before, did I feel anything but stone dead inside.

I wished I'd had the words for it all, before. Maybe it wouldn't have made the life come to me any faster, but it might have let me hold out without the mistakes I'd made, the horrible mistakes, knowing that one way or another it'd happen. *Where there's life, there's hope.* Maybe that's what people really meant, when they'd say that.

What was I now? Was I really... everything, even that which only seemed wholly separate from myself? It would kill someone, wouldn't it, to even imagine they could somehow embody all that, take it all in? And yet it was true.

It was true. Lisa, Stephen, Linc, my mother, Jessie, all them were still themselves and yet, now, they were all also me. And Amy too, the girl who had been Amy, now she was just one of a thousand million facets of this thing called myself. Multitudes upon multitudes, living, dead, undead, dead living. My libations.

"Please don't die." Naomi's voice, pleading. "Lisa, even if it is God's will, I don't want them to die—"

"I know. But they've been very sick, honey. They've been in pain. It's all right. We have to let them go."

Lisa's voice was like a knife between my ribs: her resignation, exhaustion, fathomless sorrow and grief that I'd thought I'd helped assuage for just a little while but now without meaning to I'd brought it rushing back to her, full force. If it weren't for Naomi she'd have begged me to kill her, I knew it, she'd have pleaded with me to raise my hand up just like *he* once had and strike her down, let her die. Just like I'd raised my hand up while I was still alive, still human, to strike others down. Thank God for Naomi.

Had I raised my hand up already, just now, without knowing it? Knowing what it meant, what it felt like to do that in life, would I ever have to courage deliberately to do it now?

I pulled away from them all, from Jessie where she lay cradled in Lisa's arms, from poor Naomi who'd already in six years seen too much for a lifetime. From Stephen and my mother, even though when they said so easily, so unhesitatingly *of course we're going with you, of course you'll never be so alone again* my heart grew light and buoyant, despite the dying all around me. I wept for Jessie, for all of them, knowing that it was time for them to go and even if I could stop them, I wouldn't.

I walked away to give them space and room and nobody tried to stop me. Nick, my Old Nick I thought I'd lost forever, he padded alongside me just like he had since the true beginnings of my life, a far different and better moment than my mere birth. The sound of the calliope was still wheeling mad and drunken through my mind, every separate sad gorgeous note making my head reel and ring with the sound of a thousand, a million secret harmonies, but it wasn't dizzying or crazymaking, it was just beautiful. It was a drunken crazy steadiness. It was what had always been meant to be there, in the hollow places, all along.

"Beautiful," he mused. "There's a word for it."

He'd come down the ridge, not disappearing and reappearing as he always did but simply walking, trudging toward us, like any ordinary man. He stood there before me, his feet in their mud-caked work boots wide apart in the sand; he had my father's face, this time, not the man who fathered me as my mother's price for escaping the lab but the man who called himself my dad, loved me, died when I was only five and barely knew how to imagine where he'd gone. No matter that we'd never been the same flesh and blood—I looked into his face and still swore I saw the same straight, matter-of-fact slope to both our noses, the same shape of jaw and chin, the same little quirk at the right corner of our mouths, a constant permanent uptick like a smile always waiting to happen, and I was satisfied.

"Is it the wrong word for it?" I asked.

"Not at all," he said. "Not at all. It's just that it usually takes one so much longer to learn to appreciate it."

The quirk of the lip became an actual smile, one I remembered well and not just from photographs. Hello, Daddy. I was glad he'd come back again, if only the form of him, that the rotten flesh and tarry blackened blood of him that my mother set ablaze was nothing but the shell, the discarded candy wrapper. He—it—could be anyone, of course, but he gave me my father to talk to. To show me what would happen next. Strange sort of employee's signing bonus, maybe, but I'd take it. Nick nuzzled around the legs of his jeans, wagging his tail, and he reached down and patted him with rough, easy affection.

"Why me?" I asked. Never mind that I wanted it, that I chose it without hesitation. I still wanted to know. "Why me? And why you—I mean, the person you can't remember but who you once were? Why us?"

He shrugged. "Why anyone? You were there. I was here. You

were willing. Just like I must have been, back in the day. Your friend Jessie, she'll tell you—we've talked before, long before you and I met—I don't punish, at least not on the individual level. This is no punishment. I—which, of course, is to say *you*—don't judge. I don't condemn. I merely take what I need. From each according to their ability, et cetera, did you get that far in school?"

"They didn't like to teach that stuff in school," I said.

"I'm not surprised. Mind if I smoke?"

He pulled a lighter and crushed cigarette box from his back pocket without waiting for an answer, lit up, inhaled more deeply than any human could have managed. My dad never smoked, but then he'd never appeared out of nowhere at the averted end of the world either. As he exhaled, the smoke spun like frayed grayish-white thread from his mouth, his nostrils, the pores of his face and hands and every fold and crevice of his clothes. From his eyes, like tears gone to ice and then to fog and mist.

"I, which is to say you," I repeated. "So we're... one and the same now? You and I?"

The question seemed to surprise him. "Of course. Just as we're one and the same with everyone else standing here, everything surrounding us, the whole of all and eternity—and I thought you understood all this already. They really don't teach you kids much, do they?" He inhaled again, deeply, luxuriously. "We're sharing that burden, the two of us, for the time being. I mean, you don't make a transition like that overnight. But once you've learned everything you need to know, really learned it, I can give up my share. I'll be gone. Dead. Just like your friend Florian: I'll be part of you, but all and eternity will no longer be part of *me*. And the whole of the burden will be yours."

He exhaled again, spun the lit cigarette between his fingertips, gave me a sidelong glance. "I wonder how long you'll last, when you have to do *all* the heavy lifting? A few decades, a few centuries—"

"Time's nothing," I said. Easy, dismissive. And I meant it. "Time is nothing. I'm already forgetting what it means."

Was that a bad thing? Should I have been scared about it? What would it really mean, anyway, if eternity and ten seconds were to become interchangeable for me? Maybe I'd never leave this new life, this new afterlife. Maybe I'd never have to, never get old and tired like he had. Like whoever came before him must have. But what difference did it make, really? All in due time. An eternity away.

"They can come with me, can't they?" I asked. I'd just assumed they could, but suddenly I was afraid. "Stephen, my mother—"

He shrugged. "Why not? As you folks like to say, it's their funeral." Exhale. In through the mouth, out through the nose, pores, eyelids, scalp. "Better you have some company anyway. I mean, we already know you don't do so well, left all to your own devices."

"No man is an island."

"No man is an island. They're already something *other* to you, aren't they? Human beings, I mean? Something else. So soon. It almost surprises me."

"They always were," I said, and there was a quiet relief in speaking the words out loud. Like the first time I'd ever said them to Stephen, the first he ever said them back to someone else. The first night we were together. "I never felt like one of them. Not superior, I mean—just the opposite. I was always falling short. I was never really good enough, to make it as human." Or fake it. Even that. "Maybe this is still falling short. But it's what I'm ready for. I'm already too changed to feel like one of them, if I ever were at all—"

"Doesn't mean you won't live to regret it." He folded his arms, gazing down at me with a bemused, almost grandfatherly merriment. Still, even now, enjoying a good quiet laugh at my expense. "Live and live and live to regret it. Of course, too late now."

Maybe I would. Maybe sooner than I imagined. But so what? I didn't have to do this. *You ain't gotta.* But I wanted to. Just as, too long ago to fathom, he too might have wanted to. Maybe the real crime never was that we stole from Death—willingly or not—but that Death kept stealing and stealing our willingness, our eye-open consent, from us. Maybe if just one of us said yes, just the one, everyone else could rest better with not being able to tell Death no.

"Did I... kill them?" I asked, inclining my head toward Jessie, the others. "I didn't—were they, you know, my first?"

Smoke kept streaming from his eyes, his skin, the cloth of his shirt. "Define 'I.'" he said, smiling.

But then he seemed to take pity on me. "One last benevolent gesture, courtesy of yours truly. It's what they wanted, isn't it? Weren't they just saying so? You can't rend your garments about it now."

And so soon, they would be gone. But not gone, just faded from immediate view, part of the sun and sky and trees and sand and the air everyone took into their lungs and the electrical impulses making up every thought, every memory, every feeling and longing and wish. Just like everyone, everywhere, who ever lived and died. Every atom tells a story, don't it.

Death just stood there, looking at me and Nick. Watching us watch the small, sorrowing crowd at the other end of the beach.

"There's something else I wanted to ask for," I said.

"Name it."

"A guitar." My own frivolity made me laugh, but this was important to me and I had a feeling I wouldn't get another chance. "I want—I want music. I need music. I really do." Lisa figured that out, quickly, when we first met. Poor Lisa. Even though we'd meet again, in what was already no more than a heartbeat for me, I was going to miss her so much. I never wanted to make her sad. I never wanted her to lose someone all over again. "Please."

Death just shrugged. "And here I thought you were going to demand something outrageous." He inhaled. Held it for a painful few seconds. Exhaled. "Music. That's nothing."

"Not to me, it isn't," I said.

He pivoted on his heel, studied the lab building up on the ridge like he'd never seen it before in his life. I closed my own eyes and somewhere behind my actual vision, behind the pulsing dark red trying to slip through my eyelids, I saw rooms clean as the first hours of springtime, flooded with sunlight; every window was open to the outside air and every day, even when the sky was blue-black midnight or sparkling harsh after a snowstorm or subdued and gray with rain, was a perpetual peaceful mid-May dawn. No more closed-in rooms, no more prisoner's windows stuck small and high on the topmost walls, but the hallways would still be there, more numerous and byzantine than I'd ever imagined. I could live there, if I liked. I could spend hours, years wandering through that maze of hallways, never getting lost but also never quite finding what lay at the end. In my house there were many, many rooms. And the air in all of them, even the most subterranean depths, would be so clean and sweet. So full of perpetual light.

I was ready.

"A guitar," Death repeated. "Music. That can be arranged. Most things can be, you'll find..."

The smoldering remains of his cigarette fell from his mouth, dropped to the sand; his heel crushed it out harshly, his foot making a wide encompassing sweep, like a little kid taking aim at a colony of anthills. My master, everyone's master, from before any of us were ever born. My brother. Myself. I turned my back on him, Nick following at my heels, and went to rejoin the others.

THIRTY-THREE
JESSIE

I was dying. At long last, I was actually dying.

There were footsteps above me and a throb and hum of voices, but I couldn't make out what any one person was saying, it all just blended together like the buzz of ten thousand flies—no. Lisa's voice, I could make hers out, and Amy's, and that little girl stuck to Lisa's side whose name I couldn't remember anymore. Linc was beside me and my head was on his shoulder and Renee's head was in my lap, my fingers in her hair. For a moment I thought we were back in the nature preserve at the height of the plague, but the plague was over, the apocalypse that aborted itself was over, the fight was over. Finally. Long last.

Was I scared? I wasn't sure. I just wanted this to be the end, the last, no cheats or tricks or backtracks. Not anymore.

Voices. Somebody was saying something. Linc. He raised his head up and I could feel the effort it took him, the rusty broken machinery of his body creaking and groaning to turn the gears one final time. He said my name, *Jessie*, and those mere two syllables cost him so much energy that he crashed right back into the sand. Of course it made sense, that he would die first of all of us. He'd cheated Death, been cheated out of death, for decades now, so much longer than me or Renee. I reached a hand up and touched his face.

"I'll be there soon enough," I said. "We'll all follow."

"You sure?" I saw his face and I could tell he was thinking of Billy, of Sam, of all the ones left behind. Of me, right after Joe. "You sure—we'll all—"

"Follow. I am." I patted his cheek. *Calm down, my love, calm the fuck down. You're only dying. We know this song and dance full well.* "All of us. Every one."

He saw I wasn't lying; no false words, no slop-sugar as the final thread of consciousness spooled out, frayed at the ends, unraveled into death. Saw I wasn't lying, tried to smile. The facility was deserting him.

"Soon," he said. And died.

Soon.

Lisa or someone above us gasped, and there was the stifled sound of sobs. For God's sake. As if we needed any more life. What we'd already had was plenty enough, more than enough—

Renee. Were you there, still? Renee?

"I'm here," she said. Murmuring, eyes closed, not lifting her head from my lap. Held my hand, strong, thumb pressed to the soft bit next to my palm, holding it the way you held the hand of someone you loved. Of course we loved each other all along too, of course we did. All three of us. Whatever kind of love you wanted to call it. I held back just as hard.

"I'm here," she repeated. And then, like that, she wasn't.

Murmuring sounds, all around me, susurration of the waves and high-low hum of talking and congested rainstorm dampness of crying. Stop that, Lisa. Stop. Lucy, Amy's mother, I heard her saying something I couldn't make out but surely it was something calm and sensible, she and Amy both had that way about them, and I let the sounds rush and wash over me like lake water. I didn't think Renee would go before I did—but then, she only had me left to tell goodbye. Only me.

Only me left. When did I get to go? When did I have to? Soon. I could tell. Soon.

Someone was squatting down beside me, so close I could feel her hair brush my face. Amy. She laid a hand to my cheek, weirdly grownup gesture from the kiddie, though she was already so much not what she once was and I didn't know whether to feel sad for her, glad for her, both and neither at once. She made her choice, open-eyed, and she seemed glad of it. Hell, she leapt at it. I'd never understand why she took it so hard, just because she killed a person or two, but then it must be different when you're human. I hadn't been human in such a long time—

Or maybe all of this was human: death, life, death-in-life. All of it together. Maybe we always were one. Maybe it's like I always suspected, dying did a fucking sentimental number on your brain.

"Are you okay?" Amy whispered. No dignified remove. She sounded young as she was, and scared. "Are you in pain?"

I shook my head. It was hard to do it, it took all my effort and it almost hurt but other than that, no, there wasn't any pain. "This is what I'm used to," I told her. Every word taking all my effort. "This is what I've missed."

Lisa was losing it again, kneeling over me choking and sobbing. *Jesus Christ, Lisa, seriously, get a grip. You've got a kid to take care of.* Tears and snot streamed down her face, threatening to drip right on me like scum-water from a rusty tap. We'd all see each other again, sooner than she'd ever think. I was sure of it.

"Fly right," I told her, looking her straight in the eye. I grabbed her hand, putting all the strength I had left in a hard painful grip. "Fly right."

She shuddered with the effort to pull herself together. A winter-scaled hand scrubbed and scoured at her flushed cheeks, at her eyes pink and swollen with grief. "Jessie—"

"See you soon."

I dropped my head, my hand, back to the sand. It was rushing over me in earnest this time, over and through my nostrils and mouth and lungs, but it wasn't like drowning—it was water to a fish, a fish who never knew it was a fish and spent all its time gasping and dying on the shore but now, gratefully, amazedly, opens up its gills and slides into the sea. Breath, true breathing, at long last. Deep and quiet. In through the mouth, or maybe the nose. Out through the pretty slits fanning on either side of my throat.

I told you we'd all be together again, didn't I? There they all were, gathered around me and over me, Florian and Joe and Sam and Annie and Billy and Mags and Teresa the bitch and fucking Rommel and Renee and Linc and my mother and everyone, everyone everywhere, countless thousands and millions I couldn't even start to name. Everyone was here, everyone was one. The music hadn't stopped playing in my head, the music of the old days, the dances, the wild carnival melody that still kept on flying and spiraling even with the calliope crash-landed on the ground. Nobody ever decides when it's time for a dance, you just know. Everyone knows it, all together, electricity singing flesh and traveling from each to each all around the circle until all our bones, blood, brains, melt together to become one and only. The merry-go-round was coming to a stop. The music never would. The music was all of us.

I wish I had understood that, earlier. Years ago. Lifetimes ago.

It's been a good life, though. All of it. Even the terrible parts had their core, their sliver of goodness. My last act of defiance to the universe, I couldn't speak it anymore, but I was thinking it, I was thinking it out loud: *I wouldn't change one fucking thing. Not this, not anything else.*

"Jessie—" Lisa's voice. Hand reaching to me. Eyes full of understanding and fear and grief.

The sea was claiming me. I closed my eyes, and the tide carried me away.

THIRTY-FOUR

LISA

"Jessie?"

She was gone.

I glanced up at Lucy, at the others; they'd pulled back, sad, worried, wanting to give me room but not certain, beyond the obvious physical space, just how to do that. Gone. They were all gone now. It was like she just—slipped under, quietly, like someone already oblivious being carried away by the incoming tide. Drowning. Or not drowning, but drifting. Floating. I still had her hand in mine, every finger a tiny, paper-dry, almost apologetic collection of bones. So thin, so fragile, so old even while her face had stayed unnaturally young. I leaned forward and kissed her forehead, savoring the last fleeting feel of her hair brushing against my temple, the faint scent of her skin—

—and though I had felt flesh and bone and hair just seconds before, now my lips touched nothing. Naomi and the others cried out behind me, so I knew I didn't hallucinate it: She was truly gone, she and Linc and Renee, their bodies vanished before I even sensed their dissolving. Of course. They were so old, truly, all of them, they had been dead for so long, they would all long since have crumbled into dust. Even Renee, the youngest of them. Dust and atoms like the very air, the dead all around us. Maybe I had breathed part of them in, just then, without even realizing it.

I felt numb.

I stumbled to my feet, Lucy and Stephen both running forward to help me, Amy facing me with such sorrow and kindness in her face I didn't think I could stand it. *Did you do that, just now?* I wanted to ask her, the words refusing to come out of me, but I didn't even have to bite them back because she read my thoughts, right there on my face. She shook her head.

"They went their own way," she told me, too quietly for anyone else to hear. "It wasn't me. But they didn't need my help... or his. I don't think they really needed anyone's help. It was long past time."

His help. The man who wasn't really a man, any more than Amy was any longer a girl, stood halfway across the beach watching, waiting, and even though he and she were not the slightest bit alike, when I looked at them—really looked at them, beneath that faint surface illusion of difference—I saw twins. I saw more than twins. I saw one person, one entity, that only seemed for that faint, fleeting moment, a fraction of a heartbeat in their own extra-human time, to be divided into two. But that was nothing but a trick, a reassuring mirage, for they were the same now. They were one. Oh, Amy. My Amy, my daughter, why did you do it? Why did it have to be you? Why did you let it, why did you *want* it to be you?

Naomi hovered behind Amy now, uncertain, head turned away from the waiting stranger, hugging Nick because Nick was the only truly calm one among us just then. This couldn't be happening. And of course, it was. Of course all of it was. I started to laugh. I couldn't help it.

"If you were lying," I said to Amy. "If you were lying, when you promised that I will die someday, that I'll see Karen and—" I couldn't even say her name, right then. "—my sister again—"

Of course she wasn't lying. How could I say that? How could I talk to my own child like that? Amy's arms were around my neck now, hugging me hard, and I felt such remorse for my suspicion as I hugged her back. She was my child, still, one of my three daughters, even if I had to share her with Lucy. Even if both of them were going away. I couldn't believe it. They couldn't *all* be going away. They couldn't leave me like this. This wasn't happening. But it was. We hung on and on to each other for what felt like hours and I breathed in the scent of Amy's skin, her hair, just like I did Jessie's, knowing this was the last I would ever have of it again. But for now, for now—

The stranger on the sand, Amy's hidden twin, said something I was too far away to hear. Silence. If nobody acknowledged he had spoken, Amy and I might keep this moment forever, in blessed silence. But the others heard him. They heard.

"It's time," Lucy said. So quietly, so hesitantly, I could almost pretend I hadn't heard her either.

"I think it's time," said Stephen. Only the smallest bit louder. He sounded scared. As scared as I felt.

Amy made a little sound against my shoulder: fear, or sadness, or just plain nerves, all at once. Then she pulled away, tucking a lock of hair behind my ear.

"You have to be okay," she said. It was half command, half fearful plea. "I can't do this unless I know you'll really be—"

"I have to be," I told her. It was true. I had a little girl to take care of. I couldn't fail Naomi. I had to be all right. I didn't know how anything, anywhere, could ever be all right again, but *I* had to be all right.

"You have to be okay."

"I'm going to be." I swallowed. "I have to be. I'm going to—"

"I'm scared," Amy said, and started to cry.

I stepped back and let Lucy approach instead, let Lucy and Stephen hold and comfort her, because they were her family and they were going with her and I had to practice not being able to. I had to practice it now, get used to sliding down the long, endless tunnel of loss for the rest of my life. Naomi ran up to me with tears in her own eyes and I knelt in the sand, hugging her, pretending not to notice as Nick detached himself from her side and went over to sit patiently, waiting, at Amy's feet. It was time. It was past time. This couldn't be happening.

Naomi wiped her face dry, breathed in hard, and Amy and her family, her other family, came up to us and we gathered together in a desperately tight knot. Thoughts clattered disjointedly, chaotically through my head with the uncontrollable velocity of panic, but what kept pushing to the maelstrom's surface was the memory of me and Jessie fleeing north on foot during the worst of the plague, both of us so torn up inside by its wild unreasoning hunger we'd have killed anything, anyone, for food. An old man—still human, one of the unlucky immune—crossed our path like a rabbit leaping into a snare and when I looked at him I saw nothing but meat, but Jessie let him go. She let him hurry off in stupefied terror on his rusty, breaking-down bicycle, and I screamed at her for it because we were starving, we were both starving, but we could have taken him down together. Linc, too, we might have killed for his flesh when we found him, already up in Prairie Beach helping bury the dead, except Jessie recognized him for who he was. She was a better person just then than I was, a better person so much of the time than she'd ever thought she was; for her sake, as much as for Amy's or Naomi's, I had to try to be a good person too. *Fly right.* Maybe. I'd do what I could.

"Could you leave?" I asked Amy, trying not to plead. To beg. "Could you change your mind, walk away—"

"I don't know." Amy snuffled, curling the arm she'd wrapped around her mother's shoulders into a fierce hug. They were so much alike, the two of them, a portrait of the same woman older and younger when you saw them cheek by jowl. I didn't need Naomi to look like me but still, that feeling when you looked at yourself in your own child, it was one I still missed. "Maybe I could," Amy said. "Maybe I could walk away right now. But I don't want to. Even if I'm scared. I won't." Her eyes, as she gazed at me, had a warning lurking inside them. "I won't."

I nodded. I'd known the answer before I'd ever asked.

There wasn't any putting it off anymore. The sun was high in the sky, the clouds dispersing—it was still so amazing, after what we'd been through, to see actual real earthly sunlight, smell lake water and greenery once more. Amy and I were embracing again, we couldn't say anything. I couldn't hold on long enough, it would never be long enough, so I had to let her go. She slipped her hands into her jacket pockets, that too-big ripped-up jacket she'd been wearing since I first met her back in Leyton, and she laughed once more, easy, suddenly unafraid.

"I loved it there," she told me. "The other life, I mean, the afterlife. Even as eaten up as it was, the second we first set foot on it, I loved it. That very second. It felt like somehow, I had always been meant to be there. Like I was meant to stay there. As some kind of... I don't know. Some kind of guardian. Or custodian."

So far beyond me. So far beyond all of us. So unlike that scared, angry girl, a fugitive from her own town and her own self, that I found cowering in fear of a lost dog—and yet, she still was what she was. She'd gone beyond humanity but her humanity was still there, intact, waiting to be reclaimed: a perfectly ripe apple that would never bruise or go to rot, dropped from a single tree in an endless, sealike orchard and just lying there, patiently, until she decided once more to pick it up. Just like his, her stranger-twin's. And perhaps just like all of us, living, dead, undead, dead living, all along. Maybe that's all people ever meant, when they talked about a soul.

"Goodbye," Amy said. She reached down to Naomi, shaking her hand like that of some precocious foreign dignitary. "Goodbye, Naomi. Take care of my Lisa. Have a good life."

Naomi had tears in her eyes again. She made a little choking sound, then broke away and ran over to Nick, hanging onto him for dear life. He licked her face, his tail thumping on the sand, and waited in silent, otherworldly patience until she finally let him free.

"Goodbye," Naomi said. A nearly inaudible, little record-scratch of a sound.

Lucy was embracing me now, Stephen suddenly full of adolescent awkwardness as he leaned forward to kiss me and then thought better of it, clumsily shook my hand. The goodbyes and farewells and till-we-meet-agains were floating all around me but I couldn't quite seem to hear them, and then they were walking together up the duneface, Amy and Lucy and Stephen and the man who once was Death. Nick trotted close behind them, breaking off only to caper in little circles of canine happiness. Walking away, away forever, without looking back—

"Come back!" I shouted, starting to cry again. "Amy! Please come back!"

I knew she wouldn't. Even as the words flew out of my mouth I knew she wouldn't stop, wouldn't turn around, but I couldn't help it. I didn't even know if she'd heard me, if she'd closed her ears as determinedly as she'd turned her back, and now my useless pleadings were lost to the wind. Come back, Amy, Jessie, Karen, Linc, Renee, Mom, Dad, Jim, everyone, please, just stop this horrible foolishness and *come back*—

They were up on the ridge now, near the white gravel road that snaked around the front face of the lab. Beyond my pleas, beyond earshot. They were walking toward the building now, and nobody could stop them. As they went I saw another set of figures, shadowy, undefined, though one of them seemed to be a man, the two others women. They were coming *out* of the lab, down the ridge, toward us, three afternoon-long shadows with the clumsy, staggering, entirely extinct gait of the walking undead. Closer and closer to us, to me, and yet no matter how close I couldn't manage to *see* them, to make out their faces or features. At this distance, I should have known them by sight—

I closed my eyes hard and shook my head; I didn't know what I'd just seen, or if I'd really seen it. I looked up to the ridge again, to Amy, her mother, Stephen, Nick, but they were gone. While I'd been distracted chasing shadows, chimeras, they had vanished.

No goodbyes. No last look. No more.

Gone. They were gone forever.

I could hear someone crying, sobbing loudly. Not Naomi, who stood there beside me stunned and silent. It was me. I choked back the sounds coming out of me and fought harder than I'd imagined possible to regain my composure; I had to remind myself over and over in the space of seconds that Naomi was right here, depending on me, Naomi who had also lost all her own family and Nick, the nearest thing she'd had to a pet, who she'd grown to love. Naomi had already seen me cry enough. I breathed in hard, between my teeth, and managed to get myself under control.

Was it still possible, in this new world, for people to cry and really mean it over someone they never even knew? Would that be at all possible, for Naomi's generation? If it were, then maybe we weren't quite as far in the shit as I'd thought. Just a bare inch higher up in the sewer, but enough to breathe in actual air. Fresh, clean air.

"It's all right," I said, when I felt like I could talk again. It felt better, it would feel better for years to come, simply not to look toward the ridge, up at the lab. Easier and better to turn my back. "It's all right." I cleared my throat, hoarse and sticky wet from all that crying, and straightened my shoulders, pretending everything was sorted, settled. Fake it until you make it. "It's been a bad year or two. A terrible year."

A year. *One* year. Could everything really have changed that much in a *year*? Summer, last summer, that was when the disaster really began. It couldn't be. It would take all the rest of our lives, to get used to things being what they were. "A terrible year. But things are getting sorted. They wanted to go. They'll protect us." Please let me be right. I couldn't handle it, I really couldn't, if I wasn't right. "We can start again, and move forward."

Another year. I got almost another whole year with my sister, her friends, a year I'd never have had. I can remember her dying peacefully, willingly, not stumbling across the landscape a prisoner of her own rotten body (*just like all of you*, I know she'd say, *just like all you humans face up to it or not*—but let's face it, her perspective was a little warped). I'd never have met Amy, never have had her in my life. I'd never have found Naomi. I could believe I might see Karen again, someday. I had three daughters now, not just one. I'd just have to picture the other two working outside the country. Away at school. Naomi stared up at me, her eyes shadowed like they were bruised and her shoulders sagging with weariness. All of us, children included, we were all just so tired.

"They'll protect us?" she asked.

"Yes. They'll protect us."

"Just like Jesus? And that man, the old man, the angel?"

"Yes. Just like Jesus." What place was there for Jesus, Mary, anything I'd believed in, in anything I'd just seen? I couldn't think about that now. Those thoughts were outside the country, away at school. "And we'll make everything right. We'll start all over again."

Those words brought a worn-out doubt to her face, that all the talk of angels hadn't. "*How?*" she asked.

How? I'd be asking myself that the rest of my life. But Naomi didn't have to know that, didn't need to struggle with my own anguish on top of her own. Somehow, I had no idea how, I had to give her the room to be young, to be a little girl again.

"Slowly," I said. "One step at a time." I managed a smile. "My grandmother used to say, how do you eat an elephant? One bite at a time. Just think about that, when it all feels like too much. Think about... elephants."

She considered this absurdity for a few silent moments.

"I like elephants," she said. "I had a book with pictures of them, that I got for my birthday."

I'd find her another one, in what remained of the county libraries, the ruins of bookstores. My own small, private project. A book with elephants.

"I thought we could go to Cowleston," I said. "That little town outside the other beach, where that woman Tina lives? You liked Tina, didn't you? And after everything that happened, they could probably use our help." A tornado came through. I'd just keep telling myself that: a tornado came through, knocked everything over and sideways, killed some people and destroyed some neighborhoods but you could rebuild, after a tornado. We'd been doing it long before the plague ever arrived.

Could I stand it, to live less than a mile down the road from Cowles Beach, all those memories, all those ghosts who've atomized and dispersed themselves elsewhere? Could I stand to stay here? Too many memories all around me; there was no place to run, no place to go that was free of them. Welcome to life. Welcome to answered prayers.

Was Tina even alive, after what had happened? I hoped so. I even prayed so. I had promised.

"So, what do you think?" I glanced down at Naomi. "Should we go back to that other beach, stay there? Have a house of our own?"

Naomi gazed into the distance, her brow furrowing: no wandering attention, she really was thinking it over. Weighing our options. Then she nodded.

"Will you be mad," she said, "if I do prayers with Tina? On Sunday?"

I shook my head. Please be alive, Tina. I promised. Let her give Naomi back those last things she learned from her mother, her first mother. It was only fair.

"I'm so tired of walking everywhere," Naomi said. "And now we have to walk back."

"I'll carry you," I said. I stroked her hair. "I can't promise when, but maybe someday we can have another dog—"

"I don't want another one," she said. Her face contorted for a moment, but she didn't cry. "Just Nick. But he was Amy's so he had to go with her. I don't ever want another one—"

"Someone else there might," I said gently. "If they do, you

could play with it."

Naomi thought that over. Nodded. A picture book, Tina, a dog to play with: already my promises were piling up, all these promises I had no idea if I could keep. But that was all right. The grandiose promises, the almost demented determination somehow to fulfill them, that was all part and parcel of loving a child. Of loving anyone. And sometimes, every now and then, you actually could live up to your word.

Naomi gazed up at the ridge, at the lab building, and a small shadow of disorientation crossed her face; she closed her eyes hard, shook her head like a dog shaking water from its coat. Then she turned away.

I forced myself to look too. I raised my head, turned mine eyes to the ridge; I took in the white gravel road cutting through the knee-high uncut grass, the sandy stone like Lego brick, the rundown crumbling open-air columns of the aquatorium on the opposite side. The few scrubby, lonely, wizened trees at the very top of the sand, too foolhardy to put down roots in the dirt and grass. The thick, knitted swaths of nearly untouched woodland behind the aquatorium and the lab, too far back from the dune bottom to be much more than a long horizontal shadow overlaid with shifting, frothing bands of green. The lake itself, the way it looked bluer and darker and somehow less frenetic here than on the shore in Cowles County. The broken-down Chicago skyline, so sharp and clear in the noontime sunlight that you could imagine yourself walking right over the horizon on glassy, solidified stepping-stones of lake water, slipping into the shadow of the Sears Tower. The Tuskeegee Airmen statue, its copper going patchy green as though mold encroached, sitting by the aquatorium's wide-open entranceway. I drank it all in, trying to memorize the sight of everything, because once we set out for Cowleston it might be years, might be never, before I ever saw it again.

Goodbye, Jessie, Amy. Jim. Everyone. Goodbye.

It was a long walk to Cowleston, over the county line. Miles to go before we slept. And never mind just our little village-to-be;

there were so many people, living people, needing things rebuilt and remade, whether it's homes or farms or cities or themselves. A long life ahead, a whole lifetime of hard work. Even when the enormity of what had just happened finally hit me, brought me crashing down to the ground again and again every time I tried to get up, there would be so much work to do. I would struggle to my feet, bruised, bleeding, aching in every muscle and bone. Fight. Fly right. Live.

I reached down and took Naomi's hand.

"Ready?" I asked.

ACKNOWLEDGEMENTS

To Michelle Brower and Jita Fumich, for their constant work on my behalf. To Kate Sullivan and the entire staff of Candlemark & Gleam, for allowing me to complete and share with the world the story I began in *Dust*. To all my readers who sent both praise and criticism, asked for more and waited, with admirable patience, to get it. To the employees and volunteers of the Indiana Dunes National Lakeshore and the Indiana Dunes State Park, for vital information and inspiration. To all my family, loved ones and friends, for their love, encouragement, pep talks and occasional short sharp shocks. To everyone who picks up this book, now or in the future, and finds something in it that speaks to them: I started this story, but all of you together finish it.

ABOUT THE AUTHOR

JOAN FRANCES TURNER was born in Rhode Island and grew up in the Calumet region of northwest Indiana. A graduate of Brown University and Harvard Law School, she lives near the Indiana Dunes with her family and a garden full of spring onions and tiger lilies, weather permitting.

Visit the author at www.joanfrancesturner.com.

CPSIA information can be obtained at www.ICGtesting.com
Printed in the USA
LVOW13s1739250314

378894LV00003B/725/P